A RAINBOW
OF **BLOOD**

ALSO BY PETER G. TSOURAS

Britannia's Fist: From Civil War to World War

Alexander: Invincible King of Macedonia

Montezuma: Warlord of the Aztecs

A RAINBOW OF BLOOD

THE UNION IN PERIL

Volume II of The Britannia's Fist Trilogy

Peter G. Tsouras

An Alternate History

SKYHORSE PUBLISHING

Skyhorse Publishing books may be purchased in bulk at special discounts for sales promotion, corporate gifts, fund-raising, or educational purposes. Special editions can also be created to specifications. For details, contact the Special Sales Department, Skyhorse Publishing, 307 West 36th Street, 11th Floor, New York, NY 10018 or info@skyhorsepublishing.com.

Skyhorse® and Skyhorse Publishing® are registered trademarks of Skyhorse Publishing, Inc. ®, a Delaware corporation.

www.skyhorsepublishing.com

10 9 8 7 6 5 4 3 2 1

Library of Congress Cataloging-in-Publication Data is available on file.

ISBN: 978-1-62873-697-7

Printed in the United States of America

This book is respectfully dedicated to all the men of the Bureau of Military Intelligence of the Army of the Potomac—the first practitioners of all-source intelligence, the unsung combat multiplier in the great war for the survival of the Union.

CONTENTS

ACKNOWLEDGMENTS

I have been fortunate indeed to have as a longstanding friend and colleague the soundest of sounding boards, William F. Johnson. Over endless cups of coffee, I have sought his advice and bounced my ideas off his encyclopedic knowledge of this period of military history in the development of the details and story line of *A Rainbow of Blood*. As Edward Gibbons's service in the British militia prompted him to say that he thought the Hampshire Grenadiers informed the historian, Bill's service in the U.S. Marine Corps and as an intelligence officer have combined with great good judgment to make him a both a formidable critic and an astute observer. I am indebted to his help.

INTRODUCTION

British troops swarmed through the buildings of the Washington Arsenal only to find the powder magazines empty. The Arsenal workers had removed them before they fled — all except for what they had hidden down a well. It was into the darkness of that well that a British soldier peered, torch in hand. He tossed it down to see what was at the bottom. A tremendous explosion rocked the site "whereby the officers and about thirty of the men were killed and the rest most shockingly mangled."[1]

The scene was not the beginning of the Great War in September 1863; it took place in 1814 during the second Anglo-American War when the British sacked and burned Washington. Yet the feckless action of a lone British soldier who touched off a disaster would be paralleled by the rulers of his nation as the American Civil War raged forty-nine years later.

The British establishment maintained such an active dislike for the American experiment that it looked across the Atlantic with undisguised glee at the young republic's fratricide. Great Britain's neutrality law was so loosely written and even more loosely observed that it was no hindrance to the massive trade with the Confederacy that equipped and outfitted its armies with the vast output of British industry. Even worse was the building of commerce raiders in British yards that devastated the American merchant marine. Only the greatest pressure from the U.S. government would force the British government to interfere with the practice, but even then British juries invariably ruled for the Confederates.

The last straw was when the Laird Brothers firm in Birkenhead began building for the Confederacy two armored iron warships outfitted with steel rams. Abraham Lincoln was finally forced to put aside his policy of "one war at a time" and deliver an ultimatum on September 5, 1863, threatening war if the ships were delivered. At the same time in *Britannia's Fist*'s alternate history, the USS *Gettysburg* was dispatched to sink the Laird rams if they escaped.

Events now rested on the jagged edge of war and peace. As the British soldier in 1814 had done, Lord John Russell, the British foreign minister, peered down the dark well, torch in hand. He dismissed every fact-filled brief submitted by Charles Francis Adams, the U.S. ambassador, even as he concluded that the ships must be seized as a matter not of law but of state policy. He notified Adams of this too late. A Confederate sympathizer in Lord Russell's own office was the one to actually knock the torch out of his temporizing hand and down the well. He warned the builder, and the just-completed CSS *North Carolina* fled on the morning tide. Things now automatically began to happen.

Gettysburg caught *North Carolina* off the coast of Wales and seized her in British waters. HMS *Liverpool* arrived to dispute the action. Defiances were thrown and the Battle of Moelfre Bay began. The British frigate would have overpowered the smaller American ship had not USS *Kearsarge* arrived to tip the scales. *Liverpool* died in the explosion that blew her powder magazines, taking six hundred British lives. An enraged Britain declared war.

Kearsarge fled home, pursued by a vengeful British squadron with orders to take or sink her wherever found. They followed her right through the Verrazano Narrows and into the Upper Bay of New York, despite her escort by a Russian naval squadron that had intercepted her. The battle was desperate, but the British were driven out. As the battle raged, the British ambassador delivered the declaration of war.

The British struck first. Too weak to defend British North America, British troops and Canadian militia struck simultaneously to seize Portland, Maine, and Albany, New York, by coup de main. Maine was vital to the survival of British North America. The only railroad that connected Canada with Britain ran from Halifax, Nova Scotia, down to Portland and then north to Quebec and beyond. Maine's regiments from the Army of the Potomac were just detraining in Portland for recruiting duty as the British attacked. Led by Col. Joshua Lawrence Chamberlain, they saved the city, but the British patiently set siege.

The objective of Albany had a different, though no less strategic, purpose. New York was the richest, most populous, and most industrialized state in the Union; it was vital to the American ability to wage war. From Albany the British struck down the Hudson Valley, leaving a pall of smoke in their wake as they burned the river towns and terrified New York City, America's great entrepôt. Already its population's morale had been shaken by the draft riots of July when the mostly Irish mobs had run rampant. Crack the morale of New York, and the United States would be out of the war.

At the same time, the Copperheads, the violently anti-war, Lincoln-hating Democrats of the Midwest, rose in their planned revolt to take their states out of the Union and into the Confederacy with the aid of Confederate prisoners liberated from the POW camps in Indianapolis, Chicago, and Rock Island. Chicago, the nation's second city, fell to this stab in the back. At the same time, the Royal Navy was preparing to descend on the coasts of North America to break the blockade of the South and counterblockade the North.

It was at this moment that the Union could have cracked as the storms of foreign war and rebellion crashed and broke. But it held. It was now total war. The Union could no longer fight with one hand tied behind its back. Every resource would be strained to its utmost, for it faced the greatest power of the era whose industrial capacity, with an equal population, was ten times as large. To these odds were added the second industrial power of Europe, as the French jackal, Napoleon III, sought to guarantee his conquest of Mexico by also declaring war.

By the summer of 1863, Lincoln had already done much to prepare the Union for this ultimate struggle. He had been impressed by the brilliant and decisive contribution to the victory at Gettysburg by the Bureau of Information (BMI), the first all-source intelligence organization in history. He brought its creator, Col. George H. Sharpe, to Washington in late July to replicate on the national and international stage what he had done for the Army of the Potomac — rationalize the disparate and uncoordinated efforts of the government. In short order, Sharpe created the Central Information Bureau (CIB) and established its motto: "We Share Intelligence." He utterly rejected the natural instinct to horde information as power. He would make the CIB a great combat multiplier for the Union.

Lincoln had also taken action to create another combat multiplier by removing the chief of the Army's Ordnance Bureau, Brig. Gen. James Ripley, who had obstructed every attempt to take advantage of emerging technologies such as repeating and breechloading firearms. Lincoln was a technologically astute and transformational man, but his efforts had been effectively blocked by Ripley, who would sabotage a direct presidential order to buy repeating weapons. Even Lincoln's direct purchase of the first effective machine gun, which he named "the coffee mill gun," had been countered by Ripley, who saw that every one was returned to be safely polished and stored in the Washington Arsenal.

Lincoln's nose for technological innovation had also been shown in his order to establish the Army Balloon Corps early in the Civil War. With a telegrapher in each balloon, Union commanders were able to receive real-time aerial intelligence. So effective were the balloons that they terrified the Confederates, but Lincoln could not be everywhere all the time. The war structure of the federal government and the armed forces was too new and unwieldy. With no one to watch over it, the Balloon Corps was neglected to death by the Army. Lincoln's first order to Sharpe was to get his balloons back. Sharpe did just that and was careful to subordinate the revitalized Balloon Corps to the CIB.

The survival of Portland was owed to Sharpe's suggestion that the Maine regiments be returned under the cover of recruiting. His suggestion was based on intelligence that intensive prewar British intelligence was gathering in Maine. After his arrival in Washington, Sharpe had met a British visitor over dinner, the one-eyed Lt. Col. Garnet Wolseley, the assistant quartermaster general of British North America. They both realized the other was more than represented. Sharpe was no ordinary colonel of infantry; Wolseley had soldier written all over him despite his mufti. Both recognized a formidable opponent in each other. For Wolseley would return to plan the attack on the United States and fill the intelligence role that Sharpe did across the border.

But intelligence, balloons, and repeaters, not to mention the nation's deeper resources of industry and ingenuity, were advantages that would be slow to develop. Smoke hung over the Hudson Valley as New York City screamed for help. Two army corps (XI and XII) of the Army of the Potomac had been ordered to the relief of the trapped Union Army of the Cumberland at Chattanooga, Tennessee, following its defeat at Chickamauga. They were instead diverted to New York City and designated the Army of the Hudson. Maj. Gen. Joseph Hooker was given command; it was a supreme opportunity to redeem himself after his defeat at Chancellorsville in May.

History was coming to his aid at that moment. The tramp of redcoats on the soil of their adopted land had switched the huge Irish immigrant community from its Democrat-inspired opposition to the war to its total support. In the days after the Battle of the Upper Bay, the former commander of the Irish Brigade, Brig. Gen. Thomas Francis Meagher, had recruited fifteen thousand of his countrymen to fight for the Union, the equivalent of an army corps. Lincoln had promptly promoted him and given him command of XI Corps at Hooker's suggestion. His first act was to lead a band of his Irish veterans to scotch the British raid on the Cold Spring Foundry across the Hudson from the Military Academy at West Point. The foundry was the largest producer of cannon for the Army and a strategic asset. His men returned to a victory parade in New York where flowers cascaded on their ranks; a red coat swung from each bayonet. But the British Albany Field Force had only been nicked. Its wait for New York City to panic would not be long, and it marched downriver to settle things once and for all as a huge reinforcement from the British Isles put to sea.

As the British poised to march on New York City, the ships of the Royal Navy's heavily reinforced North American and West Indian Station left their anchorage in Bermuda. Vice Adm. Sir Alexander Milne sent a strong force to break the blockade at Charleston while he led his main force to the Chesapeake Bay. It was at Charleston that the navies would fight one of the great battles of the war. Led by two of the largest armored broadside warships of the day, the British crossed the bar to get at the South Atlantic Blockading Squadron that was commanded by the father of U.S. naval ordnance, Rear Adm. John Dahlgren.

At the Third Battle of Charleston, it would be American technology that was decisive. Dahlgren's famous guns packed a bigger punch than anything the Royal Navy had, and his battle line of Passaic class monitors and the broadside *New Ironsides* outfought the two British armored leviathans in the first great battle of armored warships. Yet as glorious as the triumph of that day was, it was a strategic disaster. The blockade was as broken as if every one of

Dahlgren's ships had gone to the bottom. The loss of the forward operating pass at Port Royal made the blockade logistically unsupportable. Charleston station was abandoned as Dahlgren's force fled north to the shelter of Norfolk Navy Yard and the Chesapeake, picking up the North Atlantic Blockading Squadron at Wilmington on its retreat. Britannia still ruled the waves with her huge navy as it began to choke off American trade and hover like sentinels of ill omen off every port. The Royal Navy, smarting over its defeat, would resort to its ultimate weapon, the slow squeeze of blockade that had brought the haughty monarchs of Spain and France to heel time and time again.

Thus the alternate history of *Britannia's Fist* ended with the Union in dire peril—the blockade broken, Maine lost, Portland besieged, the Midwest in revolt, Albany seized, and New York City threatened. Throughout the Confederacy, the church bells, if they had not already been melted to make cannon, were ringing in delirious joy. The fervent hope of foreign intervention had been fulfilled with the resounding glory of an Old Testament prophecy.

If anyone thought that victory had fallen into the lap of the Confederacy, though, it was not Robert E. Lee. Hard fighting still lay ahead. He knew the men in blue had a core of resilient steel, but for the first time, the odds were now more than even.

This now is the story of *A Rainbow of Blood*.

MAPS

DRAMATIS PERSONAE

Alfred Ernest Albert, His Royal Highness. Lieutenant, Royal Navy (RN), aboard HMS *Racoon*, the nineteen-year-old second son of Queen Victoria and Prince Albert.

Alger, Russell A. Colonel, U.S. Volunteers; commander, 5th Michigan Cavalry, 2nd Brigade, Cavalry Division, Army of the Hudson, in the Hudson Valley Campaign.

Andrews, George A. Brigadier general, U.S. Volunteers; commander of the garrison of Port Hudson.

Babcock, John C. Civilian order-of-battle analyst and assistant director, Bureau of Military Information (BMI), Headquarters, Army of the Potomac.

Baker, Lafayette. Director of the Secret Service of the War Department.

Banks, Nathaniel. Major general, U.S. Volunteers; commander, District of the Gulf.

Barton, Clara. Volunteer nurse with the Union Army in the defenses of Washington.

Bazaine, François Achille. General, French Imperial Army; commander, French Forces in Mexico and of the Texas Expedition in support of the Confederacy.

Beauregard, Pierre Gustave Toutant de. General, C.S. Army; commander of the coastal defenses of South Carolina and Georgia.

Berdan, Hiram. Colonel, U.S. Volunteers; commander, Rifle Regiment.

Booth, John Wilkes. Fiery dramatic actor, brother of Edwin Booth, and a rabid Southern sympathizer.

Bragg, Braxton. General, C.S. Army; commander, Army of Tennessee.

Bright, John. Member of Parliament, one of the great reformers of the age, and advocate of the Union, derisively referred to as "the member for America."

Callaway, James E. Major, U.S. Volunteers, 21st Illinois Volunteer Infantry, assigned to the Army of the Cumberland.

Candy, Charles. Colonel, U.S. Volunteers; commander, 1st Brigade, 2nd Division, XII Corps.

Carnegie, Andrew. Railroad executive, entrepreneur, and organizer of the first train to rush troops to the defense of Washington at the outbreak of the Civil War.

Chamberlain, Joshua Lawrence. Colonel, U.S. Volunteers; commander, 1st Brigade, First Battle of Portland.

Clarke, Asia Booth. Sister of John Wilkes Booth and Edwin Booth.

Cline, Milton. Major, U.S. Volunteers, 3rd Indiana Cavalry, and senior scout of the Central Information Bureau (CIB).

Cobham, George A., Jr. Colonel, U.S. Volunteers; commander, 2nd Brigade, 2nd Division, XII Corps, Army of the Hudson.

Coles, Cowper Phipps. Captain, RN; innovator and inventor of an armored turret.

Cooke, John Rogers. Colonel, C.S. Army; commander of Cooke's brigade, Army of Northern Virginia.

Cushing, William "Will" Alonzo. Lieutenant, U.S. Navy; noted for his daring special operations.

Custer, George Armstrong. Brigadier General, U.S. Volunteers; commander, 2nd Brigade, Cavalry Division, Army of the Hudson.

Dahlgren, John. Rear admiral, U.S. Navy; commander of the Southern Blockading Squadron; known as the Father of American Naval Ordnance.

Dahlgren, Ulric. Colonel, U.S. Volunteers; hero of Gettysburg and son of Admiral Dahlgren.

Dana, Charles. Publisher and U.S. assistant secretary of war.

Davies, Henry E., Jr. Brigadier general, U.S. Volunteers; commander, 1st Brigade, Cavalry Division, Army of the Hudson.

Davis, Jefferson. President of the Confederate States of America.

Delacroix, Jean-Yves. Lieutenant, 9th Battalion, Les Voltigeurs de Quebec.

Denison, George. Lieutenant colonel, Canadian Militia; commander of the Royal Guides.

Disraeli, Benjamin. Leader of the Tory, or Conservative, Party in Great Britain.

Dow, Neal. Brigadier general, U.S. Volunteers; the colonel of the 13th Maine Regiment of the Army of the Potomac.

Doyle, Sir Charles Hastings. Major general, British Army; commander of Imperial Forces in the Maritime Provinces of British North America.

Dunlop, Hugh. Commodore, Royal Navy; commander of the coup de main against Washington.

Edward, Prince of Wales. First son of Victoria and Albert, and heir to the British throne.

Ewell, Richard. Lieutenant general, C.S. Army; commander, 2nd Corps, Army of Northern Virginia.

*Foley, Richard. Irish seaman, Royal Navy, and deserter.

Forrest, Nathan Bedford. Major general, C.S. Army; commander, Cavalry Division, Army of Tennessee.

Fox, Gustavus "Gus." U.S. assistant secretary of the Navy—essentially in modern terms, chief of naval operations.

Franklin, William B. Major general, U.S. Volunteers; commander, XIX Corps, Army of the Gulf.

Gates, Theodore B. Colonel, U.S. Volunteers; commander of the 20th New York State Militia Regiment.

Gatling, Richard. American businessman and brilliant amateur inventor of farm machinery and the automatic weapon known as the Gatling Gun.

Geary, John W. Brigadier general, U.S. Volunteers; commander, 2nd Division, XII Corps, Army of the Hudson.

Gorchakov, Aleksandr Mikhalovich. Russian foreign minister.

Gordon, John B. Brigadier general, C.S. Army; commander, Georgia Brigade, Early's division, Ewell's corps, Army of Northern Virginia.

Grant, James Hope. Lieutenant general, British Army; commander of Her Majesty's military forces in British North America; considered the best general in the Empire.

Grant, Ulysses S. Major general, U.S. Army, victor of Vicksburg, and commander of the District of the Mississippi.

Green, Thomas. Major general, C.S. Army; commander, Cavalry Division, Western Louisiana District.

Hardenburgh, Jacob. Lieutenant colonel of the 20th New York State Militia Regiment.

Herans, Otto. Lieutenant colonel, U.S. Army; commander, 2nd New York Cavalry, 1st Brigade, Cavalry Division, Army of the Hudson, at the Battle of Stottville.

*Hathaway, Michael. First lieutenant, U.S. Volunteers; commander of the guard at Mount Vernon.

Hill, Ambrose Powell. Lieutenant general, C.S. Army; commander, 3rd Corps, Army of Northern Virginia.

Hogan, Martin. Private, U.S. Volunteers; young Irish immigrant and scout for the Bureau of Military Information (BMI), Army of the Hudson.

Hooker, Joseph. Major general, U.S. Army; commander, Army of the Hudson.

Howe, Albion P. Brigadier general, U.S. Volunteers; commander, 2nd Division, VI Corps, at the battle of Kennebunk.

Ireland, David. Colonel, U.S. Volunteers; commander, 3rd Brigade, 2nd Division, XII Corps, Army of the Hudson.

Keckley, Elizabeth. Free woman of color, seamstress, and confidante of Mrs. Lincoln.

Kilpatrick, Judson. Brigadier general, U.S. Volunteers; commander of the Cavalry Division, Army of the Hudson.

Knight, Judson. Sergeant, U.S. Army; chief of scouts, Army of the Hudson.

Layard, Austin David. Member of Parliament, undersecretary to Lord Russell at the Foreign Office, and envoy to Richmond.

Lee, Robert E. General, C.S. Army; commander, Army of Northern Virginia.

Lincoln, Abraham. Sixteenth president of the United States.

Lincoln, Mary Todd. Wife of Abraham Lincoln and First Lady of the United States.

Lindsay, Sir James. Major general, British Army; commander, Brigade of Guards at the Battle of Claverack.

Lisovsky, Stefan S. Rear admiral, Russian Imperial Navy; commander of the Baltic Squadron sent to New York City.

Longstreet, James. Lieutenant general, C.S. Army; commander, 1st Corps, Army of Northern Virginia.

Lowe, Thaddeus. Scientist; colonel, U.S. Volunteers; founder and commander of the Balloon Corps.

Lydecker, Garrett L. Captain, Corps of Cadets, U.S. Military Academy at West Point.

Lyons, Lord. British ambassador to the United States.

Marx, Karl. German expatriate revolutionary and journalist living in London; foreign correspondent for the pro-Lincoln *New York Tribune*.

McCarter, Michael William. Former sergeant of the Irish Brigade, discharged for wounds after Chancellorsville.

McEntee, John. Captain, U.S. Volunteers; chief, Bureau of Military Information (BMI), Army of the Hudson.

McPhail, James L. Civilian provost marshal of Maryland and later deputy chief, Central Information Bureau (CIB).

Meade, George Gordon. Major general, U.S. Volunteers; commander, Army of the Potomac.

Meagher, Thomas Francis. Major general, U.S. Volunteers; commander, XI Corps, Army of the Hudson.

Mercier, Edouard-Henri. French Imperial ambassador to the United States.

Milne, Sir Alexander. Vice admiral, Royal Navy; commander of the North American and West Indies Station.

Moreau, Michel André. Colonel, French Imperial Army; commander, Zouave Regiment of the Guard.

Morgan, John Hunt. Colonel, C.S. Army; commander, Morgan's Cavalry Brigade, Army of Tennessee.

Morton, Oliver. Republican governor of Indiana.

Muravyov, Mikhail Nikolayevich. General, Russian Imperial Army; known as the Hangman for his brutality in suppressing the Polish Revolt.

Murphy, Frank. Second lieutenant, U.S. Volunteers; acting commander, 13th Regiment New Jersey Volunteers.

Nicolay, John. One of President Lincoln's two private secretaries.

Paulet, Frederick Lord. Major general, British Army; commander of the Albany Field Force in the invasion of New York.

Polignac, Camille Armand Jules Marie, Prince de. French prince of the House of Orleans; brigadier general, C.S. Army.

Rimsky-Korsakov, Nikolai Andreyevich. Ensign, Russian Imperial Navy, aboard *Aleksandr Nevsky*, flagship of the Russian Squadron visiting New York.

Ripley, James W. Brigadier general, U.S. Army; former director, former chief, Ordnance Bureau.

Root, Elisha K. Director, Colt Arms Factory.

Rosecrans, William "Old Rosey." Major general, U.S. Volunteers; commander, Army of the Cumberland.

Rowan, Stephen Clegg. Captain, U.S. Navy; commander, USS *New Ironsides*, and acting commander of the South Atlantic Blockading Squadron.

Russell, Lord John. British foreign minister in the Liberal Palmerston government.

Scarlet, William Lord Abinger. Lieutenant colonel; commander the Scots Guards Fusiliers.

Schurz, Carl. Major general, U.S. Volunteers; commander, Third Division, XI Corps, Army of the Hudson.

Sedgwick, John. Major general, U.S. Volunteers; commander, VI Corps, Army of the Potomac, and in independent command of the relief of Portland.

Semmes, Raphael. Captain, C.S. Navy; commander of CSS *Alabama*, the greatest of the Confederate commerce raiders.

Seward, William H. U.S. secretary of state.

Seymour, Sir Michael. Rear admiral, Royal Navy; commander of the squadron sent to destroy the U.S. Navy's South Atlantic Blockading Squadron at Charleston.

Sharpe, George H. Brigadier general, U.S. Volunteers; director of the Central Information Bureau (CIB) and commander of the 120th Regiment, New York Volunteers.

Sherman, William Tecumseh. Major general, U.S. Volunteers; commander, XVII Corps.

Slocum, Henry W. Major general, U.S. Volunteers; commander, XII Corps, Army of the Potomac and Army of the Hudson.

*****Smoke, James R. "Big Jim."** Chief agent for the Copperhead movement in Indiana and subsequent agent of Lafayette Baker's Secret Service.

Spencer, Christopher. Inventor of the Spencer repeating rifle.

Stanton, Edwin McMasters. U.S. secretary of war.

Steinwehr, Adolph von. Brigadier general, U.S. Volunteers; commander, 2nd Division, XI Corps, Army of the Hudson.

Stimers, Alban Crocker. Inspector general of ironclads, U.S. Navy.

Stoeckl, Baron Edouard de. Russian ambassador to the United States.

Tappen, John R. Major, U.S. Volunteers; acting commander, 120th Regiment, New York Volunteers.

Taylor, Richard. Lieutenant general, C.S. Army; son of President Zachary Taylor; commander, Western Louisiana District.

Thomas, George. Major general, U.S. Volunteers; "the Rock of Chickamauga," who succeeded Rosecrans as commander, Army of the Cumberland.

Victoria, Alexandrina. Queen of the United Kingdom of Great Britain and Ireland; ascended her throne on June 20, 1837.

Washburn, Cadwallader C. Major general, U.S. Volunteers; commander, XIII Corps, Army of the Gulf.

Welles, Gideon. U.S. secretary of the Navy.

Wetherall, E.R. Colonel, British Army; chief of staff to Lt. Gen. William Fenwick Williams, commander, Imperial forces in British North America.

Williams, Alpheus S. Brigadier general, U.S. Volunteers; commander, 1st Division, XII Corps, Army of the Hudson.

*Wilmoth, Michael D. Sergeant, U.S. Volunteers; senior order-of-battle analyst, Central Information Bureau (CIB), and protégé of George H. Sharpe.

Windham, Sir Charles Ashe. Major general, British Army; commander of the Portland Field Force.

Wolseley, Garnet J. Lieutenant colonel, British Army; assistant quartermaster, Imperial forces in British North America.

Wright, Horatio G. Brigadier general, U.S. Volunteers; commander, 1st Division, VI Corps.

Zeppelin, Count Ferdinand von. Captain, Prussian Army; official observer of the American Civil War.

1

Hanging Billy

MICHIGAN AVENUE, CHICAGO, ILLINOIS, 1:35 PM, OCTOBER 15, 1863
The smoke hung over the water's edge, mixed with early snow flurries that blew in from the black clouds rolling down from the north across Lake Michigan. Maj. Gen. William "Cump" Tecumseh Sherman's horse picked its way over the burning debris and the bodies that littered Michigan Avenue. Some of the bodies wore red coats. Most were in some ragged combination of butternut and gray or in nondescript civilian clothing. A gaggle of prisoners was being pushed along by the bayonets of their guards.

Sherman pointed to the group. "Separate out the Rebs and the Brits. Hang the Copperheads." His troops had known him affectionately as Uncle Billy. Ever after he would be known as Hanging Billy. He was hanging every man bearing arms without a uniform.

Copperheads! They were the virulent Lincoln-haters, mostly antiwar Democrats, loathing emancipation and determined to stop the war, overthrow the federal government, and take the Midwest out of the Union and into the Confederacy. They had plotted and prepared for the great day when, organized and trained by Rebel officers, they would storm all the Confederate prisoner-of-war camps in the Midwest and arm the liberated prisoners in their thousands. Thus Camp Morton in Chicago with seven thousand trained prisoners had fallen.

The behavior of the liberated Rebels had been correct save for sating their hunger and replacing their rags in the rich shops of the city. The Copperheads were simply out of control. Gangs had gone through Chicago with lists of prominent Unionists to murder in their own homes or to round up and shoot in the stockyards. Bodies floated down the Chicago River into Lake Michigan for days. The Copperheads had thought things out well and seized all the armories and murdered the militia officers wherever they could. Then the British and their Canadian militia allies had come steaming over the lake to add red to the garrison.

But Sherman and his XVII Corps had fallen on the stricken city with a hardness of heart that a pharaoh would have envied. Sires of a conspiracy born and nurtured in the dark had not had the stomach for a tough fight in the light of day. Many threw their weapons away but were hunted down by the Chicagoans out for revenge and shouting "Copperhead quarter!" It was martial law at its hardest, and Sherman was determined that they would never rise again against the United States.[1]

It was not only Sherman who saved the Midwest. The shrewd prescience of Lincoln's new chief of intelligence, Brig. Gen. George H. Sharpe, had been decisive in the month before the rising. He had sent his chief of scouts, Maj. Milton Cline, and two hundred specially trained cavalry to assist state authorities against the Copperhead plots.[2] Fresh on the heels of scotching the attempt to liberate the POWs at Camp Morton outside Indianapolis, Major Cline had run wild over Indiana, striking at one Copperhead concentration after another, rallying the local Unionist militias and home guards. Slowly, town by town, village by village, the Loyalist men had prevailed. And as in Chicago, there was precious little mercy shown. The people of the Midwest would always associate the rising with the sight of men hanging from trees in town squares and along country roads.

The viciousness of this cycle of murder and revenge was replicated across the region in almost every city, town, and village. That had been the first setback in the Copperhead plan—the Union men fought back. The news of Sherman's ruthlessness in Chicago suddenly collapsed the uprising everywhere else. The loyal men and the state militias mopped up the last of it, and they made Hanging Billy look like the most tender of civil libertarians. The troop trains heading to Chattanooga passed hundreds more bodies hanging from trees. Sherman had to intervene repeatedly to stop the house-to-house revenge killings by proscription lists. Those lists were voluminous for men who had been too free with their opinions before the Stab in the Back, as it was now being called.

Sherman's hellfire threats to the state authorities to rein in the excess was the only thing that put a stop to what would be known as the White Terror.[3]

CHATTANOOGA, TENNESSEE, 5:00 AM, OCTOBER 16, 1863

The men of the Army of the Cumberland called their present position "Starvation Camp." They were shivering in the last cold, wet hours before dawn. Heavy autumn rains had turned their positions into seas of mud. The army had been reduced effectively to quarter rations, and hunger obsessed every man. Their animals were dying first, in large numbers. Many of the poor creatures, unable to be fed, had been sent out of the tightening siege by the one remaining supply route through mountain and mud that was so difficult to travel that countless died on the way. Supplies coming into the army were shrinking to a trickle.

At the moment when the Union needed every one of its veteran field armies to ward off foreign invasion and new rebellion, the Army of the Cumberland lay dying of complete loss of faith in its commander more than from outright starvation. Maj. Gen. William Rosecrans—"Old Rosey"—had been undone by his defeat at Chickamauga and seemed incapable of even occasional powerful bursts of energy. Simple problem solving now seemed to elude him. None of this was lost on his men.

A wise general knew that he had only one man to defeat—his opposite number. A general defeated in his own mind carries the doom of his entire army. Yet Gen. Braxton Bragg, commanding the Confederate Army of Tennessee, failed to vigorously take advantage of his opponent's moral surrender to deliver the coup de grace. His efforts to close off the final supply route into Chattanooga were never pressed with a killer instinct. He had even sent off his most aggressive commander and the author of his victory at Chickamauga, Lt. Gen. James Longstreet, to lose himself in a mindless campaign against Knoxville in a region bare of subsistence. Bragg's remaining energy was expended on engineering the relief of his next most competent subordinate, Gen. D. H. Hill, for which he had asked Jefferson Davis himself to come to the siege lines to preside.

This and the news that Grant was coming to the rescue were unknown to the men in "Starvation Camp." It would take all Grant's skill to save them. After all the subtractions from the powerful army Grant had assembled to take Vicksburg, he was bringing with him only XV

Corps. Given Bragg's tight grip on the surrounding mountains, it would take a miracle for him to save the Army of the Cumberland. And Grant would not be on the scene with his troops in less than two weeks.

ABOARD THE RIVERBOAT *OHIO STAR* ON THE OHIO RIVER, 4:29 PM, OCTOBER 16, 1863

Grant couldn't remain still; the pain wracked his body. A vicious mount had fallen on him in New Orleans and injured him seriously a few weeks before. He hobbled up and down the riverboat's deck on crutches, anxious to get his hands on events, but he was confident in the actions he had already taken.

A wave of near panic had washed over the Army with the news of one disaster after another, but Grant was as imperturbable as a block of granite. A desperate Secretary of War Edwin M. Stanton had sent him orders appointing him commander of the Military District of the Mississippi—essentially everything east of the Appalachian Mountains, south of Canada, and down to the Gulf. It was a command that would have swallowed half of Europe. At his direction, the armies began to move. He did not give a hint of distress or uncertainty, and waves of calm and assurance seemed to radiate from him. Up the Mississippi, hundreds of steamboats and barges moved his forces north. He had appointed Cump to pacify the Midwest while he concentrated on saving the besieged Army of the Cumberland. The Union dared not lose a field army at this moment of crisis. Veterans could not be spared, and the shout of triumph from her enemies to the south and north would have demoralized loyal men and women. There had been too many disasters already.

That was why he read the daily reports from Sharpe with such intense interests. Each one was a comprehensive analysis of current intelligence, far superior to anything he had received from the overwhelmed War Department in the past. For the first time, he was able to build a complete strategic picture of the situation besetting the Union. With that in mind, he could better plan his own operations. Not that the Daily Intelligence Summaries were bearers of good news. On the contrary, they were rigorously objective and spared no bad news. That was fine with Grant. He needed facts, not sugarcoating. As his steamer puffed up river, he finally gave in to physical necessity and found a chair on the deck. He leaned his crutches on the railing, a cigar clenched in the corner of his mouth, and watched the muddy water part before the bow. In his hand was Sharpe's latest telegraphic report, fresh from the cipher clerk's rendering.

The report put the feel of the overall situation at his fingertips. He summarized it in his own mind—Bragg had invested the Army of the Cumberland as tight as a tick; the men were starting to starve. The secretary of war's representative, Charles Dana, was in Chattanooga, reporting how Rosecrans had lost his nerve and the confidence of his men. Longstreet, his old friend from the prewar Army, commanding his own I Corps, Army of Northern Virginia, had been detached to strike at Knoxsville.

Maj. Gen. George G. Meade was doing all he could to keep up with Robert E. Lee's vigorous maneuvers in northern Virginia. The Royal Navy had taken control of the southern reaches of the Chesapeake Bay, and an attack up the Potomac on Washington by its lighter ships was possible. There was evidence at this time of Rebel-British cooperation. To the north, Portland still stood siege, and the British had reinforced the investing force. Union Maj. Gen. John Sedgwick was taking his time to get his VI Corps up there.

Hmm, that sounded just like Uncle John, Grant thought. Good in a fight but slow to get into it. Maj. Gen. Joseph Hooker, on the other hand, was moving rapidly up the Hudson on its eastern shore to a collision with the British at Albany. Now Hooker had the opposite problem—he would not waste time getting into a fight, but at Chancellorsville he had lost his nerve when Lee had had the temerity to upset Hooker's plan. As Grant saw it, the problem was whether some British general would have the same effect on Hooker.[4]

Reports indicated that a large reinforcement from the British Isles was on its way to Canada. A French army had also marched up from Mexico. It was moving along the Gulf Coast and was reinforced by more troops that had landed at Galveston after a French fleet had destroyed the Navy's blockading squadron there. New Orleans was the likely target of the combined French forces. There was no word of any British or French action against the East Gulf Blockading Squadron, which had concentrated at the Pensacola Navy Yard. Rumors stated that Admiral Dahlgren's South Atlantic Blockading Squadron had been destroyed, but there were doubts as to their veracity.

The Copperhead rising in the Midwest seemed to be subsiding, beaten on every hand by Loyalist men. Grant had independent confirmation of that. He had Sherman's telegraph in his hand as well. It smelled of the fire that had burned half of Chicago. If he knew Cump, his friend would make the Midwest howl. He decided to take the immediate action of relieving Rosecrans of command of the Army of the Cumberland and replacing him with Maj. Gen. George Thomas, the IV Corps commander who had held the rearguard at Chickamauga.

Still, time was not on his side. He leaned back in his chair, rocking it back and forth as he smelled the snap in the air. Already the days were turning unseasonably cold.[5]

THE CINCINNATI TYPE FOUNDRY, CINCINNATI, OHIO, 3:22 PM, OCTOBER 15, 1863

Close to Rebel-infested Kentucky just across the Ohio River, Cincinnati had been struck hard by the Copperheads. Confederate sympathizers had burned the first factory where Richard Gatling had built his new gun in 1861; now they were determined to burn the foundry where he had just finished his first order of thirteen guns ordered by Maj. Gen. Benjamin Butler and paid for out of his own pocket. It seemed that half the city was on fire, with Copperhead mobs burning and killing. For days now, the factory workers had feared to come to work. Only Gatling and his partner, Miles Greenwood, had made it to the building, a stout brick structure with a high wall and strong gate.

It would not be strong enough. All the Confederate officers who had crossed the river to organize the mob had driven them to new frenzy. They were howling outside, and that noise rose to a roar just before the gate shuddered at a tremendous blow. Gatling and Greenwood looked at each other as they stood in front of one of the guns they had dragged into the yard. "It was a splendid-looking thing, a marvel, a curiosity, a dazzle of shining metal and sleek design, even in its fledgling state. Six steel barrels were arranged in a tight, intimidating circle and affixed on a narrow platform suspended between two large wagon wheels. Jutting from one side of the device was a hand crank."[6] This gun had been only finished two days before and not been tested.

Richard Gatling was a tenacious man as well as one of the great inventors of an age of invention. Even before the war, he had grown rich from his developments in farming machinery that had drawn amazed attention at the Crystal Palace Exposition in London. As civil war loomed, though, his thoughts turned to arms. He reasoned that he could thin the battlefield and spare lives for the Union if one man firing a quick-repeating gun could take the place of a hundred. While his logic of war was naïve, his ingenuity was as practical as they came. Thus in less than a year was born the weapon he was now quickly loading with steel cartridges as the gate groaned under the assault of the mob's battering ram. Governor Oliver Morton of Indiana had seen a display in Indianapolis the year before and become an enthusiastic booster. That had won Gatling the opportunity to have the Army test his gun in May and July. The examining officers were unusually impressed and urged its purchase in large numbers. Their report had been dead-filed by the rigid and obdurate chief of the Ordnance Bureau, Brig. Gen. James Ripley, who loathed any new idea that came across his desk. Only Butler had shown interest, but there was a limit to any general's personal pocket.

The gate failed with a crack as its crossbar snapped at the last blow. Its halves swung back to strike the brick walls with a loud crash. The mob waited only long enough to drop the ram before screeching in victory and rushing into the factory yard. Gatling's right arm spun the crank on the gun around and around as his left swiveled the barrels right to left. The gun groaned as it spat out its bullets, higher and higher the pitch the faster he turned the crank.

The mob went down in a spray of blood as if death's scythe had swung clean through them. Gatling kept on firing into the packed mass as a spray of bright shell casings spewed onto the brick pavement. The mob's bloodlust howl now turned to shrieks of terror and pain. Those in the middle turned to claw their way to safety but were held by those pressing from behind until they, too, fell to the harvest of the machine. He stopped firing, and the barrels spun slowly to a wispy smoking stop. Gatling and Greenwood were gape-mouthed by the reality of their weapon. Bodies, dead and writhing, two and even three deep, carpeted the threshold of the gate and back out into the street. There were so many that a man could walk across it without touching the ground.[7]

OFF CAPE FEAR, NORTH CAROLINA, 5:04 PM, OCTOBER 15, 1863
John Dahlgren woke from his coma to look up into his son's face, now
ringed with a new light beard of angel gold. "Papa, Papa, thank God,"
Col. Ulric Dahlgren whispered, as the surgeon looked down at the admiral, taking his pulse and beaming. The worst was past. The wound had
not festered. Luckily, no bone or nerves had been damaged, as deep as
it was.

He tried to speak, but his throat choked on its own dryness. A
water glass was pressed to his lips, and he drained it to lie back and let
his wits come back to him. He did not recognize the cabin and could feel
the ship underway. "The battle," he whispered. "The battle?" His mouth
went dry again.

"A victory, Papa!"

It took a moment for it to sink in. "Tell me."

"We crushed them, Papa. We crushed them. Only a handful of their
ships got away. *Black Prince* sank alongside *New Ironsides* a half hour after she struck. We beat two ships of the line into kindling, turned them
into torches. A third struck and is in tow. Three frigates, two corvettes,
and two sloops rounded out the Royal Navy's humbling. My God, Papa!
You've commanded the greatest naval victory in our history!"[8]

"Our losses?"

"Sloop *Pawnee*, monitor *Nahant*, I'm afraid. *Donegal* put too many
shots through *Nahant*'s deck, smashing her engines, and letting in the
ocean that took her down with all her crew." He paused, "And, yes, ironclad *Atlanta*. She rammed *Shannon* with her spar torpedo and sent her to
the bottom, but she died in the process. Cromwell went down with her.
And we lost three gunboats—*Marblehead*, *Ottawa*, and *Wissahickon*.[9]

Dahlgren looked anxious. "And the submersibles?"

"Papa, the tender picked them up, but *Resistance* shot her to pieces
just after the recovery, and she burned. Both boats were lost, but we
saved the crews."[10]

Capt. Stephen Clegg Rowan, commanding USS *New Ironsides* and
acting commander of the South Atlantic Blockading Squadron, had been
immediately informed that the admiral was awake and came down to
pay his respects. Dahlgren pressed him immediately to explain the battle. Rowan pulled up a chair. "Well, Admiral, your plan just played itself
out. Your tactics and your guns won the day. After you were wounded,

the battle broke into two parts. The ships to our front, the two monitors, and *Wabash* and *Pawnee*, kept moving in line ahead and engaging the enemy line led by *St. George* and then *Donegal*. We pounded both ships into splinters; it was amazing how fast the shells from your guns will set a wooden ship on fire. A burning ship of the line is a magnificent and sad sight, I swear. The British frigates followed them into the same meat grinder.

"We were having a tougher time with *Black Prince* and *Sans Pareil*; they had come up on either side of us after our screw was damaged. The monitors following us pounded *Sans Pareil* until she struck. The British were still game. What brave men. Their frigates and corvettes crowded in, and I think would have boarded the monitors had not our gunboats come up from Morris Island to rake them. I think the last straw was the arrival of our three monitors and more gunboats from Port Royal followed by most of the ships at the base. I think seven of the enemy got away. Their other ironclad, *Resistance*, escaped into Charleston Harbor. The navy has never won such a victory, Admiral."[11]

"Where are we now, Rowan?"

"That's the bad news, sir — off Cape Fear. The entire squadron is sailing to Norfolk. We were lucky to win at Charleston, but we could not risk a second fight against a larger force. Our supplies are low, and we can barely get everyone away. We evacuated Port Royal just in time. The last late ship out reported a large British force approaching from the southeast. They'll find nothing but the ashes of our base. I'm proud to say we got off all the troops both at Port Royal and around Charleston. They're a bit crowded and on short rations, as were we, but we were able to find room for all twelve thousand men. I'm sure they feel the accommodations are better than British hospitality."

Dahlgren said, "Yes, that's twelve thousand men to fight another day — and a fleet in being."

"We put a lot of them on them on the captured British ships. It was crowded with their surrendered crews and all the men we fished out of the water — we paroled and turned over to the Rebs 1,400 wounded prisoners. We could not care for so many. But we have over 2,500 unwounded prisoners, Admiral — 2,500 prisoners, by God!"[12]

"And one very special prisoner. It seems that we picked up Prince Alfred, Victoria's second son, wounded on *Racoon* and saved by the ship's ratings. Shows you how a good officer can win the love of his men. Why, I put him in the cabin next to yours."

At that moment, they heard the clatter of a tray of food hurled into the passageway from the next cabin. A dripping plate rolled past the open hatch to the admiral's cabin. A very English voice screamed, "Swill! Damn your eyes! Don't come back until you have a proper meal!"

A smile twitched at the corners of Dahlgren's mouth. "You were saying, Rowan?" Then, suddenly exhausted, he sank back on his pillow, but his eyes gleamed.[13]

THE HOUSE OF COMMONS, LONDON, 11:30 PM, OCTOBER 15, 1863

The House sat in dead silence. The Speaker in his red robes and Restoration wig nodded to the shrunken little man sitting in for Prime Minister Palmerston, who had been felled by the shock of the disaster at Charleston.

Foreign Secretary Lord John Russell knew in his heart the role his own inattention and missed opportunities had played in bringing this unimaginable humiliation to Crown and country. He had failed to alert the American minister, Charles Francis Adams, that the government had determined to seize the two ironclad rams being fitted out in Liverpool.[14] He had been in no hurry, unaware that things automatically had begun to happen. The Americans had sent USS *Gettysburg* to intercept the rams should they escape, as had the infamous commerce raider CSS *Alabama* the year before. He also suspected that the ship was forewarned of the order of seizure by a Confederate sympathizer in his own office. Events had spiraled out of control. His orders to seize the rams arrived too late; one of them had escaped, and *Gettysburg* as well as USS *Kearsarge* had sunk two British warships in British waters when they tried to stop the capture of the ram. The government had declared war in the upswell of public outrage and dispatched reinforcements from the Channel Squadron to Adm. Alexander Milne with orders to immediately break the blockade of Charleston. Russell had escaped censure in the debate for war by simply lying with a facility he did not know he had.

His hands were not clean, and he knew it. There was British blood on them, and he could not help obsessing about Lady Macbeth's wail that not all the perfumes of Arabia would wipe away the stain. He took refuge in confining himself to reading Milne's report, but even that was a crucifixion. The sweat beaded on his forehead though the chamber had caught the early autumn chill. He read on of the crushing defeat that was unparalleled in British history: the great ironclad, HMS *Black Prince*, sunk, and *Resistance* barely able to escape into the safety of Charleston Harbor. He read the list of the famous old names of ships of the line that had burned or struck. When he read the name *St. George*, a groan escaped the grim men on their green leather benches. The list went on and on as he read the names of frigates, corvettes, and gunboats lost.

He finished and sat down to thundering silence. The British people and their leaders had sustained a shock to the very basis of their self-esteem, their birthright to victory and success. Such a loss to their ancient enemies, the French, might have been taken better. After all, the French were due a victory simply by the law of averages. But to suffer such a humiliation from the Americans, for whom the British establishment felt such contempt, left them humiliated and perplexed beyond all measure. They had taken little notice of the flood of Britons and Irish to the American republic. They might have taken solace from the argument that they had been beaten by themselves, men of fundamentally the same blood, language, religion, and history, but after the American Revolution, they were loath to acknowledge any common root stock.

It was then that John Bright rose and faced the Speaker. The tension exploded. In moments the members were on their feet in a roar, waving arms, shouting, throwing papers. Their pent-up rage suddenly had found its outlet in this most famous friend of America in Parliament. Bright was the foremost reformer of the age and as obdurate foe of slavery as he was the champion of the rights of the common man to the franchise in the United Kingdom. From the reform of the Corn Laws to the relief of Ireland in the grip of famine, he had become a moral power in the tradition of William Wilberforce, the immortal enemy of slavery. And for all that he was a Quaker, he was the most deadly debater in the House, ready to eviscerate anyone careless enough to challenge him.

Already he was known derisively as "the member for the United States." And it was his friendship with the beleaguered Union that enraged the House. There was deeper fuel for the members' anger, though. The very men who had looked with such sympathy on the South had been long frightened of Bright, the reformer. He had made it quite clear that the success of the Union would be the proof that democracy worked.

That success would provide the irresistible moral impetus for the exten-
sion of voting rights to the British common man. It was no accident that
the very men in the British establishment who so ostentatiously favored
the South were equally opposed to Bright's reforms and its threat to their
monopoly of power.

The Speaker struck his mace of office against the floor to bring
order, and only slowly did the members resume their seats with an ill-
graced and sullen snarl. The Speaker nodded to Bright. "The chair recognizes the member for Durham." Russell's slight form seemed to shrink
even more on the ministers' bench.

Bright began. "The gentlemen are rightly shocked by the news of
Charleston. It is a sad day for British arms, and many homes will mourn
throughout the realm. But the gentlemen have no right to be shocked
that we are at war. For two years the government and privilege in this
country have goaded and insulted the American republic in its trial of
freedom against the slave power. Even more, this government and privilege have done incalculable injury to that republic, though hiding behind
a tissue of neutrality."

"Shame, shame!" an angry voice cried out from the upper benches.

"Shame, indeed, sir!" Bright shot back. "Shame that it has been
British-built warships that have savaged and ruined the merchant shipping of the republic, which has done us no injury. Shame that it is British
foundry, arsenal, and factory that have equipped the armies of the slave
power and kept them in the field far beyond the poor ability of its own
industry. Shame that it is British bacon and biscuit that feeds the armies
of the slave power while it was fifty thousand barrels of American flour,
generously donated, that has fed thousands of British mill workers and
their families destituted by that same slave power's calculation to with-
hold cotton to force this country to become its ally."

"And shame that when the great republic has remonstrated again
and again about the commerce raiders built at Birkenhead, this government has turned a blind eye. Lord Russell has told the House that the
Americans offered insufficient proofs that the purpose of the ships being
built was warlike. I have seen copies of these proofs, and there is nothing
insufficient about them. Had they been written with the finger of God
Almighty Himself, I doubt not Lord Russell would still proclaim them
insufficient. He would refer them to the opinion of Lucifer. Is there any

doubt where his sympathies lie? Has anyone forgotten his efforts to force a settlement on the Americans that would have served to achieve that independence, which the slave power has not been able to win on the field of battle. I have it on good authority that the notorious *Alabama* escaped on the warning of a friend of the slave power in the Foreign Office before the government was moved to detain the ship. Strangely, *North Carolina* seems to have bolted Liverpool in the same way."[15]

The attention of the House turned to Russell, who betrayed no outward concern, but the other cabinet ministers were not so calm. Now voices cascaded down the benches, "Answer! Answer! Answer!" Russell stood almost languidly.

"I assure the House that every consideration was given the proofs provided by Mr. Adams, the American minister. He was notified of the decision to detain the ships in proper time."

Bright shot back, "Proper time? Mr. Adams had shown me before his departure the correspondence with your lordship's office. Your own signature, sir, says otherwise. For three crucial days after you had decided to detain the rams, according to what you have told this House, Mr. Adams had no word of this decision. Instead, he could only contemplate your last correspondence, which dismissed his proofs. Is it any wonder that he then delivered his government's ultimatum and added to it the fateful lines, 'It would be superfluous of me to say this means war?' Is it any wonder that the American plan to intercept the rams at sea was then set automatically into motion?"

The House became a bedlam. It was minutes before the Speaker could regain order. Bright spoke again. "The government and privilege have willfully and fecklessly heaped up a mountain of tinder, and they are outraged that a match has fallen into it. The conflagration that rages has touched many humble homes in this country and in America, and for what, I ask the House, for what?"

"Treason!" shrieked a voice from above the ministers' bench.

Bright turned a baleful eye on its source. "Is it treason to want this country to stand back from the precipice before we go tumbling over into the abyss? For God's sake, make peace!"

A bushy-bearded, slovenly man in the gallery looked down with glee at the roiling anger of the members. His small, dark eyes glinted in delight. Yes, he thought, make peace! But not just yet. He desperately hoped the fools would not. War with the Union could deal the forces of privilege and reaction a mortal blow and free the working class of their chains. He could feel in his bones the revolutionary condition coming to a boil. Still, it would be the title of his next day's editorial in the *People's Paper*, but its main audience would be the *New York Tribune*, the largest newspaper in the world, for which he worked as a correspondent.[16] Karl Marx had composed the piece in his head before he had even left Parliament that morning.

THE WHITE HOUSE, WASHINGTON, D.C., 7:00 PM, OCTOBER 15, 1863

Baron Edouard de Stoeckl came to the point. "Mr. President, we are then agreed on the principles of the treaty of alliance between His Imperial Majesty's government and the United States." It was a statement, not a question.

Lincoln nodded and said, "We are, Baron." Secretary of State William H. Seward sat back with a look of supreme satisfaction. He had done the detailed negotiations with the Russian ambassador. The day of the Royal Navy's attack on USS *Kearsarge* in the Upper Bay of New York, Baron Stoeckl had offered an immediate alliance under sealed instructions from Czar Alexander II, to be opened only upon an attack on the United States by Great Britain or France. The devil was in the details, though, and it took two weeks of wrangling to birth terms acceptable to the world's greatest autocracy and the world's greatest democracy. Hawk-faced with a roman nose and an unruly head of hair, the little American was so thin he would not have had trouble hiding behind a rail. Yet he had been a pillar of support for Lincoln once he had figured out Lincoln would not let him run the government. Lincoln had also found a good friend in Seward.

The baron was a thorough professional in the highest traditions of European diplomatic service. His English was excellent, and he was not really a baron. The bogus title served to impress the Americans. Son of an Austrian diplomat and the daughter of the Russian dragoman in Constantinople, he had risen in the Russian service through ability and the patronage of the Russian foreign minister, Prince Aleksandr Mikhailovich Gorchakov. His tact and good advice had been much appreciated by Lincoln and Seward. In fact, it had been the Russian's good advice that had encouraged Lincoln to back off the confrontation with Great Britain over the seizure of two Confederate emissaries from *Trent*, a British mail packet, by a U.S. warship in late 1861. The baron had candidly advised Seward that the United States had violated international law in the seizure, despite the fact that it had been wildly popular in the North in the face of blatant British favor to the rebellion.

The baron's analysis of the situation and international law was so lucid and compelling that Lincoln was convinced to return the emissaries and take the political heat. It also reinforced his "one war at a time" policy. He realized that had Britain gone to war, as it seriously threatened to do, it would have crushed the Union in short order, so unprepared was it at the time. As it was, he had backed up only as far as necessary. He would not accede to the additional British demand for an apology. With the return of the emissaries, the British conveniently dropped the issue.

Baron de Stoeckl said, "His Imperial Majesty has long felt that the preservation of the American Union to be a vital objective of Russian policy. We have had a long and friendly relationship, Mr. President. Our mutual commerce has enriched both our nations. And uniquely among great nations of the world, we have no strategic conflicts."

Seward added, "At the moment of this country's birth, Russia's influence was benign. The British tried to buy mercenaries first from Catherine the Great who responded that her subjects were not for sale. German princes were not so solicitous of their subjects. Then that same monarch formed the League of Armed Neutrality to resist by force of arms British attempts to interfere with neutral commerce with the United States. Russia's latest gesture of support has been the visit of her Baltic Fleet's squadron to New York and her Pacific Squadron to San Francisco. The London *Times* simply seethed. I had not been so gratified in a long time."

Lincoln replied, "I cannot tell you, Baron, how much it meant to me when you read to me your sovereign's letter of support in the dark days of the first year of the war. It was, as I said at the time, 'the most loyal manifestation of friendship' shown by any European government. We shall never forget."[17]

The Baron picked up the cue. "Still, we must be realists, Mr. President. Nations do not go to war through sentiment and good feelings.

There must be something that engages their vital interests. And it is here that our mutual cordial relations reinforce the interest. British world hegemony threatens Russia as much as it threatens the United States. The British and the French attacked my country ten years ago as Russia was engaged in loosening the bloody grip of the Turk upon numerous Orthodox Christian peoples in the Balkans. They have now attacked you while you are engaged in a similar liberating crusade."

"Yes," Seward said to Lincoln, "the Baron has put his finger on the liberating missions of our two countries. The Czar's freeing of the serfs and your issuance of the Emancipation Proclamation in the same year are enormously powerful statements to our purpose."

It took all Lincoln could do to control himself. For once no appropriate story was at hand. Yet butter would not melt in his mouth now. "Liberating mission" indeed. He would have to ask Seward how much he actually believed in what he was saying. He suspected strongly that it was just a way for Seward to poke a sharp stick in the Lion's eye. Lincoln had no doubt of the liberating mission of the United States in this terrible war. Russia was brazen to pretend such lofty ideals while she was busy suppressing the latest Polish revolt with marked brutality. Yes, freeing any subject of the vile Turk was a humane goal by any standard, but the Russians merely meant to replace one autocrat with another. Lincoln supposed that in the balance of things, it would be an improvement. Compared to Turkish cruelty, the Russian rule was indeed liberation. Lincoln could only fall back on the aphorism that the only thing worse than fighting a war with allies is fighting a war without them.

The baron went on. "The world has not seen such a war that is beginning since the wars against Napoleon. Now England fills the roll of international tyrant. She has not made many friends by bestriding the world. The pretext upon which she goes to war, the sinking of a ship, is flimsy. All Europe knows she went to war to support the slave power in a malicious attempt to ruin her strongest commercial rival. She sees your future, and it frightens her. I assure, you, gentlemen, that the slave power is thoroughly detested throughout Europe. The English are now in a poisonous embrace, not only internationally but, our ambassador in London assures me, domestically as well.

"It is common knowledge that she has grown even richer by selling the Rebellion the weapons and supplies without which it could not have continued the war for more than six months. But let us look a few moves beyond the present in this great game, gentlemen. His Imperial Majesty's government will declare war on Britain and France with much regret. All of Europe will see that Russia was forced to do so by an unprovoked attack upon His Imperial Majesty's ships in a friendly, peaceful port.

"Then it will be a time of choosing sides. The smaller powers will, as usual, attempt to stay neutral lest they be crushed by the great powers. Without Russia, no one would come to your assistance. With Russia as your ally, your active ally, the pieces on the board will all begin to move.

"Unfortunately, the coming winter will limit the ability of Russia to support you with anything more material than official belligerence, but even that is useful. Much of the rest of the fleet will go to sea before our declaration of war is presented in London and Paris. That and the state of war will add enormously to cost of war for the enemy, as the shipping insurance rates will become crippling. Our enemies will have to begin looking both east and west at the same time.

"But when spring allows active operations, we will then be able to stress the British and French at opposite ends of the planet. You see, they were successful against us in the Crimean War because the full power of both empires could be directed against Russia at one critical point. Now they will have to split their forces at opposite ends of the planet, never quite sure which is the more important.

"The offensive operations of the Russian Imperial Army, I assure, you will provoke the entry of Austria into the war. Whether she declares war on the United States as well as Russia is uncertain. She would be foolish to do so, but the Hapsburgs have often acted fecklessly. In any case, she can apply no power against you.

"The Prussians, on the other hand, will be the critical player. With Austria in alliance with France, Prussia will see her two ancient enemies at war with Russia and the United States. These two powers have had the continued fragmentation of Germany as a primary policy. Prussia has been slowly unifying Germany, a process that holds no threat to Russia. She gains nothing by remaining neutral or by joining them. I believe that Prussia's interest lies in the defeat of France and Austria. I have no doubt the able Prussian chancellor, Otto von Bismarck, is pursuing just such a long-range policy. This war gives him the perfect opportunity to advance that plan. Prussia's intervention on our side, leading a German confederation, would tip the balance."

"Don't forget, Mr. President," Seward added, "the Germans are the most intensely anti-slavery people in Europe. The Prussian king refused to receive or allow any of his subjects to receive the Rebel emissary."

The baron resumed, "Also do not forget, sir, that it will be Prussian interest that will decide their actions. If it aligns with sentiment, so much the better. It will make the Prussians feel virtuous.

"Since our mutual enemies have gone to war to destroy the territorial integrity of the United States, the maintenance of that integrity is the primary objective of both our countries. We agree to make no separate peace. Since it is the pursuit of hegemony that impels the English to seek to destroy that integrity, His Imperial Majesty believes that the means of that hegemonic power must be destroyed. In this, both the United States and Russia can play complimentary roles. To that end, we support the conquest of Canada by the United States. Russia, in turn, will endeavor to encourage revolt in India, which the English call so charmingly the 'jewel in the crown.' They will be even more sensitive to the loss of India than Canada, for India is the cornerstone of their empire, the greatest source of wealth and position in the world. Let them worry about keeping what is theirs for a change rather than stealing what belongs to others. The threat to India coming on the heels of the Great Mutiny will ensure that the English will not dare to strip the garrison of India by so much as a drummer boy."[18]

Seward said, "And the British have a very small army, half of which is in India or scattered in penny packets across the rest of their empire. Sharpe's analysis of the strength of the British on land and sea did much to assist our negotiations."

"Indeed, Mr. President," the baron responded, "the good general has been most helpful in supplying valuable information. I have already sent it off by pouch to St. Petersburg, where I am sure it will be a valuable addition to our own efforts along these lines."

Lincoln stood up to lean one long arm against the mantle. "Canada and India, of course, Baron. Your logic is sound, but it is like serving ten years in prison; easy to say but harder to do."

"That goes without saying, Your Excellency," the baron replied dryly.

"But what about Ireland, Baron? If we wanted to detach something from the British Empire, I can think of nothing better than Ireland to cause them infinite pain."

Seward jumped in, "That attacks the integrity of the United Kingdom as profoundly as the British support of the rebellion attacks the integrity of the United States. Two can play that game." He positively relished the idea.

The baron shrugged, an act of tactful patience. "Yes, it would, but remember Archimedes's statement that he could move the earth if he had a lever long enough and firm place to stand. I am afraid that neither the United States nor Russia has the lever or the ground to make such a threat. With their superior fleet, there is no way that we can seriously threaten English control of Ireland."

The baron thought that Lincoln had accepted the obvious and moved on, though Seward, who knew him far better, was not so sure. "We are both great land powers, Mr. President, with armies of a million men, and it is with these armies that we must apply our power. You against Canada and we against India and England's friends in the Balkans."

"Of course, Baron, of course," Lincoln replied.[19]

HEADQUARTERS, CENTRAL INFORMATION BUREAU (CIB), LAFAYETTE SQUARE, WASHINGTON, D.C., 7:50 PM, OCTOBER 15, 1863

Brig. Gen. George H. Sharpe heard the familiar rap on his office door and looked up. It was Sgt. Mike Wilmoth, the young Hoosier who had become a combination secretary and the chief of his new order-of-battle office. He had come to look on him in a proud paternal way, the way a father looks on an able son with a bright future. The young man might have been lost in the dark blue mass of the Army had not an illness sent him to a Washington hospital and then to light convalescent duty with Sharpe. He quickly had brought administrative order to the new office and absorbed like a sponge the skills of an order-of-battle analyst from John C. Babcock, the man who had founded the art in the Army of the Potomac.[20]

"Sir," Wilmoth said softly, "the president desires you attend him at the White House."

Sharpe put down his papers and left immediately through the bustle of his outer offices. The CIB did not keep regular hours. He passed his deputy, Jim McPhail, in the hallway and said, "Off to see the president, Jim." McPhail just nodded and went on down the hall intent on his own business. This was no great event. Lincoln called Sharpe almost on a daily basis.

It was certainly not that Sharpe cut a Napoleonic figure. Lincoln had had enough of that type of officer. If anything, he was much the opposite—a thirty-five-year-old man of medium height, round-shouldered, with short, dark hair and a drooping mustache. What Lincoln found in Sharpe was a man with an unusually keen brain, fertile imagination, and a sly boldness in getting things done. As soon as he engaged this nondescript colonel of infantry in conversation, the man seemed to transform himself. He was sharp as an obsidian razor, it was clear from the first words. He knew his business like the best lawyer knew his brief, and the fact that both Lincoln and he were lawyers may have had something to do in the way they connected. The way Sharpe could express himself in speech and writing in the clean and direct style of a fine legal brief impressed Lincoln. There was charm there, as well—the art of winning arguments and men without making enemies—and a wit and gift for telling stories that came close to Lincoln's legendary penchant. Lincoln joked that he kept Sharpe on just to mine his stories.

Lincoln had pondered deeply over the implications of Sharpe's hand in the victory at Gettysburg and contrasted that with the confusion and lack of central control of intelligence matters at the national level. He ordered him to Washington and laid before him the offer to create for the entire U.S. government the same sort of intelligence operation under the same single guiding hand that Sharpe had done for the Army of the Potomac when he had put together the BMI, the country's first all-source intelligence entity.

Sharpe had accepted immediately. In a few months, he had replicated his old organization to serve the entire war effort. It was headquartered in the house he had rented for his family earlier on Lafayette Square right across from the White House. Luckily, his wife, May, had fled with their three children from the Washington summer back to their home in Kingston, New York, just south of Albany on the Hudson. He set up shop in the empty house. Its location had been a priceless advantage.[21]

One of his first priorities was to obey Lincoln's order, "Get me my balloons back." Lincoln had personally authorized the creation of the Army Balloon Corps after a brilliant demonstration of the capability of the wonder at the hands of the country's foremost aeronaut, Dr. Thaddeus Lowe. Lowe's balloons had done invaluable service from the Peninsula through Chancellorsville. A telegrapher and his device had been placed in the balloons, allowing the army commander to receive real-time intelligence. Unfortunately, jealous officers had harassed Lowe to the point where he went home in disgust after serving without pay at Chancellorsville. After that the corps had simply disappeared, its balloons worn out, and none of its personnel able to replace Lowe. Sharpe brought him back with the rank of colonel and command of the reconstituted Balloon Corps, and he had Lincoln's approval to subordinate it directly to his own CIB. Sharpe now added aerial reconnaissance to the growing assets of his new bureau.[22]

At the same time, he had raced to replicate the BMI in each of the other field armies of the Union. Unfortunately, the new intelligence staff of Rosecrans's Army of the Cumberland was not able to identify the arrival of Longstreet's First Corps, which had been sent by Lee to reinforce Bragg's Army of Tennessee, even though Sharpe was able to inform them that the reinforcement was on the way. The result had been the Union disaster at Chickamauga, the retreat of the Army of the Cumberland to a wasting siege at Chattanooga, which Grant was trying with meager forces to relieve.

THE WHITE HOUSE, WASHINGTON, D.C., 8:09 PM, OCTOBER 15, 1863

John Nicolay, the president's secretary, was a tired man. The president had been keeping late hours ever since the British attack, and Nicolay had been his faithful shadow. He brightened when he saw George Sharpe enter. Lincoln had come to rely on him, and the president's small but devoted staff appreciated anyone who could lighten his load.

"The president is expecting you, General. Stoeckl and Seward were with him until just now. Alliance business." Although there had been intense speculation in the press and the public assumption of a Russo–American alliance, nothing had been announced by either government. Nicolay knew Sharpe was fully privy to negotiations. "The president said to go right in, but I'd wait a few minutes. Mrs. Lincoln just beat you in, and from the sound of it—"

The door slammed open and out stormed Mary Todd Lincoln. She was a small, stout woman, a contrast to her tall, gangly husband, which brought to everyone's mind Jack Spratt and wife. Now her small mouth was pursed so tight as to almost disappear into her round face. Her dark eyes flashed. She stormed past Nicolay and Sharpe without a word. Then a voice from inside the president's study said, "Is Sharpe out there? Send him in."

Sharpe glided in quietly. Lincoln was sitting with his feet on his desk. He was wearing worn slippers, and his socks were darned. Sharpe was used to Lincoln's informality. He looked more tired than Nicolay. He said, "I've distressed Mrs. Lincoln again, Sharpe. Missed supper— again, I'm afraid."

Part of Sharpe's talent was a natural empathy. It was a talent that made him a master interrogator as well. "Our duty is hard on the ladies, sir. My own wife wants to join me here, but I have insisted she stay in Kingston. I tell her she would see almost as much of me there as if she were here."

Lincoln sighed, "I'm afraid the ladies will have to put up with a lot more." He got up and motioned Sharpe over to one of the chairs around the fireplace, where a ruby bed of coals warmed the room from the fall's early chill.

"Seward and I were just ironing out the last details of the treaty. I expect you know all about them."

"Yes, sir."

"That's why I hired you," Lincoln said. "The treaty is an absolute necessity at this time. That reminds me of two boys out in Illinois who took a short cut across an orchard. When they were in the middle of the field, they saw a vicious dog bounding toward them. One of the boys was sly enough to climb a tree, but the other ran around the tree, with the dog following. He kept running until, by making smaller circles than it was possible for his pursuer to make, he gained upon the dog sufficiently to grasp his tail. Held on to the tail with a desperate grip until nearly exhausted, then he called to the boy up the tree to come down and help.

"'What for?' said the boy.

"'I want you to help me let this dog go.'"[23]

He smiled and went on. "That's just it, Sharpe. We need Russia to help us let go of the British and French that are chasing us around the tree. And they need us to crop to help England's ambitions. If they didn't seize this opportunity, they knew they would never get another chance."

"Necessity, sir—the iron law of necessity."

"Yes, but what of the consequences down the road, Sharpe?" He picked up a copy of the *New York Herald*. "Now the *Herald* is not our friend, and for that reason bears reading. Listen to this:

> If Russia equally resents and punishes the interference of Europe in the affairs of Poland, she may be mistress of the Old World, as we shall be of the New, and then perhaps in a hundred years hence, these two immense Powers may meet upon the Pacific Ocean and, differing upon some question of the possession of Australia or New Zealand, may enter upon that Titanic contest which will forever decide the destinies of mankind.[24]

Australia and New Zealand—nonsense, but the prophecy in general may have something in it."

He got up and poked at the fire. "Now, so far, so good. Seward's got his ears open all over Europe. Finally, the expense of all those embassies might show a profit. I told him to share everything with you. How's it going?"

"Secretary Seward has been extremely cooperative, sir. Of course, he expects it to be a two-way street, so we have set up a small committee. That also includes Secretary Welles's Navy Department, too. I have determined that the motto of the Bureau will be 'We Share Intelligence'!"

"Good luck there. People tend to get mighty protective of their little hen yards. But the reason I wanted to see you was to tell you that I think the Rooshans will bear watching, too, and to suggest that you might want to pick up the slack over in Europe. The State Department people are fine at sifting all the gossip of Europe, but they don't know much about fighting. The exception was Tom Dudley, our consul in Liverpool. If it hadn't been for him, we wouldn't have a clear picture of how the Confederates were building their commerce-raiders—with the connivance of the British government. Do you think you might have work for him over there?"

"I'm way ahead of you, sir. We are planning to stand up a European office. I was going to send over Jim McPhail. But he could use someone like Dudley to direct operations against the British Isles. The problem right now is getting there. The British blockade is tightening, and with Mexico in French hands, we don't have a friendly neutral through which to pass our people and communications. It's going to make the alliance communications damned difficult, as well."

Lincoln looked at him over his reading spectacles. He had chosen Sharpe because the man had the knack of solving the very problems he identified. He said, "I think, sir, our Irish friends just might be the key that unlocks this door. It is said of them that they are welcome in every country but their own. I think we can make use of that misfortune."[25]

THE WINTER PALACE, ST. PETERSBURG, RUSSIA,
3:15 AM, OCTOBER 16, 1863

The awestruck naval courier bowed himself out of the presence of the czar of all the Russias, Alexander II. He had ridden at a gallop from the large Russian naval base at Kronstadt, just outside the capital, to bring news that Russian forces had fought a battle in the Upper Bay of New York with the hated British.

Alexander Nikolayevich was forty-five years old and in his prime. He had inherited the Crimean War from his late father Nicholas I in 1855 and spent the first year of his reign unable to stave off a humiliating defeat at the hands of the British and French. An ardent reformer, he had freed the serfs from their landlords, abolished the death penalty, and initiated a score of reforms to bring Russia out of its backwardness.

Yet in one vital respect, Alexander was a man captivated by an ancient dream woven into his soul: Constantinople—the once "God-guarded city" and the mystical root of Russia's Orthodox Christian civilization. The niece of the last Byzantine emperor had married Ivan III and from that union had been born the idea of the Third Rome. After Constantinople inherited the mantle of Rome and then fell to the vile Turk, Moscow took up the legacy as the mother of Orthodoxy. Moscow was the Third Rome, and there would be no other. No Westerner could understand the determination of every Russian to plant the cross once again on the dome of the Hagia Sophia, Justinian's great cathedral.

Alexander read the dispatch for the third time. Then he solemnly raised his right hand to his forehead, thumb and first two fingers joined and the remaining two fingers folded onto the palm, crossed himself in the Orthodox fashion from right to left, and fell to his knees before his astonished servants and family hastily roused from their beds.[26] Tears welled in his eyes. Raising his arms he exclaimed, *"Slava Bogu!"* — glory to God![27]

2

Le Bal

"Here they come!" the Union signalman shouted from his makeshift perch in a tree. For Maj. Gen. Nathaniel Banks's Army of the Gulf, used to the drabness of dark blue or butternut and gray, the sight of the advancing French was more than memorable; it was the ultimate martial fashion statement. The Confederate division on their left went hardly noticed.

On they came in a rapid, ordered advance across the open ground that stretched out before the Union positions. The quickening sound of their drums ran before them as their tricolor standards topped with their imperial eagles waved overhead. Squadrons of cavalry swarmed ahead of the infantry to drive in the Union cavalry pickets. These were the *Chasseurs d'Afrique,* bitterly named by the Mexicans, and the *Los Carcinceros Azul* (The Blue Butchers) for their ferocity and their light blue jackets above stylish baggy red trousers. Raised in North Africa from French colonists to subdue the Muslim populations, they had come by their ferocity honestly. One of their regimental colors bore the *Légion d'Honneur* for the capture of Mexican colors earlier that year. In reserve were squadrons of the *Chasseurs à Cheval* in brown tunics and Hussars in green with their lambskin busbys. Most impressive of all were the lancers in sky blue jackets and red trousers with Polish helmets and white and red pennants whipping from their lances.[1]

Behind them came the infantry, with the *lignards,* or regular infantry, of the 7th, 51st, 62nd, 81st, and 95th *Régiments de Ligne* in their new yellow-piped, dark blue tunics ending just below the belt and derisively described by critics as a masterpiece of *les stupidités du mode.* Fashionably

dressed or not, the men wearing them were hard-bitten, long-service veterans, many of whom had fought in North Africa, the Crimea, Italy, and
Mexico. Their dark blue tunics flared at the shoulders with red-fringed
epaulets; blue kepis were covered with white covers and sun guards.
Their baggy red trousers — *les pantaloons rouge* — and white gaiters had
become the mark of the French infantry since 1829. With them were
the exotic 1st, 2nd, and 3rd regiments of Zouaves, one of the numerous French units of *l'Armée d'Afrique* developed in the colonializaton of
North Africa and clothed on exotic, native models. Instead of the kepi,
they wore a blue-tasseled, red fez, a short and open blue jacket with
red piping, and an extremely baggy version of the *pantaloons rouge*, *à la
Zouave*. They were the only regiments in the French Army allowed to
grow full beards, of which they took luxurious advantage. The Zouave
regiments had seen considerable action in Napoleon III's numerous
wars and had acquired an elite reputation. The 2nd Regiment, "The
Jackals of Oran," had been the first to adorn its colors with the *Legion
d'Honneur* for capturing an Austrian color at Magenta in Italy. In the
same war, the 3rd Regiment had been famously referred to as the *furia
francese* by their Piedmontese allies.[2]

A fourth Zouave regiment was formed for the recreated Imperial
Guard of the emperor. To fill the new Guard regiment, the other Zouave
regiments had been cherry-picked during the Crimean War for their
best men. The new regiment had baptized itself in blood by storming
the Malakoff Fort, where half of them died for their first victory. At Magenta in 1859, they shattered the Austrians, winning ten crosses of the
Legion d'Honneur. They were distinguished from the other line Zouave
regiments by the yellow piping of their jackets and the red-, white-, and
blue-striped soft fez.[3] The Emperor had hinted broadly to the French
Army commander, Maj. Gen. François Achille Bazaine, that they not be
stinted of glory. The Zouaves of the Guard would not be denied.

Rounding out the French force were four battalions of skilled light
infantry, *Chasseurs à Pied*, in dark blue tunics and light blue trousers,
spread out as skirmishers ahead of the line regiments.

Napoleon III tread heavily on the glories of his incomparable uncle,
the first and, many would say, the only Napoleon. One of these was to
reissue the colors of the armies in a grand ceremony on the Champ de
Mars in 1851. The chief change was to add the imperial eagles to the

tricolor. By 1860 this was an 18 cm, cast-aluminum eagle topping a dark blue staff. The front of the color bore the words, "*L'Empereur Napoleon III au . . . Régiment,*" and on the rear the regiment's battle honors.[4]

The French colonial experience in North Africa had done more than influence the fashion of the French Army. Its harsh arena had developed deadly light cavalry. That experience also had found a perfect home for another French experiment, *La Légion Étrangère* (the Foreign Legion). Founded in 1831 as a way to rid France of foreign social undesirables, it was stationed in Algeria. Now the entire legion, a single regiment, took its place in the French line, distinguished by their white trousers. Major General Bazaine had served with this band of cutthroats and thieves, and though he appreciated their fighting skills, he had no illusions about their nature. They were the greatest source of desertion in the French Army in Mexico, and Bazaine stated matter-of-factly, "I shall have some of them shot. . . . It is quite clear that a good many of them enrolled in the corps to get a free trip, but it shall cost them dearly if they are caught."[5]

Napoleon III had another colonial rum lot to send to Mexico in a battalion of the *Infanterie Légère d'Afrique* (African Light Infantry) made up of military convicts who had served their sentences but had time left in their enlistments. Naturally, they had been sent to North Africa, where any tendency to mischief would be less noticeable than in France. It would be even less noticeable in Mexico.

Still another colonial experiment was the battalion of the *Tirailleurs Algériens* (Algerian Rifles). These were native North African Berbers and Arabs who were commonly called Turcos for their brutal fighting ability.[6] Another African contingent was a battalion of Sudanese slave soldiers, the oddest of the units sent to Mexico. Napoleon III had pressured the ruler of Egypt for black African troops, whom the French rightly believed would be more resistant to the yellow fever that was felling French troops attempting to keep open lines of communication called the Fever Road, from Mexico City through the coastal *tierra caliente* (hot land) to Vera Cruz. Napoleon had asked for a regiment of Sudanese; the pasha coughed up a battalion. Muslim slavers had sold them to the Egyptian government, which followed an ancient Muslim custom of training African slaves as soldiers. To the terror of the Mexicans, they quickly proved their worth.[7] Marching out of Galveston in their sky-blue

Zouave-type uniforms, they had excited the hard stares of the Texans and the immense curiosity of their slaves.

ONE MILE WEST OF VERMILLIONVILLE, LOUISIANA, 2:10 PM, OCTOBER 21, 1863

A long-range shot from a distant Union battery hit and bounced along the bare ground straight toward Walker's Texas Division. Every eye could see it from the moment its strike sent the dirt flying. Its second bounce took it straight into the cavalcade of French officers riding in front of the Texans. The shot tore off the legs of the lead rider's horse and then drove through the ranks of the infantry.

The stricken horse screamed in agony as it writhed on the ground, its forelegs gushing stumps. Its rider, Major General Bazaine, had leaped off with the quickness of a cat, pulled his pistol, and put his horse out of its misery. In an instant he was surrounded by his anxious aides and Confederate escorts. He laughed, "*Le bal commence, messieurs!*" and waved them off to walk over to the Texans whose ranks had dressed around the gory gauge left by the ball. He had been running a practiced eye over the ranks of these men when the shot struck.

If ever there was judge of fighting men, it was Bazaine. He had left school to enlist as a private in the French Army in North Africa and had fought in every war in which the tricolor had waved, covering himself with glory, honors, and wounds. His feats in the Crimea had earned him France's highest honor, as well as the ultimate praise from France's ancient enemy when the British had awarded him the Order of the Bath. He had been largely responsible for the destruction of the Mexican Army at Puebla at the end of May and had led the first French troops into Mexico City. The men of the Foreign Legion held an especially dear place in his esteem for he had fought and bled often with them. These Texans reminded him of them, though they were obviously cleaner and undoubtedly more virtuous. Their ranks had barely stirred when the shot plowed through them, dealing death in a spray of blood.

Bazaine inquired after the wounded and congratulated the regimental commander on the fine appearance of his men. By appearance he did not mean their ragged butternut and gray but their lean and hungry look, their gleaming rifles, and their discipline under fire. He said loud enough to be overheard, "*Les brave gens, les brave gens!*" (The brave fellows, the brave fellows!) as another horse was led up to him. He knew the compliment would leap the language barrier, as it always did. It had come as a surprise to him how many Confederates, especially from Louisiana, spoke French well.

As they rode off, he turned to the Confederate brigadier general who served as his escort and liaison. "Well, I think, Your Highness, that these men shall give the Yankees a hard time today." At the age of thirty-one, Camille Armand Jules Marie Prince de Polignac cut a magnificent figure in his uniform of Confederate gray. The Frenchman had traveled to the Southern states just before the madness of secession had intoxicated them and had offered his services to the young Confederate Army. His service in the French Army had made him a valuable commodity, and his talent had justified his rise to general officer rank and command of a brigade under Lt. Gen. Richard Taylor in the Western Louisiana District.[8]

Taylor had given him command of the small brigade of Stevens and Alexander's Texas regiments. The Texans had responded with a frontier directness that Taylor had to deal with personally. They would not serve under a Frenchman with a name they could not even pronounce. Taylor would not reverse his decision but promised that if they still had reservations after the first action, he would reconsider. It was not long before the Prince de Polignac made first-rate soldiers of them and won a grudging affection for his care and attention to their welfare, but still he had not had his test of fire. Yet Taylor had no worries and said of him "he belonged to that race of gentry whose ancestors rallied to the white plume of Henry at Ivry, and followed the charge of Condé at Rocroi."[9]

After the fall of New Orleans in April 1862 to Adm. David Farragut's bold attack up the Mississippi, Taylor's minor command with its one small division had been lucky to annoy the Union forces based there. The addition of Walker's Greyhounds to his command had doubled Taylor's force to about ten thousand men. The arrival of Bazaine's twenty thousand by ship at Galveston after the French Navy's destruction of the Union West Gulf Blockading Squadron at the battle of Galveston[10] had been a godsend to Taylor who now had a serious opportunity to recapture New Orleans. With the fall of that city, all the Union successes in gaining control of the Mississippi would be cancelled. Taylor had come within an ace of recapturing New Orleans in July when he sacked the

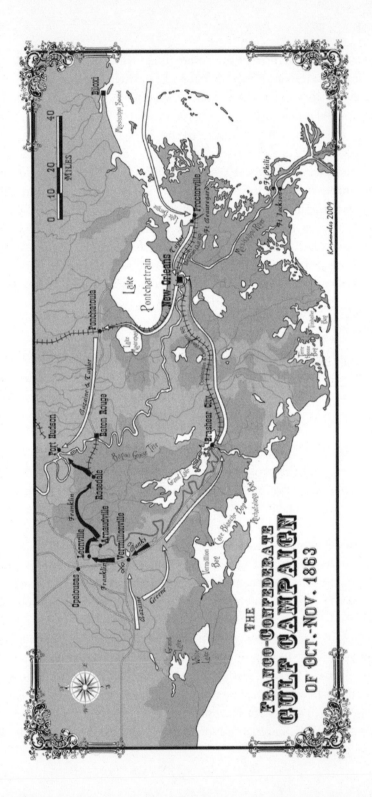

THE
FRANCO-CONFEDERATE
GULF CAMPAIGN
OF OCT.-NOV. 1863

huge Union supply base at Brashear City and marched to the outskirts of the almost undefended Crescent City. The taste of victory was nearly on the tongue when the news of the fall of Port Hudson and the imminent arrival of Banks's army turned his foray into a trap. He barely withdrew his tiny force in time.[11]

In only a few days, Taylor and Bazaine had taken each other's measure and got along well. Trusted by both commands, the Prince de Polignac had been the perfect liaison, doing everything possible to ease tensions and encourage cooperation. Bazaine had gracefully acknowledged Taylor as overall commander while Taylor had eagerly sought Bazaine's advice. Bazaine had been prepared to deal with an American novice and dreaded the complex diplomatic delicacies that would be needed to finesse the weakness of the man who was the brother-in-law of Confederate president Jefferson Davis. But Bazaine had been surprised to find in Taylor a gifted commander with shrewd tactical and strategic insights. Taylor had learned soldiering from the very best, Old Blue Light — the legendary Stonewall Jackson — who had taught him that speed and surprise are the most precious jewels of war. His relationship to Davis only gave priority and the full, unstinted support of the Confederate government to the allied effort. Napoleon III's instructions to Bazaine were to work as closely and tactfully with the Confederates as he could. A Confederate guarantee of French control of Mexico depended upon their joint and cordial success.

Taylor also burned with an ardor that was not all patriotism. This son of former president Zachary Taylor was determined to avenge the desecration of his late father's magnificent Louisiana estate, Fashion, by Union plunderers. They had not even spared his presidential papers but scattered them about the fields or sent them off as trophies to that viper's pit of Yankeedom, Boston.

It had been Taylor who had then come up with the plan that solved the unity-of-command problems. Leaving Walker's division and Polignac's brigade under Bazaine's command, he had taken the rest of his brigades aboard the same French transports that had delivered Bazaine's troops. His destination was the oddly named Lake One-Eyed. That would leave Bazaine in command of over thirty thousand allied troops. The two were about to turn on its head the old military adage that one bad general is better than the inherent disunity of two good generals sharing command. Whoever had coined that bit of wisdom had not met Banks.

And now, as if on cue, Banks had laid a priceless gift before Bazaine. He had come out to fight. Nathanial Banks was a political general, an influential Republican, former governor of Massachusetts, and Speaker of the U.S. House of Representatives. Known as the Bobbin Boy of Waltham for his close ties to the textile industry, he had been most useful to Lincoln in generating political support for the war and initiating political reconstruction in occupied Louisiana, but he was less than able as a general. His only success had been to reduce by starvation the last Confederate garrison on the Mississippi River at Port Hudson, about a hundred miles north of New Orleans. He was better known for being repeatedly drubbed by Stonewall Jackson in the Shenandoah Valley in 1862. The masses of supplies he lost to Old Blue Light earned him the title from the perpetually hungry Confederates of "Commissary Banks."

He had come out to fight, to Bazaine's amazement, when the better part of valor would have been to withdraw behind the water barrier of the maze of swamps, bayous, and lakes that paralleled the Mississippi to the east from the Gulf to north of Port Hudson. Barely twenty miles north of the Gulf, however, this barrier opened narrowly between the coastal swamps and Grand Lake and Lake Palourde in a forty-mile-long strip ending at Brashear City. Coming down from the north, Bayou Teche, a former channel of the Mississippi itself, wound through the strip emptying into the Grand Lake at Brashear City, the eastern end of the gap. Through this gap ran the only serious road between Texas and New Orleans. From the great river port to Brashear City ran a railroad. The strip was ideal defense in depth as Banks brought his supplies forward while Bazaine broke camp immediately and marched against him with the combined French-Confederate Armée de Louisiane of thirty-five thousand men. The French general counted his advantages, the weather among them. It was the driest month of the year in Louisiana, and air was as fresh and delightful as a bottle of fine wine.

ALBANY, NEW YORK, 2:20 PM, OCTOBER 21, 1863

The ruins of Albany swarmed with redcoats. Two weeks ago, the British Army in Canada had struck with complete surprise, using the railroads to rush south and overwhelm New York's state capital. Its warehouses, factories, and nearby Watervliet Arsenal had all been burned to deliver such a trauma to the citizens of the Empire State that they would clamor for peace. Now what was left of the city was the base for the British Albany Field Force, commanded by Guards major general Frederick Lord Paulet, who was sending raiding parties west to the big industrial towns and down the Hudson to scorch more holes in the state's morale. Towns along the Hudson that had gone up in flames during the War of Independence at the hands of red-coated incendiaries were again sending plumes of black smoke skyward. The might of the British Empire in its imperial battalions and Canadian militia had planted a boot on the throat of New York. In its imperial battalions, no finer troops existed. Events were building that would send the Albany Field Force south and east to threaten New York and Boston just as the French and Confederate battle line was marching to contact west of New Orleans.

Before the outbreak of hostilities, the British government had wanted the quality of the reinforcement to be taken into account in American diplomatic calculations, which was why the two Guards battalions — the 1st Battalion of the Grenadier Guards, and the 2nd Battalion of the Scots Fusilier Guards — were included. The Rifle Brigade had also sent its 1st Battalion.

Most of the regiments had their share of North American battle honors. The oldest was the Grenadier Guards, sent to Virginia in 1677 to put down Bacon's Rebellion. The 15th (York, East Riding) Regiment of Foot had fought on the Plains of Abraham with Wolfe and served during the Revolution with Howe and Clinton in the campaigns of 1776–78. The 17th (Leicestershire) Regiment of Foot was also at Quebec and served through the entire American War of Independence, with the great misfortune of being twice captured — at Stony Creek in 1779 and at Yorktown in 1783 — and both times speedily exchanged. The 16th (Bedfordshire) Regiment of Foot, fought in the War of 1812 in Canada. The 30th (Cambridgeshire) Regiment of Foot campaigned in North Carolina in 1781–82. The 47th (Lancashire) Regiment of Foot had seen hard service at Bunker's Hill in 1776 and at Saratoga in 1777, where it surrendered with the rest of Burgoyne's army.

One regiment even had its origin in what would become the United States. The 60th Regiment of Foot, the old Royal Americans, was originally raised in New York and Philadelphia in 1755 during the French and Indian War. They were also with Wolfe at Quebec. The 62nd (Wiltshire) Regiment of Foot fought in the War of 1812 in the Great Lakes campaigns. The 63rd (West Suffolk) Regiment of Foot landed with Howe on Long Island in 1776 to help drive Washington out of New York, then beat him again at Germantown and Bennington and went on to fight in South Carolina, distinguishing themselves at Eutaw Springs in 1782.[12]

Of more current importance, the battalions of the Rifle Brigade and the 17th, 30th, 47th, 62nd, and 63rd Foot had served in the Crimea, and a decade later had a core of experienced veterans. Regardless of whether they had bled in the Crimea, every British battalion could be depended upon to be obstinate in battle to the point of suicide. That refusal to never turn their back on an enemy was ingrained, despite the Duke of Wellington's comment that "all soldiers run away." It had been a rare enemy in the last hundred years able to make them do it. Their regimental anniversaries were marks of such obstinacy — Blenheim, Quebec, Minden.

British regiments usually had only a single battalion, usually numbered the first. In that case, they were simply referred to by their regimental number. A few regiments did have more than one battalion, though these were exceptions. The result was that although, for example, the title of a unit was the 30th Regiment of Foot (30th Foot, for short), it actually represented a battalion in strength, usually about eight hundred and fifty men in ten companies. Most of the battalions that had been sent to British North America had been plussed up from their depots to about a thousand men each. The term "battalion" originally meant a detachment or part of a regiment, or the organization of the regiment for combat. Occasionally, the British would raise a second, third, or fourth battalion of the same regiment. Administratively and operationally, each battalion was a separate organization. American regiments, in contrast, numbered about nine hundred and fifty men in ten companies. Battalions were only large detachments of the same regiment. There were never separate numbered battalions.

British battalions were also unique in having distinct personalities that were encouraged to foster the regimental spirit, a cohesive power unequaled in the world's armies. Nicknames were common. The 1st Battalion, Grenadier Guards, was known as the Dandies, no doubt from their parade functions in London, and the fact that, like all the Guards, they were selected for height to make a grander appearance. Other regiments' nicknames were derived from their combat history or, sometimes, in jest, to having just missed a fight. In this case, the 1/16 Foot was known as the Peacemakers, for having been shipped to Europe from Canada to fight Napoleon, only to barely miss Waterloo.

In contrast to the subdued uniform colors of the U.S. Army and C.S. Army, the regulation British tunic was a brilliant scarlet, achieved with that perfect red dye, cochineal, derived from the crushed bodies of a beetle, and first concocted by the peoples of Mesoamerica more than a thousand years ago. Facings varied by regiment—yellow, buff, green, and blue—to distinguish each regiment from another. There were also a wealth of differences in buckles and other accoutrement, especially the regimental badge worn on the front of the shako, as marks of regimental pride. Standing out from all these scarlet-clad regiments were the rifle battalions, the 1st Battalion, the Rifle Brigade, and the 4th Battalion, 60th Foot (The King's Rifle Corps) in rifle green with black and scarlet facings respectively. The Rifle Brigade was descended from the 95th Rifles of Peninsular War whose most famous officer had been the same Richard Sharpe that Wolseley had commented on at dinner with George Sharpe in Washington.[13] As a rifle unit they were unique among British regiments to carry no colors. To honor the Queen's late beloved husband, Prince Albert, they had become known in 1862 as the Prince Consort's Own.

As with most Western armies, each British battalion carried two flags—the regimental colors unique to it and the royal colors. The latter was the national or Grand Union flag. Each measured 42 by 48 inches. British regimental colors wore the color of the regimental facing, with the Great Union flag in the upper hoist corner. Exceptions were made for regiments with white or red facings—for white to prevent its confusion with a flag of surrender and red for possible confusion with a flag of no quarter. Instead, the field for such colors was the Cross of St. George, a red cross on a white field. The regimental number in Roman numerals was centered on the Grand Union flag in the upper hoist corner. Regimental badges were placed in the center, around which were the names of their battles were inscribed. With the delightful irregularity of British military tradition, the Guards regiments reversed this arrangement, with the Grand Union flag as the regimental colors, and a unique crimson and gold embroidered silk flag as the royal colors.[14]

American colors were much simpler. U.S. Army regiments carried the national colors, the Stars and Stripes, and a regimental flag, usually dark blue with a large embroidered American eagle in the center and the regimental number on a red wreath beneath. Exceptions were made for certain volunteer regiments. For example, the Irish Brigade's regiments carried the green flag of Ireland, which displayed a golden harp on an emerald green field. Battles honors were often written on the red and white stripes of the national colors. However, Confederate regiments carried only a single flag—the Stars and Bars on a square field—referred to by their opponents as "those damned red flags of rebellion."[15]

Colors were as highly prized as any Roman standard, and it was the ultimate disgrace to lose either flag in battle, which made it an extremely rare occurrence. In the past, colors had been lost when regiments had to capitulate as part of larger forces that had been trapped, such as at the battles of Saratoga and Yorktown in the American War of Independence. In combat, however, if any enemy picked up a British flag, it was usually because they found it surrounded by the dead of the regiment. By the time of the Civil War, rifled weapons had made the role of color bearer exceedingly dangerous, if not a death sentence. American regiments, North and South, usually collected a special fund for their families.

The two Scots battalions, the Scots Fusilier Guards and the 25th Foot, King's Own Scottish Borderers, did not wear kilts, which was a Highland regiment prerogative. Only the bagpipers of the former were kilted in the Royal Stuart tartan. The regimental march was "Blue Bonnets over the Border." For all their bagpipes, this battalion was more English than Scottish, having only its recruiting parties visiting Scotland, while being stationed permanently in London. In March 1861, 59 percent (557) of its 996 officers and men were English; only 272 were Scots (27 percent). The rest (14 percent) were Irish.[16]

Amid all this worship of the traditions of the regiment, the British Army had undergone important reforms after the Crimean War. The uniform had been changed after almost a century from the awkward swallowtail coat to the more comfortable tunic, which had the advantage keeping a man warmer in winter. Black trousers and a short black shako topped with a black pompom completed the new uniform. Improvements were also made in the soldier's pack to replace the traditional torture instrument the British soldier had carried for generations. The two Guards battalions stood out not just for their height but that they wore, instead of the shako, a bearskin hat eighteen inches tall and weighing only one and half pounds. Their appearance on any field would be instantly noted.

The soldier was also armed with the superb .577 caliber muzzle-loading Enfield rifle of the 1853 pattern, the product of the Royal Small Arms Factory Enfield. As a weapon, it was only rivaled by the American Springfield rifle.

The Royal Artillery had also taken the lead in introducing a break-through new artillery piece. The field artillery batteries had come equipped with the new breechloading Armstrong guns. Breechloading artillery was a military innovation that had not been adopted by either the North or the South in America, except for the handful of English Whitworth rifled guns slipped through the blockade for the Army of Northern Virginia. Quick-firing and accurate, the Armstrongs had been introduced with much promise. To Wolseley's dismay, he was discovering that they were problem-plagued. Trials had not revealed any deficiencies because the manufacturer had carefully trained the crews, but once in the hands of the Army, the problems became glaringly apparent. Sixty percent of the enlisted men were illiterate, and the simplest mechanical device confounded most. Their noncommissioned officers (NCOs) were as steeped as the officer corps in tradition and took an active dislike for such an innovation. Careful training and maintenance would have eliminated most of these problems, but the NCOs were hostile and unprepared for that sort of attention to either their men or to complicated mechanisms. They complained of having to rewrite the venerable gun drill "because the gun loaded at the wrong end." They complained that "the guns were so complicated that the ignorant gunners would never, ever learn to handle them." And, of course, officers did not train anyone.[17]

No matter how good the British infantryman was, however, there was simply not enough of "that article," as Wellington used to call him. An effective Canadian auxiliary force was vital to the defense of British North America. In early 1860, the process of consolidating the many independent companies into battalions began. The first to be so organized had been granted the title of the 1st Battalion, Prince of Wales Regiment, by Prince Edward when he had toured Canada in 1860. In early 1863, the 2nd Battalion of the Volunteer Militia was designated the 2nd Battalion, The Queen's Own Rifles of Toronto. The men were issued Enfield rifles and kit and paid for each day of drill but had to furnish their own uniforms, modeled on the new British Army uniform introduced after the Crimean War. Rifle battalions, such as the 3rd Battalion, Victoria Volunteer Rifles of Montreal, copied their Imperial counterparts by dressing in rifle green.

The affiliations with the British regimental system were instinctive in the English-speaking population and much sought after. In 1862 the six Scottish clan chiefs in Montreal raised companies that were consolidated into the 5th Volunteer Militia Battalion; its two flank companies were dressed in tartan trews. In the Maritimes, the militia had a regimental tradition. New Brunswick Regiment of Yeomanry Cavalry had been formed in 1842 as the first voluntary cavalry regiment in British North America. Prince Edward Island formed its militia companies into the Queen's Country Regiment. In Newfoundland the various militia companies were consolidated into the Royal Canadian Rifle Regiment in 1862.[18]

The cavalry troops never did consolidate into battalions; with their vast forests, Canada and the northernmost states of the Union were not the best cavalry country. The Canadian cavalry tended to be modeled more on the American experience of dragoons—ride to the fight but fight dismounted. They were usually uniformed in blue with yellow facings, wearing a brown fur busby with a white plume, and armed with saber and carbine, the latter greatly inferior to the American single-shot Sharps breechloader.

A unique troop was the Royal Guides of the Governor General's Bodyguard for Lower Canada, or Royal Guides for short. Based in Montreal, they were actually the "family" troop of Lt. Col. George Denison, whose grandfather had founded the unit in 1812. His father had commanded it as well. The fifty-five-man unit was unique in both dress and function. The family's long association with the unit had given Denison enough familiarity to encourage him to study carefully the history of cavalry as well as draw on the experiences of the war to the south. Ardently pro-Confederate, he paid special attention to Southern achievements. In Denison's creative hands, the Royal Guides became an excellent intelligence-gathering and scouting unit. They wore blue with white facings and a nickel-plated dragoon helmet with a red feather. In this case, the soldier as peacock took precedence over a scout's need for anonymity. It had not taken Wolseley long to appreciate the usefulness of the Royal Guides and the value of its commander. He and Denison became good friends, and he introduced the Canadian into his small circle of British Army intimates, men chosen for their abilities. He was one of the few men Wolseley allowed to call him "Joe."

Denison was part of a relatively small group of openly pro-Confederate Canadians. He was a through and through Imperialist and a very pugnacious man. Even after Vicksburg and Gettysburg, when such sympathies did not appear to serve Canadian interests well, he and a small group of fire-eaters continued to champion the Southern cause. Both living in Montreal, Wolseley and Denison were inevitably drawn to each other by similar opinions. "I tell you, Joe," Denison would say, "that if three and a half million Southerners can come close to beating the entire North, then what cannot three and a half million British North Americans backed by Britain achieve?"[19] It was a calculation much on Wolseley's mind.

Three Canadian militia infantry battalions were brigaded with one British battalion for wartime operations. The British were consciously following the Roman historical model in which non-Roman auxiliary cohorts served with the Roman legions. This system was followed in India, especially after the trauma of the Great Mutiny. In Canada seven such brigades were created initially. It is no wonder that when overseas, British units were referred to as "Imperial battalions." The Canadian battalions also trained with these same British battalions and quickly picked up some of the smartness, field craft, and cunning of the regulars. The Americans had failed to parcel out their regular units in a similar fashion at the beginning of the Civil War to leaven the huge masses of volunteers that had rushed to the colors; their road to professionalism had been much longer and more painful than their Canadian counterparts.

While the Canadian infantry benefited by training with the Imperial battalions, they received additional assistance from another 104 British NCOs specifically sent out as infantry training teams. The small number of Canadian cavalry was on its own in the absence of British cavalry until the arrival of a training team of fifty-eight British cavalry officers and

NCOs. As sound as these measures were, they were only a beginning. Of the twenty-three Canadian battalions established by September, one had been raised in 1859, one in 1860, twelve in 1862, and the rest only that same year of 1863. Although most battalions had been created by incorporating existing militia companies, it took time to meld a battalion-level organization together, requiring skills—especially in leadership, training, logistics, and maneuver—at a more complex level than existed in the forty- to fifty-man community-based companies. With only training together as a battalion the eight days per year allowed by provincial law, there was a definite limit to how much experience even a close association with an Imperial battalion could impart.[20]

VERMILLIONVILLE, LOUISIANA, 2:25 PM, OCTOBER 21, 1863

To say that Banks was unsettled by the quickly advancing wave of French red and blue was an understatement. He had assumed that the enemy would await his own advance, a conceit common among amateurs. Now that Bazaine had plucked the initiative from his hands, he just did not know what to do. Unfortunately, his XIII Corps commander, Maj. Gen. Cadwallader C. Washburn, was as new to that level of command as a soldier could get. He had only assumed that position because Maj. Gen. E.O.C. Ward, one of Grant's better senior commanders, had just fallen sick and had to surrender command of the corps that very day. Grant had referred to Cadwallader as "one of the best administrative officers we have." However, it would not be administration that would beat the French.[21]

That left Maj. Gen. William B. Franklin, commander of the smaller XIX Corps, as the only professional and experienced senior officer on the field. Franklin, top of his class at West Point in the same years as his friend Maj. Gen. Ulysses S. Grant, was a tough Regular Army fighter and had seen almost all the major action in the East. One admirer wrote: "He struck me as an officer of power—large with square face and head, deep-sunk, determined blue eyes, close-cropped reddish-brown hair and beard."[22] It was he "who had shared the brunt at Bull Run, who fought the rear-guard battles from the Chickahominy to the James, and held the pass of White Oak Swamp against half of Lee's army on the critical day at Glendale, who won at Crampton's Gap 'the completest victory gained to that time by any part of the Army of the Potomac. . . .'"[23] His conduct had earned him command of a third of the Army of the Potomac in the assault at Fredericksburg on Stonewall Jackson's wing of Lee's army. Franklin fought hard and skillfully, but because Burnside had frittered away the time necessary to strike hard and fast, the assault never had a chance. It was no disgrace to be bested by Jackson, and Franklin had given Old Blue Light some anxious moments that day, a feat few could boast of.

To that time, Franklin had been as loyal a subordinate as a commander could hope for, but Burnside's gross incompetence was too much. He plotted to remove Burnside. Instead, he was scapegoated for the disaster by the witch-hunting Congressional Committee on the Conduct of the War. It did not help that he had been a protégé of Maj. Gen. George B. McClellan, an object of special venom to the committee, which believed his dedication to victory left something to be desired. Ironically, another plotter, Maj. Gen. Joseph Hooker, succeeded to army command. Franklin languished in New York without an assignment for six months until Grant could find a command for him in Banks's military district.

Until he had been given XIX Corps in Banks's Louisiana command, he had worried that he might be ordered to lead black troops, the ten regiments of locally recruited blacks known as the *Corps d'Afrique*. Many of them were from old Louisiana state militia regiments of free blacks that had been mobilized by the Confederacy. Once New Orleans had fallen, they had been largely transferred to federal service, shorn of their officers. They had seen a deal of active service, and their assault on the defenses of Port Hudson, though repulsed, had been nothing less than heroic. Despite his distaste for black troops, Franklin had been appalled by the nefarious means of recruitment he had found upon his arrival. Black men had been arrested on the flimsiest charges and given a choice between enlistment or prison. Franklin's outrage at this practice had put a stop to it.

Now outside Vermillionville, Franklin immediately saw the danger they were in. The army's sixty-five-mile-long line of communications back to Brashear City was wide open. He had argued with Banks against this expedition, but "Bobbin Boy" had had his eye on the political payoff of a victory and how well that would sit in Washington. With the British rampaging in New York and Maine, the administration desperately needed a success. For Franklin, the professional officer who had slugged it out with Stonewall Jackson, every atom of his experience had rejected this move. Banks should have keyed on the defense of New Orleans by making sure the enemy could not pass through Brashear City again to threaten the city from the south. It was clear that once that barrier was passed, New Orleans would be next to impossible to defend. Holding Brashear City with its long difficult approach was the only way to defend the city.

Once again he remonstrated with Banks. "I tell you, again, General, we are in a trap. All the enemy has to do is fix our front and sweep south and cut us off from our line of communications."

Banks was one of those men who only got stubborn when confronted by his own mistakes. "We shall meet them on this field, General. Now, sir, rejoin your command."

Franklin was not through. "By God, sir, you will hear me out!" He was a forceful man, and Banks almost seemed to cringe from the power of his personality. "Not only are we about to be cut off from our communications, but you have placed us with our backs to this lake and the bayous beyond. Why, all the enemy has to do is push us back and we tumble down the bluff and right into Bayou Capucin. We must quit this field and march south immediately, sir!"

Confronted with a barrage of the obvious, Banks simply retreated into stubbornness. "Rejoin your command, sir!"

In disgust, Franklin spurred his horse away from the command group to take his place with his small corps of barely six thousand men on the right of the line just as his skirmishers were rushing back through the line of battle. In his obtuseness, Banks reminded Franklin of Burnside, the bungler of Fredericksburg. It was a telling comparison for Franklin and Burnside had been mortal enemies. He muttered to himself that since he couldn't outright shoot that damned fool Banks, he was going to work out his anger on the approaching French instead.

Bazaine had declined to oblige him. Instead of the French line, it was Walker's Texans who surged toward XIX Corps. The Frenchman had reserved the full weight of his own regiments for Washburn's large sixteen-thousand-man XIII Corps on the left. By Taylor's account, it was a veteran formation that had seen much action in the Vicksburg Campaigns. Bazaine had also given much thought to Taylor's analysis of Washburn and Franklin, and it was clear to him that he would rather attack the large veteran corps commanded by a political general than a small corps led by a pugnacious veteran. He would leave that tough nut to Walker's Greyhounds and the glory to the French.

Bazaine had Taylor's shrewd biographical intelligence analysis of Banks and his corps commanders to thank for this unfolding opportunity. He had been suspicious when Taylor's scouts reported that Banks's line of communications had been left wide open. Surely it was a trap. It was a rare European general who would have blundered so. He sent the scouts out to confirm. Once Bazaine had realized what an imbecile opposed him, he sent his large Confederate cavalry division ten miles south to cut the Union line of communications and himself marched straight for Vermillionville. He almost licked his lips.

Bazaine's first move was to send the bulk of his remaining cavalry with two battalions of *Chasseurs à Pied* south within sight of the enemy to cut the road to Brashear City. "*Oui, messieurs,*" he mused to his staff, "Let General Banks observe. It is always wise to give the enemy something to be nervous about." He also thought to himself that the nervousness would be shared by the rank and file as the word flitted through the ranks that they were cut off to the south. Amazingly, Banks had not put his cavalry division on this open flank but held it in reserve.

The men of the Union XIII Corps had a lot to think about. As word of the French cavalry's appearance on their flank spread, they could see the French line moving to engage. Their colorful ranks ate up the intervening ground as their drums beat to quicken the advance. French brigades seldom made a uniform appearance. Regiments of the line were brigaded with Zouaves or other individual units as the Foreign Legion or *Tirailleurs Algériens*. But it was more than martial splendor that closed on the American lines. It was the reputation of the French. American military models had been uniformly French — from the kepi to tactics to the popular bronze smoothbore cannon personally developed by Napoleon III himself. Any military observer of the period would have identified the French as the foremost martial race in Europe. Prussia's glory still slept.

And that reputation was swiftly closing the beaten ground between the two armies. The artillery of both sides, smoothbore and rifled, opened up, sending the first clouds of black smoke through the clear fall air and ugly death into the ranks of both armies. But the French kept coming.

At four hundred yards, the American line erupted in a sheet of flame and black smoke. Frenchmen tumbled forward or pitched backwards. An eagle standard went down only to be snatched up again. But the French kept coming as the American fire became continuous. At three hundred yards, the French line stopped and delivered its first rifle fire. American bodies crumpled. Then the French drummers beat the *pas de charge* all along the line. The air throbbed until it built to crescendo, and on they came, the field echoing with "*Vive l'Empereur!*"

HMS *CAWNPORE*, THREE DAYS OUT FROM ROYAL NAVY BASE HALIFAX, NOVA SCOTIA, 4:30 PM, OCTOBER 21, 1863

The Royal Navy troop transport lumbered through heavy seas, bearing the second great wave of reinforcements for the garrison of British North America since the Trent Affair of late 1861. Eight thousand had been sent then; twenty thousand — horse, foot, and artillery — were at sea or about to depart the British Isles, the greatest movement of the British Army since the Crimean War.

Cawnpore carried the nine hundred men of the 41st Foot fresh from the garrison of Dublin. Their officers were particularly irked over the men's appearance and conduct, for it was their lot that the ship also carried the commander of British forces in North America, Lt. Gen. James Hope Grant. The men's resentment evaporated when they realized Hope Grant, as he was commonly called, was only interested in their welfare. A historian would later write of him, "Not many men have better understood war than this kindly, pious, daring lancer who could play as skillfully on the hearts of his men as on the strings of his beloved violoncello."[24] A contemporary, the notorious Harry Flashman, had a different take, "He wasn't much of a general; it was notorious he'd never read a line outside the Bible; he was so inarticulate he could barely utter any order but 'Charge!;' his notions of discipline were to flog anything that moved. . . . But none of this mattered in the least because, you see, Hope Grant was the best fighting man in the world."[25]

If he fit the bill as the eccentric British officer, he did not care. He was an accomplished musician and a deeply thoughtful man. It was said that he chose his aides and staff for their musical abilities so that the tedium of the long voyages around the world in the service of the queen could be relieved by his heart's delight. That he had become recognized the finest of the queen's generals only added to the image.

Hope Grant had started his military life with the 9th Lancers in India, but he got his first foot on the ladder of fame as brigade-major to Lord Saltoun during the First China War. "Saltoun—a hero of Hougemont [at Waterloo] in 1815—had selected Grant for both his military and musical abilities, he himself being a keen cellist." He came out of that war with Saltoun's patronage and the CB (Companion of the Most Honourable Order of the Bath). He added wars, decorations, and promotions relentlessly—from the Second Sikh War to the Great Mutiny where he commanded the 9th, then a brigade, and finally the cavalry division with great skill and uniform success in almost every one of the great actions of the war. He earned the KCB (Knight Commander of the Most Honourable Order of the Bath) and promotion to lieutenant general, and his lancers won no fewer than fourteen Victoria Crosses. His reputation won him the command of the expeditionary force in the Second China War of 1860, where he took the Taku Forts, routed the Chinese repeatedly in open battle, and took Peking. The loot from the imperial summer palace was immense, though he distributed his huge share to his men.

He commanded the Madras Army in India 1862–63 and was then posted home to become Quartermaster General of the British Army. He did not even have time to get used to his title before Britain was plunged into war with America. His reputation in the Army and favor with the queen guaranteed him the command of British forces in North America.

Time had not rested heavily on his hands during the voyage. He had the original war plan against America developed during the Trent Affair to review as well as the astute studies of the Northern states that Wolseley had sent him. They were of even more current value now that British armies were holding Albany and besieging Portland. He was particularly interested in the maps of these areas, and of these the maps of Maine held his attention the most, for without Maine and its loop of the Grand Trunk Railroad, Canada could not be held. He was most interested in the ability of the Americans to relieve the siege of Portland and fully expected them to be undertaking it as he steamed across the pond. *Cawnpore's* destination had been Halifax, but he directed the captain to change course to Portland.

Map study had not completely consumed his time. His devotion to God was as fully a part of him as his love of music. That devotion found him on the quarterdeck as a member of an officer string quartet playing for the crew and the 41st. They were not playing Mozart, Bach, or Vivaldi. Instead, the delicate and haunting music to Henry F. Lyte's "Abide with Me" came from their instruments—a hymn beloved on both sides of the Atlantic since its writing in 1847. They were accompanied by a sweet voiced naval rating, and the beauty of their music floated upward like incense to the Almighty and seeped through the souls of the men crowding the deck:

> Abide with me; fast falls the eventide;
> The darkness deepens; Lord with me abide.
> When other helpers fail and comforts flee,
> Help of the helpless, O abide with me.
>
> Swift to its close ebbs out life's little day;
> Earth's joys grow dim; its glories pass away;
> Change and decay in all around I see;
> O Thou who changest not, abide with me.

3

Niter and a One-Eyed Lake

THE WHITE HOUSE, WASHINGTON, D.C., 1:28 PM, OCTOBER 21, 1863

The president's private secretary, John Nicolay, pointed upstairs to the parlor where Lincoln received visitors. Sharpe had become almost a member of the White House staff, which was quite aware of his standing in Lincoln's opinion. To Sharpe's amazement, he had found himself going from a staff colonel in a field army to a trusted advisor and confidant of the president. Lincoln had added the stars of a brigadier general to emphasize his favor. It was all an enormous compliment from the man who was always on the scent of good advice.

Sharpe was walking down the hallway to Lincoln's parlor when the door burst open and Senator Benjamin Wade, one of the hardest of the Hard War Republicans, strode out, his face red with anger. He barely mumbled an apology as he brushed past Sharpe.

Sharpe poked his head into the parlor. Lincoln was sitting at his desk, leaning back in his swivel chair with a look of mirth on his face. "I fear I have made Senator Wade my enemy for life," he said. "He was just here now, urging me to dismiss Grant, and in response to something he said, I answered, 'Senator, that reminds me of a story.' I had not even got one foot in the story when he said, 'It is with you all story, story! You are letting this country go to hell with your stories, sir! You are not more than a mile away from it this minute.'"

"What did you answer?" Sharpe asked.

"I asked good-naturedly if that was not just about the distance from here to the Senate Chamber. He was very angry, and grabbed up his hat and went off."[1]

Wade, like so many of the movers and shakers, missed the powerful didactic purpose of Lincoln's storytelling. His cabinet had come around to it, though the pompous did find it trying, but he also used storytelling to let a man down easily or sooth a ruffled feeling. He was as much at home telling stories to the workers at the Washington Navy Yard and the troops in the field as he was to his cabinet and the members of Congress and the endless stream of politicians and generals that flowed through his parlor. And he has the same ability to convulse a crowed of sunburned infantry as the most refined aristos of the Northeast with the same, often bawdy, story.

A raconteur like Sharpe was not alarmed. He knew that a good line was apt to have a delayed effect. "I wouldn't worry too much about Senator Wade, sir."

"Oh, I know. He's a good man under that stuffed shirt. He'll chew on my comment and come around. He won't let it come between us and our great work. That reminds me of a famous politician from Illinois, recently deceased, whose undeniable merit was blemished by an overweening vanity. If he had known how big a funeral he would have had, he would have died years ago."[2]

Sharpe had a good laugh, and then traded just as good a story. Lincoln batted back an even better one. Sharpe waited for Lincoln to bring up the reason for calling him over, and that was soon coming.

"Sharpe, did I ever tell you about the lectures I used to give on the wonders of American invention?"

Sharpe knew he was now playing straight man and answered on cue, intrigued by what would come next. "No, sir, I don't think you did."

Lincoln's eyes twinkled, "Well, if I do say so, I gave a pretty good lecture on the marvels rolling out of the brains in this country and abroad. I used to talk about the enthusiasm for invention that would infect a certain sort of fellow something powerful. I said of this type, 'He has a great passion—a perfect rage—for the *new*. His horror is for all that is old, particularly Old Fog; and if there be anything old which he can endure, it is only old whiskey and old tobacco.'[3]

"Well, Sharpe, I've been thinking that these wars we have got ourselves into require just that sort of fellow. If we are to survive, we have to have that perfect rage for the new. Old Fog just keeps us even with the enemy. Ripley was 'Old Fog' in the flesh, you know. Called everything new 'new-fangled gimcracks' and gave me a devil of a time getting those repeaters into the hands of the troops, not to mention my coffee mill gun. Replacing him last month as chief of ordnance for the Army was just a start.

"I figure, Sharpe, that the enemy might get that perfect rage for those new-fangled gimcracks, too. Now that would just tear things. As I see it, invention gives us an advantage with our monitors and repeaters, not to mention the balloons. But, Sharpe, Britain is called the 'Workshop of the World' for good reason. Why, their factories, forges, and arsenals have kept the Confederates in the field for two years without causing one British soldier or sailor to do without so much as a hardtack. Throw in the French, too. They can even fight a war on our doorstep without anyone in Paris doing without milk in his coffee. And they can do this by just being Old Fog.

"Take niter for example. We need it to make gunpowder, and they've got it in India, or most of it. And we can't buy it now. And with their blockade, we can't buy it from the new sources in Chile either. Luckily, I had Pete Dupont quietly buy up so much we have eight million pounds in reserve, but that will only last for one year or less. But to hedge our bets, I had a fellow named Isaac Diller working on a substitute based on chlorate. Well, I've spent a fortune on it, and he gets a very good powder, but they just can't grain it.[4] We had a demonstration a few days ago, and all I can say is 'small potatoes and few in a hill.' What a bust!"

Lincoln was walking around the room now as he spoke, his hands clutching his lapels. "Of course, we could do what the Rebels are doing and work through every cave and dung heap for niter, but that would be a drop in the bucket. Pete Dupont tells me, though, his chemists are working on something called guncotton, but that will still require niter. Now if we could only figure out a way to make niter here at home."

Sharpe wondered what Lincoln was up to. He had fingers in more pies than even Lincoln knew, but munitions production was not one of them.

"Pete tells me that some Germans have been working on this guncotton for twenty years, but they haven't been able to find out too much." He looked over his reading glasses, perched on the end of his nose. "Do you think you might be able to help him there?"

Sharpe grasped the thread immediately. "Of course, sir. But with the blockade, it is a time-consuming process to get our agents out of the country and to Europe. Our Irish friends, though, have a talent for slipping over the Canadian border and transforming themselves into loyal subjects of the queen. I'll see what I can do."

Lincoln said, "I have plans for the Irish as well, but we'll talk of that later." He looked away as if in lost in thought for a moment, then turned back to Sharpe.

"You see, Sharpe, if we try to match Old Fog to Old Fog with the British and French, we will lose hands down. That plays against our nature as a people. Our ancestors left Europe to get away from Old Fog for God's sake. Now that the full weight of their power has fallen upon us, we must rely on the strength of our nature, and avoid anything Old Fog like the plague, excepting, of course, old whiskey and old tobacco.

"And then there's Doctor Johnson's famous observation that the prospect of getting hanged concentrates the mind wonderfully. The British and French have done us a great favor in a way. They have swept away the doubts and the opposition. The mind of the people is wonderfully concentrated. I tell you, Sharpe, when a New York Brahmin like Theodore Roosevelt, who has avoided service in the war, begs me to allow him to raise a regiment and pay for its equipment out of his own pocket, our enemies have conjured a miracle."

Sharpe interrupted, "In all fairness, sir, I think the reason that Roosevelt did not join up before was his very Southern wife. Her brother is the same James Bulloch, the Confederate agent in Britain who built *Alabama*. A younger brother serves on her still. His wife would have left him if he had joined."

"You don't say! Well, I can sympathize. Mrs. Lincoln's brothers are all in gray, too, but I'm a luckier man than Roosevelt. There's no way Mrs. Lincoln would leave the White House." He winked at Sharpe.

His face grew long again as he picked up his earlier thread. "Of course, the Copperhead treason has made the Midwest vomit equivocation up. It's a foolhardy man who speaks out against the war now. The country is as united as it was the day after Sumter was fired upon, but now it is steeled as well. The problem, Sharpe, is to make the best use of this unity, for if we don't, it will just evaporate, and the enemy will grind us down. And they can do it, too. With a British army in Albany and a

French army marching on New Orleans, they could beat us before we even figure out what we are doing."

He went over to the desk and picked up a rifle that had been leaning against its other side. "This is what I mean, this fine repeater built by Chris Spencer." He cocked the piece in a smooth action. "I hear the boys who have them say that you can load it on Sunday and fire all week. And the Rebels are scared to death of them. It's too bad that we don't have tens of thousands of them now, but that's water under the bridge."

Sharpe spoke up, "I saw what the Sharps repeater did at Gettysburg, sir. A few companies of the Berdan's Sharpshooters laid the enemy out by the hundreds."

"Just so, just so." Lincoln was pacing back and forth in front of Sharpe faster now that he was worked up to the subject. "The problem is that Spencer just can't make them fast enough. There are too many different repeaters being made, and he can't get the machines and men to make them. That's why I've asked Andy Carnegie to look into working this knot out of the string." Sharpe had met Carnegie several months ago when he had come to Washington. Secretary of war representative Charles Dana had introduced them, called him that "little Scotch devil," and recounted how at the very beginning of the war he had marshaled the railroads to get reinforcements to Washington in the nick of time to save the city and had worked out the plan for the nation's telegraph systems to support the government. He was a man who could see to the heart of any organizational problem, conceive a solution, and then find the right men to execute it. He put a premium on initiative and good judgment.

"That's why I want you and Charlie Dana and Gus Fox, and the Army and Navy chiefs of ordnance, to work with him. The way I see it, you ferret out anything useful going on in Europe and keep an ear open if the enemy suddenly steps out of character and develops a passion for the new."

PLYMOUTH, ENGLAND, 6:20 PM, OCTOBER 21, 1863

Crowds of well-wishers and families packed the docks along with the county notables of Devon to give a rousing send-off to the 1st Devonshire Rifle Volunteers embarking for Ireland where they were to take over the Dublin garrison duties of the recently departed 41st Foot.

Although a Navy town, Plymouth had gone all out to take care of her own county volunteers. Each man received a package with needle and thread, writing paper, tins of sardines, bottles of jam, and a prayer book as he boarded the ship.

Such scenes were being reenacted all over the British Isles as Britain mobilized for the American war. Britain's small regular army of two hundred and twenty thousand had been spread around the world, with barely seventy thousand men left in the British Isles. Already more than twenty thousand of them had been sent to British North America, with many more scheduled to go despite the winter seas. The next largest concentration of troops was the fifty thousand men in India, but the embers of the Great Mutiny still glowed hot in British eyes, and the government had determined that India would not be asked for a single man. The jewel in the crown was the greatest source of Imperial wealth and could not be risked. The Mediterranean garrisons held twelve thousand men, and New Zealand and South Africa held five thousand each. Another three thousand men garrisoned Hong Kong. Only limited numbers could be drawn from these garrisons. The Maoris in New Zealand had only recently been subdued after desperate fighting, and depleting that garrison would be imprudent.

But Britain had other resources. Where France, Prussia, Austria, and Russia relied upon conscription, the British had the innate and eager patriotism of her people. Her old county militias, numbering one hundred and thirty thousand men, produced a flood of individual volunteers to fill out and expand the regular infantry battalions. In the Crimean War, ninety thousand militia members had volunteered for regular service, and ten thousand served overseas. The Yeomanry added fourteen thousand cavalry commanded by the great landowners whose tenants filled the ranks. The greatest addition to British strength was a far more recent organization, the Volunteer Rifle Corps (VRC). Barely five years before, tensions with France had boiled to the point that a French invasion was taken with deadly seriousness. In 1859 the secretary of state for war had called for the raising of the VRC in England, Wales, and Scotland. Ireland was pointedly ignored. Volunteers were to provide their own clothing and equipment, which put a firm middle-class stamp on the new formations. Most eschewed regular red for the green, gray, and black of the rifle corps to set themselves apart. The regulars were only too thankful that their scarlet would not be worn by these amateurs. The VRC was such a success that by 1862 it numbered 162,000 men, of which 134,000 were in rifle battalions, fully equaling the infantry strength of the regulars. Almost fifty thousand men were consolidated into eighty-six deployable battalions and the rest in administrative battalions. The Royal Small Arms Factory Enfield, aided by commercial arms makers, had been easily able to arm the entire force with the superb Enfield Rifle.[5]

In short order, Britain had doubled its army, a remarkable feat for a country for which conscription was anathema. Yet, as with the rapid expansion of the Union Army, the iron judgment of Socrates held—a body of men is no more an army than a pile of building materials is a house. It would take time for the regulars to absorb the militia volunteers and for the Yeomanry horse and the VRC to work up to the level where they would be more dangerous to an enemy than themselves. Until then, it would be the Thin Red Line upon which the Empire depended.

HUGHENDEN MANOR, BUCKINGHAMSHIRE, ENGLAND, 6:25 PM, OCTOBER 21, 1863

Benjamin Disraeli sat gazing into the flames that leaped and crackled in the fireplace of his library. The dancing light illuminated its "writing-tables, couches covered with yellow stain and profusely gilt, oak cabinets ornamented with caryatides, columns and entablatures of Dresden china." This room had been his joy but of late had been refuge from a world that seemed to have passed him by.[6]

To say that he was one of the most interesting men of his time would have been an understatement. He was stoop-shouldered, thin, dark-complexioned, with one very carefully arranged black curl draped over his forehead. Born into a Jewish family who had made their way to England after the expulsion from Spain, his father had him baptized into the Church of England after a dispute with his synagogue. Although an observant Anglican, he reveled in his Jewish heritage. On one occasion, he threw back an anti-Semitic insult, "Yes, I am a Jew, and when the ancestors of the right honorable gentleman were brutal savages in an unknown island, mine were priests in the temple of Solomon."

His youth had been so bohemian as to earn him the epithet of "revolting fop," but ambition had harnessed his appetites and channeled them into politics where he had risen to the leadership of the Conservative, or Tory, Party. He had become what he admired most, a country gentleman, a member of the establishment—no mean feat for a man whose father had held the Torah. Disraeli still found time to write a series of well-received novels and become noted for droll wit:

> It would have been a good dinner, if The soup had been as warm as the champagne or The beef had been as rare as the service or The brandy had been as old as the woman on his left or The woman on his right had been as Hansom as the cab he took home.[7]

He had had a circle of friends who so valued his political genius that they had bought him this estate, paid many of his debts, and found a suitably rich wife for him—prerequisites for the Tory leadership. Mary Anne was twelve years his senior, causing some cruel wit to quote the Bard, "Who cares if the bag is old as long as it's full of gold." They had shocked society and fallen deeply in love, and he liked to say that he had married for money but now would marry her again for love.

She doted on him and now fretted that he had seemed to suddenly age. Friends in the House had whispered that he nodded off more often than not. His slight frame seemed to shrink in on itself, and his dark complexion became even more sallow. The single dark curl that he so ostentatiously wore down his forehead seemed to whither away. Then war had come, and he had unexpectedly arrived at Hughenden even though the House still sat. He strode through the estate's grounds he loved so much with a quickness she had not seen in years.

That night, the noise of a carriage arriving over the gravel roadway brought him from his fire to the door. He flung it open to the shock of his butler and ran down the steps though the rain as a man in a black Quaker coat stepped out the carriage. "Bright, so good of you to come. Please, come inside. I have a good fire to take the chill off."

They paused only long enough for Bright to greet Mary Anne, who ordered coffee and a meal to be sent to the library as Disraeli slid the doors shut. He turned to look at the man who had insulted him only a few days before. The day after Bright's speech in the house, he had gone to a chophouse for a meal. Disraeli had followed him in and said,

"Bright, I would give all I ever had to have made that speech you made just now."

Bright looked at him straight and said, "Well, you might have made it if you had been honest."[8]

In relating that incident to a friend, he had said, "Politics is like war—a roughish business. We should not be over-sensitive. We have enough to do without imaginary grievances."[9] Any offense had been swallowed up by a realization that Bright was right. It was a bad war fought for the worst reasons, but the Tories had been swept up with the rest to avenge the insult to the nation. They had even more reason to press such a war. The Tories were the party of privilege and tradition, landed power of the most ancient kind, the very ones to find empathy with the South. Still, Disraeli had not made a career out of such stolid ideas but as a reformer and had dragged his party along. He had particularly generous to the United States in its fratricide. Addressing Parliament, he had said:

> When I consider the great difficulties which the statesmen of North America have to encounter, when I consider what I may call the awful emergency which they have met manfully and courageously, I think it becomes England in dealing with the government of the United States, to extend to all which they say at least a generous interpretation, and to their acts a liberal construction.[10]

They sat by the fire, letting the warmth soak in. It was a strange pairing. Everyone knew Bright was a dangerous political opponent, but no one distrusted him for he always did just what he said he would do. To put it mildly, Disraeli did not have such a reputation. "Well, Disraeli, what is it that you insist is better said in Buckinghamshire than in London?" He looked upon Disraeli as a skeptic would upon organized religion. He did not trust the man. They had had a similar encounter in 1854, and Bright's sketch of Disraeli's personality had not changed:

> This remarkable man is ambitious, most able, and without prejudices. He conceives it right to strive for a great career with such principles are in vogue in his age and country—says the politics and principles suit England must be of the "English type," but

having obtained power, would use it to found a great reputation on great services rendered to the country. He seems unable to comprehend the morality of our political course. . . .[11]

In particular Bright remembered Disraeli's candor when he once said, "We are here for fame."

Disraeli leaned back in his chair. "For a great nation to wage war, it must have leaders that understand chess, Bright. They must think three, four, five moves ahead and even more to checkmate. But war is not like chess, for the game of war ripples on beyond checkmate."

"And what are these ripples you see?"

"You don't think this war will be confined to North America, certainly?"

The doors opened, and Mary Anne walked in, followed by the servants who set a small table. Disraeli showed Bright to a seat but did not sit down himself. He began to pace. "How do we want this game to end Bright? What kind of world do we want to see when it is all done?"

Bright knew it was a rhetorical question and that Disraeli was about to answer it himself. You never knew where Disraeli would land once he leaped. His party was not in power, but he had the queen's ear and affection, for she believed "Disraeli was the only one who appreciated the prince," her late husband, Albert, the Prince Consort, who had died only the year before.[12] Disraeli had been careful to take up the cause of those talented men whom Albert had also championed, which only added to the Widow of Windsor's favor. He once admitted to a friend, "You have heard me accused me of being a flatterer. It is true. I am a flatterer. I have found it useful. Everyone likes flattery; and when you come to royalty you should lay it on with a trowel."[13]

One of Albert's men was Capt. Cowper Phipps Cole, RN, a first-class innovator who had developed the concept of an armored turret for warships almost contemporaneously with John Ericsson. His design pivoted on rollers, a far more stable design than Ericsson's jam-prone central spindle. It was no accident that the first armored, turreted, all-iron warship building in British yards laid down in April 1862 shortly after the Prince Consort's death was named HMS *Prince Albert*. She was not scheduled for launch until May 1864, and the queen was distressed at the slow rate of work.[14]

Her grief for her lost husband was compounded by anguish over her son Alfred, who had been missing since his ship went down. The palace had given the impression she was as stoic as a rock, but privately she shared this pain with Disraeli, whom she had taken into her closest circle, so much so that he was accorded marked respect even by her formidable Scots guardian, Mr. Brown.

"There will be nothing worth calling victory," Disraeli said. "We shall envy Pyrrhus. It took everything we had to defeat the Russians ten years ago. Now the bear is sniffing blood and will surely fall on us as we trade blows with the Americans. Who knows what other allies the Russians and Americans will find?"

He got up and poked the fire. "It's the Russians we have to worry about, Bright, not the Americans. They will finish with the Poles soon, and then watch out. We have interests in India, Afghanistan, and Central Asia, to which the Russians are the main threat. We have seen how close the Russians came this spring to bringing on a general war by abolishing the Kingdom of Poland. The Polish question is a diplomatic Frankenstein, created out of cadaverous remnants by the mystic blundering of Russell. And with whom does Palmerston and Russell get us into war, Bright, with whom? They have driven the Americans straight into the arms of the Russians.

"We can only hope the Poles can drag out their fight. Every Pole who dies buys time for England. No wonder the czar has not declared war after the naval battle in New York. Palmerston has had the rare good sense to treat the Russian involvement in the battle in New York Harbor as nothing more than an accident." He gave the fire a savage poke. "This will be a long and exhausting war if the Russians get into it."[15]

Bright's focus, though, was on North America. "Well, then, all the more reason to end this terrible war immediately. But, I must say, Disraeli, you have been at some pains never to let the Tories take a clear stand on the American question. I must ask you straight on. Why now? I thought you would be baying with the rest of the war hounds."

Disraeli ignored the question. "The Liberal government will lead this country into a blind alley within the year. I think the Russians will be in this by spring. I must be ready to find a way out when the country casts Liberals out. My question, then, Bright, is will you and the Radicals help bring that about?"

Bright was incredulous. "How much blood will be spilled in a year? Act now and we will support you."

Disraeli sighed. "Bright, these events have a natural rhythm which must play out. Should we try to arrest it, its force would crush us. No, we must wait despite the cost. We must cheer each victory, rally from each defeat, vote every appropriation, and point out every bungle so that the country may honestly turn to us when the time comes."

Bright stood up. He was clearly angry. "My God, Disraeli, your blood runs cold. No honest man could play so cynical a card."

Again Disraeli ignored the insult. "No doubt, Bright, no doubt. But the only way the war can be ended is without any more defeats. Nothing would dig in the heels of this nation than more catastrophes. The country's resolve will become adamantine."

He smiled darkly. "Do you remember Cobden's[16] statement at the Navy Estimates Committee in February? My God, Bright, the man was a perfect Cassandra. Everything he forecast with our ships came about. Next to you he is the most influential of the Radicals. He should not let his prophecies be forgotten."[17]

HQ, UNION GARRISON, PORTLAND, MAINE, 1:25 PM, OCTOBER 21, 1863

The leaves had turned an unusually brilliant range of colors this year in the "Forest City" of Maine. Even more brilliant than the reds, oranges, and yellows from the oaks, chestnuts, and maples were the tongues of flame that spiraled up from the burning city.

Brig. Gen. Neal Dow roamed the ruins, trailing a small staff. He commanded the garrison of the city that had stood grim siege for ten days. He knew it as a man knew his own backyard. A famous teetotaler, he had turned the city dry as mayor and put down the ensuing Portland Rum Riots with a heavy hand. Now all was forgiven as he breathed combative life into the garrison and gave stout heart to the population. He had led the Maine regiments of the Army of the Potomac back to recruit after the bloodletting of Chancellorsville and Gettysburg, a ploy of George Sharpe to quietly strengthen the vital port as Britain and the Union paused before lunging at each other. The Maine men had arrived just in time to thwart a British coup de main against the city. Dow had led the attack that had broken the British landing on the docks while Col. Joshua Chamberlain had beat back the landward attack.

The city's suffering had only begun. The British had turned Fort Gorges's heavy guns on the docks and warehouses, first while the Royal Navy's ships steamed around the Portland peninsula adding the fire of their guns. The British normally would not have fired on a defenseless port, and indeed the British naval officer who had fired on the railroad station was eventually relieved for violations of the customs of civilized warfare. But once Dow decided to defend the city, it became fair game. The British division was reinforced with heavy guns from the defenses of Halifax, and these pounded the landward defenses of the city. Already a quarter of Portland was in ruins, its population, save for able-bodied men in the militia and those with other vital skills, huddled in their cellars. At least they had not gone hungry. Portland was the port used to export the grain harvest of the Canadas, and most of it was in the city where it was being milled before being shipped to Britain. The city's bakeries produced bread and hardtack around the clock. They did not want for fuel either since the winter supply for the city had been laid in, and ruined buildings provided even more.

Dow had made good use of the ruins, organizing the men of the city to pile up the rubble along the waterfront as a barricade and blocking every street facing the bay and walling up every ground floor window. The Portlanders had responded to every demand with stoic determination. They now proudly referred to their city as Fortress Portland and took great pride that it was the sons of Maine and their own militia who manned the barricades and entrenchments.

The pounding was relentless that afternoon. The people huddling in their cellars felt the waves of concussion and watched as the dust drifted down through the floorboards from the broken floors above. Dow had climbed up a broken wall to gain a better vantage ignoring the pleas of his staff, "Get down, sir! Please, get down!"

They saw the guns on the big frigate in the harbor ripple with fire. The wall simply disintegrated as several 68-pound shot struck it. Dow was thrown off like a rag doll and buried as the broken brick cascaded down on him.

With Dow dead, command of the town fell upon Chamberlain's shoulders. By the tenth, he had not slept or changed his clothes for what seemed like an eternity. His clothes stank of burning, which at least covered up worse. The roar of the guns had become such a constant that he was instantly aware when the silence announced itself. They had stopped. It was not just a rare coincidence of timing. The silence went on. The reason was explained in short order when a messenger from the landward defenses reported that the British drummers were beating for parley, and an officer had come over under flag of truce with a formal request.

Maj. Gen. Sir Charles Hastings Doyle was requesting a meeting with the American commander. The commander of British forces in the Maritime Provinces since 1860, and now commanding the twelve thousand British and Canadian troops of the Portland Field Force, did not much like Americans. He had been a strong advocate of the occupation of Maine during the Trent Affair. It was Portland's misfortune to have him in command. This veteran of the Crimean War and former inspector of militia in Ireland was an able and intelligent soldier with a reputation for fairness and integrity. The energy with which he conducted the siege was proof of that, as was his ability to integrate the new Canadian militia battalions with the Imperial battalions.[18]

Chamberlain accepted, desperate for some opening or at least some information. The British had sealed up Portland as tight as a drum. But first he had his uniform brushed thoroughly while the best barber in the city ran the keenest razor he had ever felt over his blond stubble. After the barber removed the hot towel, he ran his hand over his face, allowing himself the momentary luxury of the smooth feel of a really close shave.

The American drummer beat parley, and Chamberlain and escort rode through a gap in the line. Almost immediately a British party left its own lines. Chamberlain thought that the British knew how to put on a military show in this sort of thing. He had made sure that his color bearer and escort were all from his own 20th Maine and were shaved and cleaned up. Maj. Ellis Spear, acting commander of 20th Maine, was his deputy.

The two parties stopped twenty yards apart as the two commanders rode forward accompanied only by a color bearer and a single escort. Doyle and Chamberlain rode alongside each other, exchanged salutes, and introduced themselves. Then Chamberlain pulled off his gauntlet and offered his hand. Doyle was taken aback. English gentlemen found this American custom of shaking hands to be mildly distasteful, but he believed that a gentleman never unwittingly gave offense. He took Chamberlain's hand.

He was the first to speak, appropriately enough as he had called for the parley. "General, may I offer my admiration for the gallant defense of the city."

It was Chamberlain's turn to be taken aback. "I appreciate the compliment, Sir Charles, but my rank is that of colonel."

Doyle smiled, "Well, sir, let me be the bearer of happy news from one soldier to another. Your newspapers have reported that Mr. Lincoln has promoted you major general of volunteers." The surprise on Chamberlain's face revealed this was certainly news to him. Doyle was pleased to be gracious, for being a general transcends nationality, but was even more pleased to discover how completely cut off Portland was if this week-old news had not penetrated. That could be a weapon in his hand if used well. It was a godsend that this American did not know that the powerful VI Corps led by the able Maj. Gen. John Sedgwick was detraining just over the state border to the south to march directly to the relief of Portland. With just the right approach, he might be able to convince Chamberlain to surrender before he had to march away either to abandon the siege or to leave just enough force behind to maintain the siege and meet Sedgwick well short of Portland. It would not do to leave a fortress in his rear with an able and aggressive commander.[19]

Doyle then said, "But, my dear general, duty requires me to lay soldierly courtesies aside. I appeal to you to surrender the city for the sake of humanity, to relieve the civilian population of their distress."

Chamberlain replied, "I assure you, Sir Charles, that the good people of Portland are snug in their cellars and well fed on good Canadian bread." He then threw back the offer. "But I am surprised at your concern for humanity when the Royal Navy fired upon a defenseless city in the dead of night without provocation. It was an outrage of the civilized conduct of war, Sir Charles."

Doyle would admit only to himself that the American was correct. The Navy had cocked that up badly. It does not do to put a vengeful spirit into your enemy. Talleyrand had put it well. It was worse than a crime; it was a mistake.

Ignoring the issue, Doyle then played upon the hopelessness of the garrison's position. "I assure you, sir, your government has far more to worry about than this one city. As you have been so obviously cut off from the blows which Her Majesty's armed forces have inflicted on your country, it is my sad duty to inform you. The British Army has taken Albany and put the entire Hudson Valley under contribution. New York City will fall within a fortnight. The Royal Navy has driven your fleet from its blockading stations along the coast of the Confederacy and has, in turn, blockaded your own coasts from Portland to the Chesapeake."

He glossed over the destruction of the British squadron at Charleston at the hands of Adm. John Dahlgren's South Atlantic Blockading Squadron. It sounded better with a selective choice of facts. Despite the tactical victory, the Americans had suffered a strategic defeat with the loss of their main forward operating base at Port Royal. Unable to sustain their blockading squadrons, they had withdrawn them to Norfolk. British ships stuffed with war material had flooded into the now open Confederate ports. Charleston harbor rode with a hundred masts, as its white gold stored for just such an event replaced the military cargos.

The obvious relish with which Doyle delivered the bad news only seemed to make Chamberlain more obdurate. His eyes narrowed as he said through clenched teeth. "I will fight you to the last cartridge from the last ruined house with the last man. Your trophy will be a corpsestrewn ruin." It was a bold front. He had acted as if his ammunition was in good supply when his men were down to barely a dozen cartridges a man and the artillery down to even fewer than a half a dozen rounds per gun. There was plenty of ammunition for the big guns at Fort Gorges, but the British held that granite pile in a tight grip.[20]

In the end, it was Chamberlain's bluff that mattered. The parley ended with his final refusal to consider surrender. Doyle was left with only the choice of bad options. He simply could not abandon the siege, and he could not allow Sedgwick to get within striking range to trap him against the garrison of Portland. He could only hope to steal away with enough men to beat Sedgwick and then rush back before Chamberlain noticed he was gone. That would be asking a lot.[21]

BOSTON ATLANTIC WORKS SHIPYARD, BOSTON, MASSACHUSETTS, 2.00 PM, OCTOBER 21, 1863

W. L. Hanscom was a naval constructor and not a very happy one. The new light draft monitor, USS *Chimo*, rode in the water with only part of her coal and none of her ammunition on board. Fully loaded, she was supposed to have fifteen inches of freeboard. Hanscom had just finished measuring the ship. She rode with barely seven inches of freeboard at the bow, and the stern was actually an inch under water. His report would read "adding the ammunition would have made her deck level with the water or submerged it. Only the arched portion of the deck along the ship's fore and aft centerline would have been out of the water — 'rather a small margin for a man to go to sea with.'"[22] A deadly understatement, indeed.

For the Navy's chief engineer, Alban Crocker Stimers, general inspector of ironclads, the news would fulfill his growing fears that had accumulated with sickening regularity for the last six months. Another ship of this shallow-draft monitor Casco class, the class namesake, would slide into the water with the same glaring result as *Chimo*. The builders could not be blamed.

Officially, Stimers reported to Rear Adm. Francis Hoyt Gregory, general superintendent of ironclads, but everything having to do with the actual construction of the ironclads was his responsibility, and now he was trying desperately to think how to shirk it. Stimers was a practical engineer and had not avoided getting his hands dirty in learning his trade. His career had ridden high with the ironclad monitors, the children of genius inventor John Ericsson. He had supervised the construction of the revolutionary turret of the experimental USS *Monitor* and accompanied her on her voyage to immortality at Hampton Roads.

Time and again, the ship was threatened with disaster during the voyage. Heavy seas poured water through the ventilators, which were only six feet above the water, soaking the leather drive belts for the ventilators. The belts snapped, and the ventilators quit, cutting off the intake of fresh air. Quickly, engine fumes poisoned the air. Stimers led the engineering department into the engine room. Men dropped from the fumes as Stimers worked heroically to restart the ventilators, finally coaxing them back into haphazard operation.[23]

Just before the battle, the ship's engineer discovered that the pony wheel for the engine that operated the turret was rusted tight and could not be freed. Stimers, who had spent his youth turning wrenches, stepped forward and freed it. During the battle with its Confederate ironclad nemesis, CSS *Virginia*, Stimers had operated the turret and then the gunnery division when the executive officer had to assume command after the wounding of the captain. When the turret had frozen, he had freed it again by the main force of his powerful body. It was extraordinary combat achievement for an engineer to execute such operational responsibility, and he had come under the eye of Assistant Secretary of the Navy Gustavus "Gus" Fox, an observer of the battle.[24]

His stock had ridden high after the battle, and he found himself brought to Washington to supervise the construction of the new ships being built on the *Monitor* model and its product improvements. He quickly became a disciple of Ericsson's, and a triumvirate of Ericsson, Fox, and Stimers emerged dedicated to rapid production of new monitors of improved classes. The first such were the ten ships of the Ericsson-designed Passaic class. They were considerable improvements over the original *Monitor* and were constructed and delivered in record time. They had been the heart of Admiral Dahlgren's victorious battle line at Charleston. Stimers accompanied the first group of Passaics to join the South Atlantic Blockading Squadron's attack on Fort Sumter in April 1863 and stayed on to supervise their repair. By then he fully deserved the reputation as the Navy's "Mr. Ironclad."

With the success of *Monitor* and *Passaic*, the Navy leaped into the modern age and let contracts for a number of classes of new monitors. John Ericsson was again the foremost designer, and he provided the plans for a light-draft Monitor class (subsequently the Casco class), of a very simple design meant to penetrate the waterways that the draft of no conventional warship could attempt. Ericsson then concentrated on two leviathan monitors, *Dictator* and *Puritan*, and thereafter had little time to spare for the shallow-draft monitors.[25]

Stimers hoped to replicate the success of the Passaic class with the new Casco class and threw himself into the project with a praiseworthy intensity. Unfortunately, he was also seized with a desire to achieve a level of perfection in a new technology that was still groping forward. In effect, he sought to out-engineer John Ericsson and, in so overreaching, injected a level of complexity and confusion that contributed significantly to what happened at the Boston Atlantic Shipyard. He was constantly sending changes to the builders who were forced to tear out and replace already completed work. Unknown to anyone, significant errors were being made in the thousands of design computations done in Stimer's office.

The builders were also experiencing the confusion and miscalculations inherent in the introduction of a new technology on an unprepared and inexperienced industrial base. None of them had built an ironclad before or even an all-iron ship. They severely underestimated the machine tools and skill levels necessary in their workforce. By late 1862, the industrial base that Ericsson had estimated could absorb such programs with ease was beginning to run into trouble. Severe competition arose over materials, machine tools, and skilled labor. The Navy had also fecklessly let a number of contracts to shipyards on the Ohio River, failing to take into account that its seasonal rise and fall as well as its winter icing would decisively influence when the hulls could be floated and the ships moved. To add to the builders' attempts to cope with all this, the government's payment system imposed a growing financial burden that strained and then exhausted their credit.

For Stimers personally, the workload was overwhelming. As one historian would note, he was dealing with everything from pay disputes to shortages of bolts:

> Simultaneously with altering the monitors in service, he was making similar changes on those under construction. He was providing both original and revised drawings for Tippecanoe-class and the light-draft (Casco-class) monitors. He was supervising twenty-nine Tippecanoes and Cascos as well as Ericsson's *Dictator* and *Puritan*. He was designing a "fast sloop of war . . . and a twin-turreted monitor. To top it off, he was subject to a court of inquiry. "Stimers cannot properly superintend the 6 vessels and the planning of others at the same time," Ericsson had opined over a year before, when Stimers had far fewer vessels to inspect. By the summer of 1863, the general inspector had been working at a killing pace for over eighteen months.[26]

All these issues came to a head as that first hull floated half-submerged with all the pathos of a dead whale. The stink traveled to Washington with such force that it brought the entire class to a halt as the Navy realized the extent of the disaster. The class that had absorbed the lion's share of money, materials, and manpower was an abject failure at the very moment when two enemy armies were marching through the United States and her coasts and ports were under tight blockade.

LAKE BORGNE, LOUISIANA, 1:50 PM, OCTOBER 21, 1863

The Tricolor snapped in the cool October breeze from the stern of the French ironclad *Gloire* as it steamed across the broad waters of Lake Borgne. The armed might of France had not flown its colors on this body since Napoleon I had sold Louisiana to the United States of Thomas Jefferson sixty years before. For the sailors, the very name was itself a piece of wry humor, for *borgne* meant "one-eyed" in French.

When named in the early eighteenth century, it had been a freshwater lake, but a century and a half of nature's fury and relentlessness had opened it to the Gulf of Mexico, and its water had become saline. Lake Pontchartrain lay to the north across a narrow neck of swamps and bayous and had almost direct access to New Orleans, but its canals and rivers were guarded by strong forts. *Gloire* and the flotilla of warships and transports ignored it and steamed west into Borgne. They had also ignored the traditional route to the great city up the winding Mississippi through its long delta. There too were the strong forts that Farragut had fought past to seize New Orleans the year before, but the forts were much more powerful now in Union hands.

Gloire had been the world's first ironclad, laid down in 1858, and had provoked the British to build the larger and more capable Warrior and Defence classes. The French ship was smaller than both at 5,530 tons; its thirty-six 6.4-inch breechloading rifled guns were less capable than the British Armstrong guns but more reliable. The British ships had been all iron-hulled while *Gloire* was a wooden hull clad with a casemate of 4.5-rolled wrought iron armor. The irony was that *Gloire* had been more successful than its British counterparts. The American monitors had sunk *Black Prince*, the second ship of the 9,200-ton Warrior class at Charleston only weeks before. *Gloire* and the four follow-on ironclads of her class had completely destroyed the U.S. Navy's unarmored West Gulf Blockading Squadron about the same time in the battle of Galveston. Behind *Gloire* was her sister ship, *Couronne*, the first iron-hulled French ship. Now both steamed on, their black guns also run out and crews at battle stations.[27]

Aboard *Gloire*, nervous Confederate lieutenant general Richard Taylor paced the captain's quarterdeck. When the French lookout shouted his sighting, Taylor swung his glass in that direction. Slowly, the three-tired stone bulk of Fort Beauregard, looming over the small port of Proctorville, came into view one gallery at a time as the ship closed.

No alert sounded from the fort. It had never been completed and was now derelict; it and the town below had never recovered from the massive hurricane of August 1860. All that was left of Proctorville was matchwood and the end of the Mexican Gulf Railroad that ran up to New Orleans, a little less than thirty miles to the north. Black work crews were languidly building a new pier and railroad terminal. *Gloire* and *Couronne* took station as close as the pilot said was prudent for their drafts, their guns covering what had once been a town. Small boats darted out from the ironclads to the beach. French Marines jumped into the surf and fanned out across the beach and into the town to clear it of a nonexistent enemy, completely ignoring the workers who took advantage of the unexpected work break to stare. A signal rocket reported all clear, and immediately the transports began lowering away dozens of small boats, soon filled with troops in faded gray and butternut. The boats scurried to the beach like a host of black water bugs.

One of the first to boats to hit the water had Taylor as a passenger. His eyes fixed on the beach, he only turned back to wave a friendly thank you to the French captain who had shouted, "*Bonne chance, Général Taylor!*" Taylor had promised him the best dinner in New Orleans, and the captain had heard very good things about the wondrous Creole seafood cuisine.

Taylor pushed that thought to the back of his mind as his brigades sorted themselves out ashore. As soon as each regiment formed, he put them on the road north. Speed, speed, and more speed. Once taught by Jackson, a soldier always felt the need for speed. He had drummed it into his subordinate commanders and now was everywhere applying his formidable presence to wherever the movement off the beach and onto the road slowed. When two brigades were ashore and moving north, Taylor rode after them. The follow-on brigades and artillery would have to catch up. They would continue through the night, and with some hard marching he would be on the outskirts of a largely undefended New Orleans by the following night. The powerful Union army that would have stopped him cold was over a hundred miles to the west as the crow flew, fixated on Bazaine's Franco-Confederate army that had marched out of Texas.

Despite the pace of the march, the men enjoyed the cool and dry marching weather, so rare in Louisiana that it buoyed their morale and put a bounce in their step. Taylor put Mouton's brigade of Louisiana regiments in the van—the 18th and 25 Louisiana, the Crescent Regiment, and Fournet's and Beard's battalions. They were marching home, and it quickened their stride even more than the weather. The Texas brigades behind, no slouches at hard marching, had to hurry to keep up. The real bounce, though, came from the sense that they were going to be in on the kill after so much frustration and defeat. They could taste it.

The prize, the first city of the South and entrepôt for the entire watershed of the Mississippi, was in their grasp. Its capture by the Union in April 1862 had been the first great crippling blow the North had inflicted on the Confederacy. The fall of the great river forts from Vicksburg to Port Hudson in July had, in Lincoln's words, allowed the "Mother of waters to run unvexed to the sea." Taylor was determined to vex Mr. Lincoln all over again.[28]

BRASHEAR CITY, LOUISIANA, 2:00 PM, OCTOBER 21, 1863

The main Union supply base in Brashear City should have been as impregnable as a fortress with all the advantages afforded by surrounding nature. The town lay sixty-five miles slightly southwest from New Orleans on the Opelousas and Great Western Railroad. There the tracks ended, and supplies were conveyed to Banks's army by wagon train along the main road that continued north another fifty-five miles up to Vermillionville and then west again to Texas. The first twenty-five miles was a narrow strip of land between Grand Lake to the north and impenetrable swamps, marshes, and bayous to the south. Winding back and forth like the coils of a snake was the marshy Bayou Teche, offering an endless series of chokepoints to even a moderately determined defender.

When Maj. Gen. Thomas Green, commanding a division of two thousand five hundred Texas cavalry, arrived at Indian Village just beyond this twenty-five mile naturally defended corridor, he had accomplished Bazaine's order to cut Banks's communications with his main supply base. Bazaine had overestimated the attention Banks would pay to the defense of the mountains of supplies accumulating at Brashear City. Instead, he had left a green brigade recently arrived from the North. The local country people swarmed to Green to tell him that almost the entire Yankee force was concentrated at Brashear City and none too alert.

Green did not hesitate. He put his regiments in motion immediately. To the shock of the Union teamsters in the long wagon trains, his lead units galloped past them, not even bothering to stop and accept their surrender, which was later taken by the regiments bringing up the rear. On the Texans galloped, so fast that they outraced the very news of their coming.[29]

4

"Well, They Might Have Stayed to See the Shooting"

VERMILLIONVILLE, LOUISIANA, 2:22 PM, OCTOBER 21, 1863

Banks never knew what hit him that afternoon. Bazaine's attack crashed into his army all along the line. The French general had reduced his tactical problem to a very simple point—it would be a shoving match with all the odds on his side. Banks could shove him westward all he wanted; the ground stretched easily and unimpeded for mile after empty mile. He would simply be falling back on his communications. However, Bazaine had only to shove Banks's corps east for a tenth of a mile before they were pushed into Lake La Pointe or fell off a short, steep plateau into the shallow river that fed into the lake at its base. Should they struggle out of that, their retreat east would carry them into the marshy waters of Bayou Teche, and beyond that Lake Grand. A very simple problem indeed.

Banks's army was positioned in line of battle on a north-south axis just east of the main road leading north from Vermillionville. Major General Franklin's XIX Corps was on the right flank, with XIII Corps on the left and the cavalry held in reserve.

Banks may have been an amateur who rejected Franklin's sound advice, but his two corps were veterans, and Bazaine's army felt their bite immediately. But they were victims of a saying by Alexander the Great's canny father, Phillip II—an army of deer commanded by a lion will always beat an army of lions commanded by a deer. They also suffered from the damned bad luck of fighting an army of lions commanded by a lion. Banks almost immediately proved the long-dead Macedonian correct by losing control of the battle. He forgot, if he had ever learned, that the primary role of the commander in battle is the allocation of the reserve. So, when Washburn tried to relieve the quickly depleted brigade

on the right of his corps, Banks countermanded the order for the replacement brigade to move into the line. However, Banks never countermanded Washburn's original order for the brigade in contact to pull out.

The Prince de Polignac saw the confusion in the opposing firing line
as it filed away to the rear, leaving a gaping hole. He rode to the front of
his two regiments, pointed his sword to the void in the enemy line, and
shouted, "*En avant, mes enfants!*" and in English, "Go, get 'em, boys!" The
Texans responded with high-keening Rebel yells, borrowed in admiration from their mortal Comanche enemies on the wild frontier. At the
sound, the neighboring French Zouaves instinctively paused in their
firing; it was savage and alien to their military style and experience. The
Yankees were all too familiar with it.

The Texans raced through the opening. Franklin was not even
aware of what was going on. He had all he could do trading hammers
and blows with Walker's Greyhounds. His men were Grant's veterans
of the Vicksburg Campaign, but they had never seen such hard fighting.
It was Franklin's great good luck that Polignac rolled up the flank of XIII
Corps instead of turning north against his own corps. Struck from flank
and rear, Washburn's brigades came apart. The prince was riding the
foaming crest of a tidal wave, his colors party desperately trying to keep
up with him. His Texans, exultant in their success, followed the gallant
chevalier of France as his ancestors had followed the plume of Henry IV.
There was no doubt that they were led by a fighting man who met every
standard of Texican manhood.

So when they saw him lurch back in the saddle, his sword flying
from his hand, a groan rose from their ranks. His aide was beside him
in an instant to prevent him from falling from his horse. Men rushed up
on foot to ease him to the ground. His regiments rushed by, stabbing
with their bayonets and bludgeoning the fleeing mass of panicked men
in blue. Bazaine watched in awe. He thought he had seen everything. He
said to his staff, "You see, *messieurs*, the *furor Texicus*. Consider it your
privilege to have witnessed it." He paused only for the briefest moment,
then announced. "Now I shall commit my reserve." He called forward
the commander of the Imperial Guard Zouave regiment and pointed
farther down the Union line that was now showing the effects of the disaster rolling up their flank. "There, Colonel Moreau, there is where you
will strike, and they will fly apart."

Walker

Armée de la Louisiane

Bazaine

Zouaves of the Guard

Harris

Franklin

Army of the Gulf

Banks

Washburn

Lake la Pointe

Vermillionville

Lee

THE
BATTLE OF
VERMILLIONVILLE
OCTOBER 22, 1863

Harrison

Karamales 2009

On the open southern flank of the battle, the two great cavalry hosts faced each other. Bazaine had placed his cavalry there to tell the enemy plainly that his line of communications had been cut. That does wonders for an enemy's confidence, he knew, and it had done just that, sending excited shouts through the XIII Corps regiments along the line as the French were advancing rapidly on them from their front. Banks had been provoked to bring his cavalry division of almost three thousand men out of reserve. He gave Brig. Gen. Albert Lee the order to drive the enemy cavalry from the field. Lee would have suggested, had Banks been anything but visibly panicked, that he now deal with the French cavalry as dismounted infantry employing their Sharps breechloading carbines to bring down so many that they would have to move off. Instead, he found himself drawing his saber and riding to the head of his thirteen regiments.

Across the field, the French commander also drew his saber as his Chasseurs à Cheval, hussars, and lancers sat stock still waiting for the command. The French would have been outnumbered had the cavalry of Harrison's brigade not reinforced them. The Texans were not used to the massed cavalry action that clearly was shaping up, but they were game for anything. While the French thought in terms of their sabers and lances, the Texans felt the handles of their revolvers.

From across the field, the French and Texans heard the Union bugle call signaling the advance at a trot. The entire Union division was quickly in motion. The French commander waited to let his horses save their strength for the last command when they would burst forward in a gallop. Let the Americans tire their horses. He would wait. After all, he was a veteran of a dozen European and North African battlefields, and he knew cavalry. When the Americans had closed half the distance between them, he gave his own order and the serried, colorful French lines flowed forward, the drabber Texans on their right flank. At the last moment, the French bugle call for the charge at the gallop sounded, and the French squadrons seemed to leap forward as sabers and lances dropped to the attack. The French were in their element, their national spirit embodied in the wild assault of mounted chivalry, the white arm of the French Army. A shout of "Urraaaah!" ripped from them seconds before five thousand horsemen crashed into each other.

In the center, Washburn was overwhelmed by the unfolding disaster, swept away by the flood of fugitives from his disintegrating front. It was then that the Zouave Regiment of the Guard swept forward in a blaze of color—big, bearded men advancing in impeccable order until Moreau bellowed across their front, "*En avant, mes enfants! En avant!*" With a shout, they charged. Behind them, Bazaine ordered a general advance. Moreau led his Zouaves against that part of the line held by the Iowa and Wisconsin regiments of one of Washburn's stoutest brigades, commanded by Col. Charles L. Harris, the last steady unit as the rest wavered.

The farmers of the 11th Wisconsin were veterans to the core, hammered into a special toughness under Grant in the Vicksburg Campaign, the same mettle as the three Iowa regiments in line with them. Their front was already littered with the fallen, but they responded with precision to the command to fire. A sheet of flame spit from the line, and the charging Zouaves went down by the hundreds. Their entire colors party was swept away as the eagle fell to the ground. Miraculously, Moreau was untouched, despite riding at the head of his regiment. He would find eight bullet holes in his uniform and cap that night. He looked back to see a guardsmen snatch up the fallen colors and rush forward. The impetus of the charge had not been broken as his Zouaves jumped over the bodies of the dead and wounded. Still, they dropped as the Americans were firing at will. The eagle went down again, and again it was retrieved to lead the crest of the attack, and for a third time it fell and rose again. Moreau found himself rolling in the dirt, his horse dead, and himself bleeding from wound in the thigh. He staggered to his feet and faced forward.

Bazaine's staff was exclaiming their admiration for the charge of the Guard Zouaves, but their general saw the American line stiffening by the example of Harris's brigade. "*Messieurs*, it will not do for the Emperor's Guards to not have their glory. Let us help them." By then, the Zouaves had fallen back a hundred yards, dragging their colonel and colors with them. French artillery rolled up on either flank to pour canister into the Wisconsin and Iowa men. They might have stood all day had not the panic on their right finally dissolved their flank brigade as the Prince de Polignac's Texans hammered their way down the line. Harris tried to refuse his right, but the 21st Iowa was swept away by the flood of fugitives. It was then that Moreau, a bandage around his thigh and mounted on a fresh horse, again ordered the *pas de charge*. The drums beat above the din of battle. Again the Zouaves came on in a rush, and again many fell, but the American fire slackened and then died away as the brigade fell back.

With that, the entire XIII Corps ceased to be a fighting formation, save for the remnant of Harris's brigade, and turned into a mass of fleeing men and vehicles. They did not see the drop of the plateau until it was too late, and the men behind pushed over hundreds of those in front. Caissons, guns, wagons, and ambulances careened over the edge to shatter at the base in a mass of splintered wood and maimed screaming horses. The thousands on foot tumbled over the precipice to leap into the shallow, marshy water of the bayou that fed into Lake La Pointe. Many more fell into the lake itself to drown splashed helplessly about.

Into this chaos, the remnants of Banks's cavalry were slowly pushed toward the lake from the south. The cavalry fight had been the most vicious of all the killing that day, for it was man-to-man fighting at sword or lance length, and a pistol was just as close in that mass of struggling men and animals. Superior French skill with saber and lance were matched with American practice with the revolver, but the unraveling of XIII Corps forced Lee to save what he could. Only parts of the 1st Louisiana (Union loyalists), 2nd Illinois, and 4th Indiana were able to cut their way out of the French encirclement. The rest were driven into the shallows of the lake to add the terror of animals and shouts of men to the miasma hanging over the battlefield.

Thousands were already surrendering. Only the survivors of Harris's Brigade kept any semblance of order as they fought backward, leaving their dead and wounded in their trail. By the time they had been pressed to the edge of the plateau, Harris realized they could go no farther. He ordered his men to throw down their weapons. Moreau rode up to him, the side of his horse soaked with the blood that oozed from his thigh, and saluted with his sword as Harris offered his. Moreau refused and said in French that he could not accept the sword of such a gallant foe. Harris didn't understand a word, but the sentiment was plain enough. He was glad of what little balm he could find.

Bazaine rode into the chaos that has long ceased being a battle as his troops were disarming the dazed Americans. Banks, most dazed of all, was led up to him by the *Chasseurs à Pied* that had captured him. In that effusion of gracious condescension at which the French excel, he greeted Banks, complimented him on his conduct of the battle, ascribed the fate of the battle to Dame Fortune, and invited him to share his dinner that night.

Barely two hundred yards from this exquisite chivalry, the Sudanese had lost all sense of restraint. They had fought through the toughest part of the battle carried forward in the last charge by the intoxication of their battle cry, "*Allah u akbar!*" They just found it easier to kill when men threw down their weapons. Possessed already of the African Muslim style of war, they were like beasts. Their French officers had done nothing to restrain them against the Mexicans and now could do nothing with them.

Even with the generals clustered around him, Bazaine could see the carnage. Banks turned white, but before he could speak, Bazaine turned his horse around and spurred into the slaughter, striking left and right with his sword at the Sudanese, crying out, *"Quels sauvages!"* His staff plunged in after him, and then Zouaves of the Guard rushed in to throw a cordon of bayonets around the Americans. With the Sudanese finally under control, Bazaine rode up to their commander, seized his sword, and snapped it like a stick.

None of this was evident to Franklin, but seeing the ruin of XIII Corps as the Prince de Polignac rolled up its flank, he realized he was on his own. He could passively accept the fate of the rest of the army or save what he could. For this old soldier, there was really no choice at all. He carefully swung back his line to face south, still engaged with Walker's division, probably the supreme tactical achievement of his life. He could not have done it had not his four batteries held the Greyhounds at bay while the infantry wheeled away. The guns literally backed up yard by yard in the technique called "firing by prolonge." Normally to move a gun, it would have to be hitched to a caisson or limber, and its crew would have to mount horses, drive away, then unlimber and set up again. In the face of an advancing enemy, it was fatal. By firing by prolonge, the gun stayed harnessed to its team, which was pointed in the direction of retreat. The harnesses remained taut so that when the gun fired, the recoil took it a few yards to the rear in the direction of the retreat. The crews simply marched back with gun instantly ready to load and fire. It was a fighting retreat that spewed canister into the oncoming enemy so continuously that even the hosts of heaven would have gave pause. And it was the margin that Franklin needed.

His gunners gave it to him, fighting their guns back yard by yard, crewmen and horses dropping from the enemy's rifle fire. Dead horses were cut out of their traces, and the surviving crewmen just kept feeding the guns. The regulars of Batteries F and L of the 1st U.S. Artillery were matched by the volunteers of the 4th Massachusetts and 25th New York Batteries. Even the toughest and most determined Red Leg[1] was not proof to Texan marksmanship, and one by one the crewmen began to drop as did their horses until there were not enough men to keep the guns firing or horses to pull it off. One after the other, guns were left in the wake of the batteries' fighting retreat. When almost half the guns were lost and three of four battery commanders dead or wounded, Franklin rode up to give the command to pull back to the new line he had established that straddled the main road that led eighteen miles north to Opelousas.

The sacrifice of the gunners had saved XIX Corps. Walker's division was too badly mangled itself to renew the attack against Franklin's new position or hang onto his rear as he retreated. Night fell not a moment too soon for Franklin. There had not been enough daylight left for Bazaine to transfer his cavalry north to cut him off. And so the cloak of darkness wrapped its thick folds about them as Franklin trudged north to safety.

THE HOME OF ASIA BOOTH CLARKE, PHILADELPHIA, PENNSYLVANIA, 1:30 PM, OCTOBER 22, 1863

There was an added pleasure to the rave reviews John Wilkes Booth was receiving for his "blood-and-thunder" performance in *The Marble Heart*, which was the role most considered his best. It was to relax in the home of his sister Asia. He reclined on her plush red settee with all the languid grace of a leopard on tree branch. Asia knew her little brother with the clarity of all big sisters.

Their father, the great lion of the American stage, the tempestuous Junius Booth, had named him well. Junius Wilkes was probably the most notorious demagogue, folk hero, and scoundrel of eighteenth-century British politics. The London mob cheered him on with "Wilkes and liberty!" for his goading of both king and parliament. His namesake's reputation had not been lost on young Booth who seemed to have acquired the same gift for the dramatic and for fiery stands against authority. Like his namesake, he could go too far. He was vociferous in his Southern sympathies, and it had got him in trouble on more than one occasion. Only a glib tongue and a ton of charm had eased him out it. John was the unusual American who, as an actor, had free passage of the lines to perform North and South.

Asia was half an indulgent mother as well. She was as susceptible to his easy charm and good looks as anyone else. John was easily the handsomest of the family and now a clear rival to his more serious brother, the great tragedian Edwin Booth, whose performance in *Macbeth* was highly regarded by the critics. John was riding a wave of success achieved far more quickly than his more somber older brother. In fact, Edwin was the subject of his conversation.

"Asia, dear, Adam Badeau said the queerest thing about Edwin in New York this summer." Badeau was an old friend of Edwin's and a journalist. He had come to provide the comforting moral support needed to rouse Edwin from his fits of depression. Badeau had gone off to war and had been badly wounded in an attack on Port Hudson. Edwin had taken him in to nurse him back to health in his own Manhattan home. He and John had carried him upstairs to a bedroom, dressed his wounds, and tended him in shifts. During the draft riots, Badeau had been afraid for the safety of his black body servant, but John had assured him he would personally see to the man's safety.

"He said that it was appalling to witness such melancholy in a man who had so much to live for. Well, you know Edwin. He *is* Hamlet, but I was worried when Badeau said that Edwin had told him that he had 'the feeling that evil is hanging over me, that I can't come to good.' What on earth could he have meant?"

Asia could only shake her head. She knew Edwin as well as John. Then John laughed, and the grimness in it startled his sister. "Imagine me, helping that wounded Yankee with my Rebel sinews. If it weren't for mother, I wouldn't enter Edwin's house. If the North conquers us, it will be by numbers only, not by native grit, not pluck, and not by devotion."

Asia was now thoroughly alarmed by this sudden revelation. "'If the North conquers us?' We are *of* the North."

John jumped up. "Not I, not I!" he shouted. "So help me Holy God! My soul, life, and possessions are for the South!"[2]

OFFICE OF THE SECRET SERVICE, WASHINGTON, D.C., 2:47 PM, OCTOBER 22, 1863

Lafayette Baker was a good judge of character, especially bad character. It was a useful talent in a man set to catch spies. It was also useful in his thuggish sideline of shaking down anyone he wanted, and the man standing in front of him, hat in hand, seemed just the sort he could use. Baker saw right through the big, bearded man's submissive body language. There was a brute.

Baker tossed aside the letters of recommendation. "I can use you, Miller. And right away. There's an actor over at Ford's Theatre who needs the fear of God and the Union put in him. Talks too damned much about his Rebel sympathies. Did you ever hear of John Booth? Brother of Edwin Booth, son of the great Junius?" Baker saw that he had clearly overestimated the man's acquaintance with culture. "Well, he's vain as a peacock, and a suggestion that his pretty face might no longer be presentable on the stage should get his attention."

Miller grinned, and his canines gleamed. Baker was pleased that he had not been wrong in his appraisal.

He was only half right. The man was a thug of the first order. But he was also a traitor, a Copperhead who had fled ahead of Sherman's rampage through the rebellious Midwest. His name was well known in Indiana, where he had been the murderous enforcer of Copperhead discipline. He was Big Jim Smoke, the man who had brutally killed the government's agent in the midst of the Copperhead conspiracy, the man who had murdered the guards outside Camp Morton in the attempt to liberate the huge Confederate prisoner-of-war camp. He had barely escaped with his life as Hooker's Horse Marines had charged into the camp on the heels of the Copperheads. And he had fled straight to Washington, where his cunning told him he would be safest in the bosom of the tyrant and his chief spy-catcher. He had gone directly from the train to activate his contacts with the Copperhead network in the capital to replenish his cash and acquire the spurious letters of recommendation that had so easily fooled Baker.

Smoke got directions for Ford's Theatre and rushed off to find this John Booth. He did not notice the nondescript black man selling peanuts on the street outside Baker's office, but then few whites paid attention to the omnipresent black population of the capital. The peanut vendor motioned to a boy playing marbles in the dirt. "Jimmy, go tell Massa Sharpe that Mr. Baker's got hisself a new man." He did not have to give any more instructions. The boy had memorized the Smoke's appearance, despite giving every indication of total absorption in his game.

COLT ARMS FACTORY, HARTFORD, CONNECTICUT, 3:02 PM, OCTOBER 21, 1863

Andrew Carnegie saw nothing but potential and opportunities as he toured the huge Colt Arms Factory with its manager, Elisha K. Root. Carnegie had heard the old man had come out of retirement to take over the management of the company when "the Colonel" — Sam Colt — died last year. His age had not relaxed his grip, and it was evident the place ran with precision and efficiency.

Not even thirty years old and with hair as white as snow and cornflower blue eyes, this shrewd Scotsman was already wealthy. He worked by the motto, "The rising man must do something exceptional, and beyond the range of his special department. *He must attract attention.*" The purpose of his visit was the perfect opportunity to attract attention on the national stage in the moment of his adopted nation's greatest peril. Carnegie's talent was not as an industrial expert or manager, but as someone who saw opportunities and sought out the men who could make things happen. He would also be sure to ask Root who his best managers were, the men with initiative and good judgment. Later, he would shamelessly try to hire them away, but that was later. He had no doubt of being able to do so. As one man described him, he "was the most genial of despots, bending men to his will by an unfailing charm. And he would not hesitate to outbid anyone for the talent he wanted."[3]

Right now it was the scale of the operation that impressed him. The Colt Arms Factory, covering six and half acres, was the largest weapon manufacturer in the world. Its main building had eight major bays each five hundred feet long by sixty wide.

> There were 400 rifling machines, with each barrel being subjected to forty-five separate operations. The rammers experienced nineteen, the hammers twenty-eight, and the stocks five, and there was a grand operating total of 454 distinct procedures within this single gun-making enterprise.[4]

The drop hammers consuming 900 horsepower via endless leather belts was deafening. Carnegie did not care. Mark Twain would describe it a few years later:

> The Colt's revolver manufactory is a Hartford institution. On every floor is a dense wilderness of strange iron machines that stretches away into remote distances and confusing perspectives —

a tangled forest of rods, bars, pulleys, wheels, and all the imagin-
able and unimaginable forms of mechanism. . . . No two machines
are alike, or designed to perform the same office. It must have
required more brains to invent all these things than would serve to
stock fifty Senates like ours.[5]

Brains, the native genius, had created the American system of man-
ufacture—interchangeable parts, specialization of skill, and that knack
for extracting ever more efficiency from every step and process. Hartford
throbbed with such factories, especially the weapon makers, including
Chris Spencer, whom Carnegie had brought along to Root's surprise.
Spencer's repeating rifle was the single best model in the world and a
competitor to the Colt revolving rifle. Carnegie was relieved that Root
greeted Spencer cordially. Spencer had worked at Colt and obviously
left on good terms. It was clear that Root both liked and respected the
young man. A mechanical genius, Spencer had, at the age of fifteen, built
a working model of a steam engine from a book. Only a few years ago
he had taken to driving to work in a steam-powered automobile of his
own invention. But it was as a gun maker that he excelled. At the age of
eighty-seven, he would learn to fly an airplane. A future friend of Mark
Twain, Spencer was probably the model for his hero in *A Connecticut
Yankee in King Arthur's Court*.

Spencer's rifle was not the product of a mature arms manufacturer,
but was a special handmade tool put together in the machine shop of
his partner's company, the Cheney Brothers Silk Mill. That partner was
a Boston neighbor of Gideon Welles, secretary of the Navy, a Hartford
man, and not surprisingly a demonstration was arranged at the Washington Navy Yard in June 1861. Admiral Dahlgren, chief of the Ordnance
Bureau at the time, personally tested it, and no sharper eye could have
been found. Dahlgren was rightly known as the Father of American Naval Ordnance for his fine line of guns, the soda bottle–shaped Dahlgrens,
which even the British had tried to buy before the war.

There was only one misfire of the five hundred brass rimfire cartridges fired, and that was found to be owed to defective fulminate. The
rifle sustained a rate of fourteen shots a minute without overheating and
did not require cleaning to continue, unlike the standard Springfield

and Enfield muzzle-loading rifles, which began to foul after a few dozen shots. It fired as well with the five hundredth shot as the first. Dahlgren ordered seven hundred on the spot.[6]

Spencer left Washington in a state of euphoria that dissipated when it sank in that the demonstration rifle was his only model and that there was no factory, machinery, or work force to fulfill the government order. In the meantime, Lincoln had heard Dahlgren's enthusiastic praise of the rifle, and there was no man whose technical judgment he trusted more. He prodded Maj. Gen. George B. McClellan, to consider the weapon. The Army's test was as positive as the Navy's, and an order for ten thousand followed in December. For the Spencer Repeating Rifle Company, it was an embarrassment of riches. The weapon's promise would be crippled by the lag in producing them as the factory only slowly took shape. It would not be until June 1863 that the initial orders could be filled. Lincoln's interest had cooled as well. The Navy had given him two demonstration models, and one would not work because of a rusted magazine tube. The other jammed with a double feed. Lincoln then halted deliveries of the weapon.

The business end of the company was not in Spencer's hands, but the continued development of the weapon was. It was make or break time for him. He walked into the White House with his rifle in his arms, right past the guards and into Lincoln's office. It was a less security-conscious age. "Mr. President, I understand you have had problems with my rifle."

The president loved firearms and was an excellent shot. He was like a little boy whenever the opportunity to handle new weapons presented itself. "Well, tell me, son, about this shooting iron," he said.

Spencer was his own best salesman. "Sir, my rifle uses the Smith & Wesson .52 caliber brass rimfire cartridge, which completely prevents gas leakage from the back because the brass casing expands on ignition to seal the chamber. It has a rolling block activated by lowering the trigger guard. This movement opens the breech and extracts the spent cartridge." Spencer cocked the weapon. Lincoln noticed the easy movement of the action. "Raising the lever causes a new cartridge, pushed into position by a spring in the seven-round tube magazine located here in the stock, to be locked into the firing chamber."

He then delivered a precise explanation of the problems Lincoln had experienced and the solutions he had arrived at with the production models.

Lincoln reached for the rifle and worked the action. "Smooth like butter," he said. "Nice balance, too, and not too heavy. About ten pounds, I'd say."

"Yes, sir. Exactly ten pounds. And 47 inches long."

"Does it bruise the shoulder with the recoil?"

"No, sir, it has an exceptionally light recoil."

As Lincoln continued to examine the rifle, Spencer decided to broach an awkward subject. "Sir, General Ripley has made it clear there will be no more orders for my rifle."

Lincoln laughed. "Reminds me of something that was said when I went shooting another rifle. Someone said, 'General Ripley says, Mr. Lincoln, that men enough can be killed with the old smooth-bore and the old cartridges, a ball and three buckshot.' Well, that was just the problem. I said, 'Just so. But our folks are not getting near enough to the enemy to do any good with them just now. We've got to get guns that carry farther.'" He held up the rifle as he finished, happy to see the grin on Spencer's face.

He had been referring to the Army's chief of the Ordnance Bureau, Brig. Gen. James Ripley, whose antipathy to anything but the standard muzzle-loading Springfield rifle had earned the nickname, Ripley van Winkle. The gruff old man dismissed the modern marvels generated by American ingenuity as nothing but "newfangled gimcracks." Lincoln had had to give him direct orders to buy them, which had been brazenly sabotaged through administrative trickery. He had been tolerated solely because the Army's pool of ordnance talent was so thin, there was simply no replacement, but even that excuse had worn thin.

Lincoln leaned over, put his hand on Spencer's knee and said, "Don't worry about Ripley. Come tomorrow and we can have a proper shooting match. You bring the cartridges, and I'll bring the audience." Spencer did not know that Ripley's days were numbered, and he would be dismissed in two months.

When Spencer arrived the next day, he found Stanton and other senior officials waiting, and they all marched out to the Mall near the unfinished Washington Monument, the president's tall hat bobbing above the group, and fired all afternoon at targets posted on a huge pile of scrap lumber about a hundred yards away. Lincoln was in a good mood as he sent round after round into the target from the kneeling and prone positions. He didn't even hear the shouts coming closer and closer. "Stop that firing! Stop that firing!" the voice cried, adorning that order with a flood of profanity. A short sergeant followed by an armed squad rushed up to the group, determined to enforce the ordnance against firing weapons on the Mall. "Thunderation and God damn! Stop that damn firing!" He pushed his way through the group, shoving aside cabinet secretaries and congressmen alike, as if he were a policeman out to arrest a drunk.

As an observer would later note, "Perhaps Mr. Lincoln heard him, and perhaps not, but his tall, gaunt form shoots up, up, up, uncoiling to its full height, and his smiling face looks down upon the explosive volunteers. Their faces, especially that of the sergeant . . . look up at his, and all their jaws seem to drop in unison. No word of command is uttered, but they 'right about face' in a second of time. Now it is double-quick, quicker, quicker, as they race back toward the avenue, leaving behind them only a confused, suppressed breath about having 'cussed Old Abe himself.'"

Lincoln's only response was, "Well, they might have stayed to see the shooting."[7]

He signed the order for twenty thousand rifles that afternoon.

COLT ARMS FACTORY, HARTFORD, CONNECTICUT, 4:35 PM, OCTOBER 21, 1863

Spencer's retelling of that story had Carnegie and Root nearly in tears after a late lunch in Root's office. Carnegie thought it was just the opening for what he had come to say.

"Well, you see, Mr. Root, the president had that much faith in Chris's rifle that even then he was willing to sign such a huge order. Now that we have been most foully attacked, the country must throw every possible advantage we have into the scales." Root was surprised at the vehemence of Carnegie's hatred for the enemy expressed in his thick Scottish brogue. Carnegie caught the surprised look and fixed him with his blue eyes, his face beginning to take the high color of the truly fair.

"Make no mistake, Mr. Root, it is not the British people I am against. No, sir. It is the monarchy and its system of privilege that has ground down the working people of those islands, causing the English, Scots, Irish, and Welsh in their millions to find a new home here, just as I have. And the Royals and their nobles, and their High Church prelates, they hate this country for it and wish us ruined.

"We have in this country the charter that the workingman of that kingdom has been fighting for years as the panacea for all Britain's woes, the bulwark of the people. So, let there be no mistake of my sentiments. God bless the United States, and God damn the British Crown."[8]

"Well, now that that is settled, Mr. Carnegie, what may I do for you, and for young Chris here?"

5

Honey, Vinegar, and Guncotton

**HEADQUARTERS, THE MAINE DIVISION, PORTLAND, MAINE,
8:47 AM, OCTOBER 22, 1863**

Chamberlain peered into the small room where the prisoner was sitting blindfolded and tied to a chair in his torn and dirty scarlet coat. He shut the door and walked back into the hallway to speak to his chief scout. The man shook his head in disbelief. "Sir, we caught him when he wandered from his camp for a piss. The thing is, well, there were only a handful of men in the encampment. Most of the tents were just empty. There were fires in all of them, but only a few men were moving from one to another feeding them. Most of the horse lines were empty, too. Most of 'em are just plain gone, General." Chamberlain discouraged the men from calling him "General," since he had not been officially notified, but after the word had got out from his escorts at the parley that he had been promoted, the men had insisted on the honor.

The scout was a very earnest man. "Don't know where they went, but I figured this officer would be of some help there."

Chamberlain seemed lost in thought for a moment, then looked the man in the eyes and said, "You've done a good job. I am in your debt." Some poor wretches felt that giving a compliment was like taking money from their pockets, but Chamberlain knew it was a coin always worth spending. The man beamed. "Now go get a meal and a good night's sleep."

Chamberlain let the prisoner's imagination run on for about another hour to give himself time to think over what would happen next. The more the man's fears played on his mind, the easier it would be. Finally, Chamberlain threw open the door, saw the man jerk in his bonds, and shouted, "Why is this officer still restrained? Free him at once!" The guards rushed by to untie the prisoner and take off the blindfold. He blinked to regain his focus, confusion and fear playing over his face. Then he saw the lithe, blond American colonel standing in front of him and noticed the mustache that drooped on either side of his mouth. The American's face radiated concern.

He spoke, "I must offer my sincerest apologies for your treatment to which an officer and a gentleman should never have been subjected."

The Canadian was clearly nonplussed. His capture and transfer into the city had not been gentle, and sitting alone in that room restrained in the dark had been even more terrifying. Now this American colonel had rescued him. What was he to make of this?

Exactly what Chamberlain intended. "You must be starving, Lieutenant. Let me make amends by offering you dinner. First I must see that you get some soap and water." He laughed. "I have completely forgotten my manners in my distress of finding you in this state. Allow me to introduce myself. I am Colonel Chamberlain." He bowed slightly. The Canadian's manners reasserted themselves as well, as soon as the formalities were invoked. "And I, sir, am Lieutenant Jean-Yves Delacroix of the 9th Battalion, Les Voltigeurs de Quebec."

"*Ah, bon!*" Chamberlain said, "We must speak French, Lieutenant. I am much out of practice in this most beautiful of all languages. You shall be my teacher." The lieutenant beamed, almost exactly as had the chief scout.

Dinner was excellent. Delacroix complimented the fine, hot bread and waxed even more pleased with the two bottles of wine that had miraculously appeared in the driest city in the United States. Chamberlain promised to offer amends to Dow's angry ghost. The sudden reversal of the lieutenant's fortune, Chamberlain's kindness, his courtesy in speaking French, the fine meal, the buzz from the wine, and the glow from the fire all put Delacroix in a mood to please. He unconsciously felt he was in the presence of a gentleman and not an enemy. Chamberlain had played on that theme by decrying the folly of war between two related peoples, though this son of Quebec might have argued the point in other circumstances of whether he was related to these Anglo-Saxons on either side of the borders. For all that difference, the Québécois were not eager for the Stars and Stripes to replace the queen's flag. They were royalists to the core. They cheered, "*Vive le roi!*" as eagerly for a Saxe-Coburg as a Bourbon. So, he was especially won over when Chamberlain proposed a toast to his gracious sovereign, Victoria Regina, Protestant heretic though she was.

Chamberlain was silently thanking George Sharpe for his briefings on interrogation techniques after Gettysburg. It was just an elaboration of the old saying that you catch more flies with honey than vinegar. Sharpe was adamantly opposed to any form of brutality, insisting that it was immoral and would indelibly stain the honor of anyone who engaged it. Worse, it would morally harm any subordinate man an officer set to such practices, and an officer had a profound responsibility to ensure the decent behavior and good character of his men. Men who did such things found their conduct affected in other areas that would soon poison their relationship with their comrades.

Practically, it simply was not reliable. A man in pain will tell you just what you want to hear. A well-treated man who was properly encouraged, cajoled, flattered, and even lied to can be played. This took skill and patience but was well worth the investment. From such techniques, Sharpe and his staff had drawn forth the priceless intelligence at Gettysburg that Lee had committed every regiment in the Army of the Northern Virginia but those in Pickett's Division, his smallest, by the night of the second day of the battle. Thus Sharpe was able to tell his commander the exact size of the enemy's reserve, decisively influencing the course of the battle.

Chamberlain deftly drew forth the information that Doyle had withdrawn almost his entire force to march south to meet Sedgwick's VI Corps, which had just left Boston. The rumors were that Doyle would drive south, beat Sedgwick, and then return as fast as he could. Delacroix added that a new general straight from England had landed hours after Doyle marched and had galloped after him. Chamberlain could barely control himself as the lieutenant complained that this new general, who was rumored to command all forces in British North America, had not paused to review the guard. Not that there was much to see. Only four Canadian militia battalions, some Royal Artillerymen, and engineers had been left to hold the siegeworks.

Chamberlain purred in reply to Delacroix, "I'm afraid we are in no position to do anything even if there were only one battalion.

The garrison is in such straits that we can barely keep watch." With a sigh he said. "I simply do not see how much longer we can hold out. But the honor of my country requires me to delay your general just a little more."

Delacroix commiserated on the sufferings of the Americans and offered his hopes that an honorable settlement would soon take place. "I am sure that Sir Charles would offer generous terms to such gallant men." He almost felt like patting the obviously depressed Chamberlain on the back.

HEADQUARTERS, CIB, LAFAYETTE SQUARE, WASHINGTON, D.C., 4:14 PM, OCTOBER 23, 1863

Sharpe's staff meeting had just broken up. He was in conversation with his chief of ciphers, one extremely talented lieutenant he had purloined from the Signal Corps camp of instruction in Georgetown, when Jim McPhail came striding down the hallway, carpetbag in hand.

"Jim!" Sharpe said, glad to see his deputy. Then he excused himself from the lieutenant and put his hand on McPhail's shoulder, "Let's talk about your trip." He caught one of his clerks in passing to tell him to have Wilmoth join them in his office.

McPhail tossed his bag in the corner and dropped into one of the stuffed chairs in front of Sharpe's desk. Sharpe leaned back against the front of desk, eager to hear his deputy's trip report. "Well, I'm all ears. God knows the papers are in a perfect twist. Every man of importance in the Union, it seems, has lined up in the White House to demand the president send the entire Army to defend his backyard."

"I was in Boston when Sedgwick's VI Corps marched through. The entire city turned out to cheer them on. I never knew Massachusetts could that excited about anything except abolition."

"I would, too, if the redcoats were as close as Portland. In fact, Jim, they're closer to Kingston." He started pacing. "As far as I know, May and the children are still there. Since the invasion, the telegraph has been restricted to war business. Half my office are New York men, and if I won't let them break the order, they won't see me do it either."

McPhail knew that Sharpe had reason to worry. He didn't want to sugarcoat it, though it would add another burden to his boss. "Surely, we can get a message to her when we send someone anywhere nearby.

I think you should get your and McEntee's families out of Kingston." Capt. John McEntee had been Sharpe's deputy in the BMI. "The reports are true. The British have been raiding down the Hudson Valley. New York City is filling with refugees. There's only the garrison of the city, and the president dare not send it forward, or the entire city will panic. If we lose New York, we lose the war."

Sharpe cut to the purpose of sending McPhail north. "What is the enemy situation, then?"

McPhail's seriousness deepened. He paused to carefully choose his words. "Our information is thin, George, damned thin."

Sharpe replied, "I did not expect miracles, Jim."

"And we didn't get any, that's for sure. When you called me down from Baltimore and offered me this job, I was overjoyed. At last we would be able to put some sense into the intelligence end of this damnable war. God knows, we have worked nothing less than a few miracles of our own putting this bureau together, but the job was too damned big to do and get our legs under us in just three months."

Sharpe said, "Well, we put the BMI together in two months and handed Hooker Bobby Lee's head on a silver platter. When I took this job, I knew the problem I had faced with standing up the BMI would shrink in comparison with the difficulties in putting together this bureau, and I was dead right."

McPhail said, "Don't be too hard on yourself. Look at what you've accomplished. You've resurrected the Balloon Corps and got Lowe to run it even though he promised never to work with the government again after being insulted and harassed out of the Army."

Sharpe commented wryly, "I think the colonel's commission had something to do with it."

"If you hadn't sent Cline and some of the 3rd Indiana Cavalry out to Indiana to sniff out that Copperhead plot, he wouldn't have been there to crush the attempt to liberate all the prisoners of war at Camp Morton. Indianapolis, as well as Chicago, would have fallen, and I don't think we could have recovered from that.

"You set up BMIs in the Army of the Cumberland, and with Grant and Banks down in Louisiana."

Sharpe shook his head. "It didn't do Rosecrans any good. We warned him in plenty of time that Longstreet was coming out to reinforce Bragg. A crushing defeat at Chickamauga and getting shut up in Chattanooga are not great advertisements for our organization, Jim."

McPhail was determined to convince Sharpe that the glass was half full. "George, Longstreet just moved too fast, and Rosecrans's scouts never were able to warn of his arrival. Rosecrans gave battle thinking he had brought Bragg's smaller army to bay. You know as well as I do that the enemy has a vote."

He could see that Sharpe needed more encouragement. "Then you were able to warn the president and Stanton of British maneuvering in preparation for their attack."

"Yes, and they fooled me. I would bet it was that damned Wolseley who planned it. They demonstrated so actively against Buffalo and Detroit that we sent reinforcements there, and then they struck at Albany and Portland. Our agents just did not catch that deception." Sharpe had been truly impressed with the way the British had, at the last minute and without any word getting out, marshaled their railroads to move most of the British and Canadian troops making their big show in the Canadian Peninsula to concentrate against Albany.

"George, we were damned lucky to get that. It takes longer than three months to set up an effective agent network in another country. All that Treasury gold we pass out up in Canada has bought us a lot of access, I must admit. But even that takes time to bear fruit."

Sharpe permitted himself a smile. "Reminds me of a story. Alexander the Great's father, Philip II, was faced with what everyone told him was an impregnable fortress. He replied, 'You mean an ass laden with silver cannot get inside?'"

"Exactly. And while we are at it, we did pick up the British interest in Portland. It was your idea to send all the Maine regiments home under the pretext of a recruitment leave. Had they not arrived when they did, the enemy would have taken the city without hardly a shot. Instead, the British Army that could be sacking Boston is tied up in the siegeworks of Portland."

"And that brings us back to the enemy situation, Jim. What will Sedgwick face when he tries to relieve Portland? What will the British send down the Hudson when they decide to take New York? And what reinforcements are arriving from England?"

"I don't have much more than what I wired Wilmoth from Boston and New York yesterday and last night," McPhail responded.

Just then, the unobtrusive Wilmoth entered and stood quietly. Sharpe had come to allow him unannounced access to him at any time. McPhail cordially nodded to him and went on. "I was handed this information just as I was getting on the train in New York. Halifax is abuzz with the expectation that a twenty-thousand-man reinforcement is about to arrive from garrisons all throughout the British Isles. With them comes General James Hope Grant to take command of all troops in British North America."

Wilmoth quietly added, "He's the best they've got. I have a file on him." He had a file on Wolseley, too. Sharpe would have been pleased to know that Wolseley had a file on him, too. The assistant quartermaster general had become the primary planner and intelligence officer for the British forces in North America, and if any man was Sharpe's counterpart, it was Wolseley.

"Jim, take a few days to pick whomever you want, and then I want you back in New York to pull this agent network together. And, Jim, I suggest you buy a stouter carpetbag to hold all the gold I will be sending with you."

McPhail laughed. "When I think of the opportunities to get rich in this job. . ."

Sharpe countered, "Well, I can write you a letter of recommendation to join Lafayette Baker's Secret Service if you want to get rich in shaking people down." Even Wilmoth permitted himself to laugh. The CIB staff mirrored their boss's contempt of Baker and his crew.

FORD'S THEATRE, 7TH STREET, WASHINGTON, D.C., 5:52 PM, OCTOBER 23, 1863

John Wilkes Booth was still in high dudgeon. He had been in an exuberant and exalted mood ever since Britain and France had declared war, absolutely sure that it spelled the doom of the United States and the triumph of the Confederacy. Now this vile, damnable notice had plunged into an incandescent anger. The government had banned actors from moving freely back and forth between the North and South. For two years, he had freely preened his pro-Southern sympathies to appreciative Southern audiences and had enjoyed the adulation that came with that, not to mention his increasingly impressive acting skills. What he did not know was that Sharpe had been behind the order.

He was giving another magnificent performance of outrage in his dressing room to the cast of his matinee performance still in their make-up. His handsome features seemed to glow with his anger. His glance took in the big, bearded man standing in the dressing room doorway, definitely not an actor. In the imperious tone he had mastered for Shakespeare, Booth demanded, "And who are you, sir?"

He noticed the man's grin was positively canine. "John Miller, Secret Service. I have a message for you from Mr. Lafayette Baker." The room immediately emptied past him. No one wanted to be anywhere around Baker or anyone who worked for him. The man closed the door behind him. It was clear that Booth was in a combative mood. But Big Jim Smoke had not come for a fight. He pulled up a chair and sat down. "I think we need to talk, sonny."

Smoke's inquiries with his Copperhead contacts had vouched for Booth's sympathies. The problem was how to bring this high-strung peacock along without scaring him off. Smoke had seen too many poseurs among the Copperheads to take anyone's protestations of support for granted. He may not have been subtle, but he was guileful. He knew vanity was a powerful weakness in any man and that that fault ran powerfully among actors. He leaned forward and said in a half whisper, "God bless the Confederacy." Booth's mouth fell open momentarily. Then he replied, his brown eyes dancing fire, "And God damn the Union!"

THE HOUSE OF COMMONS, LONDON, 12:00 AM, OCTOBER 23, 1863

The House always met late as a matter of course. Gentlemen never rose until the afternoon. The member for Rochdale, Richard Cobden, stood up to speak. Lord Clarence Paget, the secretary of the Admiralty, groaned inwardly. Cobden was a member of the Navy Committee and damned well informed and as influential a Radical as Bright. His comments before the committee over the Navy Estimates last February had come to haunt Paget.

"The secretary of the Admiralty will bear with me as I recapitulate my comments from the February Navy Estimates. I made a point of emphasizing then that we had then seventy-six thousand men and boys in the Navy. Since Charleston subtracted five thousand from that number, I think my words, which had no affect on the Admiralty and the House at that time, will make an impression now.

"'The fate of empires' said the noble lord — I will use his own words — 'will not in future depend on line-of-battle ships; they are not suited to the modern mode of warfare.'

"'I heard the late Admiral Napier declare, a short time before his death, that a line-of-battle ship struck with one of your modern percussion shells would have a hole in her side large enough, he said, to drive a wheelbarrow through. What said the honorable and gallant officer the member for Harwich (Captain Jervis)? In my own hearing, he said that a wooden line-of-battle ship, hit by these modern percussion shells, would be nothing but a slaughterhouse.'"

The House was deadly still. Sweat beaded the forehead of Lord Paget. Disraeli leaned back into the green leather of his bench and looked down at the floor. Cobden continued. "I asked any nautical man, 'Would you, if you were at war with America tomorrow, send one of your wooden line-of-battle ships, with 700 or 800 men on board, and with 30 or 40 tons of gunpowder under their feet, to meet a vessel like *Monitor*? Baronet, the member for Finsbury (Sir Morton Peto), once declared his opinion that the minister who should send a wooden line-of-battle ship to encounter these modern shell guns would deserve to be impeached.'[1]

"I have it on authority that Admiral Milne was hesitant to engage the American monitors at Charleston but was compelled by the direct instructions of the government to break the blockade at Charleston because of the demands of commercial interests in the city which demanded to carry off the countless of bales of cotton stored in that city.

"Perhaps the government thought that the broadside ironclads *Black Prince* and *Resistance* would be enough to overcome the American monitors. If so, it was a disastrous miscalculation. In losing both, the Navy lost one half of its ironclads. The noble lord was at pains in February to explain that eighteen more ironclads were under construction and should all be at sea, though not commissioned, by spring of next year. I might add that most the rest are wooden frame ships bearing armor plate. Already, the battle of Charleston has shown them to be obsolete against the turreted American ships. I ask the noble lord, how many of those eighteen ironclads are turreted?"

Paget rose slowly. "The member from Rochdale should know that *Royal Sovereign* and *Prince Albert* will be the first such ships."[2]

Cobden shot back, "Come, my lord, you neglected vital information. Pray, what is the purpose of these ships?"

Paget replied, "Coastal defense."

"Coastal defense! Well, my lord, we shall then be able to put up a stout fight when the monitors cross the ocean and steam up the Thames."

Hard laughter rolled down the benches. Paget did not know when to fold and added, "We also have the second of the two turreted warships being built by Laird Brothers which the government plans to transfer to the Navy. That is an ocean-going ship."

Disraeli rose and was recognized by the Speaker. "My lord perhaps does not appreciate the irony of his last statement. One battle, one avoidable battle, has declared to the world that our Navy is obsolete. Now the secretary of the Admiralty tells the House that we will have, at some undetermined date, one and only one modern warship able to sail the high seas and that ship is none other than the sister to the infamous *North Carolina* whose escape, due to the inexplicable neglect of the Foreign Office, has ignited this war. Perhaps my lord should take to writing novels. He certainly has far more imagination for it than I. May I recommend a publisher, my lord?" More laughter.

HEADQUARTERS, CIB, LAFAYETTE SQUARE, WASHINGTON, D.C., 6:10 PM, OCTOBER 23, 1863

Sharpe asked McPhail, "Well, was Ripley van Winkle cooperative?" On his trip north McPhail had had more to do than shore up the thin agent system in Canada.

He grinned. "I had expected him to be the cantankerous, difficult obstructionist we had all come to love as chief of the Ordnance Bureau. But, you know, shameless flattery will open doors that you could not break down with a fire ax. Oh, I laid it on thick, telling him that he was a national treasure as the single greatest expert on ordnance in the United States, and how he had a reputation for utter probity and had been an exemplary steward of the taxpayer's money. He really warmed up when I mentioned it must have taken iron self-control and dedication to duty not to be stampeded into ordering all the crackpot new weapons every charlatan had thought of.

"I actually thought I had overdone it, but the old coot was eating it up with a spoon. You know, he really is a world-class expert. My notes are extensive." He looked at Wilmoth, who seemed as eager as a child on Christmas Eve at the prospect of McPhail's details. Wilmoth's pencil hung poised over his notepad. "Ripley had been an encyclopedia of knowledge about the Royal Small Arms Factory, Enfield. He was also able to supplement what Pete Dupont has been able to tell us about the nearby Royal Powder Mills at Waltham Abbey. Even more than we thought, the British have concentrated what seems like an inordinate part of their army's war-making production in one small area.

"Ripley said that early during the Crimean War, they discovered that the weapon contractors were simply unable to fulfill their production contracts for the new Model 1853 Enfield Rifle. It was a potential catastrophe for them. So, they swallowed their pride and sent a military commission here to study our 'American Method' of production.[3] They went straight to Springfield Arsenal, which Ripley was running at the time. They were most impressed, and Ripley apparently fell all over himself to be helpful. He sent them on an extensive tour of factories of all sorts to see how we do things and especially of weapon makers such as Colt and Sharp and of the makers of our specialized weapon machine tools. He positively glowed when he repeated the comment of the commissioners that 'the Americans displayed a degree of ingenuity which English industrialists would do well to imitate.'[4] They spent a fortune on American machinery, rebuilt their facility at Enfield — which had been nothing but a repair shop — on a huge scale, and converted it into the primary producer of the small arms of the British Army. They even hired away Ripley's chief engineer to manage the new factory."

Sharpe asked, "Anyone we know?"

"James Burton, a Virginian and surely a Rebel according to Ripley."

Sharpe looked at Wilmoth who said, "We have a file on him, too."

McPhail added, "They seemed to have hired most of their talent here." He rummaged through a sheaf of papers in his carpetbag and pulled out one. "Yes, there's a fellow named Oramel Clark, foreman in the stocking department, one Caulnin, foreman in the smithy, and someone named McGee, whom Ripley thinks is Burton's assistant." He handed the paper to Wilmoth.[5]

"The factory went into full production in 1859 and turns out as many as a hundred thousand rifles a year. Ripley was sure that in wartime they could at least triple their production based on his experience at Springfield Arsenal. He also said that the private weapon makers had to follow Enfield's example and retool. The largest of these is the London Armoury Company with its pronounced Rebel sympathies. Although they've sold us a lot of Enfields early in the war, they've been supplying the Confederacy with their entire output ever since."[6]

Sharpe asked, "Where is Enfield?"

Wilmoth spoke up. "It's thirty-five miles north of London in Essex but only twenty-five miles from a port on River Crouch."

By this point, Wilmoth's encyclopedic knowledge surprised neither Sharpe nor McPhail. "A good hard ride, I would think." Sharpe leaned back on his desk and folded his arms in thought. Then he and McPhail looked at each other, seemingly arriving at the same thought that Wilmoth had already had.

McPhail went on. "Ripley also had an uncanny feel for what is going on in the British and European ordnance network. The British don't have anything like our repeaters. Ripley thinks this is a fine example of superior British prudent common sense. And he didn't have anything good to say about the Prussian needle-gun either." Another thought occurred to McPhail. "You know, I had one of our people go through Ripley's files before I went up so I could speak from some authority. Good God, George, those files are a graveyard of opportunities that have passed us by. He actually lied to General Frémont last year when he asked for some of those coffee mill guns Lincoln had forced Ripley to buy. Ripley just lied that he didn't know a thing about them, when he had actually recalled them to the Washington Arsenal."[7]

Sharpe said, "I'm way ahead of you, Jim. Someone told me they could fire a hundred twenty rounds a minute. I heard one was used once in combat and cut a Rebel cavalry squadron to pieces. You just poured the cartridges into a hopper and they fed the gun by hand crank; the hopper looked like a coffee mill, and that's what Lincoln called the gun. I thought they sounded interesting. Then they just disappeared from the

Army. Then when Lincoln gave me this job, he told me everything about how impressed he was with this gun and how Ripley had made sure nothing came of it. He could have wept in frustration.

"So, I made a few inquiries and, lo and behold, I found all sixty or so of them neatly lined up at the Arsenal, most of them brand new, oiled, and unfired. Well, I drew ten for the Ulster boys and ten for the 20th. They've been practicing at the firing ranges around Washington. The boys seem to like them, though they can be finicky. We got the designer out here to work out the bugs, and they've been fairly reliable."

Sharpe was referring to the regiment he had personally raised in August 1862—the 120th New York Volunteers, known as the Ulster Guard, and his old militia regiment, the 20th New York State Militia commanded by Col. Theodore Gates. Both regiments had been recruited form Sharpe's hometown of Kingston and the surrounding counties of Ulster and Greene. Sharpe was a man of intense loyalties and had persuaded Lincoln to transfer both regiments to the garrison of Washington. It was understood clearly, however, that the two regiments reported to Sharpe. He also had under his control those companies of the 3rd Indiana Cavalry that weren't out hunting Copperheads in the Midwest. Sharpe was doing more than taking care of his men. He was giving himself the capability to act in an emergency without having to beg for troops. He was also thinking of those situations in which the use of such troops was something the Army did not wish to know about.

McPhail nodded. "And there's another gun made by a Richard Gatling. The Army tested it twice earlier this year. I read the reports in Ripley's files, stamped with a big red 'REJECTED.' Good men on the committee, and I've rarely read such enthusiasm. They said it simply did not malfunction or overheat no matter how many rounds you fired from its six rotating barrels—two hundred a minute, I think the reports said."

"All fine and good, Jim." Sharpe was anxious to move on, but made a mental note of what McPhail had said. "We know how Ripley thinks in these matters. He can't do any more harm. But has he heard of any developments in finding an alternative to niter in the making of gunpowder?"

"Well, nothing specific on that, I'm afraid. He admitted that he knew less about propellants than ordnance."

Wilmoth spoke up again. "Mr. DuPont had something interesting there. I spoke to him a few days ago after you told me about the niter supply problem. It's guncotton."

Sharpe threw up his hands. "But I thought the British and Europeans had all given up on it because it was too unstable and dangerous."

"Mr. DuPont said he has heard that the British Army's chief chemist, Sir Frederick Abel, has made a serious advance in making guncotton safe."

McPhail asked, "What the hell is guncotton?"

Wilmoth said, "According to Mr. DuPont, it is a lightweight explosive made by soaking finely washed cotton treated with nitric and sulfuric acid."

"And why is this important?"

"Well, sir, it uses a lot less niter to make the nitric acid used in making guncotton than is used to make gunpowder."

Sharpe stood up suddenly. "You mean that our niter supply can be stretched almost indefinitely by making guncotton instead of gunpowder?"

"I think so, sir, but I'm no expert, and Mr. DuPont says it would take a lot more experimentation to turn it into a useful propellant, if it can be done at all."

"My boy!" Sharpe almost shouted, "We have the . . ." He stopped in mid-sentence as he heard his name being shouted in alarm as footsteps ran up the hall. His chief telegrapher threw open the door. "General, New Orleans has fallen!"

HEADQUARTERS, ARMIES OF THE WEST, OUTSIDE CHATTANOOGA, 7:15 PM, OCTOBER 23, 1863

Maj. Gen. Ulysses S. Grant sat on a stump with a cigar clenched in his teeth, reading the same telegraph message that had stunned Sharpe's telegrapher. Taylor had bounced into the city three days ago. The news had run along with the panic by escaping riverboat to Baton Rouge and from there to Port Hudson. The Navy had been able to carry off part of the garrison up river before the city fell.

His staff hung about him silent as the grave. He looked up and muttered to no one in particular, "How the hell did this happen? Where was Banks?" There had been no mention of Banks or his army. Grant was aware that he had marched west to meet the French. Grant had immediately wired him to pull back behind Brashear City and the city's marshy moat and not risk a battle. He did not trust Banks in an open fight with anyone who had his wits about him.

The forces at Grant's command after Vicksburg had been so powerful that the Union had ample freedom of strategic initiative. Now he was desperately short of men. Washington, at the instigation of Maj. Gen. Henry Halleck, Lincoln's Army chief of staff, and a military pedant of the first order, had overridden his desires and sent his powerful XIII Corps under command of one of his best generals, Maj. Gen. E. O. C. Ord, off to support Banks in a mission of picking up loose change in western Louisiana and eastern Texas. Then the Copperhead rebellion had diverted Sherman's tough XVII Corps to the recapture of Chicago and the pacification of the Midwest. He had been promised the shrunken XI and XII Corps from the Army of the Potomac, but they had been held back with the British in New York and Maine. All he had been able to bring to the fight was XV Corps, and he had used it to drive a difficult route to the beleaguered garrison over the loop of the Tennessee River at Brown's Ferry. But all he had done was put off the day when the last hardtack was consumed. He had replaced Rosecrans, whose spirit had never recovered from his crushing defeat at Chickamauga, with Maj. Gen. George Thomas, an obdurate man who had fought the rearguard action that had saved the remnant of the army and earned him the epithet "The Rock of Chickamauga." He now vowed to hang on until they starved. Grant knew the last hardtack in Chattanooga would be a distant memory before Thomas asked for terms.

He leaned against a tree, lost in thought, one arm on his hip, his only movement an occasional puff on the cigar. His staff relaxed. Grant had the inexplicable talent to emanate calm force from his nondescript, almost shabby self, in powerful waves. The staff had an unshakable belief in his good judgment and determination. He was relentless in pursuit of success. So indisposed was he to retreat that he would not even backtrack while traveling, preferring to cut a new route even over the most difficult terrain.

Then he walked back to the stump, sat down, and pulled out his dispatch book and a pencil from his pocket. In a precise and calm hand, he began to write. Historians would later marvel at the neat and unhurried handwriting of his dispatches, written even in the fiercest battles. The man simply could not be rattled. His ability to coldly focus even in the most hellish crisis had become legend. Finished, he gave it to his old friend and chief of staff, Col. John Rawlins. "Get this to Sherman immediately." Rawlins read it as he called for a telegrapher. "Join me with your corps at once. Turn over remaining pacification to state authorities and militia."

Grant got up and took Rawlins by the arm, "Now, John, let's see how we can get General Bragg to help us out."

"HOOKER'S DIVISION," WASHINGTON, D.C.'S RED-LIGHT DISTRICT, 9:33 PM, OCTOBER 23, 1863

No one noticed the little black boy gliding in the shadows between the brightly lit saloons and whorehouses in Washington's red-light district, known as Hooker's Division, a triple play on a nickname for the oldest profession, the bawdy general, and the unsavory reputation of his former headquarters. Jimmy was an expert and determined tracker in the urban jungle that had become wartime Washington. He had never had so much difficulty in tracking a man as the big, bearded man he has seen at Baker's that morning. Big Jim Smoke had a lifetime's experience of thuggery to hone his feral survival instincts. He could just sense his tail. If Jimmy hid in the shadows, Smoke disappeared time and time again in the crowds of soldiers and civilians that crowded the streets and wooden sidewalks or into one or another of the noisy, crowded saloons. But each time he slipped out, the shadow followed.

Jimmy was as relentless as he was careful. Sharpe's instructions had been clear. "Find out where he goes and whom he sees." He had picked up Miller's trail after the man had returned to Baker's office later that day. Now with the gas lamps flickering over the crowded street, he slipped into another shadow to wait the man's exit from Madame LeBlanc's, one of the middling whorehouses. He munched on an apple that Sergeant Wilmoth had given him as he bounded out of the BMI office, intent on Sharpe's instructions. He had the gift of patience and could wait and wait. This time he did not have to wait long. The big man pushed open the double swinging doors and looked about, then quickly strode down the sidewalk. The shadow followed.

The man abruptly turned into a darkened alley. Jimmy waited a moment and went into the darkness after him. His eyes were good in the dark, and his shoes so worn that they made no sound as he picked over the patches of bare ground between piles of garbage.

As good as his eyes were, they could not see around corners. No sooner had he glided around the edge of the building than an iron grip took him by the throat and lifted him into the air. He couldn't breathe. "Not so good, are you, nigger?" Jimmy would have screamed as the knife buried itself to the hilt in his chest and twisted, but the hand had his throat closed. He did not feel pain as the man threw his body against a wall.

6

"Because I Can't Fly!"

AMERICAN ENTRENCHMENTS, PORTLAND, MAINE, 1:55 AM, OCTOBER 24, 1863

The early morning cold of a hard autumn seemed to bite to the bone. The breath of the entire Maine Division rose in vapor wisps as they stood silent in their ranks, broken down into their sequenced assault groups. Almost three thousand veteran men in blue and another two thousand militia, men hardened quickly in the two weeks of siege, waited behind the city's landward defenses. Two days of intensive preparation had readied them for the supreme effort—the sortie to break the siege.

The opportunity for such a desperate measure had leaped almost instantly into Chamberlain's mind when his interrogation of the Canadian lieutenant revealed how weak the force guarding the British fortifications was. He must strike before Doyle returned with his division. With luck, Sedgwick would win, and that would be the end to the threat to Portland. If not, then the sortie must succeed to give the garrison a new lease on life. Chamberlain had walked down the line past each assault group, encouraging the men in his reassuring way. They in turn encouraged him by their eagerness to do this thing.

It was time now. He looked at his watch by the light of a hooded lantern behind the earthen walls. He nodded to his regimental commanders who sped off to join their men. They did not have far to go. His ten regiments were now shrunk small and did not take up too much frontage. Besides, he had grouped them into three assault groups with one infantry regiment in reserve and the 1st Maine Cavalry ready to ride through any breach in the enemy's lines.

The front ranks, heavily reinforced with militia, carried fascines —
that is, bundles of branches — to fill the ditch in front of the British positions. The militia was not expected to actually help carry the enemy
works. They were told they could withdraw after they had thrown their
fascines into the ditch. Following them were the dozens of ladder details
to cross the filled-in ditches and plant their ladders against the six-foot-
tall earthen wall. Behind them were the special assault teams chosen
from the boldest men in each regiment.

Every piece of equipment that could make noise had been left behind or padded. No lights were allowed. It was an overcast and moon-
less night, pitch black even to men who had been out in it for hours, and
a cold mist rose from the ground to further envelop them as they crossed
the beaten zone between their own positions and the enemy's. It was
a recipe for disaster. Night attacks were rare because the potential for
failure was so great. Units would get lost and sent off in the wrong direction or arrive too late. It took the tightest control to even attempt a night
attack, and to do so in such darkness would have been folly. To prevent
that, the boys in each regiment — the drummers and fifers whose eyes
were the sharpest — unrolled white bandages in the direction of the enemy to within yards of the ditch. The men would advance in their ranks,
the man behind with his hand on the shoulder of the man in front.[1]

The mass of men began to move through the sortie breaches in the
defenses in a muffled shuffle, the cold morning mist tingling their faces
and freezing where it touched the metal of their rifles and fixed bayonets. Chamberlain moved with the center group. All three groups were
focused on the enemy line held by the Canadian militia. The batteries
of the Royal Artillery were avoided. The Canadians kept poor watch by
and large, especially the newly raised battalions. The battalions Doyle
had left behind were the most recently raised and had not soldiered long
enough to have sink into their bones a great military sin — to fall asleep
on guard. Early in the war, President Lincoln had had that problem
brought home to him again and again as he had had to review the death
sentences of new soldiers for just such failings. To the distress of his generals, he invariably pardoned these boys. The Canadians would have no
such benefactor this night. The time of early morning had been chosen
not only for the cloak of night, but also to take advantage of the time
when the body demands to sleep.

It was a sound assessment, borne out as the first Union men reached the mist-shrouded ditch. The fascine men were brought forward to toss in their bundles and then fall back as the ladder details crossed the now filled-in ditch. But as the ancients liked to say, the gods are perverse. The sergeant of the guard of the 29th "Waterloo" Battalion, raised in Galt, Upper Canada, was no militiaman. Sgt. Henry Mocton had taken his discharge seven years ago from an Imperial battalion, one of the more savage schools of soldiering in the British Army. A struggling farm had improved his memories of "the Armye," and when Galt raised this battalion, he rushed to reenlist and put on the scarlet coat again. As the only veteran in the battalion, he had been much praised and had become even more disliked when these amateurs learned what real soldiering required.

At that moment, the ladder details began to move forward, Mocton's duty round took him to the guard station just above. He found Pvt. Alexander MacCauley sound asleep, huddled below the parapet all in a ball to keep warm. Mocton was about to wake him with a brutal kick when the two arms of a ladder fell upon the edge of the parapet. In moments a face appeared wearing a blue cap. In one fluid, unthinking movement, Mocton drove his bayonet through the man's left eye, twisted it, and withdrew. The body silently fell backwards and landed with a dull thud that brought cries from the men below. Mocton threw the guardpost torch over the side and looked. He could see a mass of moving shadows below and ladders to either side thick with climbing men. He pulled back, turned, cupped his hand to his mouth to shout the alarm — and choked. He looked down to see six inches of a bayonet protruding from below his breast, and then life went dark for him.

Chamberlain dropped over the parapet as the man ahead twisted his bayonet out of Mocton. Men would later say he was reckless beyond all measure for being at the point of the assault, but such a desperate enterprise needed the animating power of the leader at the spear tip to ensure that it continued to be driven home. The men in blue flowed into the advanced positions where the duty sections slept and roused them with rifle butts and the prick of bayonets in their backsides. The first shots rang out, then more, to his left and right down the line in the dark. Other parties had attacked the more alert Royal Artillery batteries from the flanks and found out how well the British gunners took to losing

Canadian Militia Camps

Back Cove

Canal Basin

British

Siege

Chamberlain

Lines

Defenses

Portland

0 250 500 1000
FEET

Portland

THE
PORTLAND SORTIE
OCTOBER 24, 1863

Karamales 2009

their guns. A gun boomed and then another. Here and there a militia-man had escaped into the dark, fleeing to his encampment in the rear. Chamberlain had drummed it into his regimental commanders that they were not to be delayed inside the enemy positions, but were to press on and overrun their camps where most of the enemy would be. The camp-fires and torches in the British works cast enough light for the assault groups to be reassembled and thrown forward through the dark to the lights of the Canadian camps.

There the militia had come groggily awake. That rarest thing in war, Napoleon's description of "two o'clock in the morning courage," was no-where to be found. Panic ran through them as they desperately tried to dress and find their weapons. Ragged lines of half-dressed men began to form, but then when the battle lines of the Maine men emerged from the dark with bayonets leveled, the militia came apart. A few ragged shots got off, but the rest of them turned and ran into the night, the odd man still carrying his rifle. It would have been a presumption against human nature to have expected anything more from men whose military experi-ence was measured in weeks. The same thing had happened to Ameri-can troops two years ago when both Union and Confederate armies were just as green. The officers ran with the rest.

But a few men who were made of bolder stuff tried to stem the race to the rear. One such field officer yelled at a man who sprinted past him, "Why are you running, soldier?"

The men yelled back over his shoulder as he disappeared into the dark, "Because I can't fly!"[2]

SAMUDA BROTHERS' POPLAR SHIPYARD, PORTSMOUTH, ENGLAND, 2:20 PM, OCTOBER 24, 1863

Lord Clarence Paget was seething behind a placid face. Her Majesty's sudden visit to the yard to inspect the construction of HMS *Prince Albert* was the last thing he or the Admiralty wanted, especially in company of that simpering courtier, Disraeli. Paget had rushed to Plymouth from London to be in attendance.

Victoria's visit was her first public appearance since the death of Albert, and had aroused the nation's interest in what had broken through her veil of deep mourning. The yard workers had wildly cheered her appearance, buoying her spirits. Disraeli had worked this wonder in persuading her to come, artfully explaining that in this time of national peril, Albert would have wanted her people to see their queen. He went on to say that there would be no better way than to support the project in which Albert had believed so deeply, Captain Coles's turret ironclad. It had taken all of his powers of persuasion to coax her from her shell.

Disraeli murmured to her, "See, mum, how they love their sovereign. They are delighted to see you amongst them again." Now the crowd began to chant, "Albert! Albert! Albert!" A suggestion to the builders from Disraeli had seeded the idea of this greeting as well as the suggestion of a paid holiday. Now Victoria glowed. The tribute to the love of her life brought public tears to her eyes for the first time in her reign of twenty-six years.

She was delighted at the flowers presented by the children of the yard workers. She had been presented a mountain of flowers in her lifetime, but these seemed most beautiful of all. She was equally delighted to be introduced to Capt. Cowper Coles, the inventor in whom her husband had had such faith. Victoria had become an even greater partisan of this slim, forty-four-year-old naval officer with the long, luxurious blond beard. He escorted her up the Union Jack-draped ramp to the ship's main deck where sat the huge, black, round turret.[3]

Coles showed her through a hatch into the empty cavernous interior brightly lit with oil lamps. The deck mounts for the guns had been installed, but the guns themselves had not yet arrived. "Your Majesty shall see how easily this turret is rotated." At a signal, eighteen men below strained on a capstan to turn its bulk smoothly 360 degrees on its rollers in a minute.

Victoria was as delighted as a child on a merry-go-round. Without looking at him, she said, "Lord Paget, pray tell me how many such ships we are building."

"Your Majesty, we have almost two dozen ironclads under construction."

"With turrets, Lord Paget?"

"Only one, mum, *Royal Sovereign* and the former Confederate ship *Severyn*."

"Why only one?"

Paget was visibly squirming now. On cue, Victoria said, "Mr. Disraeli, what is your opinion?"

Disraeli explained, "Your Majesty, ships that rely on a web of masts and lines for most of their propulsion will find the movement of a turret greatly inhibited."

"Yet, Lord Paget, this 'web of masts and lines' did not serve us as well at Charleston as the American turrets." She was glad of Disraeli's explanation.

Disraeli's face did not betray his intense amusement at Paget's distress. One tried to evade Victoria's probing questions at his own peril. He was sure to note that the dozen journalists lining the turret walls were taking down every word in shorthand.[4]

ST. LOUIS CATHEDRAL, NEW ORLEANS, 11:00 AM, OCTOBER 24, 1863

A cloud of incense wafted out of the immense double doors of the cathedral as Bazaine stepped into the bright, crisp autumn morning, the hymns of the "Te Deum" still running though his head. The crowd that packed the square and nearby streets outside erupted in a wild roar, punctuated by shouts of "*Vive Bazaine!*" and "*Vive l'empereur!*" New Orleans was pleased to show off its French face to its new heroes.

They were already comparing his victory at Vermillionville to Napoleon's at Austerlitz. On that winter's day in 1805, Napoleon had driven thousands of Russians into icy ponds to drown. At Vermillionville, Bazaine had driven thousands of Americans into the murky waters of a Southern bayou and lake to a similar fate. Let the others take up the refrain, he thought. The emperor should receive his report in a week. He knew how ambition's game would cause a sensation in Paris—30 colors, 32 guns, 9 generals, and 12,348 unwounded prisoners. Another 899 dead and 3,223 wounded had been counted on the field. They had been veteran troops and deserved better leadership.[5]

Bazaine was already toying with thoughts of the rewards to be expected from his grateful sovereign—*Le Comte de Vermillionville* or, even better, *Le Duc de Vermillionville.*

Yes, Bazaine knew the game of military ambition in the Second Empire and so was attentive to the concerns and dreams of the imperial ambition. The ostensible purpose of the alliance was to secure France's grip on Mexico. A grateful Confederacy would gladly acquiesce to what an undivided Union would never tolerate—the nullification of the Monroe Doctrine. The emperor had hinted broadly in his instructions that perhaps France could expect greater gains from the American fratricide.

Jefferson Davis was astute enough to be concerned about larger French ambitions. For that reason, he had carefully instructed Taylor to emphasize the subordinate role of the French while operating on Confederate soil. Taylor had wasted no time in bringing that subject up with Bazaine shortly after his tumultuous welcome to the newly liberated city that would deny the victor of Vermillionville nothing.

Bazaine responded with cordial grace to Taylor's recapitulation of alliance roles. "*D'accord, d'accord, Général Taylor.* That is in line with the emperor's instructions. This army is sent to support you in your own country. You command me, and I command my army, no? This is best."

Then he paused to blow a neat circle from his cigar. "Of course, His Majesty has concerns that he has confided in me."

There it was—what Taylor feared—the "yes, but." He replied, keeping his voice even, "And those concerns are?"

"Oh, General Taylor, these are minor things, matters of sentiment, I assure you. But they are matters close to our French hearts. The emperor wishes to extend his imperial protection to Louisiana due to his regard for its French history, culture, and language—the very language of this city and the one we are speaking now."

"The Confederacy, sir, will look after its own," Taylor said pointedly in English before repeating it in French.

"Ah, yes, someday, of course, but you must admit, that the very necessity of welcoming a French army indicates otherwise. No? Your Confederacy will no doubt, as is His Majesty's fervent wish, be able someday to defy the world, but in the meantime you will face a vengeful Union and, I may say between friends, the treachery of perfidious Albion, despite the temporary alliance of convenience we share with it. It is the affection for our shared history and aspirations that motivates France."

THE BATTERY, CHARLESTON, SOUTH CAROLINA,
11:00 AM, OCTOBER 24, 1863

As Bazaine emerged from St. Louis Cathedral in distant New Orleans, Jefferson Davis was waiting for the British ship that was slowly approaching the dock. He had rushed down from Richmond for the occasion when word of it reached him. It was the most wished-for event in the Confederacy, the recognition of the independence of their new country by the foremost power in the world. Davis had insisted that it be the most formal of state occasions. With him was his vice president, Gen. Pierre G. T. Beauregard and a cluster of other generals, the governor of South Carolina, an honor guard in new uniforms, and a band. The railings along the Battery had been lined with alternating Union Jacks and Confederate flags. Crowds packed the street behind the Battery, the adjacent park, and the balconies of the overlooking mansions.

Charleston had come back to life in the last two weeks. This great Southern city had been nearly choked to death by the grip of two years of blockade. Now its harbor was a forest of masts from the hundreds of ships that had raced in from Bermuda and from across the Atlantic to exchange their cargoes of war materials and luxuries for the mountains of Southern cotton from the harvests of 1861 through 1863.

The battle that had freed the city could only be heard by the crowds packing the waterfront on that fateful day. A deep and constant rumble of heavy naval guns and clouds of dark smoke from the funeral pyres of ships of the line had kept hopes balanced on a knife's edge until the 6,200-ton ironclad HMS *Resistance* had steamed into the harbor past Fort Sumter. The crowds had gone wild. Only a practiced eye could see how much distress the great ship was in or that it had struck a Confederate mine in passing the fort. Its approach was agonizingly slow, and as it came up to Auger Dock, the wounded leviathan simply settled to the bottom. Luckily, its deep draft allowed its upper decks to remain above water.

General Beauregard carried off the official welcome in gallant Southern style. In the greatest tradition of the Royal Navy, *Resistance*'s captain strolled down the gangplank as if nothing had happened, graciously, albeit briefly, accepted the thanks of the city, and then asked for assistance for his many wounded.

Those men were rushed to Confederate hospitals and private homes where they were nursed by the ladies of the city with every care. The officers were feted in every mansion, and the only officer who did not immediately have a dozen belles hanging on every word was the officer on deck, for the captain had insisted on maintaining the illusion that his ship was still all "shipshape and Bristol fashion." But even the watch officer was soon deluged with visitors, for *Resistance* had become the greatest tourist attraction in the South. In a week, a dozen ships of the Royal Navy rode into the harbor among the mass of civilian shipping. The "women of the town" experienced a lucrative but exhausting bonanza. One of the ships brought the news of the imminent arrival of a ranking representative of the British government, and the news had drawn Davis from Richmond like a magnet.

Now, Jefferson Davis paced the stone parapet of the Battery as the ship came up to the dock with its distinguished passengers clustered on deck, flanked by scarlet-coated Royal Marines. The guns along the Battery fired the salute, the band struck up "God Save the Queen," and the crowd cheered. No one seemed to notice the nearby HMS *Resistance* with its upper decks barely above the water.

The Southern press immediately immortalized the meeting on the dock of President Davis and Her Majesty's representative, Austin David Layard. Their private meeting was much less satisfactory. Foreign Minister Russell had carefully chosen Layard for this mission. Layard had been his undersecretary at the Foreign Office and a member of Parliament. No one was more informed of the government's policies.

Russell was aware of Layard's overt Southern sympathies, but that was a sentiment shared by most in the British establishment. What he did not realize was that Layard had done more to start this war than anyone else. It was Layard's warning that allowed the infamous Confederate commerce raider, CSS *Alabama* to escape from Liverpool in 1862 just when American pressure was building for its seizure. The depredations of the *Alabama* and her sister ships had forced Lincoln to demand the seizure of the two ironclads building for the Confederacy in September. Layard had warned the builders and their Confederate accomplice in time for one of them to escape. Its escape and subsequent interception by the USS *Gettysburg* in British waters had provoked the battle with the frigate HMS *Liverpool*. The destruction of the British ship with heavy loss of life was the casus belli for the British declaration of war against the United States. Davis was more informed of Layard's role than even Russell through his agent in Britain, Capt. James Bulloch, Layard's contact. Davis considered Layard's appointment to be a mark of distinction and compliment to the Confederacy, unaware of Russell's ignorance of his activities. He was prepared to treat Layard as a hero.

For that reason, Davis was stunned by Layard's official message. It was clear to him that Layard had the impossible task of attempting to square a circle. "I regret that Her Majesty's government is unable at this time to offer your government formal recognition or alliance."

Davis's response was unprintable.

Layard attempted to explain, but even his aplomb was unsettled by the seething anger of the sharp-faced man in front of him. "Honor left Great Britain no other recourse after the attack on one of Her Majesty's warships in British waters than to go to war to avenge this outrage." If his role in this chain of events bothered him, it was not apparent. "The nation will support a war against the United States for this reason, sir. At this time, it will not support a war to maintain slavery."

Davis shot back, "Such distinctions are a fantasy, Mr. Layard. This war has already become indivisible by such artful distinctions. And I assure you, sir, from my own considerable experience, war is a great destroyer of assumptions. The iron law of necessity demands recognition and alliance. You would hamstring yourself without them."

Layard resumed. "As I said, Mr. Davis, at this time, we are not prepared to offer recognition and alliance. But Her Majesty's government recognizes that the force of events will alter perceptions of necessity at some point in the future. Only then will recognition and alliance be possible."

"Alliance already exists de facto, Mr. Layard. You fought a battle to break the blockade. Your ships ride in Charleston Harbor and have the full use of the Navy Yard. Your wounded are cared for in our hospitals. Royal arsenals and factories supply our armies. Your armies already occupy territory of our mutual enemy, and you have blockaded his coast. What would you call this state of affairs?"

"That is the purpose of my visit—to fashion a de facto cooperation that will serve the practical necessities of alliance. The difference between de facto and de jure, sir, is often a gossamer."

For the first time, the flicker of a smile played on Davis's face. "Tell that to a bastard, Mr. Layard."

"Ah, Mr. Davis, there is always the possibility that rightful legitimacy will be discovered in due time."

UNION RAILROAD STATION, INDIANAPOLIS, INDIANA, 2:44 PM, OCTOBER 24, 1863

Sherman's aides could not take their eyes off the crowds of men at the station as the general's train slowly came to a stop. There must have been at least two thousand, most in faded blue with a bedroll or knapsack, but most without weapons. They were not in any military formation, but they showed the innate sense of order of veterans. "It's been like this at every station since we left Chicago," one officer said.

It was the crowds of men in faded blue that raised the morale of Sherman's troops as they sped south. These were discharged veterans, men who had enlisted for two years in 1861 and had been discharged. They had gone home satisfied that they had done their share and vowing never to rejoin the Army. With them were thousands more who had been invalided home for wounds or sickness. There was more than one limp or cough among them still. Now they were back, trudging down the roads, gathering at the railroad stations demanding to be sent back to their regiments, and taking the oath of enlistment from any military or naval officer they could find. Entire discharged regiments assembled in their original camps of instruction and marched in step to the railroads, their tattered colors drawn from the state houses or from the place of honor in the home of some beloved commander. Even deserters came back in response to Sherman's blanket amnesty. Trains were commandeered to move this growing host. Sherman would arrive to reinforce Grant, not with a single corps but with an army.

As the train slowed to a halt at the bunting-draped main station building, Sherman could see what was obviously a delegation of civilians, chief among them the tall and rotund figure of Governor Morton. A band was playing "Rally Round the Flag, Boys!" to sea of men in blue. In the midst of crowd was what first appeared to be several batteries of artillery. A closer look showed the barrels to be circlets of heavy rifle barrels mounted on what looked like light artillery gun carriages.

As soon as Sherman emerged from the car, the throng erupted into hearty soldier cheers. Morton stepped forward, the platform boards creaking under his weight. He thrust out his hand to Sherman and the crowd cheered even more. Morton may not have been a soldier, but he knew public relations. "Wave, General, wave. Use the moment." It was hard for Sherman, who loathed anything smacking of a politician's oily pretence, but he waved. Now the crowd was chanting, "Billy! Billy! Billy!" It washed over him with the force of nature.

Morton linked arms with Sherman as he waved his hat at the crowd. He whispered into Sherman's ear, "Indiana has another gift for the Army, General. I want you to meet Richard Gatling."

MILL ROW, MANCHESTER, ENGLAND, 3:50 P.M. OCTOBER 24, 1863

Edward, His Royal Highness the Prince of Wales, had had to beg his mother to give him some role in supporting the war. She had not forgiven him for his father's death. Prince Albert had gone to his son's sickbed and caught there the typhoid that killed him. It had taken the intercession of the government to plead with the queen that he allowed to do his part to strengthen national resolve.

The sinking of HMS *Liverpool* in British waters by two American warships had filled the British public with an incandescent rage. It had been worth John Bright's life to speak out, but speak he did. Here and there, when the first enthusiastic rush of patriotism had worn down, thoughts of the consequences of the war became hard to ignore. And the most glaring of these was that Great Britain had essentially gone to war in support of the slaveholding South and was now in de facto alliance. The loss of *Liverpool* was the poisoned fruit of British support of the Confederacy and only the ostensible cause of war. Too many men had become rich over that support, and too many more had had their prejudices against American democracy flattered by that support. The establishment — privilege — had done everything to bring on this war. And now that it had come, privilege began to worry.

So Mill Row, the mill worker's row cottages for one of the big cotton manufacturers in Manchester, had been chosen by the government for a visit by His Royal Highness to encourage support for the war. Despite the tens of thousands unemployed by the Confederate cotton embargo, Army enlistments had slowed to a trickle. The crowd that came to see him had been large but distressingly restrained with its applause after he read the speech prepared for him, and that clearly was not due to the ingrained good manners of the British. After the speech, he walked down Mill Row in one of those rare exposures to the common people that only the necessity of war could provoke. He stopped every few yards to speak to someone in the respectful crowd. It was painfully obvious that he did not have the common touch, but he was the queen's son, and there was a deep reverence for Victoria.

He stopped by a young man, not more than twenty-two years old, who seemed sound enough to be a soldier and had that Everyman look that is more disguise than window. Edward thought him a suitable stage for his performance. "Well, my good fellow, will you enlist today and make Manchester proud?"

The young man doffed his cap and bowed slightly. Then he said plainly, "No, sir."

"No, sir?" Edward blurted out in surprise. "And why not?" Edward had stepped into the trap that only the most experienced and quick-witted politician can extricate himself from. And Edward was neither. Don't ask a question you don't know the answer to or don't want to hear.

The young man's gaze seemed harden. "Have you ever watched your child starve, sir?" His knuckles clutching his hat were white.

Edward was speechless, but his entourage gasped. No one asked him anything with such raw emotional bluntness, much less the type of person who normally cleaned his boots. If such a person addressed a question to him, it was invariably for instruction in meeting his needs.

"I named her Vicky, sir, after your mother, I did. She was God's gift, always laughing, golden curls. And when the slaveholders cut off the cotton and put me out of work, I watched her starve. I could find no work. I watched the flesh melt from her bones and her hair turn to straw." He voice caught.

Edward could only murmur, "I'm so sorry, my good man."

"She didn't die, sir, though the reaper was walking to my door, for sure."

"Well, then . . ."

"You see, sir, it was American bread that saved her and the pennies of the Americans who felt more pity for us than the slaveholders did."

Edward's entourage could see a disaster in the making and tried to move him on, but it was as if the prince had been glued to the cobbles as the crowd pressed in to hear every word. All he could mutter was something about standing up for your country.

"I love my country, sir, but my country would have let my child starve, like it did the Irish. Only the Americans showed pity."

The crowd had hung on every word and packed in tight. It began to buzz. Another man spoke up. "It is shame on this country to fight for the slaveholders. This is not our war."

Then another voice louder, "Privilege will see us all slaves!"

Another voice shouted, "I have family in America. We are shedding our own blood!" It was a rare member of the lower orders that did not have kin in North America. The buzz became a roar, and the crowd began to seethe. It was then that the chief constable acted to force a path for the prince and his entourage and insist they leave immediately.

The next day's lead article in *The People's Paper* carried the headline, under the byline of Karl Marx, "Mill Workers Demand End to the American War." He knew that the paper would be on the next packet for Canada and then smuggled to the United States where it would be reprinted in the *New York Tribune*, the formidable anti-slavery and pro-Lincoln engine of opinion. It was almost as if Karl Marx had a direct line to Abraham Lincoln himself.

That evening, the papers from London arrived in Dublin where Marx's report was read with perhaps even more interest than it would be in New York. Ireland had bled away over half her population of over eight million in the last fifteen years, and the green land was still stricken by the nightmare of the Great Famine that left almost two million corpses strewn about its empty cottages, country roads, and poorhouses. Another two million had fled ahead of grim starvation, many to Canada and Australia but most to the United States. Memories among the survivors of the starving time were bone deep with a permanent fester of hatred for the government that had ignored their plight, more anxious not to interfere with the working of a free market. It was remarked that the British showed more care for their dusky colonial subjects than their fellow Christians right across the Irish Sea. Safe and snug in Britain, privilege had not seen the convoys of grain being exported from the starving country, trailing thousands of emaciated beggars fended off by the bayonets of the redcoat escorts.

The wrath of outraged England at the loss of HMS *Liverpool* had not flared so brightly in Ireland outside the Protestant Anglo-Irish world. But the country by and large was still loyal, if only out of habit, and would shoulder the burden of this new cousin's war. But not all. Underneath the veneer of loyalty, the seeds of fifty years and more of the growth of Irish nationalism were sprouting. "Ireland's centuries-old dream of independence materialized in the collective form of a body of Irish rebels on 'the old sod and the new sod—America—alike.'" They came to be called Fenians by the British, a blanket term for any of the Irish who advocated independence. But the British were inexplicably blind to the spread of the movement.

They were especially blind where their own power concentrated. The British garrison of Ireland was shot through with Fenians. Just before the war, a quarter of the garrison's twenty-six thousand men had taken the Fenian oath "to free the Irish people from seven hundred years of oppressive British colonial rule or to die in the struggle."[6] So many Irish in the garrison of their own country was not unusual, for Ireland had been the prime recruiting ground for the Crown. Only a few decades earlier, before the Great Famine winnowed the Irish so cruelly, Ireland supplied fully half the enlisted strength of the British Army. Only the loss of half of its population since then had allowed that figure to drop below fifty percent for the first time. Now, ten thousand men of that garrison were on at sea on their way to Canada, some of them serenaded by the music of hymns, Mozart, and Bach.

OFFICE OF THE SECRET SERVICE, WASHINGTON, D.C., 4:47 PM, OCTOBER 24, 1863

"Well, Miller, you're in luck. The president's bodyguard has gone missing, and I'm short a man to fill that post." Lafayette Baker normally had quite a pack of agents at hand, but he had run the cupboard bare with the explosion of enemies, except for this new Midwesterner. And the man had done well in the assignment he had been given. That sniveling, noisy actor had shut up most ostentatiously.

Yes, luck was not what Big Jim Smoke had counted on when he had knifed the bodyguard and dumped his body into the Potomac River after the two stumbled out of an Alexandria dockside tavern two nights ago. He counted on the odds. If they ever found the body, it would be unrecognizable. The Copperhead organization in Washington had not been decapitated as it had been everywhere else. It was used to lying low in the den of the enemy, but its links farther south into Rebeldom had not been neglected. Shadowy orders had flowed north: weaken or penetrate the security around Seward, Stanton, and Lincoln.

Baker went on, "It's actually the easiest duty in Washington. Just sit outside his office or follow him around and keep the office seekers off him. And there's some free entertainment. He likes to go to the theater a lot."

KENNEBUNK, MAINE, 10:18 AM, OCTOBER 25, 1863

As soon as Hope Grant caught up with the British Portland Force marching south to meet the American VI Corps, the column picked up its pace. As commander of all of Her Majesty's forces in British North America, he immediately assumed command. As an old cavalryman, he knew the value of speed. In this he was much like the late Stonewall Jackson. He pushed his Imperial and Canadian battalions down the Portland Road. Scouts reported the advance of the Americans coming north also on the Portland Road. John Sedgwick knew how to hard-march his men as well as Grant. The forced march of the VI Corps to Gettysburg on July 2 had been an achievement by any standard. They numbered fifteen thousand men and forty-two guns. They were tough as nails.[7]

Grant's study of the map pointed to the little town of Kennebunk, bisected by its eponymous river, as the likely point where the two columns would meet. The river was crossed by Durrell's Bridge, which connected the two halves of the town, and seven shipyards clustered down both banks. Kennebunk was a major shipbuilding center, and building materials lined the streets and roads leading to the river. Doyle could tell him little of the enemy that he faced other than its high reputation as a fighting formation and its commander as a fighting general. Almost immediately, Grant sent a courier off to the coast to make contact with whatever Royal Navy ships were blockading Kennebunk at Kennebunkport, a few miles downriver.

For Sedgwick's part, he had no idea that he was about to meet the foremost British general of the age. His last information had Doyle still at Portland. Grant had had the foresight to cut the telegraph and race ahead of any warning. The Brunswick Regiment of Yeomanry Cavalry was effectively screening his advance—until they were hit hard by the small cavalry brigade attached to Segdwick's corps. At the first sound of gunfire to his front, Grant deployed his battalions and moved forward. It was not long before the Canadian cavalry came flying past. The Union cavalry were close behind, but the closely wooded road had masked the red lines from them until the last moment. A volley from the 17th Foot brought down the head of the column in a tangle of bodies and screaming, flailing horses. Grant ordered them forward, and the red ranks surged ahead, bayonets at the level.

Sedgwick's first knowledge of the British was when some of his cavalry came tearing back through Kennebunk to tell him that they had run into redcoats only a few miles north. No one ever accused Uncle John of being a Napoleon, but he was steady and unflappable, attributed by some to an utter lack of imagination. But he knew what to do in a fight. His first division was approaching the bridge over the Kennebunk River. The others were strung out for miles to the south. He sent couriers after them to hurry the pace.

The first men over the bridge would be Horatio G. Wright's 1st Division. Sedgwick wanted his best to land the first punch. Wright had only recently been given division command after a brilliant record in the West. The man was slated for a corps command one day, and Meade had been eager to find him a division. Meade had other reasons. Wright would be senior to the 2nd Division commander, Brig. Gen. Albion P. Howe, who had the great talent of alienating just about everyone above him in the chain of command. Howe and Sedgwick simply did not get along. Howe was also a partisan of Hooker's, whom Meade has succeeded, and then a partisan of Sickles in the controversies surrounding Gettysburg, going so far as to testify against Meade before the House's witch-hunting Committee on the Conduct of the War. It was inevitable that Howe would come to be called "Perfidious Albion."

PORT HUDSON, LOUISIANA, 12:33 PM, OCTOBER 25, 1863

It had been the retreat through a green hell. The exhausted survivors of Franklin's XIX Corps struggled into the defenses of Port Hudson as the black faces of the Corps d'Afrique looked on their shambling ranks with wide eyes. It had only been a fifty-mile march, but miles down roads that were barely tracks through the great stinking expanse of swamp, marsh, and bayou. One by one its wagons and guns had been abandoned and at last even its ambulances full of groaning misery. The wounded had been mounted on the horses or carried in litters.

On the road north from Vermillionville to Opelousas, Franklin had gone northeast to Leonville to cross Bayou Teche, then back south to

Araudville and from there the great "muck march," as the men would call it, to the Bayou Grosse Pointe and across. It was there that Franklin heard the news of the fall of New Orleans and the imminent fall of Baton Rouge. That dashed his hopes of taking the railroad from Rosedale to West Baton Rouge. He would have to take his worn-out men another fifteen miles north through more hellish swamp country to safety in the fortifications of Port Hudson. Along with Vicksburg, Port Hudson had been one of the two strong fortresses keeping the Mississippi out of Union hands. It had fallen four days after Vicksburg. Now he realized it would have to serve the Union, hopefully better than it had served the Confederacy.

Franklin was thankful to find the river below Port Hudson filled by the U.S. Navy. A good part of the river squadrons that had fought so hard to free the Mississippi were there. The sailors was glad of the chance to do something useful in the midst of catastrophe and ferry Franklin's men over to Port Hudson. It was a nervous post commander, Brig. Gen. George A. Andrews, who met Franklin at the landing. All he could talk about was how the French army and fleet were about to march upriver and overrun the fort. Franklin smelled the man's panic and pulled him by the arm over to a quiet place. "General, this fort will hold, by God. This fort will hold. And you are going to help me do it." All Andrews seemed to need was someone to take charge, and Franklin had done just that. "First thing, I need to get my men fed and the wounded to hospital." Andrews's panic had not let him neglect the military administration he was very good at.

"I've already given orders, sir. Every cook at this post is slaving away, and more tents are going up at the hospital. We've already been overrun by refugees up from New Orleans, so we were doing a lot of this anyway. The Navy's brought thousands to here and Baton Rouge."

"What is the strength of the garrison?"

"Besides four artillery batteries and a cavalry regiment, I have a brigade of infantry of the Corps d'Afrique — about three and half thousand men in all."

"I have one of my own brigades at Baton Rouge, "said Franklin, "but the place can't be held against a superior force. The last I saw of Banks, he was with XIII Corps as it was being crushed by the French. Do you have any word from him?

"Nothing, General."

"Then who is in command of the Department of the Gulf?"

"Why, I expect you are, sir."

KENNEBUNK, MAINE, 1:29 PM, OCTOBER 25, 1863

Big white flakes were falling in the first snow of the season as the command group galloped along Main Street north of the bridge. The sound of gunfire up ahead seemed muffled by the falling white blanket when a shell burst overhead in an orange spasm that spewed black iron fragments. Sedgwick rose up from the saddle and then toppled over to the ground without a sound. His staff rushed to him, but the gaping hole in his forehead told them there was nothing to be done. He had been riding beside a regiment pushing forward to the fight and was waving them on with his hat. They had seen him go down and groaned as one man. VI Corps loved "Uncle John" and would not take this kindly.[8]

The 1st Division had barely passed over the bridge when the British hit the head of the column on the edge of town. Hope Grant's map reconnaissance told him the bridge was key terrain feature, a choke point that delayed passage of large bodies of men and vehicles. If he could catch part of the enemy's force on the near side and smash it, then the remainder would retreat. He did not need to destroy the enemy, just keep them from relieving Portland. Without Portland, Canada could not be held.

His timing had been flawless. He had driven back the enemy cavalry and then marched so quickly that he was able to catch the Americans before they were even halfway across the bridge and still in column. That had been the easy part. Speed, surprise, and the grit to slug it out toe to toe had been the secret of his success against Sepoy and Chinaman. Against the Americans it might not be enough.

Speed had brought Grant's red battalions sweeping up to Kennebunk. The British breechloading Armstrong guns were very accurate at a long distance, and their first volley killed Sedgwick and burst over the stone spans of Durrell's Bridge, which was packed with men of the 49th Pennsylvania and the guns of the Battery F, 5th U.S. Artillery. The bridge exploded into a bloody shamble, clogged with dead and wounded men and horses, and guns, caissons, and limbers overturned by their dying and wounded animals.

THE
BATTLE OF
KENNEBUNK
OCTOBER 25, 1863

0 250 500   1000
FEET

XXX
Portland H. Grant

Niagara

Halifax

Wright
captured

Kennebunk

Torbert

XX
1
Wright

Sedgwick
killed

Sherbrooke

Bartlet

High St

Russell

XX
3
Terry

XXX
VI
Sedgwick

HMS Bacchante

XX
2
Howe

US Route 1

Dog Brook

Kennebunk River

Wright now found himself on the north side of the river with only two brigades. His last brigade and the other two divisions were stacked up on High Street on the other side of the river as men desperately tried to clear the bridge. Wright was ignorant of both Sedgwick's death and the severing of the corps column because he was urging on Brig. Gen. Alfred T. A. Torbert's New Jersey Brigade in the lead. He knew the enemy was ahead from the reports of the cavalry and was determined to get his division out of town and deployed. Grant had the opposite purpose. The last thing he wanted was for the Americans to deploy outside the town; then they would be able to feed their entire force into the fight and have numbers on their side. No, he must hit them in the town and force them back to the bridge. It was a race, pure and simple.

That was why Wright rode past the 1st New Jersey, his lead regiment, to personally reconnoiter the ground ahead for the battle. Behind him rode his escort, a hundred men of the 1st Vermont Cavalry. Almost as soon as they turned off Main Street to the Portland Road, they ran into the Canadian 54th Sherbrooke Battalion blocking the road. Their volley ripped into the head of the cavalry column, tumbling men and horses in a kicking, screaming knot on the road. As the survivors turned back, skirmishers went forward to round up prisoners. Pinned under his horse, Wright found himself looking up into the blued point of a Canadian bayonet. Beyond the honor of capturing a general officer, the Sherbrooke men had done a great service to Grant. They had decapitated VI Corps. With Sedgwick dead and Wright captured, command would have devolved on Albion Howe, had he known of the fate of the other two. But he was still south of the bridge with his division. VI Corps would fight that day without a commander.[9]

Sweeping in from the south, the 17th (Leicestershire) Foot, almost a thousand men strong, struck Wright's lead regiment, the 1st New Jersey, just as it exited the town. The British were known as the Bengal Tigers from their service in India, and an apt nickname it was. Their volley shattered the far smaller New Jersey regiment, and their bayonet charge finished them off. They pushed down Main Street to collide with the next regiment, the 4th New Jersey, which stubbornly blocked the road. Two more Canadian militia battalions came up to feel the flanks.

Grant himself led the 63rd (West Suffolk) Regiment of Foot known as the Blood Suckers, with its three Canadian militia battalions of the Niagara Brigade to attack into the town from the west. They drove straight to the bridge to run into Wright's third brigade, which had just cleared the wreckage and was beginning to stream across. The 5th Wisconsin double-timed off the bridge to wheel into line to face the Niagaras.

Wisconsin regiments were particularly tough. Wisconsin was the only state to keep its original regiments up to strength rather than raise new regiments as the old ones shrank due to casualties and illness. Regiments were kept strong, and the fighting skills and spirit of the old hands was passed to the new men. Now, seven hundred Wisconsin men, flanked by battery of the Rhode Island Light Artillery, leveled their rifles and fired into the red-coated column coming down Stover Street. The six guns followed in ten seconds to catch the men in the back of the column. The 58th Compton Battalion disintegrated from the blows. The Wisconsin men pushed up the street in pursuit where they ran into the Blood Suckers coming their way. Both columns fired at the same time. The 5th Wisconsin's colonel and lieutenant colonel both went down, as did the commander of the 63rd. Now it was a soldier's fight as the men spread out among the houses and yards. A company was too big to control as the fighting went house to house. It was close-quarters work with pistol, rifle butt, and bayonet as groups of men broke into a house or fired from its windows, and rushed across small yards. The 119th Pennsylvania fed into the fight just as more Canadian militia were flanking through the alleys.[10]

For Grant, it was just like the fighting in the Great Mutiny, storming one position after another, except that the Americans gave as good as they got, and often as not threw the British out of a house and were thrown out in turn. This was his first time fighting a Western opponent. He didn't count the Russians; they were just blond Orientals, but brave and stolid. And this opponent spoke English, for which Grant allowed himself a moment of pride in the descendents of his own land. Only a brief moment. He had a more pressing problem. The Sherbrooke Brigade had been stopped, soaked up in the house-to-house fighting. The town and its shipyards, filled with wood, were already beginning to burn. His only reserve was the remnants of the 62nd Foot that Chamberlain had savaged at the First Battle of Portland—only four hundred Imperial troops. His Canadian battalions were doing well in their first action, but they were no match for the veterans of VI Corps.

At the same time, the head of Third Division was approaching the bridge with the Second Division right behind. They were double-timing forward, rifles over their shoulders, bayonets a flowing blued-black ribbon above the moving columns. They moved with a veteran smoothness, ten thousand men, more than enough to tip the scales against Grant's force.

Grant saw all this from the steeple of a church and knew that his gamble had failed. It was only a matter of time before the enemy crossed the bridge in such numbers as to overwhelm him. His face set as he turned to an aide to give the order to disengage, when a shrill whistle rent the air. He looked south and saw a warship approaching, its funnels streaming black smoke. It seemed to fill the river as it turned the bend. She was the screw frigate, HMS *Bacchante*, and never was the arrival of the Royal Navy more opportune.[11] All through the noise of battle, everyone stopped to hear the whistle shriek. Grant had a bird's-eye view as the wooden ship came up to within two hundred yards of the bridge and swung amidships in the deep river to present her broadside. The whole ship shuddered when she fired her portside battery of fifteen 8-inch naval rifles and ten 32-pounders. The bridge blew apart, scattering stone and men into the air. Its spans collapsed into the river with hundreds of men and horses. For a brief moment, the noise of the battle died, but only for a moment, for again *Bacchante*'s whistle shrieked in triumph.[12]

7

"Lee Is Coming!"

MOUNT VERNON ESTATE, VIRGINIA, 4:10 PM, OCTOBER 25, 1863

The lieutenant kept the guards at their posts by sheer force of cool example. He stood square in the center of the gate to Mount Vernon. His two guards stood at either gatepost at order arms. In front of him a Confederate cavalry troop stood stock still, their only motion the swishing of their horses' tails. The troop's officer was a slim Californian from San Francisco who had come back across the continent to defend the Union. Fate had placed him in command of the small guard force placed on George Washington's estate eight miles south of Alexandria.

Great battles had passed the lieutenant by as he stood his post. Both sides had put Mount Vernon off limits to their troops, and the Union had placed a guard to make sure neither side violated the sacred ground. Both Blue and Gray revered Washington, and it had been an honorable but uneventful duty for the lieutenant and his handful of men. The gentle but iron-willed ladies of the Mount Vernon Ladies' Association, who had rescued the estate from decay just before the war, had been most kind to them. The ladies themselves had camped out in the mansion itself to make sure no harm came to it. The war that had seemed far away now stood right in front of him.

The clatter of more approaching horses turned the Confederate cavalry commander in his saddle. He straightened up immediately and called his command to attention. The command staff of the Army of Northern Virginia rode up, its simple yellow headquarters flag with the black initials "ANV" waving above to blend with the first of the leaves turning in the unusual early autumn cold.

No one could mistake Lee on his big gray horse, Traveller. He dismounted in front of the gate, followed by a single aide. There was no Union soldier who had not seen a likeness of Lee. He took a step forward. The lieutenant cried out, "Present arms!" The bayoneted rifles rose in one swift movement with a snap that would have impressed the Grenadier Guards. The lieutenant had filled the boring hours with drill and ceremony. He brought his own sword to present arms as well. Lee returned the salute. "Order, arms!" The rifle butts slammed into the ground and the lieutenant's sword swept to the side before he returned it to his scabbard.

Lee's brown eyes misted up a bit. "Lieutenant, I beg your permission to present my respects at the tomb of General Washington."[1]

MOUNT EAGLE, ALEXANDRIA, VA, 4:49 PM, OCTOBER 25, 1863

From this high point in the defenses of Washington, one of Colonel Lowe's balloons floated in a light breeze. A guest in the balloon was a twenty-five-year-old Prussian count, Capt. Ferdinand von Zeppelin, a military observer. Zeppelin had been fascinated with the balloons and had been introduced to Lowe through one of his German-born assistants. Lowe had taken to the engaging young man and gladly approved his request to ascend with him.[2] From this vantage point, they all could see the entire region in the crisp fall air. What was clear from that altitude was what was going to be called the Washington Races. The fate of the capital rested on who would win.

That race was between the butternut and gray columns of Lee's army and the blue of Meade's army. Lee had sidestepped Meade in series of rapid maneuvers that would be studied for generations. Meade's already sharp tongue had been honed to the edge of a surgical scalpel by the stress of the last ten days as Lee had worked him away from Washington. His staff felt the edge of that tongue as Meade summoned every last bit of his considerable professional talents, but he knew in his heart that he had been outclassed. Now those Rebel columns had moved like quicksilver around him to the south to march up parallel to the Potomac. Alexandria, with its huge depots, railroad yards, and hospitals, was within Lee's grasp if he could get through the ring of forts that had grown up around the capital. Once that ring was pierced and

Alexandria taken, Lee would sweep up the few miles of the Virginia shore of the Potomac until he was opposite Washington.

Lee knew the exact spot on the Virginia shore from which to direct his artillery. Arlington House overlooked the city from a hill and would give him perfect observation of Washington. It had been his wife's property; Lee had carefully managed it back from his father-in-law's mismanagement. Shortly after the firing on Fort Sumter, the Union Army had occupied the estate and used the mansion as the headquarters to oversee the construction of the ring of fortifications around Washington. The Lees had left most of their property in the mansion when Lee had moved to Richmond to offer his services to the new Confederacy. Wolseley himself had been affected by Lee's account of the vandalizing of his estate, during which tears had coursed down his face. Since the Lees had moved to Richmond

> every injury that it was possible to inflict, the Northerners have heaped upon him. His house on the Pamunky river was burnt to the ground and the slaves carried away, many of them by force; while his residence on the Arlington Heights was not only gutted of its furniture, but even the very relics of George Washington were stolen from it and paraded in triumph in the saloons of New York and Boston.[3]

Furniture or no, the Lees were about to come home.

Almost from the moment Lee had given Meade the slip, Sharpe had ordered out his own scouts and Hooker's Horse Marines. But it was Lowe's telegram warning of the glint from a river of moving bayonets that had brought Sharpe at a gallop from Washington to ascend with Lowe and Zeppelin over Mount Eagle, south of Cameron Run. From their balloon they could see the enemy columns pushing up the Mount Vernon and Telegraph roads toward Alexandria. They looked to the west for any sign of Meade's men and saw heavy road traffic in the distance on the Leesburg and Alexandria Turnpike, but whose? A line of Lowe's balloons extended for miles in a ring around Washington to the south and west to give complete coverage of the enemy's approach. They were Lowe's large Union-class balloons, each of thirty-two thousand cubic-foot capacity able to lift five men, about seven hundred and fifty pounds, in a wicker basket, and secured by four strong cables.[4]

At last the morning sun illuminated the color of the approaching host, and it was not Union blue. The telegraph operator in the balloon clicked the message that flashed down the wire and out along the lines in every direction: "Lee is coming!"

Panic had swept through Washington. The railroads leading north to Baltimore were packed with frightened civilians, not the least of which were the few of members of Congress who were in Washington during recess. Refugees poured across the bridges into Washington from the Virginia side as Alexandria was evacuated of nonessential personnel. At the same time, troops from the city's defenses on its Maryland side crossed the bridges into Virginia to strengthen the forts. Army engineers set the bridges over the Potomac and the Alexandria warehouses for demolition. Even Stanton, who had been a rock under the pounding from Britannia's fist, was overwhelmed as the rebellion approached to the gates of Washington.

Navy Secretary Gideon Welles, who had more reason to be demoralized, stubbornly refused to give in to doubt. Nothing but bad news had come over the wires in the last week. The French Navy had suddenly appeared off Galveston the week before and destroyed the entire West Gulf Blockading Squadron. Nothing had been heard of the East Gulf Blockading Squadron off Mobile. But rumors had run up the coast and leaped out of Rebeldom with triumph that Dahlgren's squadron had been destroyed as well off Charleston. Three days ago, the Royal Navy had swept into Hampton Roads and come up Chesapeake Bay in a forest of sails, including at least one of its huge ironclads, famous black-hulled *Warrior*. The light American ships had either been run down by the British or prudently retreated up the shallow rivers like the James where the deep-draft enemy ships could not follow. The large naval base at Norfolk had been blockaded. At every hand, fearful voices had said it was 1814 all over again—when the Royal Navy had ravaged the settlements of the great bay and made the country drink shame and humiliation to the dregs.

Welles faced down Stanton, who insisted that Lincoln evacuate the capital before Lee and the British arrived. "Stanton, I told you last year when you were in a panic that the Rebel ironclad *Virginia* was about to ascend the river and subdue the entire capital that it drew too much water to get past Kettle Bottom Shoals. And that's fifty miles down the river. If *Virginia* couldn't make it with twenty-three feet of draft, how do you expect those British monsters with twenty-six feet of draft to do it?"[5]

Stanton was literally wringing his hands, "But the British got up the river in 1814!"

Welles snorted in contempt. "Yes, and it took them twenty days to get through Kettle Bottom because they kept grounding on the shoals, and they have bigger ships today. I guarantee you will not see *Warrior* coming up the river. If any of their ships get through, it will be their smaller ships. We still have the river forts and gunboats and plenty of guns at the Navy Yard."

"But . . ."

"Stanton, let me worry about the Navy. I would think you have as much as you can handle with Lee."

A clerk ran in and handed Lincoln a telegram. He raised his hand, "I have a telegram from Sharpe." The room went silent. "Lee himself is on his way up from Mount Vernon; Sharpe expects the rebels to be in front of the forts within an hour. Let us pray the forts hold until Meade arrives."

Lincoln had good reason for his confidence in the dense ring of fortifications around the capital. Since his arrival in Washington,

> . . . from a few isolated works covering bridges or commanding a few especially important points, was developed a connected system of fortification by which every prominent point, at intervals of 800 to 1,000 yards, was occupied by an inclosed [sic] field-fort, every important approach or depress of ground, unseen from the forts, swept by a battery of field-guns, and the whole connected by rifle-trenches which were in fact lines of infantry parapet, furnishing emplacement for two ranks of men and affording covered communication along the line, while roads were opened wherever necessary, so that troops and artillery could be moved rapidly form one point of the immense periphery to another, or under cover, from point to point along the line.[6]

WASHINGTON, D.C.
OCTOBER 1863

Karminac 2004

Geminal Bridge

Branch

Navy Yard Bridge

Washington Navy Yard

Eastern

U.S. Capitol

Washington Arsenal

Ford's Theatre

Willard's Hotel

Tiber Creek

River

Central Information Bureau

Lafayette Square

White House

War Department

Washington Monument

Long Bridge

Ft Jackson

Potomac

Rock Creek

Georgetown

These defenses had much to defend besides the seat of government. Although Alexandria served as a major subsidiary depot for supplies, Washington itself was the Union's primary and largest logistics center. As one observer noted:

> Hardly had war begun when camps, warehouses, depots, immense stacks of ammunition, food, equipment and long rows of cannon, caissons, wagons and ambulances began sprouting up all over town in vacant lots and open spaces. Centers of activity included the Navy Yard, the Army Arsenal and the Potomac wharves at Sixth and Seventh Streets SW. By 1863 another hub of activity had grown along the Maryland Avenue railroad yards. These busy centers lined the southern rim of the city fronting on the Anacostia and Potomac Rivers.[7]

Ships unloaded off the Potomac along the Arsenal wharves and off the Eastern Branch south of the Navy Yard where the channel was deepest.[8]

The area of Foggy Bottom saw the concentration of a mass of supplies, equipment and material, and storehouses. There was also a remount depot for approximately thirty thousand horses and mules. The large open area near the unfinished Washington Monument was a huge slaughtering yard for cattle. Near the Capitol, another collection of supply warehouses and yards grew up along Tiber Creek near the Baltimore and Ohio Railroad depot and repair yards. More facilities of every kind were scattered throughout the rest of the city.[9] Originally named Goose Creek, this tributary of the Potomac had been given its grander title in hopeful emulation of *la città eterna*. It had later been converted into the Washington Canal, which was crossed at intervals by high iron bridges. It failed in its purpose as a major thoroughfare and degenerated into an open sewer that emptied into the Potomac just south of the Presidential Park, which led north to the White House.

The Washington Arsenal was the largest of the government's twenty-eight arsenals and armories and specialized in the assembly and storage of munitions and the storage of artillery. Its complex of buildings—foundries, workshops, laboratories, and magazines—occupied the southern tip of the city where the Potomac and Eastern Branch Rivers met. It had a large workforce, including over one hundred women and two hundred boys whose fine motor skills were preferred for the delicate tasks of assembling the munitions, which ranged from rifle cartridges to artillery shells.

Outside its gates lay a number of captured bronze guns from the victories of Saratoga, Yorktown, Niagara, and Vera Cruz. When the British marched on Washington in 1814, Arsenal workers had hidden gunpowder down a well. A large party of British soldiers swarmed over the site, and one carelessly threw a lighted match down the well onto the gunpowder bags, destroying every building in the Arsenal.[10]

The Navy Yard in southeast Washington lay along the Eastern Branch to the uppermost point of navigation. Directly above it was an old, rickety, wooden bridge that connected Washington to Maryland. The Navy Yard was the premier of the Navy's great yards, and its vast foundries and dry docks were a major production center for Dahlgren guns and the more complicated mechanical devices of war. It was there that Lowe's gas-generating equipment was fabricated by the teams of skilled mechanics and artisans and where those same teams had built the experimental Alligator-class submarines that Dahlgren had used so well at Charleston. The Yard's facilities were so complete that entire ships could be built, repaired, or converted from merchant to naval service there as *Gettysburg* had been. The Navy Yard was a major military objective in itself.

When the war began, Washington's population had been about seventy-five thousand; in the subsequent two and a half years, it had almost doubled and had provoked a vast spate of building. Nevertheless, a view of the city's street plan would still have been misleading. The neat grid did not reflect reality. Much of the land of the city was still uninhabited. That was especially true of the large section south of Tiber Creek, which was called "The Island" because it was bound largely by the creek and the Potomac. Its most important and only civic building was the Gothic Smithsonian Institution. Along the ends of 6th Street and 7th Street, SW, were the wharves and docks for the river and sea traffic that connected the city to Alexandria, Aquia Creek, the Chesapeake Bay, and finally the sea.[11] The Island also contained the most important military installation in the District of Columbia—the Washington Arsenal. Just outside the southeastern outlet of the canal into the Eastern Branch was the Washington Navy Yard. Outside each installation, small communities had grown up to house their employees and the military personnel assigned to them. The Marine Barracks were only a block beyond the Navy Yard. The country between these installations and the rest of the city was largely uninhabited. An omnibus to the rest of the city connected the Yard.[12] Thus two of the country's most important military installations were self-contained and not physically part of the city. They were also on the southern and southeastern edge of the city and most easily accessible to an attack up the Potomac.

The most densely built-up part of the city ran east and north of the canal. Across the canal and along 10th Street, NW, was Hooker's Division. The canal emptied into the Potomac where the forlorn stub of the incomplete Washington Monument stood almost on the water's edge. Running just inland from the monument was the major thoroughfare of 14th Street, which connected to the immense wooden Long Bridge that spanned the Potomac. Earlier that year, the Army had constructed a railroad bridge to parallel the Long Bridge. A few houses and a hotel clustered around the bridge entrance. Small guardposts at either end of the bridge checked all traffic.[13]

The fall of Washington now would not only paralyze the national government, but would also disorder the logistics of the war effort and bring it to a halt. "These depots, the arsenal, the large Quartermaster and Subsistence depots in the city, and the branch Quartermaster depot in Alexandria served the country, the nearby armies, and the army activities in and near the city."[14]

As the Cabinet officers left the White House, Stanton noticed the military guard around the building was much heavier than the small detachment that had been there before. He accosted the officer of the guard and demanded to know who had assigned these men. His jaw set when told it was the 120th New York Volunteers. Stanton turned his formidable personality on the young man. "And who ordered you here, Captain?"

"General Sharpe did, Mr. Secretary."

The first thing Stanton did on his return to his office was to call in Lafayette Baker. Stanton paced back and forth in front of his fireplace.

"Baker, I want you to increase the number of detectives you have protecting the president."

Baker had been fully aware of how Sharpe's New Yorkers had taken over security of the White House. That was getting too close to Baker's responsibility to protect the president himself. It did not take a genius to know that someone was crowding his territory, in more ways than one. He had already identified Sharpe as a rival and therefore an enemy, especially after he became aware of inquiries that seemed to point back at Sharpe about Baker's own extrajudicial methods that poured money into his pockets.

Baker was quick off the mark. Stanton had offered him an opportunity to reassert his power, and he snatched at it. "Yes, Mr. Secretary. I have already seen to it two days ago. The new man's done excellent work already. Comes from Indiana with the highest recommendations as a bodyguard."

"Keep an eye on this, Baker. Take nothing for granted."[15]

THE DOCKS, 7TH STREET, SW, WASHINGTON, D.C., 5:22 AM, OCTOBER 26, 1863

Booth reveled in the melodrama of their meeting. For him, the passions of the stage were indistinguishable from those of life and death. Now, under the gas lamplight on the river docks with the mist rising off the river from the kiss of the cold fall air on the water, he was in his element. He waved his silver-headed cane as if it were a sword. Smoke, for his part, did not suffer from such flights of imagination; it was not a survival trait in his line of work. Booth was a tool in his larger plan, a tiresome tool that required more tact to handle than Smoke liked to expend, but he was all he had to work with. If he had thought to look back on the efforts to reel Booth into the plan and keep him on it, he would have marveled at how he had risen to the occasion. But Smoke was not a man for reflection; he was a man to follow orders, the subject of their meeting under the gaslight.

"Our chances are good," Smoke said. "Lincoln regularly walks to the War Department or to Sharpe's office to see the telegraph traffic. The way our friends have been stirring things up, he's back and forth all day. I'm the only one with him. We just have to be waiting for him. Just as we planned."

Booth stabbed the metal tip of his cane at the cobbles. "Excellent. Almost as predictable as an entry stage right." This time he flourished the cane as if were a wand. "His exit will be more in the way of a magician's disappearing act."

"Damn it, Booth. What have I told you? No play-acting. We do it fast and quiet. The last thing we need is an audience."

Booth came down from his high quickly, "Of course, of course. Just as we planned."

Then Smoke took Booth by the upper arms and looked intently at him. "This morning, Booth. This morning. It has to be this morning. The wagon is waiting."

Booth seemed to shrink away at first. All the fine and heroic talk of kidnapping the president had played to his vanity. He had shown an unexpected attention to the details of the act and had coolly played his part in their brief rehearsals. But now was the moment when he had to fix his courage to the sticking point. The whole thing hung in the mist.

Then, as if leaping onto the stage from a height, Booth took a step forward and grasped Smoke's hand. He cast his perfect pitch voice to carry just in the space between them, "*Sic semper tyrannis!*"[16]

HEADQUARTERS, CENTRAL INFORMATION BUREAU (CIB), LAFAYETTE SQUARE, WASHINGTON, D.C., 6:30 AM, OCTOBER 26, 1863

Much of the infantry garrison of Washington had already been stripped to reinforce Hooker and Sedgwick in the north, leaving mostly the heavy artillery regiments that manned the forts. Every fort and redoubt was on full alert and was tied to Sharpe's intelligence operation by telegraph, signal station, or messenger. The balloons went up again in the morning to the relief of the artillerymen who looked on them almost as if they were guardian angels. Their officers knew full well what the eyes in the sky could do for them. They would need every advantage now that the infantry regiments that had manned the miles of trenches and works between the forts were largely gone. They were lucky if there was one rifleman to twenty feet of trench line—not enough to stop a determined charge.

Sharpe had left Lowe in full charge of the balloons with the assistance of a few of his officers. He returned to his headquarters on Lafayette Square, arriving just as Lincoln walked across the square, tipping his tall hat to the statue of Andrew Jackson rearing on his charger. Looking up at the bronze visage of the sharp-nosed Tennessean, he said, "Wish you were here, General."[17]

Sharpe had just come in and thrown his hat onto a chair when the guard at the front door shouted inside, "President coming!" Sharpe met him on the steps as the guards presented arms. Sharpe was pleased that his boys from the 120th New York had responded smartly. "Sharpe, I hear you have as good a telegraph set up here as at the War Department Telegraph Office; I thought I would come over to see what turns up."

"Glad to have you, sir." Sharpe's smile fell from his face as Lincoln went in and he got a good look at the new bodyguard. He'd never seen this man before. He was big and burly with a coarse face and beard. He did not like the look of him. Their eyes met and for a brief moment, Sharpe saw something savage in those eyes, which then furtively looked away.

That gaze subconsciously triggered the memory of a story he had been told after he had arrived in Washington. It was about an old black slave named Oola. She was a frightening, wizened woman said to come by slave ship from Africa before the turn of the century. She terrified the other slaves with her piercing glance and her reputation of the evil eye and the ability to conjure spells. It was in early 1861, the time when the Lincolns were settling into the White House, when the issue of war and peace hung in the balance between North and South. At that time, a great comet had hung in the sky over the East. Old Oola had said, "You see dat great fire sword, blazin' in de sky? Dat's a great war comin' and de handle's to'rd de Norf and de point to'rd de Souf and de Norf's gwine take dat sword and cut de Souf's heart out. But dat Lincum man, chilluns, if he takes de sword, he's gwine perish by it."[18] Sharpe shook it off and attended the president.

Lincoln settled himself into a stuffed chair in the telegraph room as the analysts rushed down the hallway from room to room, comparing notes and the latest information. Sergeant Wilmoth came and handed Sharpe the latest telegram. Lincoln's interest perked up. "Young man, it's good to see you again. What do you hear from your mother in Indianapolis?" Wilmoth smiled from ear to ear and said all was well. The president had been an increasingly frequent visitor since he realized that Sharpe's headquarters was the place to find out what was going on. He had taken a personal interest in the bright young man who seemed to have the whole of Lee's army at his fingertips. Sharpe's faith in Wilmoth's knowledge and good judgment was even stronger, and he asked Wilmoth to brief them both on what he had been able to put together over the night.[19]

The young sergeant calmly and clearly laid out their findings. "Late last night, the situation clarified after all the day's messages came from our cavalry pickets, the signal stations, and the Balloon Corps. Hill's corps marched past Mount Vernon late yesterday. We expect it to lead the attack on Alexandria. Ewell's corps is swinging to the west and coming down the Columbia Turnpike, we think, to cut Alexandria off from the north and drive to the river. Some of Stuart's cavalry is screening both corps and raiding north as well, though his entire division does not appear to be present. We estimate that they will attack sometime today."

A look of consternation flew across Lincoln's face. "It is morning already. How will we get what troops we have to reinforce those forts in Lee's path?"

Without missing a beat, Wilmoth said, "This morning I notified General Augur of this and recommended he reinforce in that direction. I took the liberty of signing your name, General." He looked straight into Sharpe's eyes.

Sharpe suppressed a smile. "You took the liberty of signing my name, Sergeant?"

"Yes, sir, I did."

"What made you think you had the authority to set such critical things in motion? They pay generals to make those decisions."

"My information was correct, there was no time to lose, and you were not here, sir."

Sharpe stepped forward, put his hands on his hips, and cocked his head forward to look the sergeant in the face. He said, "And continue to do so when in your good judgment such action is necessary. You have my permission, forward and backward." He winked and then broke into a broad smile.

As they laughed, the guns began to rumble to echo up the river and over the city. The three of them stopped and stared out the window.

MOUNT EAGLE, ALEXANDRIA, VA, 7:15 AM, OCTOBER 26, 1863

Lt. Gen. Ambrose Powell Hill had been riding among his troops, deeply echeloned in the terrain that they had occupied after dark. Morale had not been this high since the men had crossed the Potomac far upriver in June, serenaded by their bands, on the way to Gettysburg. Victory finally lay just ahead. Just a few weeks ago it seemed the Yankee's coils had been slowly crushing the South; it would be just a matter of time. Now it was the Union's turn, feeling the torch of an enemy trampling across her soil, her own people in revolt in the Midwest, and her ports shut by the Royal Navy's blockade. There was much grim satisfaction in the ranks. Now Washington itself lay just a few miles to the north across the river. One last battle, one last supreme effort, and it would all be over.

Hill had forced himself into the saddle. He could not miss this battle because of sickness. There had been too much talk already about how he always seemed to take sick before a fight. No one, not even he, knew it was the gonorrhea spiking up through stress. The sun was coming up over the Potomac, sending the long fall rays to glint softly among the bayonets of his men packed together waiting for the order to move. As the sun topped the trees on the eastern side of the river, a balloon rose to their front to hover over the center of the Union fortifications.

"Damned things," he said to himself. "Thought they were gone after Chancellorsville." They had not seen them in Pennsylvania. He hated them. He was impatient to get going, sickness or not. That balloon made him feel uneasy, like some hovering black bird of ill omen. He turned in his saddle. Where was the order to attack? Move quick, strike quick, he had always believed. Where was that order? He turned to an aide, "Ride to General Lee and say we must move at once!"

He heard the gun just as the aide spurred his horse. A shell burst in the field two hundred yards behind the men who sheltered behind in a rise of the ground and were invisible from the forts. A second shell fell a hundred yards closer. The ranks rustled nervously. There was a pause, and when nothing happened, the men relaxed.

Inside the forts, the gunners adjusted the elevation of their huge 15-inch Rodman guns as the gun captain shouted the corrections based on the telegraph message that had come from the balloon overhead. "Fire!" The guns recoiled as they spat their enormous projectiles to fall on the

Alexander II, tsar of Russia
and a man possessed of
a powerful dream.
Author's Collection

Baron Edouard de
Stoeckl, Russia's very
capable ambassador
to the United States.
Library of Congress

Richard Gatling would first use his deadly invention, the Gatling Gun, in the defense of his own factory. *National Park Service*

Gen. Mikhail "The Hangman" Muravyov, scourge of the Poles. *Author's Collection*

Maj. Gen. François Achille Bazaine, commander of the French Armée de Louisiane. *Author's Collection*

The French Navy enters Lake Borgne escorting Lt. Gen. Richard Taylor's Confederate landing force. *Author's Collection*

The Prince de Polignac,
the hero of Vermillionville.
Author's Collection

Maj. Gen. William B.
Franklin, commander,
XIX Corps of the
Army of the Gulf.
Library of Congress

French infantry of the line in action at Vermillionville. *Author's Collection*

French soldier comforting the wounded at Vermillionville. *Author's Collection*

Soldiers of the Corps d'Afrique, the black militia regiments of Confederate Louisiana recruited into federal service. *Library of Congress*

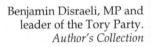

Benjamin Disraeli, MP and leader of the Tory Party. *Author's Collection*

Queen Victoria, who came out of mourning to encourage a nation at war. *Library of Congress*

Karl Marx, foreign correspondent for the *New York Tribune*, of which Abraham Lincoln was an avid reader. *Author's Collection*

John Wilkes Booth, rising tragic actor who wore his loyalty to the South none too discreetly. *Library of Congress*

Brig. Gen. George H. Sharpe, Lincoln's chief intelligence officer. *Author's Collection*

Christopher Spencer's rifle was the finest repeating weapon of the war. *Author's Collection*

A demonstration of Ager's coffee mill gun to officers of the 120th New York. *National Park Service*

Maj. Gen. Joshua Lawrence Chamberlain, the hero of Portland. *Library of Congress*

Maj. Gen. Sir Charles Hastings Doyle, who commanded at the siege of Portland. *Author's Collection*

Lt. Gen. James Hope Grant,
Victoria's finest general
and victor at Kennebunk.
Author's Collection

Maj. Gen. "Uncle" John
Sedgwick, commander,
VI Corps at Kennebunk.
Library of Congress

Maj. Gen. Joseph Hooker, commander, Army of the Hudson, who met destiny at a place called Claverack. *Library of Congress*

Maj. Gen. Thomas Francis Meagher, commander, XI Corps, Army of the Hudson. *Library of Congress*

Maj. Gen. Frederick Lord Paulet, commander, Hudson Field Force, at Claverack. *Author's Collection*

Lt. Col. Garnet Wolseley, assistant quartermaster general of Canada, on the road to glory. *Library of Congress*

The statue of Andrew Jackson in Lafayette Park in Washington, D.C.
Library of Congress

Col. Thaddeus Lowe resurrected his Army Balloon Corps in time for the defense of Washington. *Library of Congress*

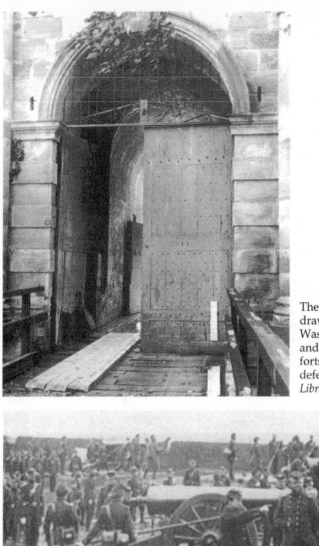

The main gate and drawbridge to Fort Washington, the first and greatest of the forts used in the naval defense of Washington. *Library of Congress*

Fort Runyon on the Virginia side of the Potomac, the key to the defense of Washington. *Library of Congress*

Hooker and his staff as the British attack sweeps forward at Claverack.
Library of Congress

The Washington Navy Yard in Washington, D.C., was the preeminent naval
establishment of the United States. *Library of Congress*

The Long Bridge, crossing the Potomac River from Virginia to the heart of Washington. *Library of Congress*

The Long Bridge Hotel, where Lincoln watched the last act in the battle for the nation's capital. *Library of Congress*

reverse slopes of the gentle hills to the south. They laced into Hill's dense ranks in a line of orange-red pulses of energy that flared before the sound could be heard. Hill did not have to wait years for the gonorrhea to kill him. A jagged fragment of shell cut him nearly in two.[20]

HEADQUARTERS, BMI, WASHINGTON, D.C., 7:17 AM, OCTOBER 26, 1863

Lincoln covered his tenseness that morning by likening the telegrams as they came in to hotcakes right off the griddle and so good they could be gobbled up without any molasses. As the morning went on, he noted they were getting tastier and tastier all by themselves. Hill's attempted attack had been disrupted by the artillery's indirect and adjusted firing by balloon observation. Where the Confederates had been able to move forward and press home their attacks between the forts, the defenders had been able to direct their meager infantry reserves to stop them. Lt. Gen. Richard Ewell's attacks down the Columbia Turnpike had run into the same web of forts supported by balloon intelligence. The high morale of their attacks had not been enough but left only a carpet of bodies in front of the fortifications. The day ended badly for Lee who could see the roof of Arlington House on its hill. It pained him to see that the beautiful groves that had once surrounded it had been chopped down, surely to build the very forts that stood in his way.

The fighting stopped as the sun set and the balloons settled to earth. The good news clicked over the telegraph and was read with immense relief in the headquarters on Lafayette Square. Lincoln picked up his hat to go and looked out the window. The shadows had faded into night and the statue of Jackson in the square was lit by a few gas lamps, picking out the obdurate image of the hawk-faced warrior president. "Well, General, it's been one of my better days. It reminds me of the boy who was talking to another as to whether General Jackson could ever get to Heaven. Said the boy, 'He'd get there if he had a mind to.' I think we will prevail if we have 'a mind to.'"[21]

Over Sharpe's shoulder, Lincoln saw Sergeant Wilmoth absorbed in writing at his desk. "It occurs to me that a lieutenant's shoulder straps would look just fine on young Wilmoth. Good night, General." Sharpe bid him goodnight and watched as the tall figure in black walked across the square with his hulking bodyguard trailing discreetly behind. Sharpe saw him tip his hat as he passed the statue before the bulk of the body-guard blocked his view. A wave of unease came over Sharpe.[22]

A man had been lounging on a park bench under one of the gas lamps near the Jackson statue. The lamplight made the polished silver head of his cane gleam. He got up and gracefully took off his hat as Lincoln passed, lost in his thoughts. A wagon rumbled up from an alley nearby. The man got up and followed Lincoln.

Sharpe motioned to the guards, "See him home safely, boys." They hurried down the stairs, trailing arms at a run to catch up with the tall figure. The man from the park bench froze as the soldiers rushed past him, their blued bayonets picking up the lamplight's glint. He slipped into the shadows. The wagon turned sharply away.

HEADQUARTERS, ARMY OF NORTHERN VIRGINIA, ARLINGTON MILL, VIRGINIA, ON THE COLUMBIA TURNPIKE, 8:25 PM, OCTOBER 26, 1863

Night had fallen on the countryside along with bitter disappointment around the campfires of the Army of Northern Virginia. Nowhere was the disappointment as keen as it was in Lee's tent. Lee's only comfort at the moment was the fresh coffee his aide and adjutant, Major Walter H. Taylor, had brought him, courtesy of a Federal supply warehouse. Lee would not touch such little pleasures unless assured that most had been distributed to the men first, and even then he would more often deny himself. But at this moment, it was a most necessary comfort.

"Major Taylor, had General Longstreet been with us, he would have remonstrated most strongly not to attack prepared positions. And after Gettysburg, I would have to agree with him, but we had victory within our grasp, and I thought it worth the terrible cost. We have no choice but to try again tomorrow. But we must not play our hand the same way again."

Just then, the soft caress of a hymn wafted through the still night of the camp. Lee stood up and walked to the tent entrance and placed his hand on the pole as he listened.

Not a brief glance I beg, a passing word;
But as Thou dwell'st with Thy disciples, Lord,

Familiar, condescending, patient, free.
Come not to sojourn, but abide with me.

Come not in terrors, as the King of kings,
But kind and good, with healing in Thy wings,
Tears for all woes, a heart for every plea—
Come, Friend of sinners, and thus bide with me.

Thou on my head in early youth didst smile;
And, though rebellious and perverse meanwhile,
Thou hast not left me, oft as I left Thee,
On to the close, O Lord, abide with me.

Yes, he thought to himself. Thou hast not left me, oft as I left Thee. He was humbled at the glory of Christ's love. He said to the night itself, "We are all sinners. Can God forgive us this war?"

Major Taylor said, "Sir?"

Lee turned with a father's smile to the young man. "That line of the hymn, 'On to the close,' Major Taylor, 'On to the close.' May God give us that close."[23]

Lee sighed as the hymn ended and with it, his hope-filled exaltation. He had more to oppress his thoughts than the failure of the day's assaults. Yes, he had outwitted Meade and stolen a march on Washington, but Meade would not stay fooled long, especially with screams of help raging over the wires to him. Lee had sent Stuart and most of his cavalry and an infantry division to hold Meade as long as he could. That would give him one more day and one more chance to break through to the river and bring Washington under fire. With that, the enemy's capital would cease functioning. With so many other blows, this could well be the one that shattered the Union's will to stay in the fight. The Washington area was also the logistics hub from which Meade's army and all other Union efforts against him were centered. His only frustration was that the Potomac lay as a barrier to actually occupying the city. He could not assume that a single bridge would remain standing when he reached the river.

"Are the Stonewall Brigade's preparations progressing well?" Lee asked. Before Taylor could answer, the noise of horses riding up to the command group was heard along with fragment of a statement, "must see General Lee immediately." Lee looked up from his field desk as Colonel Marshall, his senior aide, and a cloaked man entered.

"General Lee, may I present Captain Hancock, Royal Navy, emissary of Vice Admiral Milne."

THE OLD SENATE HOUSE, KINGSTON, NEW YORK, 10:15 AM, OCTOBER 27, 1863

Hooker waved his hat as he rode his white charger through the dense crowds that rushed to cheer him through the streets of Kingston, New York's first capital after the Revolution sundered royal authority. The crowd was swelled with refugees from nearby Rondout, Kingston's river port, which was now ashes and ruins, courtesy of a British raid. Tom Meagher rode at his side, waving to the delighted throngs. He leaned over to Hooker and said, "A little early for the victory parade, General, don't you think?"

Meagher's remark was not lost on Hooker, who smiled and waved back at the crowd as the band played behind him, and his color bearer was careful to shake out the magnificent army command flag Hooker had had specially made in New York. "Oh, Tom, enjoy it," he laughed. "It's all a matter of morale. Must give the people hope, you know. Then every hand will turn out to help us."

He pulled up at the stone Senate House and drew his sword to return the salute of the home guard that had turned out to defend the town if the British raid had come inland. Mostly they were invalids from the local regiments off with Meade—the 20th New York State Militia, the 120th and 156th New York Volunteer Infantry Regiments. He remembered then that the 120th was Sharpe's old regiment. A one-armed captain returned the salute with his surviving left hand.

Hooker gave a short speech to the thunderous applause of the sea of faces massed before the Senate House. It crossed his mind that these people might be as devoted to him when it came time to vote for president one of these days. He introduced Meagher, the victor of Cold Spring. The trees seem to shake with the applause and shouts of the people, scattering their red and gold leaves.[24]

Hooker knew he had made the right decision to give Meagher command of XI Corps. If any unit needed a heroic leader who carried victory fresh on the tip of his sword, it was the damned Dutch. The Irishman had that rare touch for the grand statement. After Cold Spring, he had returned to New York City and paraded his "Glorious 200" down 5th Avenue, every man carrying a red coat dangling from the tip of his bayonet to sway in unison with the perfect step of the men. New York loved it, roaring its delight in a deafening din that echoed off the tall buildings that lined the avenue. The last flowers of the year fell like a rainbow rain on the Irishmen. Young women who would not have given them the time of day a month ago ran up to them to plant kisses on their cheeks. Grown men and women who had starved in the Great Hunger burst into tears as the emerald green flag with its golden harp and the Stars and Stripes marched by, followed by the swaying red coats. After that day, not a business window could be found posting that old sign stating, "No Irish Need Apply."[25]

GOVERNOR'S MANSION, ALBANY, 10:30 AM, OCTOBER 27, 1863

Lord Paulet was not happy to see Wolseley. On the assistant quartermaster's advice, he had lost a company of the Scots Fusilier Guards at Cold Spring. He didn't give a damn about the Canadians that were lost. Her Majesty would not thank him for losing so many of her big Guardsmen—and to the bloody Irish! He would never live this down.

Still, he could not dismiss the man out of hand; Wolseley had the ear of the commander of Her Majesty's forces in North America. He was also the protégé of Maj. Gen. Hope Grant, a man whose star was very much on the rise. So Paulet weighed how much he could risk slighting the man and decided not much—at this time.

He was relieved that his judgment had held him back. One of Wolseley's first comments when they sat down for business was that Hope Grant was on his way with almost twenty thousand men to assume command in British North America. "The home garrisons have been stripped to assemble this force. The object, my lord, is to hold Albany through the winter. We sit in the center of this state and paralyze it for months. With Maine in our hands and New York under our thumb—not to mention their Great Lake States in revolt, the Confederates pressing from the south, and the Royal Navy blockading their ports—they will be hard pressed everywhere. A coherent defense will become increasingly difficult to the point of impossibility. We must sit in Albany long enough for the Royal Navy's blockade to do its work of disintegration of their economy.

"Your raids keep them off balance. I told General Williams that you took the raid on Cold Spring entirely on my suggestion and assurance that it was undefended." Wolseley paused to run his finger down the map of the Hudson Valley to where the latest information pushed Hooker's rapidly advancing army. "Because we must hold Albany, my lord, you will have to accept battle with Hooker and defeat him before winter closes down fighting. We are reinforcing you with two more brigades. With the three you already have, you should be a match for Hooker.

"One more thing, my lord. Our coup de main to seize Portland did not succeed. We have had to settle into siege. Unfortunately, we do not have the heavy artillery to break into the city. Jonathan is bringing up a strong corps to relieve the city. This is where it gets sticky. If we do not take Portland, we lose the railroad link between the Maritimes and the rest of Canada, and our problems then begin to multiply. We had hoped to funnel Grant's reinforcements through Portland. Now we may have to move them either up the St. Lawrence or through a smaller port we have taken above Portland and march them around the city to pick up the railroad. Either way, reinforcements will not reach you before you must fight Hooker. And we cannot reinforce you more strongly unless we give up our grip on Portland. It all depends on you defeating Hooker, my lord."[26]

Paulet was reconsidering his opinion of Wolseley. A victory in a pitched battle would certainly take the Palace's mind off the loss of the Scots. Then again, the Widow of Windsor had an uncannily good memory for little things like that.

BATON ROUGE, LOUISIANA, 2:33 PM, OCTOBER 27, 1863

Taylor's Confederates marched into the state capital to a welcome that was more unrestrained than that afforded them in the Crescent City only ten days ago. Leaving Bazaine to bring up the French Army, he had struck north just after the "Te Deum" was sung in the St. Louis Cathedral. For all his speed, he was hours too late. The Union garrison was marching out of the northern edge of the town just as his men entered it from the south, having just put the finishing touches to their orders from Franklin.

Already tall plumes of black smoke, streaked with orange flames, were billowing skyward from the burning warehouses, depots, and docks. Baton Rouge had been thick with the logistics of the Union Army, for it had served for a year as the base of operations in Banks's attempts to take Port Hudson. Pursuit was out of the question. The sky was raining sparks that threatened to ignite the entire city, and Taylor had no choice but to send his men to put out the dozens of fires starting everywhere in the wooden city.

Franklin had done his work well. He had emptied the supplies accumulated in the city almost immediately after arriving in Port Hudson. Every boat on the river and every wagon he could lay his hands on had been bent to this task. He had hoped to delay the inevitable attack on Port Hudson until reinforcements had rebuilt the army to enable him to march south and meet Taylor and Bazaine in the open field. Vermillionville would not be the last word in the war in Louisiana.

He would have been less optimistic had he known that that Bazaine was coming quickly behind Taylor, for both generals had also taken seriously the reinforcement of Port Hudson. They had hoped to concentrate fifty thousand men to seize Port Hudson before that happened. The French Army had marched to Brashear City after Vermillionville, entrained there for New Orleans, and stopped only long enough to parade through the city and take on supplies and reinforcements from the French ships now crowding the docks.

Here the situation got complicated. There was no railroad or decent road from New Orleans to Baton Rouge. The river had been the mighty highway that had substituted for both. Had they the use of the river, they surely would have made Franklin's position hopeless, but on its muddy waters, the U.S. Navy still reigned. Rear Adm. David Porter was gathering the gunboats and ironclads that been so vital in the long campaigns to seize control of the river and cut the Confederacy in two. After Vicksburg and Port Hudson had fallen in July, they had been scattered up and down the river to patrol its length. Now Porter was gathering them back, but it would take time.

What had been its weakness at sea against the French was now a clear advantage on the river. Originally, almost all of the American ships had been merchant ships that had been converted for war; their mission was to blockade Southern ports and run down blockade runners.

They were nothing like the purpose-built warships of the regular Navy in size and armament. Against the new ironclads, ships-of-the-line, and frigates of the French, they had no chance. But these same large French ships had deep drafts that prevented them from crossing the bar at the mouth of the Mississippi, the same problem faced by Admiral Farragut in April 1862 when his flagship, USS *Hartford*, could barely pass. So the French leviathans, including the ironclads *Gloire*, *Couronne*, *Normandie*, and *Invincible*, uselessly sailed the Gulf, unable to come to grips with the Americans.[27] The shallower-draft French sloops and corvettes were able to come up the river with the squadron's supply ships, but they quickly discovered that operations on the river, with its shifting channels, mud-flats, and snags, were a world apart from those on blue water.

With the river closed to them, the allies had no choice but to move north by the Great Northern Railroad, detrain at the small station at Ponchatoula, then march the forty miles west to Port Hudson. From the observation tower at Port Hudson, Franklin could see a distant pall of smoke hanging over Baton Rouge and the river thick with boats coming north loaded with the supplies that would see him through the trial to come. He said, "Thank God for the Navy."

BROWN'S FERRY, TENNESSEE, 3:42 PM, OCTOBER 27, 1863

When you begin to starve, all you can think of is food. So it was not sur-prising when several thousand men in the trapped Army of the Cumber-land volunteered for special duty that would take them out of besieged Chattanooga. It was Maj. James Calloway would do the choosing. For him, there was no dilemma—he chose the 81st Indiana.

As the fighting raged at Chickamauga the month before, the com-mander of this hard-luck Hoosier regiment had been relieved on the spot for gross incompetence. Calloway was snatched away from his 21st Illinois to take command at a desperate moment of what was considered a bad regiment. Then something miraculous happened. The 81st fought like lions. Calloway's presence had been electric. Under the power of his charismatic hand, the regiment morphed almost instantly into an outfit so stubborn and tough that they became the division rear guard in the fighting retreat that helped save the Army of the Cumberland on that deadly day.

When Grant ordered Thomas to provide an officer and volunteers to train on Mr. Gatling's guns that were arriving with Sherman's corps, someone at Army headquarters remembered Calloway's request to be allowed to recruit a new cavalry regiment to be armed with repeating weapons. Calloway had no sooner picked his men on the 26th than they were hustled out of the pocket the next morning and across the Tennessee River to Brown's Ferry where they were to marry up with the mysterious new equipment they were to train on. The first thing Calloway did was to see his men fed the first good meal they had had in over a month. Only the night before, Thomas had taken matters into his own hands and seized Brown's Ferry on a loop of the Tennessee River in a daring night operation that opened a robust supply line to his withering army. As Calloway's men ate, they watched a solid stream of supply wagons crossing the pontoons across the river.

An officer sought Calloway out to give him his written orders and introduce him to Gatling. What looked like a strange artillery battery drove off the road to park in an open field with a bluff to its back. He marched the men to the field where they took a good look at the strange weapons, shining bundles of brass-bound heavy rifle barrels mounted on light artillery carriages. They viewed them with a healthy dose of soldier skepticism. Too many promises of wonder weapons had floated through the Army for the last two years, and all evaporated into nothing but hot air. More than one eyebrow arched as Gatling described the weapon, its operation, and its effect. Skepticism soured to sheer disbelief.

All of that changed in the instant Gatling began to turn the crank. The barrels spun in whirring circles of fire, and the targets simulating a Confederate battle line disintegrated into flying splinters and scraps of cloth with not one left standing. The firing ceased, but the barrels kept on spinning with a smooth mechanical whir, finally slowing to stop.

8

Fateful Night

The officers who looked out from the fort's parapets in the dark, cool, early morning had their attention fixed on the Confederate artillery attack on the fort that covered Arlington Hill a mile and a half to the north. They did not see the men crawling forward in the darkness toward them. The first wave of engineers carried gunpowder charges to blow up the thick abattis, axes to chop through what was left, and ropes to drag it away. Men crawled behind them dragging rough ladders; the infantry followed, their metal accoutrements blackened or tied up with rags to prevent rattling. The officers had thrown away their scabbards to avoid unnecessary noise and to symbolize that this was all or nothing.

The men of the Stonewall Brigade stopped to wait for the engineer first wave to go forward. All around them were the dead of that day's assault, stiffening as the last of life's warmth fled. The wounded were there, too, moaning softly. But one man in the trench before the infantry parapet was in agony beyond endurance, shrieking Christ's travail on the Cross, "My God, why hast thou forsaken me!" The poor wretch went on and on, but no man dared leave his place to go to aid, though it left a thousand souls in torment. Hard men wept into their hands.

After a while, even orders lost their hold, and a dozen men had begun crawling forward when lights appeared on the parapet. A woman's voice gave orders as if she were used to command. Moments later, a gate opened, and a party with a stretcher came out led by a woman with a lantern. They found the wounded man. The nearest men pressed to the ground saw her kneel by the man and take his hand. The screaming stopped. A voice louder than the rest said, "We must hurry, ma'am. The Colonel does not know we are outside the wall." The party put the man on the stretcher and heaved it to their shoulders as the woman held the lamp in one hand and the man's hand in the other. They quickly disappeared through the gate.

Relief washed over the men lying on the ground. They were warmed though the ground was cold and their clothes worn thin. At least they had eaten well, the first time in a very long time, courtesy of fat Union warehouses. They were stacked up in column of regiments, some of the most famous in the Confederacy. Some of the men had been with the immortal Stonewall from the beginning and remembered his words when they were sore-pressed at Second Manassas and he commanded the 2nd Corps, and their new commander begged for support. "The Stonewall Brigade! Go back, and give my compliments to them and tell the Stonewall Brigade to maintain her reputation."[1] Not many were there then that had made it through all the following battles but enough to make the moment grow in the retelling, so much that the men who came after believed they had been there, too. They lay there waiting for the opportunity to once more maintain their reputation. With Washington just behind the line of forts and over the river, they hoped it would be the last time.

GUNSTON HALL PLANTATION, 1:15 AM, OCTOBER 28, 1863

Four miles down the Potomac from Mount Vernon, the Gunston Hall manor house overlooked the waters of Pohick and Accotink Bays. Small boats and barges filled the two small inlets. Confederate infantry were boarding from a half dozen landings. Their crews of British sailors bent expertly at the oars and pushed off. The craft had been swept up from the U.S. Navy and commercial traffic as Milne's ships overran Hampton Roads. They had trailed the special striking force Milne had selected for his descent on Washington. He knew that his large ships would never make it over Kettle Bottom Shoals; the Royal Navy had made good use of its numerous peacetime port visits over the years.

From the mansion's porch, Captain Hancock and Confederate colonel John Rogers Cooke watched the lanterns on the boats move across the dark water as if they were crosses between water bugs and fireflies. Before his spectacular demise, Hill had selected Cooke's brigade for this mission for two reasons — the brigade was his reserve, not attached to any division, and he had complete faith in the intelligence, initiative, and fighting spirit of its commander. Cooke was born at Jefferson Barracks in Missouri in 1833. He was the son of Virginian general Philip St. George Cooke. When war came, his father honored his oath to the Union, and the younger Cooke resigned his commission to offer his sword to his mother state, severing all family ties. He had commanded the 27th North Carolina at Antietam with such grit as to earn the admiration of the Army. Ordered to hold a line at all costs, he had replied that though ammunition was exhausted, he would hold it as long as he had a single man with a bayonet left. It had come close to that. His regiment lost eighteen of twenty-six officers holding that line. He was nearly one of the dead when he received a bullet wound in the forehead. A Prussian officer serving with James E. B. Stuart, his brother-in-law, said it was "the most beautiful wound I ever saw." Now he commanded four North Carolina regiments — 15th, 27th, 46th, and 48th — of whom he was im-mensely proud. They had a mission that would earn them and the South eternal glory.[2]

For command of the naval descent on Washington, Milne's choice of commander fell on Commodore Hugh Dunlop, another veteran of the Crimean War in Russian waters who had also ably commanded the Jamaica Station. Milne selected a flotilla of sloops and gunboats for their shallow draft. Dunlop's force included the 17-gun corvette *Greyhound*, and the sloops *Icarus*, *Peterel*, *Spiteful*, *Racer*, and *Hydra*. Philomel-class gunvessels, gunboats of 570 tons with five guns — such as *Landrail*, *Steady*, and *Cygnet*, and the smaller Cheerful-class *Nettle* and *Onyx* with two guns each — had been brought from the harbor defenses of Bermuda for just this mission. Distributed among the ships was a Royal Marine battalion fresh from the Channel Fleet.[3]

These ships had also crowded into the two bays, a warlike assem-blage the Potomac had not seen since McClellan's vast waterborne in-vasion of the Peninsula partly sailed down the river the last year. Fully appreciating the sight was a six-man cavalry patrol of the 3rd Indiana. They had trailed the Confederate infantry brigade as it marched away from Hill's corps in the night. Four crept up to the water's edge, leaving two to hold the horses among the trees. They could see the ships and boats thick on the water, lit by their lanterns and the starry night. Boats slipped by them, the English of their boatswains' orders clear in the still air. In fifteen minutes, they had seen enough. Their sergeant signaled to withdraw when a gentle splashing in the water drew them back to the ground. Someone was swimming to the bank with a practiced sailor's stroke. He found his footing as the water shallowed and hunched over to scramble up the bank—and right into the sergeant's pistol. The dripping man spoke first in a whisper, "Faith, and is this my welcome to the New World?"

"Shut your gob, Paddy." The pistol found the small of his back. "Now, move and be quiet."

What the scouts had seen was the fruit of much planning. On the news that the Royal Navy filled the lower Chesapeake, Lee had instantly departed down the Northern Neck to the bay to request a meeting with Milne. The admiral pulled out all the stops to honor Lee as he climbed aboard his flagship, HMS *Nile*. A full compliment of sideboys stood to as Lee was piped aboard. A Marine honor guard—a full company—presented arms as a naval band played "Dixie." The deck was crowded with Royal Navy officers eager to see the Southern legend. They were not disappointed in his bearing, immaculate uniform, and the courtliness of his greeting to Milne. But Milne and Lee did not linger on deck. A cold wind blew down the bay, and they had much to talk about in the admiral's cabin.[4]

From that meeting came the plan that was now unfolding below Gunston Hall. Lee's offer to cooperate in a strike on Washington was eagerly accepted by Milne, for it solved two of his three major problems. Lee supplied the pilots who would take his ships easily through the shoals, and his land attack would seriously distract the garrison of the Union capital. His third problem, and the one that would most seriously prevent his approach to Washington, was the city's naval fortifications. Although there were sixty-eight forts in the land defenses of the capital, there were only two naval forts meant to defend the city from an attack from the river. They were just below the city on either side of the Potomac. Battery Rogers at Jones Point was on the southern edge of Alexandria about six miles from the Washington Arsenal. Fort Foote was on the Maryland shore about one mile south of Battery Rogers. Both forts were only a quarter mile from the main ship channel. It would be a deadly gauntlet. Rogers and Foote were reported to be armed with 15-inch Rodman guns; Foote was also reported to have four 200-pounder Parrott rifles. One hit could sink a sloop and turn the gunvessels into kindling.[5]

Here again Lee was most helpful. His intelligence indicated that only the Rodmans had been emplaced. He suggested that if he were able to take Alexandria and Battery Rogers, Washington would be defenseless from attack up the river.

First they had to overcome one other major obstacle before getting to Washington, and it was just up the river from where Cooke's Brigade was loading. It was the massive masonry fortification of Fort Washington on the Maryland side of the river. It commanded the channel sixteen miles below Washington and would be difficult to pass. It stood high on a hill with its guns pointing directly at any hostile ship coming up the river. Just below the fort, the main ship channel took a turn directly toward it to pass right under its walls. Its many guns would be firing down to strike through the decks. Ships' guns, in turn, could not be elevated sufficiently to strike that high. Sink two or three ships in the channel, and they could block it for the rest.

But again, Lee was helpful. He said that as much as it pained him to associate the name Washington with failure, the fort had an ignominious history. In 1814, when Admiral Cochrane's ships had come up the river, the fort's commander had lost his nerve, spiked his guns, and fled, giving free passage to the Royal Navy. Lee suggested the fort might be better addressed from the landward side. After all, he had heard that the Royal Marines had seized Fort Gorges in Portland Harbor by just such a bold move. He offered to assist by providing men whose accents would not be thought amiss at night by the guards. Lee added, "You might learn from our own misfortune at Vicksburg, when the Union Navy ran the forts at night with scarcely a loss."

Milne came away from his conference with Lee confident. He had always favored this plan, but now its odds had gone up considerably. He was sure that by striking both by land and river at the same time, the chances of actually taking the city rose to the realm of the possible. And that would surely end the war at a single stroke.[6]

CHATTANOOGA, TENNESSEE, 2:00 AM, OCTOBER 28, 1863

The cigar fell out of Grant's mouth. He had lit it after his aide woke him to say Thomas and his intelligence officer were insistent to see him.

Colonel Rawlins had not been far behind. "You're serious?" Grant asked, incredulity written over his face.

The captain almost smirked. "Absolutely, sir. The information comes from interrogations of deserters from every corps in the Army of Tennessee, from intercepts of Confederate signals, and from one of the headquarters staff body servants."

Rawlins just burst out laughing and slapped his thigh with his hat. "I'll be damned! Just shot him, you said?"

"Yes, sir. It seems that Forrest warned Bragg right after Chickamauga. Barged right into his tent, fury on his face, at Bragg's refusal to let him pursue Rosecrans. He cornered Bragg in the back of his tent, and said, 'I ought to slap your face and make you resent it. Don't you ever give me another order!'"

Bragg's problem had not been limited to Forrest's outrage. He had completely lost the confidence of his corps commanders, who had been alienated by his acid tongue, ornery disposition, and hesitation in battle. He had especially angered Longstreet, who had won the battle for him. All four corps commanders had begged Bragg to pursue Rosecrans as the Army of the Cumberland had disintegrated and fled the field, save for the obdurate Thomas and his command. They even produced a private who had been captured early in the battle and had escaped in the confusion of the rout to describe the chaos. Bragg had sneered at him and asked, "What qualifies you to identify a retreat?"

The private had shot back, "Because I've campaigned with you all summer."

After serving with Lee, Longstreet could have only contempt for Bragg. He had then done the unthinkable for a general. He persuaded the other corps commanders to join him in an official request to Jefferson Davis that he relieve Bragg. Davis had been so alarmed that he had rushed to Tennessee to mediate the fate of his friend and confidant from their Army days. The evidence damned Bragg, but no general would put himself forward to seek command, unwilling to be tainted with ambition's stab in the back. Davis took the easiest course and the one he had wished to take; he confirmed Bragg in command. Davis had to give a sop to Longstreet, who refused to serve under Bragg. He gave permission for him to take his corps on an independent operation to take Lexington, Kentucky.

Emboldened by this backhanded statement of support, Bragg attempted to relieve Forrest, the most feared cavalry commander in the Confederate Army. Of course, he had not so lost his wits as to try to relieve Forrest in person. He had sent an aide with the order and then promptly found a reason to inspect the siegeworks farthest from Forrest's command. Finding Bragg was no problem for the legendary Yankee hunter. Mounted on his black stallion, he overtook Bragg and his staff on a forest road.

One blow of Forrest's gauntlets across Bragg's face nearly unseated him from his horse. Forrest grabbed him by the golden stars on his collar and threw him to the ground. His own bodyguard had immediately drawn down on Bragg's stunned staff. "I told you, you miserable cur, never to give me another order." He dismounted with the fluid grace of a predator and took the dazed Bragg by the collar again and dragged him down the road. Then he walked back twenty paces and turned. "I have slapped your face, Bragg. Now you have the opportunity to reply like a man." Bragg just shook, his terror-wide eyes owling above his gray-streaked bearded face. "Draw your pistol, sir, or I will shoot you down in the road."

The two groups of horsemen broke their mesmerized attention to rush their mounts into the woods. No one wanted to be on the road when shots were fired.

Forrest drew his pistol, raised and cocked it. Bragg soiled himself. His hand trembled as he drew his own sidearm. Forrest said to his aide, "Kindly count to three." Then to Bragg, "You know the rules. Defend yourself at three."

"ONE . . . TWO . . . THREE!"

In one fluid motion, Forrest's arm extended and he fired. Bragg screamed and fell onto the road holding his boot. Forrest had purposely shot him in the foot.

He turned his back as his orderly brought up his horse. As he mounted, he said to on one in particular, "That creature needs some attention," and off he galloped.

Grant just shook his head as he relit his cigar. "Thought I'd heard everything," but he was already thinking of Longstreet, Bragg's successor. Grant grew thoughtful and gave a long pull on the cigar. "Too bad I had counted on General Bragg to keep on helping us." Longstreet, who had been best man at his wedding, would take a lot of beating. If any man was to go down bristle end first, it would be him. Grant wouldn't put it past his old friend to actually win.

HUDSON, NEW YORK, 3:00 AM, OCTOBER 28, 1863

In the morning darkness, British troops arrived in the burned-out shell of Port Hudson. Paulet had cause to regret the torching of the town; it now served as a poor base upon which to anchor his campaign against Hooker. Amid the blackened walls there was scarcely a single whole roof to cover a hospital or headquarters, much less the supplies and munitions that would need care from the elements. There were still enough people living among the ruins to act as guides to show the way to the top of Academy or Prospect Hill just south of town. It was the dominant terrain and would give an observer a view for miles inland as well as to the north over the rolling farmland and wooded hills.

Once motivated, Lord Paulet was all speed. He immediately set in motion his small army, "The Albany Field Force," to deploy thirty miles south of Albany to Hudson. He began shuttling them quickly by boat and railroad, faster and easier than a hard march overland. By the end of the next day, he would have almost twenty-two thousand men there. He was determined to block and defeat Hooker on this spot. It was clear that had he waited for Hooker in Albany, the American would simply swing east and cut the railroad that connected him to Montreal. He would be trapped. If he then were to hold Albany, he had to do it from a point much farther south. He would anchor himself on the river. Maybe ten miles or less to the east of Hudson, the gentle, rolling countryside rose suddenly in steep, wooded hills to meet Berkshire County in neighboring Massachusetts. But just south of Hudson, the terrain narrowed to three miles between the hills south of the port and the rising ground to the east. Even that narrow avenue of approach was conveniently bisected by a large body of water, Bell Pond, at Linlithgo Mills.

Nature had made a fine bottleneck for the British, and Paulet had determined to cork it. Hooker would have this relatively narrow route to cross if he wanted to attack Albany or cut British communications with Canada. This was the best place for Paulet to meet and defeat him. If Hooker wanted to play a game of maneuver on this restricted stage of hill and dale, Paulet could play that, too. Five miles southeast of Hudson lay the village of Claverack with a creek of the same name curling south of it and turning north as it reached the high ground south of Hudson. Four miles south was Linlithgo Mills. Claverack would make a good forward headquarters. If he had time, he would throw his army into building in miniature the Lines of Torres Vedras, the strings of forts and trenches that Wellington built in Portugal to stall an invading French army in 1809. He would then let Hooker mark time until the winter snows shut down operations for the year. He rather liked the idea of copying the Iron Duke. He would be sure to hint at the comparison.

Paulet took comfort in the fact that his men were fresh and had suffered few casualties, other than in the affair at Cold Spring. His Imperial and Canadian battalions were at almost full strength, unlike their American counterparts whose units had been shrunk from battle and disease to small remnants of their original number. A veteran American regiment was lucky to have four hundred men. The Imperial battalions numbered just under a thousand men, about the size of many war-shrunken Union brigades. They had had been reinforced by drafts from their depots to full strength. Proper camp hygiene and good medical care had kept the wastage low, and there had been only a handful of deserters. The Canadian battalions numbered about five hundred men at full strength, which most of them were. Paulet had been surprised when Wolseley told him that the Americans had no real system for the replenishment of their regiments. General McClellan, that great organizer, had set one up, but Secretary of War Stanton had discontinued it in 1862, thinking that the war would be over quickly and that the troops on hand would suffice to win the war.

As Wolseley had explained, the Americans could not bring themselves to plan for a long war. Thereafter, instead of recruiting replacements, the various state governors simply raised new regiments, an enormous source of patronage. As the old regiments melted away from casualties and disease, their combat experience disappeared with them. New and inexperienced regiments took their place. The new men, unable to learn from veterans at their elbows, made all the same mistakes over again—at great cost. The Confederates had stopped raising new regiments when they had instituted a draconian conscription in 1862 and sent the conscripts and volunteers to the old, established formations. That helped explain their unusually high combat effectiveness.

The only exception to the state policy of raising new regiments was Wisconsin. Luckily, he would face none of them; they were all in the West.[7] Instead, he would face a large number of Germans whose sad propensity to being routed when their flanks were turned he looked forward to repeating.

Paulet was a creature of Army politics and a member of the Guards clique; his regiment was the Coldstream Guards, a battalion of which he had recently commanded. Despite this, he was not the sort who thought a good turnout weighed far more than brains. He knew his way around a battlefield better than most Guardsmen, who seldom deployed on active campaigning. He had served throughout the Crimean War and had had a horse shot out of him at the Battle of Alma. He also knew Hooker's reputation as a fighting general who had failed in independent campaign when his opponent had seized the moral ascendancy. Wolseley had been the source of this intelligence of the enemy—a useful man, useful, indeed.[8]

CLAVERACK, NEW YORK, 3:10 AM, OCTOBER 28, 1863

The Wolverines, as the men of Brig. Gen. George Armstrong Custer's Michigan Cavalry Brigade liked to call themselves, rode into the sleepy crossroads town. Only the brigade scouts had preceded their twenty-three-year-old, yellow-haired general. Aggressive beyond a fault, a natural leader with a gift for seizing the main chance, Custer had been jumped from lieutenant to brevet brigadier by Meade just before Gettysburg. Anxious to put pugnacious young men in command of cavalry, the normally cautious Meade had taken full advantage of the authority to promote talent, given to him by a terrified Washington. Meade had never regretted the decision. In repeated charges, Custer had blunted Stuart's courageous cavalry maneuver against the Union rear on the third day of Gettysburg. Meade did regret, however, that the cavalry division with Custer and his Wolverines had been sent to reinforce Hooker.

More scouts went out in the direction of Hudson as well as north. Hooker's orders were to find the British. His last reports put Paulet still in Albany, which was just too good to be true. One does not normally ascribe folly to an enemy, and Hooker would have been delighted for Paulet to stay in Albany to be stranded when his communications were cut, but he did not think his enemy would be so obliging. Custer's job was to throw light on this quandary.

That was also Capt. John McEntee's problem. McEntee had been Sharpe's deputy before Lincoln had pulled him to Washington. As McEntee was another son of the Hudson Valley, Sharpe knew he was the right man to put Hooker's intelligence support in place. Energetic, precise, shrewd, honest to a fault, and dedicated to the service of the Republic, McEntee had added implacable revenge to his characteristics when he rode with Hooker and Meagher through the ruins of Rondout, his hometown. With him were a half dozen scouts who had been chosen from the Army of the Potomac. They were all New York men like McEntee. Their chief was the six-foot-tall, red-haired, pockmarked Sgt. Judson Knight, now chief of scouts for the Army of the Hudson, a man whose wits were as fast as his reflexes in a gunfight. With him was Martin Hogan, a young Irishman no older than Custer himself and as game as Knight.[9]

Luck would take Knight and Hogan toward Hudson that early morning. They had barely gone a mile when they came across a boy of ten on horseback. He pulled up fast when he saw them, turned his horse, and put his heels into its side to race back into the dark. He had barely got a dozen yards when Hogan's hand reached over to grab the reins and pulled them up short. "Well, boyo, and where would you be going at a time when you should be snug in your bed?"

He grinned at the wide-eyed boy who pulled at the reins and shouted, "Let me go, you English bastard!"

Hogan was truly at a loss for words, a most unusual thing for an Irishman. He didn't know what to be more shocked at—being called an English bastard or being called an English bastard by a ten-year-old. He hadn't even gotten around to considering the enormity of the boy's insult.

Knight rode up. "Now, Martin, don't scare the lad. But, son, that is a mighty good question my friend just asked."

Knight's Upstate New York accent seemed to relieve the boy. "You're an American?"

"Sure am, boy, and Upstate born and bred. And U.S. Army, too." The boy looked askance at their civilian clothes.

"Don't let these clothes put you off. Now why are you about at this hour?"

"The English are in Hudson, sir!" the boy blurted out. "Hundreds of them. More and more keep landing from boats and getting off the train, too."[10]

WASHINGTON NAVY YARD, 3:15 AM, OCTOBER 28, 1863

Lowe, with the eager Zeppelin still in tow, had come back across the river at nightfall. The balloons had come down with the sun, but he had more work to do. Two of his six balloons were still held in reserve at the Navy Yard, and he wanted to see them ready to go up the next morning. It took at least three hours of preparation to produce the pure hydrogen gas necessary to lift a balloon, and he needed to start now if they were to go up by early morning.

Not only were the designs of Lowe's balloons superior to anyone else's, but he was the only one to design the support vehicle mounting the equipment, the Lowe Generator, that could produce the necessary hydrogen. By doing this, he had made the Balloon Corps truly mobile, able to follow the Army anywhere its normal wagons could go. His headquarters was the Navy Yard because it was there that the hydrogen-producing equipment was built by the Yard mechanics who seemed to be able to turn their hands to anything.

The Lowe Generator was a strong, wooden, metal-reinforced tank set on a standard Army escort wagon. Auxiliary boxes for the complex processes of cooling and purifying the gas were connected by copper couples and a short rubber hose:

> The process for making gas with this apparatus was simple and rapid. It required, however, a thorough knowledge of the proper mixture of materials, and careful handling of the equipment. For a single inflation, four barrels of fine iron filings or borings, each weighing approximately 834 pounds, or a total of 3,300 pounds, were introduced into the tank through the manhole at the top. This material was spread as evenly as possible. The tank was then filled with water to within about two feet from the top. This done, the manhole was closed and the wingknobs tightly fastened. Ten carboys of sulphuric acid, averaging 161 pounds each, or a total of approximately 1,600 pounds, were poured into the tank by means of a siphon inserted into the cooper funnel. The siphon was made

of lead, to resist attack by the acid. The acid was fed in according to a prescribed schedule and rate: five carboys at first, followed by a waiting period equal to the time expended in pouring the acid; then three more carboys, followed by a second time interval; and finally the remaining two carboys. The times delays between pouring were adopted to prevent too rapid a generation of gas, which might strain the walls of the tank. The generated gas then passed through the copper elbow coupling at the forward end of the rubber hose which conveyed it into the water cooler, from which it again passed into the lime purifier which absorbed the impurities and foreign gases. As a result, the gas which flowed from the lime solution into the balloon was almost pure hydrogen.[11]

The support teams of the two reserve balloons had been well trained, but this was their first operational inflation, and Lowe wanted to be there to make sure things went right. Lowe was relieved to see that both teams needed little supervision and seemed quite eager to get their balloons, named *Eagle II* and *Washington*, into the fight. Zeppelin, with the energy of youth, had stuck with him and eagerly took notes under the light of a lantern during the entire process.

Lowe could then spare a moment or two to watch the rest of the bustle that filled the Yard even at this early morning hour. Under the lights of lamps and torches, men were fitting guns onto the gunboats tied up at the docks and loading ammunition. Other heavy naval guns were being emplaced to defend the Yard itself or trundled across the city to bear on the Virginia side of the river. It reminded him of an anthill in which streams of disciplined insects bore streamed in and out of the nest. One such stream was transferring shells by wagon from the huge brick Yard buildings to the boats and new gun emplacements along the docks. A wagon wobbled out of line suddenly as a wheel shattered with a loud crack, followed by the louder cursing of the wagon driver. Before he could bring up the team, the wagon sagged, spilling out a dozen shell boxes. One of the boxes splintered, and its shell came spinning over toward Lowe, coming to rest only a foot away. He noted a dab of red paint on it.

A sailor came running over to retrieve the shell. He doffed his cap to Lowe. "Beg pardon, sir."

Ever curious, Lowe said. "Just a moment. What is the red paint on the shell?"

"Oh, that, sir. That means the shell is loaded."

"And that strip of lead?"

"That's the fuse patch, sir."

"And what does that do?"

"That protects the fuse. Just before the shell is put into the gun's barrel, the loader removes it to show the gun captain that the fuse has been uncovered."

"Then what?"

"Then the loader sets the fuse."

"Then what?"

"Well, sir, then they fire the gun."

Lowe smiled. "Thank you, sailor."[12]

The man waited expectantly for Lowe to ask another question or terminate the conversation when a young officer walked over to see why an Army colonel was speaking to a sailor, especially when that sailor was supposed to be loading ammunition.

"Sir, is there a problem here?"

Lowe was struck by the presence of the young officer. He was slender and tall—about six feet—erect, shoulders thrown back, and his brown hair fell to his shoulders. His light blue gray eyes were arresting, and his manner radiated force, strength, and ability.[13]

Lowe shrewdly appraised him and suddenly realized there was almost a sensation of magnetism between them. He replied, "Not at all, lieutenant. This shell fell out the wagon and rolled my way, and I had a few questions about it."

The lieutenant nodded at the sailor who fled, as much as one can flee with a 72-pound nine-inch shell. He was putting his fingers to his cap to take his leave when Lowe asked another question.

"Lieutenant, I was not able to ask to the man how the shell was ignited. Can you illuminate the process for me?"

"Why, of course, sir. If you noticed the lead caps on the shell . . ." Lowe nodded. "It's for safety. Directly underneath the fuse patch, or the safety cover, is some mealed powder. This is ignited by the hot gases in the gun's bore as it is fired. Inertia causes the lead safety plug at the base of the fuse to fall away into the powder inside the shell. The burning mealed powder in turn ignites the fuse, which can be set at 3 1/2, 5, 7, 10, or 15 minutes. The fuse burns down to the powder in the shell and ignites it, causing it to explode."[14]

"Very good, Lieutenant. Now, how would you get the shell to explode if it were dropped from a height?"

The lieutenant burst out laughing and then apologized. "Why, sir, who ever heard of such a thing? Dropping a shell from a building?" Then, intrigued by the odd question, his eye wandered to the inflating balloons. He grasped Lowe's intent immediately and explained the priming procedure. He suggested, "Two things would be needed. The lead safety cap would have to be removed as in firing the shell, of course, but you would need to have removed the lead safety plug at the base of the fuse before inserting the fuse into the shell. Then just before the shell was dropped, the mealed powder would have to be ignited by hand. Whatever did you have in mind, sir?"

Lowe smiled. "Just an idle question, Lieutenant. Thank you for your help."

The lieutenant saluted and turned to go, then stopped, and turned back to Lowe. He looked beyond Lowe at the gas generators and the fabric of the balloons spread over a rack to keep it from the ground.

"It could work, but you would need a man who knows fuses. And I don't know how many of the shells your basket could hold because the nine-inch alone weighs seventy-two pounds. Two of them would be the weight of a man. Grenades would be easier. We have some here, the Ketcham grenades. Anyone can use them."

Zeppelin had been as fast on the uptake and asked, "*Herr Oberst*, it vood be a great honor if I could ascend ven you take *diese Bomben mit Ihnen*.[15]

THE WHITE HOUSE, WASHINGTON, D.C., 4:10 AM, OCTOBER 28, 1863

Maj. John Tappen circled the White House, inspecting his guards. Tappen was the acting commander of Sharpe's regiment, the 120th New York. The two were old friends from their prewar militia service. Sharpe now wanted the whole regiment to stand by. Two full companies stood guard while the other eight slept on the lawn with their weapons. Hooker's Horse Marines, except those Sharpe had sent outside the lines to scout, were bivouacked in nearby Presidential Park. Tappen would have felt better if the old 20th had been with them, but the crisis on the Hudson had stripped the Washington forts of much of their infantry and all of the New York regiments that could be spared. The 20th was now somewhere in New York, force-marching to join Hooker. Its commander, Col. Theodore Gates, had been impressed with Tappen's use of the coffee mill guns in training and had drawn a dozen for his regiment with Sharpe's support. The two regiments had practiced at the target ranges together on a regular basis. Tappen thought his old friends should be catching up with Hooker right soon. He believed that New York men would see a lot of fighting no matter where they were.[16]

Tappen had placed four pairs of coffee mill guns to cover each corner of the buildings and its grounds. The crews slept by their guns, too. He stopped to pat one of the pieces on its long barrel. The men had taken to these infernal machines with such enthusiasm that practically every man had volunteered for the crews. To keep them all happy, he had run the whole regiment through training on them. Every man had checked out in one crew position or another. It was easy to understand the men's delight. The guns shredded the targets on the firing ranges. More than one man had said, "If we had had these at Gettysburg, Bobby Lee wouldn't have had a man to get back over the Potomac."[17]

RED HOOK, NEW YORK, 5:00 AM, OCTOBER 28, 1863

It was not even light yet when the regiment got back on the road. They had been hurrying to catch up to Hooker's command ever since they left Washington. Gates had given them barely three hours sleep, but thanks to the good people of Red Hook, no man had had to sleep outdoors in the frosty night. The people had had a hearty breakfast waiting for them as soon as their adjutants began to rouse them. There were no complaints either. These were all New York men.

The townspeople came to ask what the strange little cannons were trailing behind a single horse. They were glad to show off "Old Abe's" coffee mill guns and explain to the locals' wonderment that they could easily fire one hundred and fifty bullets a minute—as much as seventy-five riflemen. Even more, the guns fired from a steady rest and were not subject to the propensity of men to fire high or wide of the mark when worked up by a fight. One officer said, to the amazement of all, that each gun was worth a half regiment in firepower.

At Cold Spring, they had been joined by the Corps of Cadets—four hundred young men in their old fashioned, gray, swallow-tailed uniforms with a tall black shako. The veterans had looked askance at the "Kay Dets." West Point officers, with their insistence on discipline, were not always popular among the rank and file, and these budding officers did not even have the benefit of having "seen the elephant." Still, the soldiers had to admit they marched better than anyone thought possible. At least that was something.

Veterans and cadets had to gulp down those wonderful breakfasts—flapjacks, butter, bacon, ham, hot bread, and preserves (apricot, peach, raspberry), and lots of hot coffee, with cream of all things—as their officers NCOs shouted to hurry. That left the fruit pies and cakes untasted, but the women wrapped the slices in cloth napkins and pressed them into the men's haversacks, along with fresh bread, cheese, and sausages. Most men left the town with the kiss of a pretty girl on cheek or lips. It would be a long time before any man forgot Red Hook.[18]

9

Perilous Morning

FORT BERRY, VIRGINIA, THE DEFENSES OF WASHINGTON, 4:00 AM, OCTOBER 28, 1863

The whispered command crept from man to man across the line of Confederate engineers lying on the cold ground in front of the infantry parapet just south of Fort Berry. They rose, stiff from the chill, but moved forward quickly to drag off the abattis. Other men rushed through the gaps to find the stout gate in the parapet. To their amazement, it swung in at a touch on well-oiled hinges. The rescue party that had saved the screaming man had forgotten to secure it. Battles are won by such accidents. They rushed through without a second thought.

The infantry stood up in a mass to follow, when a shot rang out— then another and another. The alarm was given, but it was too late— there were too few Union infantry to make much difference. In minutes, the 2nd Virginia had followed the engineers through, then the 4th, 27th, 33rd, and 5th Virginia like a downpour through a spout. Guns from Fort Berry fired laterally down the front of the parapet but missed most of the men who had scrambled into the ditch in front of the position waiting to get through the gate. Once inside the defenses, the regiments peeled left and right, trying to overrun the forts on either side. Berry was one of the few unenclosed forts and fell quickly to the 2nd Virginia in a rush of bayonets. There they found a medical wagon and tent; a plain-faced, dark-haired woman was standing by a man on a stretcher. As they passed, each man doffed his cap, saying, "Thank you kindly, ma'am," or "God bless you, ma'am." Once the fort was secured, the colonel came up to her, took off his hat, and bowed. "On behalf of my men, ma'am, I wish to thank you for your Christian charity in helping this poor man. I have ordered my regimental surgeon to your assistance."

"Thank you, Colonel," she replied. "I'm afraid he will have more than one patient today."

"Fortunes of war, ma'am. Fortunes of war." Then he paused and asked, "May I know your name, ma'am? The men would like to know if this angel of mercy has a name."

"Barton, Colonel. My name is Clara Barton."

HEADQUARTERS, ARMY OF THE HUDSON, FIVE MILES SOUTH OF LINLITHGO MILLS, NEW YORK, 6:05 AM, OCTOBER 28, 1863

Few men had gone through the soul-searching ordeal that Joe Hooker had put himself through after his failure at Chancellorsville last May. What had made it so bitter was to realize that Sharpe's intelligence effort had put Lee in his hand. That hand had flinched and let Lee not only escape the trap but turn it around on him. So when Sharpe's man, Captain McEntee, briefed him on the reports of his scouts, Hooker, not normally a religious man, instinctively thanked God for giving him a second chance. It was up to him.

McEntee, with the big chief of scouts Judson Knight standing behind him, quickly drew the enemy situation. Paulet's forces were rapidly assembling at Hudson, brought down by steamer and railroad from Albany. The scouts estimated that at least ten thousand or more were already at Hudson, but there could be more. Canadian cavalry had pushed up the road to Claverack barely two hours ago and were driven back by Custer. The young brigadier had sent a regiment of his Michigan cavalry off to cut the railroad about five miles above Hudson. He had sent back a half dozen Canadian prisoners whom McEntee had personally interrogated. From them he was able to tell Hooker that at least three of the big enemy brigades, each almost the size of a Union division, were already concentrated in Hudson. The Guards and some cavalry were there, too. He concluded by presenting Hooker with a nickel-plated dragoon helmet. "Courtesy of Private Hogan, General. He and Knight found a pair of enemy scouts in the woods outside your headquarters. Unfortunately, they declined to be taken prisoner."[1]

Hooker took the helmet and turned it over, evidently pleased. It would make a fine mantel trophy. McEntee added, "We can't place this unit, sir. The uniform is not quite the same as the rest of the Canadian cavalry."

"Well, we are all peacocks, you know," Hooker said. "And most of the time it means absolutely nothing but vanity. Though why a scout would wear something this shiny, I don't know."

"If there's one thing Colonel Sharpe taught me, General, it's to look for patterns and their absence. This helmet is an aberration. And Sergeant Knight said he could tell good scouts when he saw them. It was only luck that he and Hogan stumbled on them."

Another variable, thought Hooker. "Get your scouts out, Captain. Let's see if we can catch any more of them. I expect Knight and Hogan can make a pretty penny selling these things as souvenirs."

Hooker went back to his maps. He had spent much time studying the maps of this region of Upstate and questioning locals. Now, with McEntee's fine work, the pieces were falling into place. Yet, as he stared at the shiny souvenir, he worried about the two men Knight and Hogan had killed. He did not want some fancy dan in a shiny helmet giving Paulet the same sort of information about him that Knight had just given him about Paulet.[2]

FORT WASHINGTON, MARYLAND, 6:15 AM, OCTOBER 28, 1863

The Royal Marine captain had hoped to bounce into the fort just as Capt. George Bazalgette, whose fame had already spread through the fleet, had taken Fort Gorges at Portland. Hoped but not expected. His company was part of the battalion brought over with the ships of the Channel Fleet. Guiding them were Confederate soldiers, Marylanders native to this shore, provided by Lee. The guides were completely at home on the small roads they traveled after landing a few miles south of the fort. Nevertheless, it had taken more than three hours, in the last darkness before dawn, to get where they were concealed behind a small rise just in front of the main gate on its north side with the river on their right. He was worried that he was cutting it too fine. He had less than an hour before dawn. It had been impressed upon him that his flares must go up at least an hour before dawn to give the flotilla time to run the guns of the fort in the darkness. Already he was late, and being late was the greatest sin an officer could commit.

The captain admitted that the description of the fort had been correct — strong masonry structure, much like the larger forts in Europe. A moat girdled the landward sides of the fort and a bastion covered the gate on the river side. Amazingly, the drawbridge was down, though the gate remained closed. He ordered two men with the signal rockets to position themselves just behind the hill.

His men wore their dark blue overcoats as had the Marines at Fort Gorges. The Marylanders were game for his gambit. He marched them straight up to the bridge. They were challenged smartly. One of the Marylanders in a blue Yankee greatcoat replied, in what the Americans had the temerity to describe as English, that they were the 27th Maine, come to reinforce the garrison. Lee's current intelligence indicated that this regiment was assigned to the defenses of Washington.

A man from the wall announced he was officer of the guard and asked them to repeat themselves. The Marylander officer shouted up again that they were the 27th Maine come to reinforce the garrison. On the wall, the officer of the guard muttered to his sergeant, "I'll be damned if they're the 27th Maine. I served with them, and they were a nine-month regiment, mustered out in July. That man speaks just like the locals around here, too. Call the colonel." He looked over the wall at the column by the drawbridge and said to himself. "Maine men — my Massachusetts ass if they're Maine men."

The Royal Marine officer was getting nervous. Fifteen minutes had passed since they had hailed the fort. There was barely a half hour of darkness left. He was more than nervous — alarmed would be a better word, for he saw time slipping away. He shouldn't be, he told himself. In every army, things went up and then down the chain of command, a time-consuming process. Ten more minutes went by. He did not see or hear the men of the garrison filing slowly up the walls to hide behind the parapet, nor the cannon being pushed through the inside of the gate house. The Marylander officer said to him quietly, "I think they have not taken the bait. Best get out of this as soon as we can."

"No, we wait."

The Marylander was about to say something rude when the small door in the gate opened, and an officer stepped out. "Come on in," he beckoned. "Sure glad to see you. We need all the help we can get. The cooks have put breakfast and coffee on for you." Then he stepped back inside the door.

The RM officer nodded to the Marylander who just shrugged. They were halfway across the bridge when the great double doors of the gate began to open, creaking on their hinges. In the lamplight that flooded through the opening doors, they saw the muzzle of a cannon. The last thing they heard was the command, "Fire!"

Double canister swept everyone off the bridge. The doors slammed shut, and the men on the parapet jumped up and began to fire into the recoiling survivors. On the rise behind, the two Marines with the rockets followed their orders. Two red rockets shot up into the air.

THE POTOMAC RIVER, JUST BELOW FORT WASHINGTON, 6:35 AM, OCTOBER 28, 1863

The British ships had been waiting for that signal, moving slowly up riverline ahead, the sloops first, then the gunvessels. The infantry-laden boats and barges would be escorted up the distant Virginia shore by the two small gunboats, *Nettle* and *Onyx*, where their shallow draft would allow them to go where the larger British ships could not.

Commodore Dunlop had had no great faith that the fort would fall, but he had hoped that the attempt would be enough of a distraction to enable him to run the fort before the defender's attention could refocus. It would be a damned tricky business whatever happened. He was leading his flotilla up the river two hours after the low tide had ebbed. The main channel made a sudden angle from the center of the river to starboard as it approached the fort and then swerved to parallel the fort, running right under its guns. The remaining broad expanse of the river was extremely shallow. If they stuck to the main channel, they could speed through. It was then that the operation would sink or swim, the outcome depending upon the pilots supplied by Lee.

Greyhound leading the first division, true to her name, dashed ahead and passed the fort without notice. *Peterel* was next, followed by *Desperate*. Each had followed the running lights of the ship ahead. They were clean through when the garrison's guns came to life. The diversion at the gate had worked well enough to draw most of the garrison out of their beds to defend the gate, leaving only a few guards to peer down at the broad expanse of the water. The moon had already set the night before, and the only illumination came faintly from the stars. The dawn would be creeping over the wood line to the east, its first faint light more confusing to the eye than night itself. Dunlop had factored this into his plan if they should be late. But chance had given him all her favors when the first division got clean through. The guards had seen the sparks from the ships' funnels, sounded the alarm, and thrown torches into the piles of wood along the shore. The garrison had rushed to the guns. The gunners did not fire wildly into the darkness but adjusted their pieces to the plots of their preset range tables for ships passing below through the main ship channel.

Chance now played against the British and confused the lead pilot of the second division, doubly unnerved by the guns firing down at them. He directed *Racer* too far west and ran her into the shallow river mud. Taking her lead, *Icarus* followed to stick herself fast as well. Just in time, *Spiteful*'s captain turned her back into the main channel, signaling frantically to the following gunvessel division to follow her closely.

The darkness still held off the approaching half light. The garrison had long practiced on well-drawn firing tables that raked the river approaches to the fort and the main channel beneath it. *Spiteful* took two hits as she steamed past. The gunvesssel *Steady* was hit repeatedly and began to settle. The other two gunvessels pushed past her and out of the range of the fort's guns. With most of the enemy flotilla safely run past their guns, the gunners of Fort Washington took special pleasure in turning the stranded *Racer* and *Icarus* into matchwood as the dawn revealed them. The shells started fires amid the wreckage, and soon two ship's funeral pyres were sending their smoke into the morning air.[3]

LAYFAYETTE SQUARE, 5:40 AM, OCTOBER 28, 1863

Sharpe took the patrol leader's report himself. Despite the uproar on the other side of the Potomac, he listened intently when Hooker's Horse Marines brought him news of the joint forces of a Confederate brigade and a British flotilla just sixteen miles below Washington. The sergeant finished his report, "We barely got back through our lines just south of Alexandria and on the road to the Long Bridge when the Rebs broke through from the west, sir."

"Good report. Now let's talk to the prisoner."

The sailor, who had been in the background, perked right up. "It's a deserter I am, your lordship, strictly speaking. I said to myself, Richard Foley, 'Foley, it's about time you absolved yourself of allegiance to Her

Majesty and quit her service.' And every fourth man in the Royal Navy an Irishman, and a great shame it is with England's boot on poor Ireland's throat. That's just what I did, your lordship, deserted from *Nettle*, I did. Now, I says to myself, 'Foley, it's time to became an American like so many of your kin.' And, so, you see, your lordship, it's both a deserter and recruit I am and not a prisoner."

Sharpe would have enjoyed this conversation if the whole world did not seem to have started crashing down, "There's only room in this conversation for one lawyer, Foley, and it is not you. If you have any hope of becoming an American and not being turned over to the British after this war is over, you will tell me what you know of the strength and purpose of these ships."

That threat cut right through the blarney, and Sharpe discovered that he had before him an observant and shrewd man. The room had grown silent as Foley listed the ships and the flotilla's mission and the particular mission of his own vessel to escort the Confederate infantry, ending with, "And I heard the officers say they would love to watch the White House burn just as their grandfathers had."

The telegraph clattered with the alarm to the War Department and the headquarters of Major General Augur, commander of the Washington defenses. Sharpe sent his cavalry sergeant with the warning dashing to the Navy Yard. He saw the man's horse strike sparks on the cobbles as he himself ran across Lafayette Park to the White House. He found Lincoln walking down the graveled driveway with his new bodyguard following. He gave the man a hard look, and the man returned it, bold and angry. He was relieved to see Major Tappen and a squad walking just behind.

"Mr. President, I'm glad I found you. I must speak with you."

"Sharpe, when I see a general sprinting toward me, I take it he has something to say I should listen to."

"Alone, out of earshot, sir." The bodyguard tried to follow, but a look from Sharpe stopped him. "Sir, you've heard the guns across the river. The Rebels have broken through the fort barrier. I do not know how seriously, but they have cut off the Long Bridge. A British flotilla is coming up the river, and as we speak probably is trying to fight its way past Fort Washington. They are escorting a train of barges filled with Rebel infantry, which my scouts estimate to be a brigade. If they get past the forts, this city will be at their mercy. For that reason, Mr. President, you must be prepared to leave the city. My men will escort you."

Lincoln paused and looked over Sharpe's shoulder. "You know, Sharpe, every day when I come to visit you, I pass the statue of Andrew Jackson rearing there on his horse. And I tell him I wish he were here. You know how much he hated the British and the very thought of secession." He smiled to himself. "That reminds me of the first time the hotheads in Charleston talked big of secession in the '30s. Jackson didn't waffle and let the fuse burn down to this terrible war we have now like Buchanan.[4] No, sir. He said that if they so much as tried it, he would march into South Carolina and hang the first Rebel from the first tree with the first rope. Well, that shut them up for almost thirty years. Someday when I met my maker, I would have to explain to Jackson how I ran away. I can't imagine that he would have. And I can't imagine that I would let the old general down." He put his hand on Sharpe's shoulder. "The president of the United States will not abandon the capital of the Union."

He let the gravity of what he had said sink in. "Now, Sharpe, let's see what else we can do to avoid the awful sight of my ugly carcass being run out of town."

ALEXANDRIA, VIRGINIA, 7:10 AM, OCTOBER 28, 1863

Lieutenant General Ewell poured his corps through the hole punched by the Stonewall Brigade. He turned Maj. Gen. Jubal Early's division toward the Long Bridge and Maj. Gen. Edward Johnson's toward Alexandria. The sound of fighting drifting south was the signal Hill's corps, now commanded by Maj. Gen. Richard Anderson, was waiting for; he launched his corps in another assault on the forts defending Alexandria.

Brig. Gen. George H. Steuart took Johnson's lead brigades south parallel to the Potomac, ruthlessly driving all civilian refugee traffic off the road and capturing dozens of wagons supplying the forts from the vast munitions warehouses across the river in the Washington Arsenal.[5] The cost was heavy; artillery from the remaining forts raked his column of Maryland, North Carolina, and Virginia regiments as he hurried his men along at the double time. The fiery Marylander was in a hurry. His orders were to drive through the town and take Battery Rogers to help the British come up the river and assault Washington. He was finally out of artillery range a mile from the town, but he kept up the pace. Those who dropped out were the price of getting there on time.

His men pounded into a town that was in complete panic. With its railroad yard, supply depots, warehouses, and hospitals, it was the transportation heart of the Union's war effort in the East. Now trains were pulling out of the yard, their cars packed with refugees and soldiers. Wagon trains sent to empty the warehouses and ambulances to evacuate the wounded clogged streets fast filling with people. The rumble of guns to the north and south roiled the crowds with fear. Discipline was breaking down among the rear-echelon troops who had never heard a shot fired in anger. The quartermaster officer was suddenly confronted with defending the town — without the combat troops to do it.

THE ANGLO-CONFEDERATE
ATTACK ON
WASHINGTON
OCTOBER 27-28, 1863

Steuart marched his men straight through the chaos, leaving the follow-on brigades to sort it out. The deep sound of the big coastal and naval guns at Battery Rogers came from the river. The battery was in the right place. It sat at the base of the long finger of land called Jones Point that jutted out into the Potomac, narrowing it sharply. Its guns could rake anything that came up the river to pass Alexandria. Little *Nettle* and *Onyx* had crossed the wide mouth of Hunting Creek just below Alexandria to take the battery under fire. With their four relatively small guns, they steamed to within three hundred yards of the battery's huge 15-inch Rodman and six Parrott rifles to slug it out. Not a few men on board the ships must have repeated the famous line of the British grenadier about to receive the volley of the French Guards at Fontenoy in 1745, "May the Lord make us truly thankful for what we are about to receive."[6] The senior captain knew that he had no chance in such an exchange, but his primary mission was to engage the battery so that the rest of the flotilla could steam past and up to Washington. Battery Rogers was the Royal Navy's last obstacle to putting the Yankee capital under its guns.

Commodore Dunlop also had expected an expensive fight to get past the huge armament of Fort Foote, which was a mile south of Battery Rogers on the Maryland side of the river. To his amazement, they steamed past without taking a shot. He did not know that the huge guns reported to be at the fort were scheduled to be installed the following week. As they moved past the silent fort, the fight for Battery Rogers was in earnest. The ship channel would take his ships straight into that action. He could see that *Onyx* was already going down by the head, its bronze propeller glistening in the morning light as it was raised in the air. He did not think *Nettle* could last long enough to give him time to steam past.

Steuart's men were seeing more than panicked Yankees now. The townspeople were coming out to cheer them, especially when they discovered that there were three Virginia regiments in the column. After two years of harsh occupation, they were overjoyed to see their own boys striding proudly down their streets. There had been altogether too much of New York and Massachusetts's swagger. They looked for their own 17th Virginia but could not find them; they languished at that moment in the defenses of Richmond.[7] But these boys would do. Lee, whose hometown was Alexandria, had been sure to find them the guides they needed to go straight to Battery Rogers. They hurried down the main thoroughfare of Washington Street until they came to Jefferson Street, where they turned east to rush down to the river. They burst through the battery's unguarded gate just as the gun crews were cheering the death of *Onyx*.

From *Greyhound*, Dunlop saw the guns go silent, then the Stars and Stripes pulled down to be replaced by Confederate colors, the Stars and Bars in the upper left corner on a field of white. Infantry swarmed the parapets to wave their hats and cheer on the British. The crews of the passing ships returned their cheers. Washington was a little more than four miles upriver. The thunder of Lee's guns bounced over the water. Victory was offering her laurels.

WASHINGTON NAVY YARD, WASHINGTON, D.C., 7:00 AM, OCTOBER 28, 1863

As the rumble of guns came closer up the river, the activity at the Navy Yard leaped into a higher gear. Unlike the huge Army supply complex at Alexandria, the Navy Yard was more like a single, well-functioning ship." Her crew, the mechanics, and naval personnel had worked well together for a long time and bonded into a single crew, though larger than any ship's company. Like a good crew, they did not panic but went about their duties with zeal and efficiency, every man proud to pull his own weight and not let the ship down.

Three gunboats pushed off down the Eastern Branch to block the river. A battery of Dahlgren eleven- and nine-inchers pointed downriver, manned by the test crews. Anyone who did not have a gun crewman's job was handed a rifle and formed into the Navy Yard battalion. The Yard intended to fight.

Lowe's balloons were filled and ready to ascend. The Yard commander ordered him up the instant he could go. Lowe noted that the wind had been blowing to the south-southeast. In twenty minutes, he, a telegrapher, and Zeppelin were floating above the city, held taut by four strong cables as the dawn's light flooded over the city. The strong, slanted autumn morning sun illuminated the panorama in gold. He thought it would have been more scenic but for the banks of rising gunpowder smoke and the moving masses on land and ships on the river. He began to dictate to the telegraph operator.

The British ships—he counted seven—were approaching the confluence of the Potomac and the Eastern Branch. Behind them trailed a mass of small boats and barges crammed with infantry. A Confederate flag waved over Battery Rogers as a ship went through its last agonies a few hundred yards away and disappeared beneath the water. Alexandria was covered by a growing pall of smoke. The forts south of it were holding out against strong attacks. North of the town, masses of Rebel infantry were encircling Fort Runyon, which covered access to the Long Bridge. Rebel guns were pounding away at the fort, which was holding its own, wreathing the area in black powder smoke. The rest of the fort system on the Virginia side still flew the Stars and Stripes. He trained his glass far to the west and swept the horizon. Where was Meade? Where was Meade?

Lowe shut his glass. "Well, Count, I think we need to let some gas out this bag and get on the ground as soon as we can." He did not realize that aboard *Greyhound* off the coast of Alexandria, an officer had pointed out the floating balloon and observed to Dunlop that it was probably hovering over their very objective, the Navy Yard—less than five miles away. It seemed like a promising sign to Dunlop. After losing four ships—three at Fort Washington and one at Battery Rogers—he knew his margin had shrunk, but the defenses of the city had been run and there were no other fortifications to stop him. His first objective was to bring the Arsenal under his guns and land Colonel Cooke's infantry from their small boats and barges along 6th and 7th Street docks on the Potomac. Then he would steam up the Eastern Branch and pound the Navy Yard into submission or ruins.[8]

SOUTH OF HUDSON, NEW YORK, 7:30 AM, OCTOBER 28, 1863

The Army of the Hudson sprang to life with reveille. Hooker had had them up two hours before dawn and fed a good breakfast. Now their columns were moving north toward contact with the enemy. The cavalry division had clattered out of its makeshift camps first, one brigade going to reinforce Custer and the other to swing wide to the east and cut off the railroad connecting Albany to Canada. Hooker aimed XII Corps for Claverack to put them in Paulet's path, while XI Corps took a parallel route inland through the hills. There was no shortage of local scouts eager to guide them over the country roads. He had told Meagher, "Tom, your Germans might enjoy falling on someone else's flank and rear for a change."

Meagher had laughed at that. Yes, the Germans would enjoy erasing their shame by the very tactics that had inflicted it. "Meagher of the Sword" and the "Damned Dutch" might have seemed like the oddest of matches, the spirited and mercurial Gael and the straight-forward, stolid Teutons — but they had worked on each other in that indescribable way that made magic in a failed organization. It had helped immensely that Meagher spoke passable German and peppered his talks to them with references to the heroes of Germany. Around the campfires, Meagher would roam and speak to them of Arminius (Hermann) who destroyed the three Roman legions at the Teutoburger Wald as *Der deutsche Tat für Europe* — the German deed for Europe to free it from a tyrant. They too were heroes in *Der deutsche Tat für Amerika*. In return they called him by the name *Unser Mauer* — Our Wall, for his thickset, powerful frame. And unlike the late Stonewall Jackson who stood like a stone wall, *Unser Mauer* was the kind that fell on you.[9]

He appealed to their love of freedom, the very thing that had driven so many of them out of their fatherland after the failed revolutions of 1848. These were not Prussian Junkers with the Army and militarism in their bones. They were the men who had supported the Frankfurt Assembly and its efforts to define German nationalism in a liberal sense. They had offered the Prussian king the German imperial throne, and he had refused it for its revolutionary contamination. So Meagher was on common grounds with these men; their fires burned with the same blue flame whether it was "freedom" in an Irish brogue or *freiheit* in Rhenish, Hessian, and Prussian accents.[10]

They were light in their step now as they pushed off through the countryside, radiant in all its fall colors, glowing now in the clear morning light. It was all he could do to keep them from singing — it was a herculean task to keep German soldiers from singing as they marched, but for him they did it.

Five miles to the north of Hudson, the commander of the 5th Michigan Cavalry, Col. Russell A. Alger, watched from the trees as a locomotive came down the tracks of the Hudson River Railroad from Albany.

It slowed to turn one of the few bends in the otherwise straight line of tracks that ran along the river's edge. Ahead, the rails had been removed; the engineer never even saw it in time to put on the breaks. The engine shot off the tracks and went crashing down the shale embankment, its whistle screaming in the paralyzed engineer's hand. It fell on its side in a shriek of rending metal and slid into the river where the hot boiler met the water and exploded in a howl of escaping steam. Five cars followed it off the tracks and down the embankment, spewing red-coated men before crashing into the water. The rest skidded off the tracks to crash into each other in a jumble of smashed and overturned cars.

Alger grinned as he punched one gauntleted fist into another. Custer would have loved to have seen that. He leaped onto his horse and charged down into the wreckage, followed by his Wolverines.[11]

Custer would indeed have been delighted to have been there, but at the same moment, he had his hands full with only the 1st, 6th, and 7th Michigan of his old brigade, and 1st Vermont recently attached—barely thirteen hundred men—trying to slow down an advance by the enemy's cavalry and infantry in at least division strength. Paulet had not wasted a moment when Custer had driven his cavalry in and immediately threw his 1st Division and cavalry right back at the Wolverines. Hooker's presence this close had surprised him, and he knew he had to get away from the river to acquire maneuver room. The rest of his force, his 2nd Division, would have to follow as it arrived by river and train. Word of the destruction of the train to the north had not reached him.

He had expected to have almost 22,000 men (47 percent Imperial troops and 53 percent Canadians) and 84 guns to meet Hooker's force, which he correctly estimated at about the same strength. Instead, he was heading into a fight less one division of about 7,500 men. It made him feel like he had only one boot on, a feeling he unknowingly shared with Longstreet at Gettysburg when the Confederate general had to fight without Pickett's division.[12] His major combat units at hand would be his 1st Division, the Brigade of Guards, 500 inexperienced cavalry, and 68 guns (see Appendix C). If his 2nd Division was to get into the fight, the survivors of the wrecked train would have to pull themselves together and join the other brigades coming behind, which would have to detrain and all force-march toward the sound of the guns. Unfortunately for him, the 5th Michigan was picketing the road south to intercept any messengers that might tell him what had happened to his other boot.[13]

Custer had led more than one sharp counterattack in person with the 1st Michigan when the enemy pressed too hard. The time was coming when he would have to break contact or become decisively engaged, and the latter would destroy his short brigade. That time did not come. At the last moment, the 5th New York galloped up for the fight; this was their home, and they wanted a big piece of Custer's action. They were the lead regiment in the cavalry brigade Hooker had sent to reinforce him. The horse artillery batteries wheeled into line just behind them. Brig. Gen. Henry Davies, Jr. rode up. "Well, George, it looks like you saved some of the fight for us. Hooker should be up with XII Corps in an hour or less. Then the party will really begin."[14]

Behind him appeared their division commander, Brig. Gen. Judson Kilpatrick. Custer and Davis looked briefly at each other and looked away. Kilpatrick was a fighting man, but reckless with his mouth, the truth, and the welfare of his men, hence his nickname, "Kill Calvary Kilpatrick." No one had forgotten how he had thrown away the life of the brilliant young cavalry brigadier Elon Farnsworth at Gettysburg. He had made a completely unwarranted slight at the man's courage. Farnsworth had charged unbroken Confederate infantry to put the lie to the slur and died for it.[15]

HMS *NETTLE*, APPROACHING THE WASHINGTON ARSENAL, 7:30 AM, OCTOBER 28, 1863

The captain of *Nettle* was elated at the scene on the Arsenal wharves as his gunboat came up. Wagons were rushing munitions up to a number of barges, and teams of black laborers were transferring them—all very orderly. One barge had pulled away to steam away upriver to directly supply Fort Runyon on the Virginia side. The sight of *Nettle's* Union Jack flapping in the southeast wind panicked the Arsenal workers. They fled from the docks while the teamsters tried to turn their wagons in the press of fleeing men. Bullets started to whiz over the ship. A few of the Union guards had stuck to their posts and decided to put up a fight. One of them was a good enough shot to drop *Nettle's* helmsman at the captain's side. Guards on the escaping barge added their fire as *Nettle* lurched to port with the wheel unmanned.

The captain jumped to grab the swinging wheel and put his boat back on course. He had strict orders to support the Confederate infantry that was trailing *Nettle* in their boats in their mission to seize the Arsenal intact. That meant not firing on its warehouses, but that did not mean he could not clear the docks of snipers. Unfortunately, he did not stop to consider that the docks themselves were piled high with powder and munitions.

Lowe's ground crews were hard at work, raising the second balloon while lowering Lowe's. They had met at about 500 feet above the Navy Yard when a thunderous explosion drew every head south. The men aboard the British flotilla stopped as the wave of the explosion rocked their ships. More explosions ripped the air and shuddered through the earth as the Arsenal's huge store of munitions ignited building by building. Bullets set off by the millions and whizzed through the air when flame touched their paper cartridges. The explosions blew shells of all calibers to arc out and fall like iron hail. Even the fighting on the Virginia side of the Potomac stopped as every man turned to the fiery spectacle. Cheers echoed from the massed Confederates around Fort Runyon. Lee and his ordnance officers were less pleased. They had counted on the spoils of the Arsenal to pump new blood into the Army of Northern Virginia for months to come.

Of course, the source of the explosion was to causes recriminations for decades. Commodore Dunlop maintained until his death that he gave no orders to fire upon the Arsenal. Some have blamed the men of the 27th North Carolina for firing on the Arsenal docks from their barges. Colonel Cooke was also adamant that he gave no orders for destruction. Both men insisted that they had orders to capture the Arsenal intact. Unfortunately, the commander of the Yard also died in the explosion, and the few survivors could shed no light on the cause.[16]

Such speculations were a luxury for the future—and the survivors. The serial explosions had shaken the city and shattered every third pane of glass. Shells and burning debris were falling into the city itself, starting fires seemingly everywhere. The streets quickly filled with the remaining inhabitants. Terrified civilians crowded every street leading out of the city into Maryland. Many soldiers from the vast quartermaster and commissary establishments deserted and joined the rush. Panic was not confined to the human inhabitants alone. Shells and debris fell among the vast herds in the Foggy Bottom stockyards, driving the animals to a frenzied rush that broke through their pens and into the streets. Roofs were blazing throughout half of the city. Lee's laurels, it seemed, would be a fiery wreath.

From Lowe's balloon, the view seemed straight from Judgment Day—the Arsenal was a sea of flames and smoke, the streets were filled with terrified refugees and animals, and the city itself was beginning to burn here and there. Greek words filled Professor Lowe's mind as he searched for a description—*catastrophia, cataclysma, o telos* (the end). But it was not the end of miseries, for only just then did the fires find the gunpowder bunkers at the Arsenal where thousands of tons of gunpowder had been stored. It was more than an explosion—it was a wave of power that pulsed outward to push the balloons nearly horizontal until their cables almost snapped. The occupants hung on for dear life. Lowe tried to catch his telegrapher as the man was blown out of the basket and plunged screaming to earth. He was barely able to keep Zeppelin from following him.[17]

The sound followed the force wave. Men remembered it as if the crack of doom itself had been sounded. What they recalled even more clearly was the immense cloud that funneled into the sky in a vast column, higher and higher until it rushed laterally as well as upwards in a great rounded head—some said like a mushroom. Lightning was seen sending its yellow bolts inside the cloud.

The force of the explosion had staggered Dunlop's ships, which were cruising right off the Arsenal and beginning to steam up the Eastern Branch. *Nettle* had disintegrated in the blast. *Peterel* had been doused with flaming debris and set on fire. The rest had had men blown overboard, eardrums punctured, their vessels' rigging shredded, and fires started. The British ships were simply stunned. The Confederate infantry in their boats and barges had been farther back down the main channel and not suffered as much. Colonel Cooke would write from his vantage point that "Hell had opened up its mouth like a volcano."[18]

Lowe had seen enough and signaled for the winches to resume pulling him down. Once on the ground, he bounded out of the basket to ensure that there was enough gas to go up again. The crews were still at their station, terror in their eyes, but the sergeants kept the men at their work. Lowe desperately wanted to find that naval officer who had told him about the fuses. He looked around the yard with its rushing men. "Sir!" Lowe turned around to see him. "I thought you might want these," and pointed to a pile of ammunition boxes labeled as nine-inch shells and 5-pound Ketchum hand grenades.

Lowe could have kissed him on the spot but couldn't spare the time. "Start loading! We can take five of the shells and a hundred of the grenades. That and two men will give us the maximum weight the balloon can lift. Hurry, man—for God's sake, hurry!" They carried the boxes by their rope handles to the basket. Zeppelin dragged boxes of grenades over to help.

Lowe paused long enough to ask, "Your name, Lieutenant? If we are going to ascend, we should know each other's name. I'm Thaddeus Lowe."

The lieutenant just grinned and said, "Cushing, sir. Will Cushing."[19]

CLAVERACK, NEW YORK, 8:05 AM, OCTOBER 28, 1863

Hooker on his white horse, his color bearer, and a small escort galloped into Claverack as the cavalry was rapidly retreating into it in from the opposite direction. It was obvious from the number of wounded clinging to their saddles that they had been through a hard fight. It was equally clear that they were still in good order and had a lot more fight left in them. Hooker raised his hat and waved so the men would recognize him. They were glad to see their commander so near the smell of powder and waved their carbines and pointed him out.

He found a knot of officers around Custer, his long blond hair and red bandana unmistakable. "Well, Custer, I hope you've set up a good fight for us."

Custer, all whiplash energy, laughed and pointed in the direction of Hudson. "The British Army will be here in ten minutes, General. Of course, there aren't quite as many of them as there were two hours ago. I estimate they've got at least ten thousand men on the field. Watch out for their artillery. It's best and fastest I've ever seen."

Hooker rubbed his jaw. "Those must be their Armstrongs. Well, I have a few surprises myself." He motioned to an aide. "Tell General Slocum to bring up XII Corps at the double quick." Then to Custer, "Let's go forward."[20]

Hooker was not the only man who had a reputation to win back that day. Henry Slocum had vacillated about coming to the aid of the embattled I and XI Corps on the first day at Gettysburg and had earned the epithet of "Slow Come." At the age of thirty-six, he had been the youngest corps commander in the Army of the Potomac, and upon Hooker's relief after Chancellorsville that May he was the most senior of the corps commanders. Seniority would have given him command of the Army, but his unassertiveness ensured that was never seriously considered. He had served through the Chancellorsville campaign and so despised Hooker that he had attempted to resign twice when placed under his command again, but Lincoln had refused, reminding Slocum that in this hour of national peril, no one had the right to such luxuries. Hooker's aide found him halted with his corps four miles to the rear at Linlithgo Mills. He had to repeat Hooker's order several times as Slocum conferred with his staff. Finally, with the column still at a halt, the aide galloped back to Claverack.[21]

At the same time, Hooker and Custer had found a perfect vantage to view the British advance, an apple orchard on a small hill outside the town. The last of the cavalry was pulling out. Not far beyond them was a red line of skirmishers pressing forward. Well-aimed artillery shells fell along the road and caught a dozen cavalrymen, sending them and their horses flying across the freshly harvested field. Two pieces of field artillery rode up to the orchard and unlimbered to slow down the advance a bit. Before they could fire, British artillery was lacing the copse. Hooker's standard bearer was blown out of his saddle by a six-inch-long iron fragment. Shells smothered the two guns. A limber with its dead horses around it was hit and exploded.[22]

The enemy was coming straight from the direction of Hudson across the open ground. They could have taken a slower but more covered route in the orchards and woody hills just to the east, but speed was obviously uppermost in his enemy's mind. Speed was uppermost in Hooker's mind also—Slocum's speed. If he did not get over the creek in time, then the enemy would force his cavalry back through Claverack and back south over the creek. Then somebody would have to attack over the creek, and the defender would have it as an obstacle in front of him. Not that it was much of one—shallow and banks none too steep— but it could be enough. Hooker had also noticed as he rode over the little bridge crossing the creek that apple orchards grew north and south of it just to the west. He had also noticed just before he approached the bridge that a large hollow lay less than half a mile south of the creek.

Hooker had added all this to his calculations. "Custer, get your men strung out on either side of the town behind any wrinkle in the ground that will give them protection from the guns. Slocum should be up to fill in and allow you to pull back into reserve. Go, now."[23] Custer dashed off while Hooker just leaned forward in the saddle and scanned the field with his field glasses. Beyond the skirmishers a wave of dense scarlet battalions was moving forward in beautiful order. As an old soldier, Hooker had to admire such drill. But Americans would have been covering the ground much faster. He thought, Good, Lord Paulet, give me more time.

Hooker only quit the orchard when the enemy's skirmishers were four hundred yards away. Bullets whistled past him as he whipped his horse back to Claverack, fully expecting to find Slocum deploying. He pulled up by Custer with not an infantryman in sight just as his aide rode up to answer the question that enraged Hooker: where was Slocum? The artillery had found them again and was falling across the village. A trooper rode up on a wounded horse that whinnied in pain. The rider desperately tried to calm her, but her wound was too much. She fell to her knees and rolled over to claw at the air with her hooves. The rider had jumped off just in time. He stepped over to the horse and shot it, then reported to Custer. "Sir, they've flanked us to the north with some cavalry. We're pulling back trying to delay, but the colonel said to tell you that unless you want to get yourself captured, get out of town."

Hooker said, "Sounds like good advice. Pull back out of town a half mile on the other side of that creek. There are orchards on the other side that will give you some shelter." His fair complexion now reddened. "Now, let me see what happened to General Slocum." He spurred his horse out of town.[24]

Lord Paulet's horse picked its way gingerly through the dead men and horses of the guns on the copse that had held Hooker only fifteen minutes before. Wolseley was part of his party, too large a party, he thought. Still, Wolseley had been impressed by Paulet's conduct of the battle so far. As soon as he realized American cavalry was on his flank, Paulet had lashed out and promptly put his troops in motion for a collision. There was no hope now that the Americans would give them time to build their miniature "Lines of Torres Vedras" from the river to the hills. Paulet had a fight on his hands, and he had stepped up punching. The troops had behaved splendidly and executed every movement with great skill, though the Canadian cavalry had suffered heavily from their inexperience and the firepower of Custer's repeaters. There would be a special commendation for the Royal Artillery, who were handling their Armstrongs with great precision and a speed Wolseley had never seen before in muzzle-loading guns. What he did not see was the rate of mal-function as improperly closed and rusted breeches blew back. He was impressed with the Canadians; their close association with the British regulars had paid off. They had pushed their skirmish lines forward ag-gressively and pressed on despite casualties. The sight of blood had not unnerved them. So far, so good.

But the fight had only begun. The enemy cavalry had fought a su-perb delaying action and inflicted heavy casualties with their carbines. The American infantry had not appeared yet. Paulet was saving the Bri-gade of Guards for that. From the orchard, they could see the Imperial and Canadian battalions sweeping by toward the village down the road. They cheered their commander as they passed him. Wolseley would remember that moment as Paulet gallantly lifted his cap as Britannia's scarlet might surged past.[25]

10

"Prettiest Parade I've Ever Seen"

THE WHITE HOUSE, WASHINGTON, D.C., 8:07 AM, OCTOBER 28, 1863
After their meeting that morning, Sharpe had left Lincoln to return to his headquarters. The president had reminded him that the 120th and Hooker's Horse Marines were about the only fighting men in the city not defending the forts. As the sound of gunfire echoed over the river, he suggested that they might be needed for something more than guard duty. Save for one company, Sharpe sent Tappen off with the men and their coffee mill guns to the southern end of the Presidential Park, which led down to where the Washington Canal fed into the Potomac.

The blast from the exploding Arsenal shattered the headquarters windows. Everyone rushed out to gape at the huge clouds and flames rising from the south. Wilmoth, with his brand-new second lieutenant's shoulder straps, came running minutes later with a telegram.

"Sir, Lowe's balloon over the Navy Yard reports British ships coming up the East Branch and a flotilla of boats coming up the Potomac side."

Sharpe grabbed the young man by the shoulders. "Run to the White House. Show this to the president. Tell him, Andy Jackson's statue be damned—he and his family must be ready to leave the city immediately. Tell him I will hogtie him if I have to."

Wilmoth's eyes went wide, and he tore off across the square with the telegram in hand.[1]

The explosion of the Arsenal had sent flaming debris through the roof of the White House. Mrs. Lincoln was in shrieking hysteria after a jagged, twenty-pound piece of iron crashed through the window and gouged its way across her breakfast table. Her black seamstress and confidante, Mrs. Elizabeth Keckley, ran out of the house to find the president, who had started to walk over to the War Department. She caught him before he had gotten too far and blurted out the scene. He rushed back immediately, his burly bodyguard trying to keep up as those long legs raced to the White House.

The building was in an uproar after a half dozen projectiles had fallen through the roof, setting fires and terrifying the staff. There was no one then at the entrance to greet the president. Keckley followed Lincoln up the stairs with the bodyguard. Lincoln traced the wailing to the family breakfast room and found Mary cringing in the corner, clutching twelve-year-old Tad. A haze of smoke filled the air. The silver and china had been thrown about the room, and the table had a gashed, splintered furrow across it. The shard of shell had struck the small stove that was used to warm the room from the early chill and torn it open, spilling coals across the carpet and onto the drapes, which were now on fire. Lincoln took it all in at a glance and pulled the heavy velvet curtains down off their rods. He threw a chair through a window, smashing glass and frame, used the curtain rod as pole to pick up the blazing curtains, and threw the blazing bundle out. Keckley stamped out the burning carpet. Behind them, the bodyguard had slowed his walk up the stairs as he deliberately pulled his pistol from his holster.

Amazingly, no one barred his way. The servants and staff and the few soldiers were busy fighting the fires that had started in half a dozen places. Screams and shouts seemed to fade from the bodyguard's consciousness as he reached the top of the stairs, so fixed was he on his purpose. Smoke wafted out of the breakfast room. Mary's wails had turned to sobs, soothed by her husband's voice and strong arms around her.

Big Jim Smoke walked into the room and saw the family in the corner. The president had put Mary on a settee and was kneeling in front of her while Tad was holding one of her hands. Smoke walked over and raised the pistol slowly to point at the back of Lincoln's head. Big Jim was not the man to recite some heroic Latin or Greek twaddle at a time like this. He was just a killer. If anything, he grunted softly, determined and cool. He was good at this. In fact, it was his only talent.

Tad saw him pointing the gun and jumped up. Smoke caught the movement out the corner of his eye and flinched as he fired.

Lincoln collapsed onto his wife. The boy shouted, "Pa!" Wide-eyed, Mary stared over her fallen husband at the snarling beast with the smoking pistol. She threw her arms around Lincoln's bloody head, trying uselessly to protect him.

Smoke stepped forward to shoot again. Tad flew at him screaming and grabbed his gun arm. The big man simply threw the boy off to fly across the floor. Then he raised the pistol again as Mary, paralyzed by terror, just shook her head, silently mouthing, "No, no," as she clutched her husband closer.[2]

Wilmoth ran into the chaos of the White House and grabbed a servant. "Where's the president?" The woman pointed upstairs. The sound of the first shot echoed from above. Wilmoth took the stairs three at a time. He heard a boy's scream of rage and followed it. He was in time to see Smoke hurl Tad across the room and raise his pistol again. Wilmoth threw himself feet first into the back of Smoke's knees. Smoke fell backward and landed hard, dropping the gun. Wilmoth rolled over and leaped to his feet. Smoke recovered just as fast and went for his pistol. The young man jumped on him, and they rolled over the floor, the smoking carpet, and the shattered breakfast plates. Wilmoth was agile, but Smoke had a hundred pounds of muscle on him. Gradually, he pinned the younger man and grabbed for the barrel of his pistol with his one free hand. He hit Wilmoth across the face and drew back his arm for another blow.[3]

A hand gripped his arm with iron strength. Smoke looked up in total surprise as Lincoln whipped him up and off the dazed lieutenant. Smoke had never been handled like this. Blood ran down Lincoln's face from the graze on the side of his head. His eyes were black coals and his jaw set like a vise. His grip squeezed the pistol from Smoke's hand. His other hand balled to a fist that staggered Smoke with a blow to the face. Smoke careened back against the wall. He shook his head to recover his wits. Then he shouted, pulled a knife, and charged.

The same powerful grip seized his wrist once more as the other hand punched Smoke again in the face. But Smoke shook it off and lowered his head to match strength with strength. Lincoln topped him by a head, but Smoke was heavier and built like a bull. He twisted his wrist to break free of Lincoln's hold. It never occurred to him that he was grappling with a man who had been one of the finest wrestlers in Illinois in his youth. And that youth had built strength like a steel cable in the man.

Lincoln threw a leg behind Smoke's knee and pushed. They both crashed to the floor with Lincoln on top. Lincoln grabbed Smoke's head in both hands and slammed it into the floor repeatedly. The big man's eyes flashed terror, and his arms flailed as his hands clutched wildly at his tormentor. Lincoln kept pounding Smoke's head into the floor even after the light had winked out of his eyes, and a thick pool of blood ran dark over the floor.[4]

WASHINGTON NAVY YARD, 8:30 AM, OCTOBER 28, 1863

It was a crestfallen Zeppelin who waved good luck as Lowe and Cushing ascended over the Navy Yard. There was room only for two men and the munitions, and Lowe needed Cushing's knowledge of fuses more than Zeppelin's enthusiasm. Lowe was thankful that the winds had continued to the southeast and floated him directly over the Eastern Branch.

They had barely made it aloft when three British ships, *Greyhound*, *Racer*, and *Spiteful*, began to pound it out with the Dahlgren battery defending the Yard. British shells found rich targets in the Yard's huge dry docks and foundries. Soon the immense wooden shell of the dry dock was on fire, as was the Yard commander's white wooden quarters. Looking down, Lowe saw a cannonball shatter one of his gas generators, spewing iron filings and acid. The residual hydrogen flamed. Several of his ground crew littered the ground around the wreckage. The rest stuck to their positions around the huge winches that tethered the balloons to the ground. The Yard's scratch gun crews threw themselves into action, and the smoke of their guns drifted over the river.

The British ships had landed Royal Marines and armed sailors south of the Yard, who were marching up to take it from the rear. On Lowe's other balloon that had already been floating over the Yard, the telegrapher had been kept continually clattering away with his dots and dashes. The electrical impulses ran down the wire to the Yard's telegraph and straight into the Yard commander's hand. The messages had told him already that only three British ships were coming up the Eastern Branch. They outgunned his battery, but his Dahlgrens carried bigger punches. It was still anybody's fight.

He had no idea that Lowe was about to deliver a few aerial punches to the defense of the Yard. He was more concerned with the British landing force, which the message estimated at four hundred men. He turned to the Marine captain at his side and showed him the message. "Off with you now, Captain. You know what to do."[5]

Lowe thought he knew what he was to do, too—drop the shells on the British ships. Simple enough, but he had not thought through the even simpler requirement to light the shells before they were dropped. As they were ascending over the smoke-hazed river, he suddenly remembered that he never carried anything combustible on a hydrogen-filled balloon for obvious reasons. It was a far more dramatic end than he contemplated. That left the grenades, which did not need to have a flame applied. But 5-pound grenades would be flea bites to the Royal Navy.

The lieutenant laughed and pulled a box of matches from his pocket and rattled it. "Not to worry, Professor. We are set."

"But there's a chance the flame will ignite the hydrogen in the balloon."

"I take a chance every time I go to sea, and you take one every time you go up in one of these. Besides, we're up here already," Cushing said as he peered down, a grin lighting his face. He pointed down at a British sloop directly below them. "What a lovely target she is, too."

He bent down and opened the first box. He pulled off the lead safety cover and exposed the powder. Then he carefully unscrewed the fuse, taking care not to spill the powder. He then pulled the lead safety plug off the bottom of the fuse and very carefully screwed the fuse back into the shell.

"Now, it should be ready to go." Cushing squatted in the basket holding the shell. Lowe huddled over him and struck a match, his teeth clenched, waiting for a trace of escaping hydrogen to ignite and flare off the balloon. "Touch it here." The lieutenant indicated the powder. The flame caused it to sizzle and flare. The lieutenant immediately rose, lifting the 72-pound shell with the power of his legs, and heaved it over the side.

They both peered down to see it fall, leaving a trail of sparks. It fell toward the ship, but the ship had a mind of its own and steamed on. The shell fell just astern. The water did not drench the fuse before the fire reached the powder charge; the river heaved up to the stern of the ship from the explosion.

"Damn!" Cushing shouted and threw his hat down to spiral through the air. He broke open another box and prepared the fuse. Lowe huddled over him to light the powder. He could see the lieutenant's lips moving. Down went the shell toward the next ship in line that steamed up to join the fight. The black, smoking orb struck right amidship. It bounced across the deck and down an open hatch. Lowe and the lieutenant held their breaths. They didn't see it bowling over two powder monkeys as it bounced down the ladder into the bowels of the ship. The lieutenant cursed again and began to tear open the third box.

They didn't see the explosion. It was confined below decks and killed or wounded fifteen men. The captain would have been happy for that if it would have spared him what came next. The exploding shell ignited the powder charges dropped by the powder monkeys, and the flames shot down, catching one boy after another with his load of powder until it reached the copper-lined powder room. The lieutenant had just dropped the third shell when they saw the ship lurch up out of the water as a geyser of flame shot up through her decks. *Racer's* boilers exploded next. Her back broke, and the two ends floated away, burning furiously.

Lowe and Cushing shouted and threw themselves into each other's arms and barely refrained from jumping up and down on the basket's wicker floor.[6]

LINLITHGO MILLS, NEW YORK, 9:26 AM, OCTOBER 28, 1863

Slocum saw Hooker's white horse galloping down the road toward him. He groaned to himself. He had advanced barely a mile since the aide had reached him. He was moving at the regular march pace, which was evident to anyone, even a galloping general.

Hooker did not return Slocum's salute. His fair complexion had flushed bright red, and rage played across his face. He stood up in his stirrups and leaned forward. "Explain yourself, General!"

"I was bringing my corps up in good order, General."

"Good order be damned! Did you not hear the sound of the guns only a few miles to your front?"

"It was not clearly a battle. I heard little–"

"By God, sir, I heard your hearing failed at Gettysburg, too!"

Slocum's hatred for Hooker flared and got the better of his normally passive nature. "I'll not be insulted by a whore-chaser and drunkard. You dare call me coward after you lost your nerve at Chancellorsville? Remember, I was on that field, and you were nowhere near Gettysburg."

Slocum's escort and staff were transfixed by the drama at the head of the column, which had now stopped even its desultory advance. The sound of the guns was becoming louder by the minute as the generals cursed each other.

It did not last long. Hooker shut down the invective by relieving Slocum and telling him to quit the Army immediately. He turned to the corps chief of staff and announced that he himself would command XII Corps. His orders came out in a torrent, and the aides raced down the column to pass them on. Within minutes, the column began to move. It had all happened too fast for the men down the column to know why Slocum was riding past them to the rear.[7]

When Hooker was satisfied that the corps' two divisions were moving out smartly, he rode back to the fighting with the corps staff. He turned to the chief of staff and smiled. "You know, Colonel, I used to be a pretty good corps commander. Let's see if I still have the touch."

At the same time, Lord Paulet and his staff were riding through Claverack with the Brigade of Guards in column following. The rest of his force had swept on ahead on either side of the town. It was there that the messenger reached him with the news that the railroad to Albany had been cut, and that enemy cavalry was on his rear. One of Lieutenant Colonel Denison's scouts also reported seeing a column of British and Canadian prisoners, estimated to be 800 men, being hurried south by American cavalry.[8] He had expected his second division of three brigades, another 7,800 men, to add to the 12,000 he had on the field.[9] He was a good enough soldier to know that his plans had been thrown seriously awry. He could no longer depend on the arrival of his second division. Wolseley was quick to also point out, "My lord, the enemy cavalry continues to conduct a skilled delay that draws us forward into the dark. We need information before we advance farther."

"Why, Wolseley, information? Look ahead of you, man. There is the enemy. What more information do I need? But you will have noticed how well the American cavalry has kept our smaller cavalry force at bay. I do not think there is much more the Royal Guides can do now. I will commend Denison, of course. He has kept me fully informed of the enemy's position, strength, and movement."

"But, my lord, it is precisely the strength and ability of the enemy cavalry that will blind us to any surprises."

Paulet waved him off. He took another look and said, "I think it is time the mountain stopped moving toward Mohammed. Let him come to us, as the story says."

Paulet was right. Hooker was advancing swiftly with nine thousand men of XII Corps to relieve Kilpatrick's three thousand cavalrymen. It did not take long for Paulet to study them in detail from a church steeple in Claverack, dark blue columns breaking out into line and heading in a directly toward Hudson. If Hooker pushed the British flank away from the river port, Paulet would lose his base and have to retreat overland toward Albany on foot. He took a moment to watch them move and observed, "Gentlemen, they are a ragged lot."

Wolseley's single eye saw more than Paulet's two. "Yes, my lord, not particularly neat. They would be disqualified on that ground alone on maneuver at Aldershot. But we are not at Aldershot. And do notice, my lord, how swiftly they cover ground."[10]

LONG BRIDGE GUARDPOST, WASHINGTON, D.C., 9:32 AM, OCTOBER 28, 1863

It was a scared body of men guarding the Washington end of the Long Bridge—four guns and fifty infantry, all intent on the battle raging across the river. The last thing they expected was the keening shriek of the Rebel yell coming at them from the rear. They turned to see a wave of men in butternut and brown coming at them with the bayonet. Scarcely a shot was fired as they threw down their weapons. Colonel Cooke strode among the guns as his Tar Heels tore away the barrier thrown across the bridge's end. "Hurry, boys, hurry! General Lee is expecting us." In minutes, he was leading three of his four regiments across the bridge. He left the fourth behind to hold the approaches.

The battle for Fort Runyon on the Virginia side was reaching its climax as Cooke's thousand men were double-timing across the Long Bridge through the shadows of the overhead trestle beams. The capture of Fort Berry early that morning had allowed Lee, the master military engineer, to pick apart the intricate and layered forts and connecting parapets with a speed the defenders never thought possible. He had been helped by the transfer of so many of the garrison's infantry to reinforce Hooker and Sedgwick and repel the British in New York and Maine. Now only one fort barred his access to the Long Bridge and his way into Washington.

Fort Runyon was located astride the important junction of the Washington-Alexandria and Columbia turnpikes, a half mile south of the Long Bridge. It was the largest fort in the defenses of the capital, covered 12 acres and had a perimeter of 1,484 yards manned by a garrison of 2,100 and 21 guns. It was Washington's final defense, and it was putting up a tough fight. Every assault had been repelled, despite a continuous pounding by Lee's artillery. Even the heavier guns dragged from fallen forts were not able to silence the garrison. The explosion of the Arsenal had sent everyone's spirits soaring earlier, and the next assault had gone in with renewed enthusiasm. Unfortunately, the garrison's spirit had not been diminished by the cataclysmic display. And hanging hatefully in the air behind the fort was one of those balloons that telegraphed the assembly for every assault.

A mile south of Runyon, Lee was pacing back and forth on the parapet of Fort Scott as he watched the survivors of the last assault fall back. His staff noticed he was showing something more than his taste for a good fight—nervousness that had never been there before. He found his nearest aide and said, "Go to General Stuart and ask him where General Meade and his army are. I must know."

Scarcely had the man galloped off when a voice from the fort's observation tower yelled down. "General Lee! General Lee!" Everyone looked up, and Lee took off his hat to show where he was. The Confederate signalman in the tower was pointing northeast. "General Lee, there's a column coming across the bridge right fast. It's ours!"[11]

CLAVERACK CREEK, NEW YORK, 10:15 AM, OCTOBER 28, 1863

Hooker threw his first division, commanded by Brig. Gen. John W. Geary, against Paulet's right in the half mile of open ground between the Becraft Hills south of Hudson and the orchards that straddled the creek. Paulet had posted his Niagara Brigade here with one Canadian battalion in the orchard. Horse artillery galloped up to unlimber and send their shells across the creek. Then came the wave of infantry. Hooker rode up to the bank with his staff to watch the attack go in and wave the men on with his hat. The men marched on in grim silence. They hardly cheered anymore. They had seen too much. But that same experience had made them veteran infantry. They knew their business, and cheering was for amateurs. But here was Hooker, his blond hair shining in the sun, astride his white charger, and they were impressed. Hooker noted a special eagerness in the five New York regiments of Col. David Ireland's brigade.

As he rode in front of his line, the colonel of the 25th Foot watched the blue wave veer to the right of his line and head straight for the Canadian 19th Battalion. He was puzzled as their line broke up with groups here and there going to ground wherever the earth wrinkled. The group under cover would fire, and another group rushed forward. There were too many to be light infantry. What was this attack by rushes? He grew alarmed as the enemy's artillery concentrated on his men where they stood on the northern bank of the creek. That was the point. He did not see the Americans slipping through the orchards to get close to his Borderers. He never felt the bullet that went through his brain.

Just as the senior British officer on that side of the field slid lifeless from his horse, Geary seemed to lead a charmed life. For all of his six foot and six inches and 260 pounds, the Union division commander knew how to make the best use of ground to get close to an enemy without getting hurt. Geary's body seemed to attract lead, and his body wore the scars of ten wounds from two wars. They were a cumulative lesson he had taken to heart. A Mexican War veteran but not a regular Army man, he had raised two Pennsylvania regiments and risen by merit to command a good division. His timely reinforcement of Culp's Hill at Gettysburg had saved the position. Now he was using the gently rolling farmland to get his command as close as possible to the enemy without having to cross an unnecessary inch of the beaten zone, that clear and deadly space over which men had to advance while under fire. The average soldier heartily endorsed that approach, and in every theater of the war had responded to the killing power of modern weapons with a strong dose of applied common sense. Instead of attacking in tight ranks, they rushed from cover to cover in small groups while others covered them with fire. It was not a lesson the British had learned in the Crimea or the Mutiny, much less in China.

Geary's regiments were working in pairs. One would rush forward to the next fold while another from the edge of the previous position would fire. To a parade ground soldier, it was hideously disjointed and defied every sense of military order. It was also the voice of experience. The Americans had too much experience of the killing range of their rifled weapons. The British were firing by volleys ineffectually. Their targets had gone to earth before the command to fire could be given. Yet the aimed fire of the Americans from behind whatever shelter they could find was dropping red-coated bodies as they stood in their ranks. Geary had passed on Hooker's instructions to concentrate on the Canadians. He understood at once that these glorified militiamen had not really soldiered as much as marauded through the Hudson Valley. Hooker had said to him, "Give them a full dose of war, Geary. Don't let them learn by little sips. Make them gag on it all at once. Peel them away from the British."[12]

Col. David Ireland's brigade rose from its latest covered position and with the shout of "Out! Out!" fired a volley and rushed forward. The Canadian 19th Battalion opposite, already shredded by shell fire, staggered back from the shock, almost every third man down. It was too much for men whose battalion had only been formed that March to drill together a scant eight days. They broke. The New Yorkers chased after them, leaping into the creek and up the other bank, bayoneting every man they caught before rounding up a hundred prisoners. Then Ireland swung them around to roll up the Borderers. The commander of the brigade reserve, 10th Battalion, the Royal Regiment of Toronto, brought his men up smartly to cover the flank and walked right into Ireland's charge. With better officers and more time together as a battalion, they stood their ground. But Ireland's New York regiments had been worked up into a rage at the burned towns they had marched through. "Out! Out!" They shouted before tearing off a cartridge paper end with their teeth. "Out! Out!" It was the same rage that came from the Saxon shield wall as they shouted, "Out! Out!" to the Norman knights massing below on Hastings Field. But this time the invader would have no lucky arrow to win the battle. In fifteen minutes, half the Toronto men were lying dead or wounded where they had stood, the survivors falling back onto their Imperial battalion's flank, followed by shouts of, "Out! Out!"[13]

From his vantage point, Hooker was more than pleased at the collapse of the enemy flank. He hoped he would not have to wait long for Paulet to take the bait and commit his reserve, the Guards. As soon as it moved to the flank, he would hit with Brig. Gen. Alpheus S. Williams's 1st Division and collapse the other flank. By then Meagher and his XI Corps should be coming down on their rear. Unfortunately, Meagher would be delayed.

WASHINGTON NAVY YARD, WASHINGTON, D.C., 10:10 AM, OCTOBER 28, 1863

It took almost an hour for the wind to shift enough to place Lowe's balloon over another British ship. No stouter ship ever flew the Union Jack than HMS *Spiteful*. The terrifying destruction of *Racer* had only egged her on. She came right up to the Navy Yard dock, her side wheels foaming, firing directly into the Dahlgren battery. Her gun crews worked with the speed and precision of steam piston arms, though the Dahlgren shells had torn great holes in her and strewn the red-painted decks with splinters and bodies. Her funnel had been shot off, leaving only a stump that spread smoke over the deck instead of into the air above. She slowly got the upper hand as *Greyhound* drew near to lend her guns to the fight. Powerful as the American guns were, they were practically naked. There had been no time to build proper earthworks to shelter them. Scanty piles of bricks and timbers were no substitute at this range. One Dahlgren was dismounted by a 32-pounder's ball. Another crew was swept away by the deck-mounted carronade. A wagon with powder charges rushing up to the battery exploded from another hit, decimating the rest of the gun crews and hurling bodies like rag dolls in every direction. The blast threw the body of the Yard commander over his guns and into the water only yards from *Spiteful*. Her gun crews rushed to the ship's sides to raise a cheer.

Lowe and Cushing watched in horror as the battery died. They had only two shells and the boxes of grenades left. Frantically, they tore open the last two boxes. The lieutenant's hands raced over the first shell as he prepared and lit it. In one fluid motion, the lieutenant rose and hung it over the side to center it on the ship. *Spiteful* was directly below. He let go. The two stared over the basket edge as the shell fell straight down to the ship. The seconds seemed to last forever as it fell. It was a perfect hit on the quarterdeck between the guns. Then it just bounced over the side to sink to the bottom, the river water racing through the mealed powder and overtaking the slow flame.[14]

The two did not waste time on a "damn" but prepared the last shell. *Spiteful* was steaming up to the dock now. Seconds mattered or she would no longer be beneath the balloon. *Spiteful*'s captain had seen the shell bounced across his deck and knew he had to get his ship out of the way. His Marines were shooting at the balloon and its crew. In record time, Cushing had the shell suspended over the side of the basket. Lowe held him by the belt as the lieutenant leaned over the side and extended his arms to give him an extra foot. Down it went, sparks flying off its burning fuse. It hit barely on the stern deck and bounced forward amidships in an arc that ended in the funnel's stump. Down it went into the smoking opening.

Lowe and Cushing were peering over the edge of the basket as the shell disappeared. Then the ship shuddered, and red flame shot out of the funnel stump. Inside, the engines had disintegrated when the shell exploded to rupture the boilers, flooding the engineering compartment with scalding steam. *Spiteful* just drifted on momentum now to crash into the wharf. The funnel stump was a fire spout, and flames licked over the decks. Men jumped over the side onto the wharf to scramble over the scattered piles of bricks and timbers that had defended the battery so poorly. The captain was the last man off as his ship became a torch.[15]

HEADQUARTERS, CENTRAL INFORMATION BUREAU, LAFAYETTE SQUARE, WASHINGTON, D.C., 10:30 AM, OCTOBER 28, 1863

Sharpe rushed out of his headquarters and had one foot in the stirrup when he saw the president striding across the square, forcing two soldier guards and Wilmoth to run after him. Immediately, Sharpe noticed the drawn pistol in his lieutenant's hand and that Lincoln was wearing a bloody bandage instead of his normal stovepipe hat. Sharpe threw the reins to a guard and ran over to greet him. He was shocked to see the caked blood on the president's head and face.

"Mr. President!" he barely had time to say when Lincoln waved him off. There was a hardness to his face, an anger Sharpe had never seen before. "Sir, what has happened?"

"I don't think Mr. Baker will be picking my bodyguards any longer. I think you should pick up that office, General." A few words of explanation left Sharpe shaken.

"Sir, I should never have removed Major Tappen's men. I hold myself responsible."

"Nonsense, Sharpe. The military guard has always been there to protect me from the outside. All the army outside the White House would not have protected me from an enemy inside. But Providence averted the assassin's hand. Providence and this young man." He pulled Wilmoth forward. Sharpe saw the deep gash across his forehead. For the first time, Lincoln's face softened. He smiled and said, "Every time I see this young man, he gets promoted. I thought that Lieutenant Colonel Wilmoth just rolls off the tongue better than Captain Wilmoth. That reminds me—" He paused. "That reminds me that we need action now."

"If we are not too late, Mr. President. Lowe's balloon reports that the enemy landed at the 6th and 7th Street wharves, dashed up to the Long Bridge, seized it, then marched across to the Virginia side. I expect they're going to attack Fort Runyon from the rear. If they succeed, you will see Lee riding up to your house within an hour or two. I was about to join my regiment."

"Well, Sharpe, I see you have another horse here. Let's go."

Sharpe mounted up. This was a man you did not argue with.

Before the two men left, Mrs. Keckley came running up to Lincoln and handed him his stovepipe hat. "Mrs. Lincoln said you would need this, Mr. President." And off she went.

They found the 120th and the Horse Marines under the shelter of the trees at the south end of the Presidential Park. As they rode up, Tappen called the regiment to attention and presented arms. As three hundred rifles snapped to present honors, Lincoln lifted his hat in acknowledgment. There were gasps at the sight of his bloody bandage.

Sharpe sent the Horse Marines out first to scout the approaches to the Long Bridge. As soon as the cavalry galloped off, he ordered Tappen to move out after them. The column marched out of the Presidential Gardens and onto 14th Street with its dozen coffee mill guns. Word spread of the attempted assassination and Lincoln's killing of the assassin. The men were extraordinarily impressed.

The few refugees still in the city made way for them. Here and there a house burned, flames spreading to the others on either side with no one left to put out the fires. The rumble of guns echoed up from the fighting at the Navy Yard, but the noise of battle from across the river drowned out that fight the nearer they got. The column crossed the fetid Tiber Creek canal over one of its arched iron bridges and marched across the base of the Mall with the Washington Monument on their right, closed off by the wooden slaughter-pen walls. All they could see from the tree-lined street was the observation balloon floating high behind Fort Runyon. Rising sharply above the rumble of cannon across the river not too far ahead was the crackle of small arms.

Two of Sharpe's cavalrymen came dashing down the street toward them. They pulled up sharply. A lieutenant gasped out, "General, the bridge is held by a regiment with four guns. We're engaging from the few nearby houses."

A man in the ranks cried out, "Look, my God, look!" All eyes went forward. The balloon above Fort Runyon had flared in an intense yellow-orange flame. The burning remnant of the balloon and its basket plummeted downward, throwing the four men aboard out to twist and writhe on fire as they plunged to their deaths.[16]

On the Virginia side, a Confederate sniper stood up in awe at what he had done with the handful of explosive bullets he had been issued. His friends whooped and pounded his back in exaltation.

They had more to celebrate. Cooke's column had rushed through Fort Jackson, defending the Virginia end of the Long Bridge. Its garrison had been taken totally unaware. Cooke's regiments had rushed the next half mile and blown their way through Fort Runyon's rear gate while the garrison's attention had been fixed to its front and flanks. The fort fell quickly. Lee wasted no time sending a fresh brigade straight for the Long Bridge. In twenty minutes, the first double-timing ranks reached the edge of the mile-long bridge and thundered onto its planks.

At the head of the column, the gallant figure of Brig. Gen. John B. Gordon led his six Georgia regiments. Gordon had laughed as he spurred his black charger onto the bridge and under the sign that said, "Walk Your Horses." Lee had recommended Gordon for this role, for no man in the two years of war had proven more able to ride speed and audacity to success than the handsome Georgian. At the rear of the brigade, his division commander, Major General Early, hurried on the regiments of his other brigades. Lee rode over to sit Traveller next to Early. When he appeared, the columns cheered wildly, waving their hats. They could taste sweet victory as they were driving into the heart of the hated Union, a living dagger. All they had to do was cross that one wooden mile.

At that moment, the Tar Heels of the 15th on the Washington end of the bridge were huddled behind their barricades trying to return the rapid repeater fire from enemies hidden in the nearby houses. Twenty men already had been picked off. Their colonel, William McCrae, looked nervously at his watch, repeating to himself Cooke's last words, "Hold until relieved. Hold until relieved."

STOTTVILLE, NEW YORK, 10:45 AM, OCTOBER 28, 1863

When two enemies unexpectedly find each other on the same road, it is called a meeting engagement. And that is just what Maj. Gen. Adolph von Steinwehr realized when his 2nd Division entered Stottville from the east and ran straight into an enemy brigade that had just entered the town from the west. Von Steinwehr's was the lead division of Meagher's XI Corps. Early that morning, Meagher had led his two divisions in a long march to the east in order to swing west above Hudson and then descend on the British from the rear. Hooker's plan was to hold the British with XII Corps while XI Corps encircled them. It was a good plan, but the enemy had a plan, too, as Hooker had discovered at Chancellorsville. In this case, though, the British arrived because of an interrupted plan. When Custer's Wolverines had cut the railroad from Albany, Paulet's last two brigades detrained where the track was broken, joined up with the survivors of the brigade from the wrecked train, and struck out on the most direct road to Hudson. That took them into the small town of Stottville.

Von Steinwehr was a good soldier. Born in Brunswick, Germany, he had earned a commission in the Prussian Army and served six years before resigning to immigrate to America. He got into the war by raising a regiment of German Americans and rose through ability to command a division. It was his division that had the worst luck in American military history to hold the right flank at both Chancellorsville and Gettysburg. He had played both bad hands well, and his reputation had not suffered. His superiors continued to think of him as "cool, collected, and judicious." He was uniformly admired as intelligent and agreeable.

It was his coolness that mattered now. For in a meeting engagement, the commander who strikes first and hardest seizes the moral and physical ascendancy. Luckily, he had a lead regiment willing to take the bit in its teeth, the 154th New York—the Hardtack Regiment—recruited from all over the state. The corps scouts had come racing back to the head of the column as it entered Stottville from the east, spreading the word that the road through the town heading south was full of marching redcoats. Von Steinwehr rode to the head of the regiment and pointed with his sword. *"Die Fienden sind da! Vorwaerts!"* No translation was necessary.

They emerged from a side street straight onto marching Canadians who were too surprised to do anything. The 154th fired point blank at the length of a rifle, and the Canadian column came apart. The New Yorkers charged with the bayonet onto the street among the startled enemy. Other of von Steinwehr's regiments came down the few parallel streets of the small town and broke the enemy column again and again. Hundreds of prisoners were taken at the first rush as the rest of the Canadian battalions streamed in panic up the opposite side streets. At the end of the column, a British Armstrong battery blocked the narrow street for the fugitives who piled up against it and pinned it in place, unable to turn about or deploy. Von Steinwehr's regiments fired into the helpless mass from the side streets. The gunners were desperate to save their guns but could not move them for the mass of panicked Canadians. Their horses fell one by one in their traces and the gunners by their guns.

Victory had its price; von Steinwehr's lead brigade was scattered all over the town, rounding up prisoners and chasing the running Canadian militia. He had struck the three Canadian battalions brigaded with the 15th Foot, known as the Snappers, and its attached battery. The British were at the head of the column and escaped the attack, but true to their nickname, they snapped back to attack into the town. They drove the scattered Americans back down the main street, freeing many of their prisoners and taking many of their own. The Snappers pushed past the guns, dead horses, and gunners to drive von Steinwehr's men back into the small town square. The 33rd New Jersey were in their way. These men had only been mustered in as a new regiment six weeks before and came apart when the Snappers came at them with the bayonet. Half surrendered on the spot, and the rest fled down the street. The fleeing men ran through the 27th Pennsylvania. Originally one of the German regiments, its losses had been so large that it had just received a draft of 170 conscripts. The new men bolted, and the rest followed.

The tables had been turned on von Steinwehr. His 1st Brigade was disintegrating, being driven like cattle by British bayonets. He committed his reserve regiment, the 134th New York, to block them as he organized the rest of the men, who had been forced back into the square, to cover each of the exits. The 134th had been raised mostly in Schenectady County just to the north of Albany. Their towns and villages had not escaped the enemy's torch, and they knew it. This fight was close to home, and they were not about to run away. They gaffed off the fleeing New Jersey men and stopped the Snappers' advance with a steady volley. At the other end of the square, von Steinwehr was just in time with the Germans of the 73rd Pennsylvania to hold off an attack by the second enemy brigade built around the 47th Foot. His second brigade arrived in time to fight back another attack. The British commander was a bruiser.

Von Steinwehr was in a fix. His division had numbered barely twenty-seven hundred men, and he had taken on two enemy brigades, each one equal to his own force. The fact that they were in the middle of this small town was to their advantage as the men instinctively turned each house into a little fort. The sound of smashing glass competed with the gunfire as riflemen broke out windows. There were no regiments marching up against each other in open order, but rushes by companies or platoons through backyards, gardens, and alleyways, or from one house to another. Guns found no fields of fire. Any gun pushed close enough to fire into a house risked its crew to small arms fire. The fighting was now house by house, and here and there the houses began to burn.

Meagher had been with his 3rd Division, commanded by Maj. Gen. Carl Schurz, when his scouts came pounding up the column with the news of the British in Stottville. Schurz was another German immigrant who, unlike von Steinwehr, had no conventional military background but was the most prominent of the "Forty-Eighters"—the German leaders of the Revolution of 1848. A staunch Republican, he had been on the committee that nominated Lincoln at the 1860 convention. He, too, had raised German troops for the Union and, with political favor, had risen to command a division. His experience had been dogged with defeat also. Meagher rushed the division forward, flying ahead to fling himself into the crisis of the battle with his Cold Spring Irish battalion at his heels.

CLAVERACK, NEW YORK, 11:05 AM, OCTOBER 28, 1863

Ironically, both Lord Paulet and Hooker were expecting reinforcement from the north. Barely minutes apart, each man's attention was called to the pall of smoke from burning Stottville, visible despite the cold, mizzling rain that was settling in.

Paulet had reacted coolly to Hooker's breaking of his right. Wolseley admitted to himself that there was much to admire in the general's imperturbability and his refusal to let his opponent control the initiative. Paulet had simply pulled the flank back. Hooker had expected him to throw in his reserve, but Paulet was keeping that for his own knockout punch. Instead, Paulet ordered a general advance of his center and left, two large brigades built around the Peacemakers of the 16th Foot and the Rifles, over five thousand men supported by four Armstrong batteries. On the open flank to the north, a half dozen troops of Canadian cavalry were strung out.

The redcoat battalions swung out toward Claverack Creek in a formation that would have done a parade for the sovereign credit. Over their heads, the Armstrong gunners fired their shells to prepare the way. From the other side, Brig. Gen. Alpheus Williams leaned forward in his saddle to say to Hooker, "Prettiest parade I've ever seen. Though, truth to tell, General, the Rebs were grander in their way in their big charge at Gettysburg."

The men in the ranks were in awe of the sight but were able to give it a cool, professional look. The bright array with the royal and regimental colors floating above each battalion was something they were not used to with their gray and butternut enemies. On those fields, the only colors were those "damned red flags of Rebellion," the square Stars and Bars. Hooker walked his horse quietly behind the ranks of Williams's infantry, listening for the comments.

"I thought they all wore red," one voice said. "Why are some of them in green?"

"Getting ready for Christmas, I reckon," answered a wag.

A young man, his voice not all that sure, said, "I heard it's not enough to kill the British infantry. You gotta knock 'em down, too."

"Damned nice targets, sonny — that's all," one of the older men said, and he punctuated it with a gooey wad of tobacco spat into the stubble. The men within earshot all laughed.

Hooker smiled and rode on. He stopped at the next regiment, where the men were on bended knee as one of them sang in a clear voice,

> I fear no foe, with Thee at hand to bless;
> Ills have no weight, and tears no bitterness.
> Where is death's sting? Where, grave, thy victory?
> I triumph still, if Thou abide with me.
>
> Hold Thou Thy cross before my closing eyes;
> Shine through the gloom and point me to the skies.
> Heaven's morning breaks, and earth's vain shadows flee;
> In life, in death, O Lord, abide with me.

There was something about that calm devotion that cut to Hooker's core. He had never been much for religion and had blasphemed mightily. Many had not forgotten how he had boasted before Chancellorsville that not even God Almighty could save Lee from his power. But the God of Battles had humbled him in his great pride. Then he did something the old Hooker would have laughed at. He prayed, "Lord, abide with me also."[17]

He then looked up at the scarlet and green host approaching and remembered another prayer, one Professor Dennis Hart Mahan had taught them at West Point, an army commander's prayer if there ever was one. Sir Jacob Hill had said it at the battle of Edgehill in the English Civil War — "Oh Lord! Thou knowest how busy I must be this day: if I forget Thee, do not Thou forget me. March on, boys!"[18]

His own artillery had opened up, and sudden black puffs of smoke told where a shell had burst in the red ranks, sending bodies flying or spinning to the earth. The ranks closed with fluid ease. And it just wasn't the Imperial battalions. The Canadian battalions were their oldest and best trained, and it showed. In the 1st Montreal Brigade marched the 1st

Battalion, Prince of Wales Regiment, the 2nd Battalion, Queen's Own Rifles of Toronto, and the Montreal Scots of the 5th Battalion, Royal Light Infantry of Montreal, with their flank companies in plaid trews keeping up smartly with their Imperial battalion, the 1/Rifles. To their left, in the 2nd Montreal Brigade, the 3rd Battalion, Victoria Volunteer Rifles of Montreal; the 4th Battalion, Chasseurs Canadiens; and the 6th Battalion Hochelaga Light Infantry kept up the pace set by the Peacemakers of the 1/16 Foot. It was a magnificent fight—Imperial and colonial power and pride, advancing across the creek, drums beating, lines clean and steady. Little knots of scarlet and green-clad bodies marked their trail.

Lord Paulet rode along their front with his staff, his hat raised in salute as he passed.

11

Click, Bang!

WASHINGTON NAVY YARD, WASHINGTON, D.C.,
11:10 AM, OCTOBER 28, 1863

Lowe and Cushing had spent the last two hours as silent observers of the ongoing struggle for Washington. Smoke from the burning Arsenal floated downriver and over to the Maryland shore. Both their shells and reachable targets were exhausted. The remaining British sloop, *Greyhound*, kept well out from the balloon's shadow, which did not keep her Marines from taking an occasional potshot. The bullets had passed with little effect through the wickerwork basket, but had holed the balloon in a number of places. Miraculously, neither of them had been hit, though Lowe had lost a boot heel to a bullet. The loss of lift was slow, but it was inexorably carrying them lower and lower. The largest weight they had aboard were the boxes of hand grenades. He could have tossed them over the side to counter the loss of gas, but something stayed his hand.

In the meantime, their attention was drawn to the fighting to the south as the Royal Marine battalion made its way through the streets to the Navy Yard. The American Marines and armed sailors were outnumbered more than three to one but fought a stubborn retreat house by house. But a retreat it still was as the British pressed them closer and closer to the Yard. It appeared that what the ships of the Royal Navy could not achieve from the river, her Marines would do by land. Already several of the largest buildings in the Yard were ablaze. The huge wooden dry dock sent a massive pillar of fire and smoke into the sky to add to the many churning up from the stricken Arsenal and the general pall from the burning city. The roof of one of the great brick foundry buildings was also burning, dropping flaming timbers and shingles several stories to the floor of the interior. In the water near the dock, the remains of *Spiteful* burned as well. The smoke swirled up thick around the balloon. At times it hid the chaos on the ground.[1]

The battle pushed down M Street past the Yard's brick walls to its turreted entrance gate, littering its way with blue- and red-clad bodies. The Americans made their stand around the gate. Lowe lost sight of them by that time; the descending balloon no longer gave him the height to see over the walls at the fighting on the other side, though the red of the enemy was evident in some of the surrounding buildings. Lowe had decided to signal his ground crew to haul them down—at least they could join the fight on the ground—when he felt the breeze pick up and begin to shift. It pulled the balloon slowly south from over the water to drift over the Yard as it swung on its four heavy cables. With the wind strong to the south, the balloon crossed the Yard wall to hover over M Street. Lowe scribbled a note, put it in a weighted metal message cylinder, tied it to a colored streamer, and threw it inside the gate. It struck the ground directly in front of a sailor who was standing ready with a rifle should the gate be forced. The man looked up to see Lowe leaning over the side of the basket waving frantically. He picked the case up, opened it, and read. Suddenly, he ran to an officer and handed it to him. Here was a great advantage over the British. The vast majority of men in the American services could read. The officer handed it back to the sailor, who dashed off down the street in the direction of where Lowe's ground crew worked the great windlasses that controlled the four cables holding the balloon fast.

The balloon continued to leak, bringing them downward so gradually that there seemed to be no danger. At the normal height of one thousand feet, men assumed the size of ants. At five hundred feet, they were only miniature humans. The fighting was clearly desperate. The Americans had been forced back to the main gate and were fighting from an arc around it. As much as the gate looked like a castle, it was all for appearance and had no fighting battlements. The gate had to be defended from the front. Bodies were piling up as the ring of defenders shrank back while the enemy drew closer, concentrating their fire on a smaller and smaller group.

Suddenly the balloon began to move down the street as the windlasses let out more of their cable. In minutes, the two were hovering over

THE
FIGHT FOR THE
NAVY YARD
OCTOBER 28, 1863

Note: Ships and balloon not to scale

Kmuralis 2009

to Surratsville

Navy Yard Bridge

Georgia Avenue

Navy Yard

Marines

Royal

Lowe

HMS Racer

HMS Greyhound

HMS Spiteful

US transport

Eastern Branch

South Capitol Street

Sunk U.S. gunboats

the gate itself, now unmistakable to the enemy below. Bullets whizzed up at the dying balloon like a swarm of angry bees, holing it in dozens of places. Lowe felt the sting of a bullet and sagged to the basket floor, the blood gushing down his leg. Cushing tore a strip from his coat and made a tourniquet with a board from the broken ammunition box. They were now at three hundred feet.

Lowe leaned on the basket wall, willing himself to fight off the shock trying to creep over him. His hand grasped the grenade box and felt the cool, oblong body of one of the 5-pound Ketchums. Instinctively, his fingers closed on it. Cushing looked at him. "We're too far away to drop them. Wait."

The lieutenant spun around and fell to his knees clutching his left forearm. Blood trickled down his sleeve to soak his white shirt cuff. He looked at Lowe and smiled. "Well, Colonel, we've had quite a run."

They heard the shrill commands of officers below. "What is it?" asked Lowe. The lieutenant peered over the basket. "Looks like they're going to charge." Lowe held up a grenade by the rod that connected the bomb to the fins. He pulled the safety off and handed it to Cushing. The lieutenant pulled himself up to his feet, nursing his wounded forearm. The enemy was rushing the gate below with bayonets while others fired in support from buildings across the street.

Cushing pulled back his right arm and threw the grenade straight out to give it the maximum reach. It arced out and then curved down and fell in front of the officer leading the attack. Its contact fuse struck the brick pavement and exploded. The officer and two men went down. The rest surged past. Cushing felt Lowe strike his leg with another grenade. He threw it, and then a third, and more as fast as Lowe could strip the safeties and hand them up. They sailed out and down every five to eight seconds, thinning the Royal Marines' numbers but not their determination. A score closed on the gate with the bayonet to meet the last of the U.S. Marines standing over their dead and wounded. The bayonets flicked out and back like viper tongues, both sides were experts in the deadly drill with cold steel. More of the British ran from their firing support positions to reinforce the attack on the gate. The Americans were wedged back in the narrow opening, barely a half dozen on their feet stabbing and parrying, leaving the red-coated bodies to lie among the blue. The Royal Marines would not be stopped, and they had the numbers.

"More grenades!" Cushing shouted as he threw them down as fast as he could into the red mass pushing through the gate. A few exploded, but most just struck the packed Royal Marines, and their bodies were not resistant enough to detonate the fuses. The impact of a 5-pound metal object from two hundred feet was dangerous enough but only as much as so many rocks. Another bullet tore through his shoulder. He swayed on his feet before sinking to his knees, pressing his head against the wicker basket.

From below came the cries of "Board 'em! Board 'em!" and then a volley of pistol shots. Cushing turned to Lowe, "Hear that? Did you hear that?" Lowe just looked bewildered until Cushing shouted, "The Navy's here!"[2]

What Lowe and Cushing couldn't see from the basket floor was the rush of the blue jackets of the Navy armed with cutlasses and revolvers to reinforce the gate. They pushed past the exhausted Marines to fire their pistols into the packed British almost through the gate. With six shots at point blank range, the Navy Colts were great killers. Lowe and Cushing sank bleeding to the basket floor as the balloon was giving up the ghost, its descent accelerating as the weight of its fabric overpowered the remaining gas. At fifty feet, it collapsed and fell over the basket; both plummeted directly over the gate. The basket impaled itself on a turret's point to sag to one side, pulled down by the weight of the fabric spilling to the ground. Blood dripped through the torn wicker onto the turret's gray slate tiles.[3]

LONG BRIDGE HOTEL, WASHINGTON, D.C., 11:10 AM, OCTOBER 28, 1863

Sharpe bounded up the stairs, jumping over the debris strewn by the cannonballs from the guns that were now in Rebel hands defending the approach to the Long Bridge. The hotel was only a hundred yards from the Confederate barricades. Sharpe was led into a room at the top of the stairs by one of his Horse Marines who had a dripping wad of tobacco in his cheek. Sharpe saw several more men shooting out through windows. One of them suddenly threw his arms up and fell backward, a clean red hole in his forehead. Sharpe crawled over to one of the splintered holes in the wall. He peered though at an angle so as not present a straight shot to any Rebel Daniel Boone.

The hotel groaned as another cannonball smashed through. The Tar Heels were behind the barricades effectively adding their rifle fire to that of the guns. A dozen of the Rebels were strewn in the street after an attempt to charge the houses had left them as testaments to the volume and accuracy of the repeater's fire. But the rest were snug behind their barricade, returning a volume of fire equal to the few Hoosiers in the house windows. They had only to hold until relieved.

Sharpe scrambled out of the room and climbed the ladder to the attic, and from there out a window onto the reverse roof. He crawled up and over the shingles to poke his head over the roof peak near the chimney and laid his glasses on the edge. He could see right down the Long Bridge to the Virginia shore. A bullet splintered a shingle just below his glasses. Another sung overhead. His presence was known, but he needed to see what was happening. In quick succession, the Stars and Stripes fell from the fort's flagpole. The Stars and Bars rose quickly in its place. A mass of men closed on the bridge, their red battle flags clustered over them. That was enough, especially when another bullet blew splinters into his face. He slid down the roof and climbed back into the house to fly down the stairs.

Tappen was waiting, kneeling behind the next house. As soon as he saw Sharpe dash out the door, he ran over to meet him. Every eye in the regiment turned to follow the two men. The 120th was strung out, hiding behind the flimsy wooden buildings on 15th Street, one street over from that leading directly to the bridge. Lincoln, too, came over to the two, hemmed in by four guards, human shields. Sharpe had come to terms with the man's insistence to come along, but he had put the fear of God into the guard detail that if anything happened to Lincoln, it better be because they were all dead. [4]

Lincoln was too late to hear Sharpe's orders as Tappen ran past him, and Sharpe was not inclined to take the time to explain. Lincoln could only watch, and he had the good sense not to slow down with questions men about to go into battle. Instead, all he had to do was observe as Tappen's brief commands were translated into a burst of action. The crew of a coffee mill gun pulled their piece toward the back of

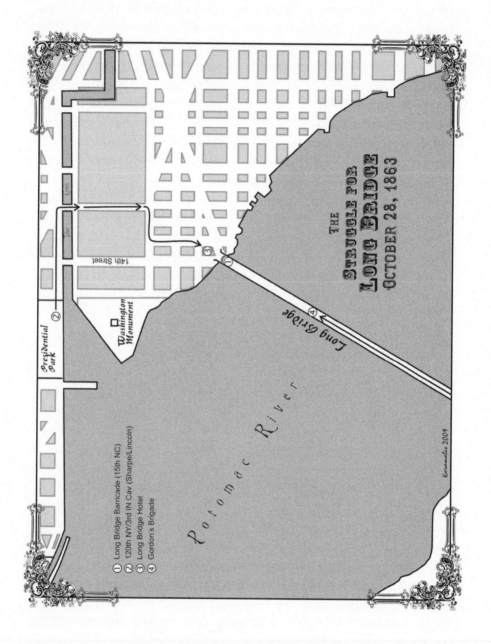

THE
STRUGGLE FOR
LONG BRIDGE
OCTOBER 28, 1863

① Long Bridge Barricade (15th NC)
② 120th NY/3rd IN Cav (Sharpe/Lincoln)
③ Long Bridge Hotel
④ Gordon's Brigade

Presidential Park

Washington Monument

14th Street

Long Bridge

Potomac River

Kimandes 2009

the hotel and quickly manhandled it through the door. Lincoln peered in after them and saw the grunting men begin to drag it from step to step up the stairs. The gun captain kicked wreckage off the treads to clear the way. Once on the landing, he looked into the first bedroom where the two cavalrymen were firing from the windows. He waved to them, but they only glanced his way. He was turning to help pull the gun in when the room exploded. Splinters, pieces of lathe, and plaster flew through the door. He threw himself to the floor. The dust had not even begun to settle when he looked in again. "Mother of God," he muttered and crossed himself. The cavalrymen were bloody bundles of rags slumped against the opposite wall where the bursting shell had thrown them. Another large hole gaped in the wall.

"Bring it in, boys," the gun captain said, pointing to the new hole in the wall. He moved to look out the hole when a bullet came through to nick his ear. He clapped his hand to it and felt the blood ooze through his fingers. Now it was personal. Waving his fist through the hole, he shouted, "Shoot at me, will you!" Then turning to the crew, he said, "Push her up right here!" The gun slid through the debris and poked its barrel out the hole. The gunner depressed its elevation to sight on the cannon crews behind the barricade.

"Load!" shouted the gun captain. A loader put the ammunition into the hopper. The gunner began to turn the crank to feed the cartridges into the revolving cylinder. In turn, the cylinder fed the first cartridge into the chamber. The gunner looked at the gun captain. "Fire," he said. The crank turned, struck the firing cap, and the first bullet shot from the barrel. The next turn of the crank ejected the cartridge case and fed another bullet into the chamber. To the ear it was, "click-bang, click-bang, click bang."[5] That first bullet went straight into the clustered Rebel gunners. Now the gunner rotated the crank faster and faster, until the click-bang blurred into the sound of a high-speed machine hammer. He only stopped when there were no more men standing by the gun. He swiveled the barrel left to take another gun crew under fire. He stitched the stream of bullets first into the enemy gunner, who had just pulled the lanyard back to fire the gun. The gunner's arm went slack as the bullets disintegrated his head. The gun captain rushed over to pick up the lanyard but walked into the bullet stream and was knocked over the gun traces. Only the men quick enough to throw themselves behind the barricade survived.[6]

By now, three other coffee mill guns were in action, sweeping the riflemen from their firing positions behind the barricade. The Tar Heels' first rank simply melted away as the guns swept back and forth, throwing the dead and wounded, struck in the upper chest or head, back into the second rank. The survivors fell to the ground and huddled behind the barricade, shocked by the speed and violence of the assault. These were veterans, but they had never seen such a storm of bullets. It was the moment Tappen had been waiting for. The sword rasped from his scabbard. The men who had been kneeling behind the houses now jumped to their feet. He led them in a run in a column of companies. Not a man fell to enemy fire as they closed the distance. The first rank easily topped the barricade and jumped down inside. The struggle was short.[7]

Lincoln looked carefully around the building to see the Rebel prisoners being double-timed out of the barricade and rushed up 14th Street under guard to get them out of the way of temptation before they recovered from their shock. The New Yorkers dragged the guns back through the barricade to their original positions to defend the bridge. The coffee mill gun crews on signal rushed their pieces down to the barricade and lined it from end to end next to the cannons. Wagons rushed up to unload boxes of ammunition to be stacked next to each gun. Sharpe stood on the barricade and looked down the bridge at the Confederate battle flags filling the first half of the bridge. They seemed to be rushing forward on the crest of a human wave. Tappen put four companies behind the guns and three on either side of the bridge to fire laterally into it.

Lincoln was the last to come forward, his big stride comically constrained by his guards whom he topped by at least two heads. He came up to Sharpe, his stovepipe hat towering higher than anything but the colors posted behind them. The breeze to the south gently unfurled the national flag. Someone shouted, "Here they come!"[8]

FORT RUNYON, VIRGINIA SIDE OF THE WASHINGTON DEFENSES, 11:15 AM, OCTOBER 28, 1863

From the fort's battered observation tower, Lee and his staff had the grandest view of Early's division surging onto the Long Bridge, their red battle flags waving aggressively above the tight-packed columns. A horseman whipped his lathered animal through the broken gates, shouting, "Where is General Lee? Where is General Lee?" Lee put down his glasses to watch the young cavalry courier take the steps two at a time onto the platform. He could not be more than sixteen, the peach-fuzz bloom of early Southern chivalrous manhood on him, despite the sweat and dirt and the ragged uniform.

"Sir!" he saluted. "Message from General Stuart." Suddenly, he realized that he truly was in the presence of Lee. He could not have been more transfixed if he had been in front of Saint Peter at the Pearly Gates.

"Yes, my boy?" Lee said gently.

The boy came to life suddenly. "'Hurry, for God's sake, hurry! Meade is pressing me hard at Reston.' Those were General Stuart's exact words just as he told me to say them, General Lee."

LINLITHGO MILLS, NEW YORK, 11:12 AM, OCTOBER 28, 1863

Colonel Gates pushed his little column on. They were now only a half dozen miles away from the rumble of the battle ahead and were about to enter it sooner than expected. In the orchard ahead, through which the road ran with Bell Pond to the right, thirty men with nickeled helmets were deployed, their carbines sighted on the head of the column. Denison's men had slipped around the battle to intercept and slow down any reinforcements. Their mission was to fire on any enemy column, force it to deploy, fall back to the next position, and repeat the process. The Canadian cavalry commander had not hesitated to disregard Lord Paulet's orders to pull his men back. His close study of cavalry tactics in the American war had convinced him that he was right. Besides, he had always cherished the saying, "It is easier to beg forgiveness than seek permission."[9]

Denison's tactics were sound, but he had not taken into account that the American infantry had learned a thing or two. Gates had just turned his horse to ride back down the column when the Canadian volley struck the color guard at the head of his column; his own horse went down, spilling him over the muddy the ground. His lieutenant colonel's horse was also down, but Jacob Hardenburgh leaped off in time to land on his feet. He scooped up the fallen colors, passed them to eager hands, and gave the orders he had given countless time in training, "Skirmishers, forward!" The two lead companies broke to the right and left and, deployed in open order, advanced quickly in an arc meant to pierce the orchard at either end and close inward.

Hardenburgh ran over to Gates and helped him to his feet. "Just like old times, Colonel."

Gates tried to wipe some of the mud off, thinking ahead. "Whoever is shooting at us will slow us down no matter how fast we push them." He turned to look back at the rest of the companies advancing in column behind the skirmishers. "Take command of the cadets. They're young and quick. Take them to the left at the run and get around these fellows. Take them in the rear if you can. If you can't, press on and report to Hooker. Get those boys into the fight."

CLAVERACK, NEW YORK, 11:25 AM, OCTOBER 28, 1863

On the field at Claverack that morning, no one had to announce that the British were coming. Their advancing red line, relieved by the green of the Imperial and Canadian Rifles, which so mesmerized the Union infantry, was quickly accompanied by the roar of the Royal Artillery's Armstrong batteries. It was little comfort to the XII Corps men that only three of four guns were still firing after the first ten minutes. Improperly sealed breeches had blown back in the heat of combat, but the fire of the rest was worse than anything the Americans had ever faced—rapid, accurate, and lethal. Before the first Imperial and Canadian skirmishers splashed across the shallow water of the creek, the ranks of XII Corps had been savaged. Even the veterans were shaken by their casualties, while the replacements were wide-eyed with terror. Yet their ranks closed up.

They watched the enemy's lines sweep down to the creek bank, wade through the water to their knees, and mount the near bank. That was the signal. As soon as they stepped out onto the bank, a burst of fire from the American ranks at four hundred yards struck them. Bodies pitched forward or fell back down the bank to roll in the water. They dressed their ranks and moved on toward the Americans, who were now firing at will. It was a deadly irony that many of the Americans were killing Imperial and Canadian troops with the fine Enfield rifle eagerly sold to the Union and Confederacy alike by the merchants of London and Manchester.

THE
BATTLE OF
CLAVERACK (PHASE 2)
OCTOBER 28, 1863

Custer

Davis

Claverack

Hudson

Claverack Creek

Grenadier Gds
Scots Fusilier Gds

Grenadier Guards

Kavanides 2009

The American gunners were throwing case shot — tin cans of large iron balls — into them at this range, sweeping away whole sections. The Imperial battalions simply closed up without losing a moment. For the Canadians, this was their first time facing serious danger. Raiding Hudson Valley river ports had not prepared them for this awful baptism. It took longer for their inexperienced officers and NCOs to rally their ranks and get them moving forward again, but move they did. From his vantage point in the rear, Paulet and his staff were encouraged by how well the Canadian battalions were behaving their first time under fire. The Canadian officers on his staff, sensitive to any hint of condescension, were buoyed by Paulet's praise. Indeed, it was a praiseworthy performance for green troops to cross that beaten zone with such cohesion.

But by the time the attacking battalions had closed to within two hundred yards, they began to disappear into roiling clouds of black-powder smoke hanging in the still, misting air. The only evidence of their existence was the trail of green- and red-coated dead and wounded marking their advance and their colors waving through rents in the smoke clouds. From within the cloud, the noise of gunfire intensified like the rattle of hail on a metal roof; the guns had fallen silent for lack of targets.

The Imperial and Canadian battalions halted individually to return fire for the first time. Their volley fire coming through the smoke cut into the American regiments, which had been on the giving end of mayhem so far. Within the cloud, men were now firing at will at only the most fleeting of targets, glimpses of scarlet, green, or blue uniforms and flash of the enemy's muskets. Most fired level into where the enemy's fire appeared to come from.[10]

Regardless of the uniform, the same scenes were shared by every man with a rifle on that field. A soldier reached into his cartridge box and pulled out a paper cartridge. He tore it open with his teeth, smearing his face with the powder, and with a hand steady or not, he poured it down the barrel held in front of him, its butt on the ground, followed by the bullet at the bottom of the cartridge. Next he extracted the ramrod from its groove under the rifle and rammed the bullet down the barrel with his right arm to form a tight seal. It was the right forearm so often raised in the air that accounted for the single largest number of wounds in this war. He then took a copper cap from his cap box and fitted it over the nipple of the breech and cocked his piece. Then he raised it to aim down primitive sights and fired. He could repeat this entire process two or even three times a minute, but all too often he fired high or wide or just kept on reloading without firing until his weapon was useless or exploded when finally fired. Green troops made these mistakes frequently but veterans were not immune. On the field of Gettysburg, thousands of rifles were recovered with multiple bullets rammed down their barrels.

Men would later say that it was Lundy's Lane all over again—the brutal toe-to-toe slugging match between a British regulars and Canadian militia on one hand and American regulars and militia on the other during the U.S. invasion of Ontario in the War of 1812. Claverack was just that sort of fight from which neither side would budge.[11]

The red battalions inched forward, and the Canadians lost much of their cohesion in the smoke for want of that instinct of men long accustomed to drilling, marching, and fighting in a formation. But it bespoke no loss of aggressiveness. Where the red and blue lines suddenly revealed themselves to each other at arm's length, bayonets and rifle butts stabbed and were swung in screaming blurs until the smoke closed in on them again. The innate stubbornness of the English-speaking fighting man was aroused and bloody-minded that day, locked in an endless frenzy made surreal by the cloaking, bitter smoke. It did not help that almost everyone on that field, save for the French Canadians, spoke the same language.

Although Hooker and Paulet were a study in contrasts, they both grasped the essential and decisive role of the commander in battle—the allocation of the reserve. Paulet felt the pressure to make this decision coming from two directions at the same time. His right-hand brigade had been half broken by the attack of Ireland's New York brigade, and now Geary's 2nd Brigade was attacking. The 15th Foot and a few surviving Canadian companies could not hold out long against the vengeful New York regiments who had tasted blood. If they went under, Geary's whole division would roll up Paulet's main line locked in its slugging match with the rest of Hooker's men. It was there across the creek that the main fight was frozen in stalemate. Only the commitment of the Guards in reserve could upset that bloody balance.

The two thousand Guardsmen stood silently in their ranks. They were big, powerful men, the very personification of regimental confidence, and afflicted with a large dose of arrogance. Anything but victory was incomprehensible, and they fully expected to be the ones to clinch it. Yet even these men could not be in two places at once. And that was Paulet's dilemma — shore up his right or throw the dice for a decisive win on the left and center. He was discovering another example of the barb in most military aphorisms, such as the commander's chief role in battle was the allocation of the reserve. The aphorism was simple; its practical application was something else.

It seemed to Wolseley that Paulet was taking entirely too long to make up his mind as the Borderers melted away, refusing to take a step backward to save themselves. The Borderers had been his father's regiment. As a child, he had come to revere it through his father's stories.[12] It was tearing at him to see it slowly dying, but he knew they could not hold forever, certainly not as long as Paulet was taking to make up his mind. "My Lord," he said. "May I suggest that the Scots Fusilier Guards would be most useful on the right at this moment."

A look of relief came over Paulet's face. "Very well, Wolseley. Would you be good enough to inform General Lindsay?" Paulet had suddenly realized the relief that comes when someone else makes the decision that has baffled you. It was also a way to get rid of Wolseley and his baleful eye. He would have elaborated on his instruction, but Wolseley was already galloping across the field to the Guards.

He found Maj. Gen. Sir James Lindsay conferring with his battalion commanders. They all nodded coolly to him. Pearson of the Dandies was a particular snob who had not let Wolseley's rising star in the Army caution his disdain. In happy contrast, the colonel of the Scots Fusiliers Guards, Lt. Col. William Scarlett, Lord Abinger, was pleased beyond measure at his orders. He had smarted badly over the loss of a company on the Cold Spring raid — an endless stream of salt rubbed into him by the fact that it had been at the hands of that Fenian rabble. He turned his horse and trotted over to his command. "The battalion will fix bayonets!"

The bagpipes skirled "Blue Bonnets Over the Border" as the Fusiliers advanced on line to the rescue of the Borderers. Wolseley rode with them and was glad to see that he did not have to encourage Lieutenant Colonel Scarlett to move out quickly.[13] The tension among the Fusiliers had been immense. They had had to watch their regiment's 2nd Battalion go off to glory in the Crimea. This would be their baptism by fire, as much as that of the Canadian militia battalions. But they were fighting men whose lineage went back to their establishment as the 3rd Foot Guards in 1661. They knew the consequence of taking the Queen's shilling. More important, the eyes of the regiment, alive and dead for two centuries, were on them. This was the test of who they were.

Ahead of them, the Borderers and Canadians had shrunk to a band around their colors as Geary committed his 2nd Brigade to relieve the Ireland's New Yorkers. Col. Charles Candy led his Ohio and Pennsylvania regiments to cross the creek and overwhelm the remnants of the Borderers. The fame of being the first American commander to take British colors in this war got the better of him. He was too intent on that shrunken band of Borderers to see doom marching through the drifting powder smoke or hear the keening of the pipes above the rattle of fire. Candy's men were just beginning to descend the embankment of the creek when the Fusiliers emerged from the apple trees on the other side. A sheet of flame from almost five hundred rifles shot over the creek, catching the Americans in disorder. The second rank fired. At that range, it was sheer slaughter. The Fusiliers did not stop to watch, but reloaded and fired again. Scarlett shouted, "The Fusiliers will advance!" The regiment leveled bayonets and stepped down into the smoky creek bed, water up to their calves. Only as they waded across did they discover what they had done. Bodies clogged the water, which ran red to pink, piled on each other, spilling down the gentle slope on the other side. The Fusiliers topped the slope and moved forward over more bodies and out of the smoke to see the survivors stumbling back the way they had come. The right was saved.[14]

STOTTVILLE, NEW YORK, 11:30 A.M., OCTOBER 28, 1863

Lt. Col. Otto Heraus sucked in his breath as the 2nd New York "Harris Light" Cavalry topped the hill overlooking Stottville from the north. It was rare sight—a burning town in the middle of a raging battle. Laid out below were the enemy reserve companies and two batteries of guns firing into the town. From the look of it, Meagher was not having things all his own way. Hooker had detached Heraus's regiment from Kilpatrick's 1st Brigade and given it to Meagher, "To help you on your way, Tom. I should have had the good sense to keep my cavalry close at Chancellorsville instead of sending them off on that fool's errand halfway to

Richmond. They should have been there to secure the roads through that damned jungle for my infantry."

Meagher had had the good sense to keep them close as well and not let them prance off into the distance where they would not be at hand. His last command to Heraus as he rushed off to the fight in the town was to circle around from the north. "See what mischief you can do. Use your own judgment, but get into this fight." And the 2nd New York was capable of no little mischief; they prided themselves for having kept General Stuart off the army's back at Gettysburg. Recruited from around Yaphank in Suffolk County, about fifty miles east of New York City, they were not Upstate men, but they felt the violation of New York nonetheless.

Heraus drew the regiment, all 347 men, in two lines and descended at a trot for the row of twelve enemy guns. It would be close work. It had been a war in which the saber had given way to the pistol and the carbine. But now it was cold steel time. At three hundred yards, the trot became a gallop. At one hundred yards, the sabers fell from shoulders to point as the men leaned forward in their saddles and their horses' hooves tore up the pasture grass. The British gunners had not noticed the approaching tide until they were within thirty yards, so intent were they on serving their guns.

By then it was too late. The New York men rode through them, hacking and stabbing at the blue-coated gunners who tried to fight them off with rammers and short swords. They discovered that trying to take guns away from the Royal Artillery was not a task for the faint of heart. The gunners had been trained to go after horses' legs with their thick, short swords, and horse after horse went down as the melee swirled around the guns and limbers. Heraus's men were switching to their Colt revolvers, deadly at such close range, dropping the gunners who clustered around their guns.

In the middle of this chaos, a Royal Artillery officer stood his ground, coolly picking off one cavalryman after another with his revolver. He turned, aimed at Heraus, and fired. The colonel felt the blow in his shoulder, and his bloody saber dropped from his hands. The officer looked at him and aimed once more. Heraus could only stare. Then a horseman rode by, and his glinting saber cut the officer from neck to collarbone in a flash. In ten minutes, it was all over. All the gunners were dead, wounded, prisoner, or fleeing across pasture and field.[15]

THE LONG BRIDGE, WASHINGTON, D.C., 11:30 AM, OCTOBER 28, 1863

"Mr. President, for the last time, I cannot fight this action and look out for you at the same time. If I must, sir, I will tie you up like a Christmas turkey and have you bodily carried away."

"All right, General Sharpe," Lincoln said, enjoying the picture of the chief executive in that state. "I will not add to your burdens. I will wait in the hotel over there. The one with all the holes in the side. Maybe the bar is open."

"And you," Sharpe said, turning to the guard detail, "Stay as close as ticks." His glare got them scurrying across the street, urging the bemused president along. There was a method to Lincoln's agreeableness. When he bent his head to enter the upstairs bedroom, he said, "Hello, boys, don't let me bother you," to the coffee mill gun crew. They rushed to upright a chair for him and dragged the bodies of the dead cavalrymen out into the hallway. Someone showed up from the kitchen with coffee. Lincoln pulled the chair up to the hole in the wall, as good a view of the dense Confederate column coming over the bridge as anyone had that day. He passed the coffeepot to the men on the gun, who gulped it down before passing it back to him.

He could clearly see the Confederate officer at the very head of the column on a black horse waving his sword. It would only be minutes now.

CLAVERACK, NEW YORK, 11:35 AM, OCTOBER 28, 1863

The drizzle stopped, and the wind picked up, blowing the smoke off the field. Now with clear targets again, the artillery on both sides began throwing metal across the field. As proficient as the American gunners were, the British Armstrongs that still worked were outshooting them in both speed and accuracy. The older Canadian muzzle-loaders were neither, but they were reliable and added to the hail of shot and shell landing amid the Americans. The Imperial batteries concentrated their fire first on the American batteries, and when they had silenced or driven off enough, turned their attention to the infantry. The American infantry had held their own against their British and Canadian cousins, but the artillery was like hammers that smashed great holes in their ranks.

William's twelve regiments averaged barely three hundred and seventy men apiece, smaller than even the Canadian battalions. It did not take a lot to deplete one of these units when the fighting was hard, and it was hard all up and down the line. Lines of bodies marked the firing lines of both sides across the beaten zone, but neither side had been able to build up enough infantry firepower to beat down the other anywhere along the line.

Hooker was everywhere on the field that day, throwing his small reserves anywhere the line needed to be strengthened. Gnawing on him was the question, "Where was Meagher?" He had had no word of him. Only the smoke from the burning town to the north gave even a hint. If the British had checked him there, it would have been Chancellorsville all over again. All he could do was fight the fight he was in. So he kept the regiments of Geary's remaining small brigade ready, commanded by Col. George A. Cobham, Jr., to relieve any hard-hit unit. One such was the 13th New Jersey, so badly cut up by the enemy's guns and those green-clad devils in front of them that it was commanded by the only re- maining officer on his feet, 1st Lt. Franklin Murphy, who clutched his left arm to his breast, nursing a nasty wound to the forearm.[16]

At this moment, chance threw its sword on the scales. Hooker sent two messengers galloping away with instructions: one for the 13th New Jersey to be relieved, the other for Cobham's 29th Pennsylvania to move right into place. The first was quicker than the second, and Murphy promptly pulled his men out without thought of whether their replace- ment was at hand. From the other side, it was as if a gap miraculously had appeared in the enemy line. Only seconds passed before the com- mand was given, "The Prince of Wales Regiment will advance!" Win- nowed almost as badly as the New Jersey regiment opposite, the premier battalion of the Canadian militia stepped over the bodies of their mates and across the beaten zone, bayonets leveled. Their colonel took the lead, shouting, "Come on, the Prince of Wales!" He broke into a run, his cap on his sword point, and the battalion followed in a scarlet flood. They jumped over the bodies of the New Jersey men who lay in the battle line where they had fallen.

Then the Canadians turned on the next American regiment in line and wrapped around its rear. The 97th Indiana just crumbled. Engaged in their front and fired on upon from the rear, many surrendered or simply fled. When the Canadians charged, the neighboring Rifles advanced as well. They beat back the opposing 2nd Massachusetts and 3rd Wisconsin. Soon the entire British line was attacking just as the American line had begun to come apart.

The sight of the advance amid American disarray sent a wave of elation through Paulet's command group. This was the moment he had been waiting for. He turned to one of his aides. "Captain Brown, please inform Sir James that he may send in the Grenadier Guards." Capt. Geoffrey Brown saluted with an elegance and style unusual in a big man. "Brown," Paulet added, "I wouldn't blame you if you went in with the Preston and his Dandies. The opportunity of a lifetime, eh?" Brown spurred his horse to where the Guards were waiting as another aide rode off to the artillery to concentrate on the Americans remaining in the center. Paulet liked "young Geoff," as he called him. The man had a saucy way and added a certain style to Paulet's staff. Paulet said to no one in particular as Brown rode off, "Bears an uncanny resemblance to Harry Flashman. A bold lot these Flashmans. Lucky, too."[17]

Hooker was finding being a corps commander harder than he remembered. And where the hell was Meagher? Williams's division was falling back in disorder with the enemy in close pursuit. Its center was yawning open, filling with men in rifle green and scarlet. Visions of Chancellorsville and Jackson's crushing blows loomed up before him. "Not again, not again," he said under his breath. "No, by God, not again!" Turning to an aide, he said, "Tell Kilpatrick to flank them and come in from the rear. I need his cavalry to take pressure off the center. Be quick, man. Ride!" The young lieutenant dashed off.

Hooker rode up to the three Pennsylvania regiments of Cobham's brigade, his last reserve on the field. They were small regiments by this stage of the war, barely one thousand men altogether. They had all served with Hooker at Chancellorsville; there was many an unforgiving opinion in their ranks that had come grudgingly around as he led them north. He stood up in his stirrups and took off his wide-brimmed black hat so that his blond hair was plain for all to see. "Pennsylvania, it is up to you! Forward!" The brigade stepped off with Hooker trotting to the front with Cobham beside him. They were advancing through the path of flight of the breaking regiments to their front. Men raced past in groups or individually. Many a man clutched a bleeding arm or shoulder or limped on a shot leg; many were helping the wounded off the field. A remnant, though—the steel core of broken regiments—retired backward, their faces to the enemy, stopping to fire and then back again to reload and fire once more.

The last of these men stopped just in front of Hooker to turn once more and shake his fist at the enemy. The ranks of the Pennsylvania men pushed past him and into the bullets of the Rifles. Here and there men pitched forward or tumbled backward. Shells burst among them, but they kept going, stopping only by regiments to fire and then start forward again. Men in rifle green now began to fall, adding to the Rifles' butcher's bill. They stood their ground and returned a steady and accurate fire. It was a rare man among the Rifles who could miss a mark at that range. The Peacemakers of the 16th Foot came up to join their firing line. Now it would be, in the Duke of Wellington's words, "a hard pounding, and we shall see who can pound the hardest." But the attack of Cobham's Pennsylvanians bought enough time for the regiments that had fallen back to reorder themselves and return to the fight, especially the New York men of the 107th and 150th Regiments.

Kilpatrick needed no time to reflect on Hooker's orders. He had been itching to get back into the fight ever since Hooker had arrived with XII Corps and ordered his division into reserve. He had already scouted the enemy flank and practically drooled at the opportunity of falling on it and driving through their guns and trains. The only thing he had to worry about was the Canadian cavalry, as few as they were, strung out on the flank, and a few train guards. They may have been pretty in their blue with yellow facings and brown busbys, but under Denison's influence they knew how to patrol an open flank. Beyond them, Denison's Royal Guides had been lurking behind Hooker's army. It was a pair of them that brought the first word of Kilpatrick's move. Before Kilpatrick got close enough to put his brigades on line, the Canadian scouts had brought the word of his advance.

Their ten troops had only been formed into squadrons for the invasion, and they had had barely two weeks to get used to each other, but they formed up well enough. Their two small squadrons did not even have four hundred men left after Custer had so roughly handled them earlier that morning, but they were still game. There was really not much else they could do except flee, but that was not much on the mind of

Lieutenant Colonel Denison, who was now in command. His scouts after had ridden up to Paulet's command group and made their report. Paulet chose not to comment on the fact that he had ordered Denison to pull his men into reserve. He seemed not to have noticed that the Royal Guides who formed his escort had shrunk to a dozen men. He simply acknowledged his mistake by asking Denison to take charge of the cavalry and hold up the Americans as long as he could. For a man who believed so much in the role of cavalry in the dismounted skirmishing role, it was a superb irony, he told himself, to be leading a good old-fashioned stirrup-to-stirrup affair against odds that made the Charge of the Light Brigade look like fair play.[18]

Paulet did more than send Denison off to lead a forlorn hope. He ordered two batteries to turn about and cover the rear and sent world to the 2nd Montreal Brigade to detach its reserve, the 4th Battalion, Chasseurs Canadien, to face about. To Sir James Lindsay, he sent the order to turn the Grenadier Guards about as well. The aides had barely galloped off when a dark tide appeared on the flank—twenty-five hundred cavalrymen in line of regiments approached, their guidons and battle flags whipping behind them as they trotted forward. Paulet now had done everything he could. He could only watch Denison's fine steed burn its way across the field to the Canadian cavalry.

At that moment, Captain Brown rode up, immensely relieved at his good luck that the Dandies had been recalled from their attack. But it was a case of "from the frying pan into the fire," for Paulet noticed him and said, "Brown, ride after Denison and tell him to strike them in the flank." For his part, Brown was not impressed with the order and had begun to turn a light shade of green under his thick sideburns as he saw the mass of American cavalry trotting toward the little Canadian band. Try as he might, no excuse would pop into his head, and he came to the awful conclusion that he might actually have to ride down into that. It only took a long, puzzled look from Paulet for him to make up his mind to actually obey his orders. Hopefully, he thought as he spurred his charger down the hill, something might turn up.

THE LONG BRIDGE, WASHINGTON, D.C., 11:40 AM, OCTOBER 28, 1863
Lincoln stared out the jagged hole in the wall, past the defenders, and down the Long Bridge to the column of men rushing across. He had

never seen Confederate battle flags so close, except as trophies. But in the hands of their bearers, the effect was entirely different. The Army of Northern Virginia, he had come to believe, was a pure embodiment of American valor in its own way — more the pity, for in this characteristic there was no North or South.

He could make out a man on a black horse at their head. Brave man. Why wasn't Sharpe firing, he wondered. They were halfway across. He found himself holding his breath. He glanced at the men with him. Each was similarly transfixed by the sight. Closer and closer they came, a glittering hedge of bayonets, held at left shoulder arms, and he could see the man and horse more clearly. His magnificent, spirited black seemed to dance as it trotted, the perfect match to the man who rode it. Brave horse, brave man.

Brig. Gen. John B. Gordon did not know he had such an exalted observer. If he had, he would have saluted with his sword, honor to honor. But now he had only time for the barricade visible at the bridge end and the sight of the half-finished Capitol dome on its hill. That dome meant the end of this unending river of blood. He turned back in his saddle and pointed with his sword, "Come on, Georgia! Home is just beyond that dome!" The men had caught the excitement of the moment as well. A roar rose up from the lead regiments.

They had given the command for their own ruin. At that moment, Sharpe shouted, "Fire!" The click-bang, click-bang, click-bang of the turning crank handles melted into a machine staccato as the eleven coffee mill guns poured their fire down the bridge.

CLAVERACK, NEW YORK, 12:05 AM, OCTOBER 28, 1863

Wolseley had never believed that the Grenadier Guards could move as fast as Preston led them to throw themselves across the army's rear in a double line. The Chasseurs Canadiens followed to link up on their right. But for all that speed, it was Denison's gallant band that gave them those extra minutes to get in line. That and the trains.

The sight of the enemy trains, hundreds of wagons strung out in the open along the road to Hudson, was too much for Kilpatrick to resist; he turned Davies's brigade on it. The commissaries, quartermasters, and Canadian train guards never had a chance. Saber and the .44 Colt pistol killed and killed as the cavalrymen hunted amid the wagons and limbers. Panicked teamsters whipped their horses to escape down the road but were shot or sabered out of their seats as their wagons careened on to crash into each other. Hundreds surrendered or fled down the road toward the bridge over the northern arm of Claverack Creek. A few ran south to run through the silent ranks of the Guards.

Paulet and his officers watched in shock as the cavalry swarmed the trains. Denison's cavalry had been too far away to intervene. But they were close enough for Denison to launch them in the path of Custer's Wolverines, who were coming forward in column of regiments—1st, 6th, and 7th Michigan, and 1st Vermont. It was three to one. From Paulet's staff came murmurs of, "Brave fellows," and "Good luck, Canada," from the British officers. The Canadians could not speak; their hearts were in their mouths.[19]

As obedient as horses are, they will not run into each other on purpose, but when hundreds of horses attempt to occupy the same space at a gallop, awful things happen.[20] Scores of animals, despite their frantic attempts to swerve, collided, throwing their riders into a kicking, flailing equine brawl as the Canadians and the leading 1st Michigan melted into each other. The fighting became hundreds of running duels as man sought out man with saber or pistol. Two such were Denison and Custer. The American, with his flowing blond hair and red bandana, drew the eye. Their sabers locked as they hacked, parried, and thrust at each other. Then the 6th Michigan crashed into the melee. The last two regiments swung wide on either side to come in behind.

Paulet and his staff watched in horror as the trap began to close. No one had paid attention to the lone rider dashing toward the fray, but seconds before the two wings of the American cavalry joined, that rider sped through the gap. Someone pointed him out by his scarlet jacket. "By God, it's young Geoff!" Paulet shouted. One American had raced ahead to intercept him, but Brown's charger rode him down. Then he disappeared into the swirling melee.

From Paulet's hill, the nickeled helmets of the Royal Guides disappeared from view one by one in the swirling mass of horses. Inside the chaos, the two commanders had been swept away from their duel by tide of the 6th Michigan. Three of the Wolverines closed on Denison. He thrust his saber into one man's throat and hacked the second out of his saddle, but the third drove his saber into Denison's side. He pulled it out to deliver the killing stroke as Denison sagged forward over his horse's neck. But the trooper screamed as his forearms flew off, slashed through by one of the last of the Royal Guides. Now the remaining four circled their wounded chief, fighting off attack after attack, like heroes on the plains of Troy defending a wounded chieftain. And one by one, they fell around him.[21]

From a distance, none of this was apparent. All eyes were on Brown's scarlet figure darting through the dark blue mass of the American cavalry. They were too far away to see that he artfully dodged through the enemy, who was startled to see a lone Englishman in their midst. It was a supreme demonstration of horsemanship that he managed to ride through so many of the enemy without coming within saber's length of a single one. Of course, he did not hear the cheering from Paulet and his staff, especially loud when he passed through the last of the Americans and galloped off into the woods. Thus, a new legend of the British Army was born—"The Ride of the Gallant Geoff," a poem to be written by Alfred Lord Tennyson himself and memorized by generations of British schoolboys.[22]

What Paulet could not see was the violent argument Davies and Custer were now having with Kilpatrick. They were opposed to continuing the attack on horseback against unbroken infantry. Kilpatrick finally ordered them back to their commands. After a few minutes, the mass of twenty-five hundred cavalry began to move forward at a trot. The artillery opened the show by sending shell to burst into them, but they might as well have been trying to stop a stampede. The cavalry picked up speed, the sound of their approach rising like the roar of an oncoming flood. In their path, the Grenadier Guards stood stock still, an example the Chasseurs did not quite attain.

Five hundred yards, and the Guards did not move; four hundred yards; three hundred yards, and still the Guards stood like statues. The ranks of the Chasseurs rippled with nervousness. At one hundred yards, the French broke with cries of "*Sauve qui peut!*" (Save yourselves!) and fled to the safety of the orchards to the rear. Preston sneered to an aide, "Now I'm sure that is the only time on a battlefield when that phrase has NOT been to Her Majesty's advantage." Fifty yards. Thirty. Twenty. Ten.

A sheet of flame flared from the Guards, and the first rank of horses and men collapsed in a bloody tangle of kicking hooves and mangled bodies. A second sheet of flame brought the next rank to ruin. The press of the rear ranks piled into the dead and dying, unable to get through or come to a complete stop. As the rattle of ramrods came from the second rank, the first had shouldered their muskets and aimed. "Fire!" Another volley struck the milling mass of horses and men. The noise of screaming horses and wounded men being trampled filled the minute between each volley. Custer blessed the Guardsman who shot Kilpatrick out of the saddle to end the folly.

ON THE ROAD BETWEEN STOTTVILLE AND HUDSON, NEW YORK, 12:20 AM, OCTOBER 28, 1863

Meagher pushed his corps south along the road to Hudson. It was only three miles from Stottville, but it might as well have been as far as Dublin as long as the British 2nd Division was willing to fight it out. The odds had been even, but only the loss of their artillery and the exhaustion of their ammunition had forced the redcoats to withdraw back up the rail line. The rumble of guns to the south drew Meagher on, riding up and down the ranks, imploring his men to keep up the pace. For the men, who should have been exhausted by the desperate fight they had just had, the sound of the guns was a magnet, and they needed little coaxing.

The column flowed to the crossroads between Hudson and Claverack and immediately intercepted survivors of the British train. Meagher sent one regiment with the prisoners to secure the town, and headed east with the main column, the 2nd New York Cavalry in the lead. They had barely ridden over the Claverack Creek Bridge when they ran into the detritus of Kilpatrick's charge. Custer, now in command of the wrecked cavalry division, met Meagher there.

"By God, I told that damned fool that we needed infantry. Or we should have dismounted to fight on foot and come through the orchards and woods. He wouldn't listen and had to have his glory. Damn him and his ambition."

Meagher leaned over to take Custer by the shoulder. "That milk is spilled, General. Get your men together to support me as I go in."[23]

THE LONG BRIDGE, WASHINGTON, D.C., 12:30 AM, OCTOBER 28, 1863

The Georgians never got beyond the point on the bridge where Gordon and his black went down. The bridge had been wide enough for two regiments, four men abreast. However, the bodies piled up to build a barricade of the dead and wounded as the coffee mill guns chattered away. The four cannons at the barricade fired solid shot through the packed, stationary mass, tearing hideous paths that spewed fountains of blood and body parts. All the while, the riflemen of the 120th fired diagonally from the riverbanks into the side of the column. The Confederates in front could not move back for the press on them from the rear. They just packed tighter as the bullets plunged into them.

Lincoln leaned over and lowered his head into his hands.

HOOKER'S HEADQUARTERS, OUTSIDE CLAVERACK, NEW YORK, 12:43 AM, OCTOBER 28, 1863

Hooker was more than desperate. XII Corps had been fought out and was barely holding on. He could hear the fighting from beyond Claverack and see the smoke, but he had no idea what it meant. Was it Kilpatrick or Meagher or both? His hopes had soared when the noise and smoke had risen in the British rear. Then those hopes had crashed when the noise died out and cheers had rippled up and down the enemy's ranks.

An aide tugged at his sleeve and pointed to the rear and the head of a small column double-timing down the road. He was startled to recognize the old-fashioned gray swallowtail coats, white trousers, and tall, black shakos that he had not worn since he had been commissioned in the Class of 1837. The sight triggered a flood of memories of his youth in the Corps, a time when the world was new and the future bright. For a moment, it almost seemed that he was a young man waiting in those ranks again.

An officer walked ahead. He stopped by some of the walking wounded on the road who pointed up to him. Hooker spurred his horse over and recognized Lieutenant Colonel Hardenburgh. The 20th had been part of the Army of the Potomac's provost guard when Hooker had been in command, and for that reason, its officers were much around headquarters. He was glad of a familiar and reliable face. Sharpe had wired Hooker in New York City that the 20th was on the way, but he never thought they would arrive in time. Hardenburgh reported that the 20th was behind them, slowed by enemy cavalry.

Hooker thanked him and rode over to the cadets, who were leaning on their rifles, a bit blown by their run through field, creek, and woods. The captain of the cadets, Garrett L. Lydecker, called them to attention. Tired or not, they snapped with credit to their reputation for smartness in drill, despite being spattered with mud and having sweat running down their faces from under their shakos. Hooker looked them over and said, "West Point, I shall need you today."

Whether he had anything more to say, the cadets were not to know because Captain McEntee rode up to report a sudden change. He pointed back toward the bridge. Out of the orchard on the other side, the head of another scarlet column emerged as skirmishers ran over the bridge to deploy. "General, they've got to be the Grenadier Guards. I'm convinced Paulet has committed his reserve. The prisoners we have taken say the Guards were in reserve."

Hooker's face darkened. "If that is the case, Captain, we are in worse trouble than it appears. The firing we heard in their rear behind the town has stopped. That can only mean Kilpatrick failed, or Meagher, or both, otherwise Paulet wouldn't be sending in the Guards." Hooker was right. After the cavalry division had been stopped cold by the Guards and retreated off the field, Paulet had turned the Guards right around to throw them at Hooker's weakened line. He knew this was his last chance to win the fight, and he needed a clear win. With his trains savaged, a draw was as bad as a defeat. He would have nowhere to go and no means to sustain himself unless he could make his way back to the river and depart by the boats that brought him.

Hooker was desperate. He had no reserves except the cadets. Williams's division was barely holding on, and Geary had had his hands full pulling Candy's brigade back together to put it back into the fight. Ireland's men were still fighting it out with the remnants of the enemy's Kingston Brigade and the Scots Fusilier Guards. Neither Hooker nor Paulet could pull a single man from that fight.

After the Scots Fusilier Guards had knocked Candy's brigade back on its ear, Scarlett had reinforced the survivors of the Kingston Brigade. Wolseley rode to the brave stand of the Borderers' colors and found himself the senior officer present. Not an officer above lieutenant was left standing in the half circle formed by the survivors. Concentric rings of bodies in scarlet showed the positions of the battalion as it had contracted inward from the attacks of Ireland's men. He took command, and no one argued. If he spared a split second's time to think that this was his father's regiment, he was not to remember. It was not much of a command by that point, but had it been only a handful, he would have done no different. There were scarcely four hundred of the original thousand Borderers, and not more than six hundred Canadians left of their three battalions.

Back on the left, the British artillery had picked up to prepare the way for the Guards. The knot of horsemen with the army and corps flags was an obvious target, and the shells began to burst nearby as the gunners sought the range. And find it they did, bursting a shell right above the cadets, spewing shards of jagged iron among them. Hooker turned to see the disordered ranks and the bodies strewn about, their gray and white uniforms blotched with blood. With a voice that had hardly even broken, a boy was screaming as his entrails spilled onto the ground. Another cadet was cradling him in his arms while others stood around, stunned and pale. The cadet captain pushed among them, and with a deft touch, hardly raising his voice, got them in order as an ambulance from the nearby field hospital rushed over. Many had fought at Cold Spring, but that had been an ambush. Here they saw their own blood. Better now than when he had to send them in. But right now they needed to get away from the blood and that poor boy. Hooker called out, "Hardenburgh! Take them into that apple orchard." He pointed to the trees two hundred yards back down Claverack Road. "Keep them under cover until I need you." He galloped off with his staff on his heels as shells burst just above where they had been.

It was clear to him that after the Guards crossed the bridge, they would take the small Pennsylvanian brigade in the flank, and that's all it would take. The Pennsylvanians had given their all to stop the advance of the Rifles and the rest of the 2nd Montreal Brigade cold. To be taken in the flank by almost one thousand Guardsmen would be too much.

The situation was just as clear to Paulet, who had crossed the bridge with his staff behind the Guards. Like Hooker he would place himself at the crisis of the battle. And like Hooker he knew how desperate the situation was. His right had nearly collapsed, center and left had been fought to a standstill, his small force of cavalry was wiped out, his trains had been savaged, and his 2nd Division had disappeared. It would have been a comfort to each had they known the other's plight. Hooker's appraisal would have been that his right and center had been fought out, his left repulsed, his cavalry defeated, his other corps missing, and reserves exhausted except for the few hundred cadets hiding in an apple orchard.

Those boys scrambled in among the trees only to find it full with a field hospital that groaned and shrieked with its work, artillery limbers, field kitchens, and a prison pen with a few dozen men in scarlet sitting dejected amid the discarded apples of the season's picking, whose ferment filled the orchard with its sweet, sour tang. The cadets had barely time to catch their breath and watch from among the trees as one of the great sights on any battlefield unfolded, the attack of the Grenadier Guards. For cadets who prided themselves on drill, watching the evolutions of the Guards as they formed for the attack on the Pennsylvanian brigade filled them with awe. The Guards were magnificent, keeping perfect alignment on their colors and seeming to shrug off the shells that spilled men from their ranks as the nearest American artillery battery concentrated on them. The ranks of big men effortlessly closed up and kept moving forward. In the rear of the battalion, its drummers banged out, under the stern eye of the drum major, a virtuoso performance of their regimental quick march, "The British Grenadiers," clearly audible to the cadets in the trees. So well known was the song that many Americans knew the words that had accompanied the building of the empire upon which the sun never set:

> Some talk of Alexander, and some of Hercules
> Of Hector and Lysander, and such great names as these.
> But of all the world's great heroes, there's none that can compare.
> With a tow, row, row, row, row, row, to the British Grenadiers.

Behind the Guards, the brigade's attached Armstrong battery raced across the bridge to deploy its guns in support. And the Grenadiers began to wheel from companies in column to a battalion front. And the drummers played:

> *Those heroes of antiquity ne'er saw a cannonball,*
> *Or knew the force of powder to slay their foes withal.*
> *But our brave boys do know it, and banish all their fears,*
> *Sing tow, row, row, row, row, row, for the British Grenadiers.*

The fighting nearest them seemed to come to a stop as first the Rifles, the Queen's Own Rifles, and the Scots of the 5th Royal Light Infantry of Montreal began to cheer. And the drummers played on:

> *Whene'er we are commanded to storm the palisades,*
> *Our leaders march with fusees, and we with hand grenades.*
> *We throw them from the glacis, about the enemies' ears.*
> *Sing tow, row, row, row, row, row, for the British Grenadiers.*

The Pennsylvanian brigade in its thinned ranks stared in dread silence to their left at the approaching spectacle. And the drummers played on:

> *And when the siege is over, we to the town repair.*
> *The townsmen cry, "Hurrah, boys, here comes a Grenadier!"*
> *Here come the Grenadiers, my boys, who know no doubts or fears!*
> *Then sing tow, row, row, row, row, row, for the British Grenadiers.*

An observer could not be faulted for thinking that the very weight of history itself was being raised to strike the American left. For on the royal colors of this regiment were names such as Tangier, Namur, Gibraltar, Blenheim, Oudenarde, Malplaquet, Dettington, Linselles, Egmont-op-Zee, Corunna, Barrossa, Nive, Peninusla, Waterloo. Yes, Waterloo, where they broke the Grenadiers of the French Old Guard and were renamed Grenadiers themselves, their cap badge a flaming bomb. And the drummers played on:

> *Then let us fill a bumper, and drink a health to those*
> *Who carry caps and pouches, and wear the loupèd clothes.*
> *May they and their commanders live happy all their years.*
> *With a tow, row, row, row, row, row, for the British Grenadiers.*

Fluttering above the center of the Guards were their colors—the scarlet silk royal colors with the crown embroidered in gold in its center, and the regimental colors, based on the Great Union flag, the marriage of the crosses of St. George of England and St. Andrew of Scotland. In the center vertical bar were the embroidered crown and unicorn, and on the horizontal bar on either side were the crowded names of all the fields upon which the Guards had fought—and won.

The mesmerized gaze of the cadets was broken as Hooker's white horse carried the general through the trees among them. He looked down at Hardenburgh and returned the salute of the cadet captain. He spurred his horse out of the orchard to look for a moment, then turned his horse halfway to them. Standing in his stirrups, he pointed to the enemy. "West Point, seize those colors!"

Hardenburgh's practiced eye counted barely a few hundred yards to those colors. There was no time to lose. He turned to see the boys had instinctively formed their ranks. Hardenburgh stepped out of the trees and drew his sword, Cadet Captain Lydecker behind him.

Across the field, Paulet was directly behind the Guards with Brigadier General Lindsay, watching the men swing left toward the Pennsylvanians' flank. An aide said, "My Lord, look there at the orchard. The enemy has emerged."

Paulet stopped to see the small band march forward in their old-fashioned uniforms and good order. He scanned their front with his glasses. "A waste. The Guards will march right over them. If Hooker thinks their fire will delay the Guards–" Then he leaned forward and squinted his eyes to focus them better. The enemy had gone from the march to the double-quick, then his bayonets at the level to a run. "Look, they are charging the Guards!"

Colonel Preston was just as surprised to see this small band racing toward his battalion. They were lucky to be one-third his number. He halted the battalion when the cadets were barely a hundred yards away. If the steady fire of the Guards could break a cavalry division's charge, it would wipe out these few. "Fire!" A volley sent the cadets' first ranks tumbling into the newly turned earth of the field. Hands reached down to pick up their colors before they struck the ground as the rest jumped over the bodies and swept on, converging on the British colors in the center of the line. Hardenburgh fell wounded among his boys, staring into the open gray eyes of the one who lay only inches from him.[24]

Cadet Lydecker was still on his feet, his athletic body glory in motion as the cadets followed him. At twenty yards, the second rank of the Guards fired. The first rank had loaded and was readying to fire again when out of the smoke the handful of survivors still led by their captain closed the last few feet. They met a fence of steel. British bayonet work was the terror of battlefields. But even the Guards could not kill them all, and their very momentum crashed through the two-man rank to the British colors. Lydecker parried with his sword the bayonet of the first-rank man and shot the second-rank man before he could be stabbed from the side. He was through with a handful of his cadets, the colors almost within reach. The color guards on either side moved in front of the color bearers. He shot one and lunged through the hole as the cadet behind him killed another. He could see the lines in the bearded face of the color bearer. The man's eyes had narrowed, and he did not flinch. The scarlet and gold silken folds of the colors were within reach. Lydecker brought up his sword, and the world went black.[25]

ALONG CLAVERACK CREEK, NEW YORK, 12.45 AM, OCTOBER 28, 1863

The subaltern of the Scots Fusilier Guards brought his horse to stop north of the creek. His jaw dropped as he saw the blue regiments coming down from the direction of Hudson with their colors whipping in the wind on a mile front. It was excusable if he completely forgot Lord Paulet's instructions to his colonel. He turned his horse and galloped back to where the Scots and the remnants of the Borderers and Canadians were fighting off Geary's renewed attack. He found Scarlett on the ground, surrounded by his staff as his life ebbed out through a gaping hole in his breast. It was suicide to be sitting on a horse as a well-aimed American bullet had just proved. The subaltern leaped off his own just before the animal screamed at the impact of a half dozen rounds. The close-range fire splintered the apple trees, their branches falling amid the dead and wounded. Groups of Americans rushed the line in a swirl of steel and clubbed rifles only to be driven back by the bayonet work of the Fusiliers.

Frantic to relay his warning to someone in authority, the subaltern stumbled into a one-eyed staff lieutenant colonel who was giving encouragement up and down the firing line. Bullets whizzed around the oblivious man. The line seemed to stiffen and its fire redoubled as he passed. The subaltern took him by the arm and shouted into his ear his warning—that and the fact that he was now senior officer on the field.

To disengage from an aggressive, able enemy is one of the most perilous of all maneuvers in war. Only the steadiest troops in the hands of the coolest commander can pull it off. But Wolseley was thinking several steps ahead of even this. He calculated that the enemy approaching from the direction of Hudson was Hooker's missing corps, and if the subaltern had judged the distance correctly, they would close on the rear of the army in short order. New York would consume its second British army in eighty-six years.[26] Wolseley was in no mood to tolerate any panic. When a French Canadian seeing the Fusilier Guards falling back by companies rushed by shouting, "*La Garde recule!*" (The Guard retreats!), Wolseley shot him dead on the spot.[27]

Colonel Ireland's tired New York regiments were the first to detect a lessening of fire on their front. What they could not see immediately was the retreat[28] by companies of the surviving Borderers and Canadians behind the shield of the Scots Fusilier Guards, who themselves were pulling back by alternate companies through the orchards. The Borderers and Canadians were filtering through the shattered and abandoned trains, filling their ammunition pouches and haversacks. Some were driving away wagons of ammunition. The Americans had come and gone so quickly through the trains that many of the wagons were still left with their unharmed teams in harness. The artillery was driving by section at a time, filling their limbers where they could. Wolseley had thought ahead of this as well. If men ever made haste, it was these men, exhausted as they were, for plainly visible in the shortening distance to the north were Meagher's men, fresh from their victory at Stottville. The Royal Artillery batteries supporting the fighting south of Claverack had also been warned by now and were turning their guns north.

None of this was apparent to Hooker, whose focus was the suicidal charge of the cadets. They had bought him minutes, seemingly for nothing—his reserves were exhausted. But the Guards' commander did not know that and was loath to leave the orchard open on his flank. Preston peeled off two companies from his support line to clean out the orchard. They would be in the trees in five minutes, seven or eight if Hooker was lucky. He turned to an aide, "Warn the hospital and get those prisoners on the road south. Then–"

He turned to look back. He heard the unmistakable sign of infantry on the double—the pounding feet, the rattle of equipment. Up through the trees rode a field officer. Behind trotted the infantry. Colonel Gates rode up, saluted. "General, the 20th New York State Militia has arrived. General Sharpe sends his compliments along with our new toys." He pointed to the coffee mill guns jolting by. "Where do you want us, General?"

Hooker slapped his hat against his leg. "By God, sir, I want you to stop them." He pointed to the mass of the Grenadier Guards wheeling to attack the Pennsylvanian brigade and its two companies coming directly at them. Gates's veterans uncoiled their column with the fluid grace of long practice. The companies left room for the coffee mill gun crews to wheel their weapons between the companies in three four-gun batteries. Hooker watched, fascinated by the strange guns. Sharpe had alerted him that they were something special, but he had expected little more than toys.

It was not toys that opened up when Gates gave the command. The tree line shot flame at the two Grenadier companies—250 riflemen and 12 coffee mill guns—the firepower of a brigade and more. Click-bang turned into a staccato scream. The scarlet ranks melted away. It was a massacre. Hooker gaped at the destruction.

The look on Paulet's face from the other side of the field was even more stunned. He did not have time to recover. His mounted party was too prominent a target and drew the fire of a coffee mill battery. The steady, level stream of bullets scythed through men and horses until only wounded animals thrashed on the ground amid the dead and wounded. Paulet and Lindsay were both dead. The Albany Field Force had been decapitated in thirty seconds.

But the Dandies marched on, oblivious to the slaughter of the generals. Preston rode directly behind the colors as the battalion wheeled past the orchard. The guns struck them in the flank and rear. The big Guardsmen crumpled or pitched forward, struck from behind. Preston and his horse went down as the guns converged on the scarlet colors. The color bearers and guard fell to the ground with no one left living near to pick up the fallen staffs. Fifty yards to the rear, the support line watched the destruction but continued marching. A subaltern and a pair of Grenadiers ran forward to retrieve the colors only to be shot to pieces themselves. Still, the support line marched forward into the fire of the guns, which had few targets left in what had been the main attack line. At last the line stopped on the command of the battalion major and attempted to turn front to return fire on the orchard. The major and the other officers fell as the line disintegrated in the fire of the guns.

Hooker was at Gates's side during all this. "Stubborn to the end, Gates. The Queen will mourn this day for sure, but by God, the woman will have nothing to be ashamed of." Not more than a hundred Grenadiers were left standing, but standing they were, returning fire until the guns swept the last of them to the ground. The dark, turned earth of the field was strewn with bright scarlet and the darker color of blood.[29]

A deadly stillness hung over the field. Both the nearby 1st Montreal Brigade and the Pennsylvanians had been witnesses to the destruction of the Grenadier Guards. The stillness was broken by a spontaneous cheer from the Americans, whose hats were sailing through the air. The cheer was taken up all along the line until it thundered louder than the guns. A shiver ran through the Imperial and Canadian battalions.

They would have done more than shiver had they also known that Meagher's XI Corps and the cavalry division were closing on their rear. For Wolseley, it was a race to get his battered command out of the way of that onrushing mass in dark blue without being slowed down by Geary's regiments close on his rear. He was puzzled for a moment, then hurried his men on faster when the guns to the north went silent and the noise of wild cheering took its place. He kept Geary's men off with sudden bayonet charges as he displaced his companies back. He was impressed with the sureness of the Fusiliers, who executed the difficult maneuver with quickness and skill even as the bullets and shells winnowed their ranks. As much as the moment filled his attention, he had thought to get the remnants of the Borderers and Canadians and the artillery into the protection of the village, which could be turned into a strong point behind which the army could retreat.

Meagher had anticipated him and sent Custer into the town first. His dismounted cavalrymen were waiting with their repeaters, more than eager to get even after their bloody repulse. They waited until the first battery was within a hundred yards. It was a target few had ever thought they would have—six guns, caissons, limbers, and over a hundred men in the dark blue of the Royal Artillery and as many horses crowding the road. The men riding the lead horses of the gun teams lashed their beasts forward. They rushed into a wall of lead. Horses crashed to the ground, dragging down the others in their traces, overturning vehicles and guns, spilling the riders until the column was a tangled, writhing mass of ruin. The infantry behind them stopped dead in its tracks, the men too tired and beaten up to push on. They went to earth where they could.

But Wolseley was guided by the ability to see at one glance what is vital, that greatest of military talents, the coup d'oeil. As the Fusiliers and batteries formed a rear guard, Wolseley kicked and prodded the Borderers and Canadians back to their feet and ordered another battery to fire on the town. He led the bayonet attack that drove Custer's men through the village streets and hedges.

He barely had time to lean on a fence and gasp for breath when an officer found him to report the destruction of the Grenadiers and the deaths of Paulet and Lindsay. The man could find no other senior officer after riding along the battle line across the creek. Just then he heard the crash of firing outside the town as Meagher's regiments closed on the Fusiliers. Over the creek, the firing also took up again as Williams's division went over into the attack. It seemed to Wolseley that death's head was grinning at him, savoring its joke—that he had acceded to his life's wish of command of an army in a desperate struggle only to surrender it. He looked at the death's head straight on with that single ice-blue eye and said, "Not today."[30]

FORT ALBANY, VIRGINIA, 12:33 PM, OCTOBER 28, 1863

From the fort's observation tower, Lee had no doubts that his long shot had failed. The carnage on Long Bridge had put paid to his daring coup de main against Washington. He buried that hope without another thought and turned to what he must do to save the army. He would have to move quickly to extricate Ewell's corps. Every courier from J. E. B. Stuart had been more and more insistent. Meade's army was getting closer and closer. He took barely a moment to once more gaze at Arlington House on its hill. He realized then that he and Mary would never see it again.

12

The Serpent's Eye

Hooker warmed his hands at the fireplace and then turned to let the fire's heat warm his backside, one of the great pleasures of a wintry day. He looked through the windows of his comfortable headquarters at the blizzard raging outside, the storm that had rung its white curtain down so unseasonably on the war. The Army of the Hudson was snugly quartered from Plattsburgh to Albany. He knew how to take care of his men, and they deserved it. It was their hard fighting that made him the hero of the nation and the darling of New York. He swirled a brandy in its glass, took a sip, and savored it. Mixed with fame, it was heady beyond measure. The sight of a petticoat thrown over a chair the previous night added just the right ingredient to the bouquet. Another reward of fame.[1]

His victory would later be immortalized in a famous painting—the meeting of Hooker and Meagher on the victorious field of Claverack where the two leaned over in their saddles to embrace as the Ulster Guard wildly waved the colors of the Grenadier Guards. Hooker would dine out on this victory for the rest of his life, and if it had been such a "close-run thing" as Waterloo, why, he would be careful to mention that to add to that fame. And, of course, that fame shone all the brighter when he praised his hard-bitten and gallant foe. His favorite story was about his visit to the field hospitals after nightfall when he encountered a number of wounded Grenadiers. He asked them why they had not immediately retreated when taken under such fire. One had replied promptly, "Why, sir, we are the Grenadier Guards."[2]

And that was only the truth. Their steadfast valor had ennobled his victory. It did chafe him that the survivors had escaped annihilation and fought their way clear in good order, despite the fact that their senior officers were dead or wounded. He took some wry satisfaction from remembering the observation from one of his history courses taught on the ancient Greeks at West Point by old Professor Mahan, "What the gods give with one hand, they take away with the other." Captain McEntee's interrogation of prisoners revealed that it had been a one-eyed colonel who had led the enemy off the field, warding off every attempt to snare the survivors. Night had closed off pursuit and saved the enemy. Hooker had known the Army of the Hudson was too savaged by the day's fighting to pursue even a kindergarten class. He was lucky to have half the men at hand that he had taken into battle that morning, and they were drained. Most had fallen asleep on their arms already. The clang of doom would not have stirred them.[3]

Hooker put his bloodied army on the road two days later. Fighting Joe's pursuit was quickened by the drumbeat of the newspapers cry for vengeance. He was their hero of the hour, Chancellorsville now conveniently forgotten. Wolseley had not cooperated and had made his speedy retreat between Lake Champlain and the Adirondacks, pulling the remaining Imperial troops out of Albany and picking up the Canadian militia companies that had been garrisoning each railroad station as he went. It was a masterful and heroic retreat, one that the British specialized in on occasion and wrung so much glory from. It would take its place with Sir John Moore's retreat to Corunna. Wolseley kept his force together, dodging and parrying Custer's cavalry and more than once fighting right through their blocking positions. Still, Custer delayed him enough at Plattsburgh for Hooker to come within a hair of bringing him to bay, but the Anglo-Irishman wiggled out of a decisive engagement and crossed the border into Lower Canada the next day and manned the fortifications there.

Hooker was too good a politician to let that stop him. He had to be the first American general to take the war to the enemy, yet his infantry was too weak to assault the British in their defenses. Instead, he sent Custer through the woods on logging trails to raise hell along the railway that ran between Richelieu and St. John. Wolseley was not spooked. He could smell the snow in the air. It was Custer who barely got his men out through the snowstorms.[4]

His back still to the delicious warmth of the fire, Hooker was doing some serious thinking about that one-eyed colonel who had snatched complete victory from him. He ordered McEntee to find out everything he could about him and was gratified to find out that Sharpe's interest in him was, if anything, greater. He had just finished reading Sharpe's report that had come in over the wire. That one-eyed lieutenant colonel was Garnet Wolseley, who had been jumped up to brigadier; the British have the great knack of finding heroes in the midst of their disasters. His name was on everyone's lips in London, a balm for defeat. There was also a list of those mentioned in dispatches. He would have to find out about the man who topped the list after Wolseley. Who was this fellow Brown?

HEADQUARTERS, HER MAJESTY'S FORCES IN NORTH AMERICA, MONTREAL, 9:10 AM, NOVEMBER 9, 1863

The St. Lawrence River flowed dull gray below them. From the height of the stone fortress built by Louis XIV to protect New France, Hope Grant and Wolseley looked down on the snow-blanketed slate roofs of Montreal, over the river, and to the south. In their minds' eyes, they were seeing Hooker's army in winter quarters. When the snow melted, Hooker would lead it north to Montreal. The American dream of conquering Canada now seemed all too real.

They would have to get past Grant and his violoncello first. Claverack had stunned Canada, and only Grant's triumph at Kennebunk had given them hope that the Stars and Stripes would not be flying from Halifax to Lake Superior by spring. Grant had been all energy from the moment of his arrival, not least in bracing up the Canadians for the terrible campaigns of 1864.

But then something of a miracle happened. The Canadian legislature voted vast sums for defense, called up the Sedentary Militia, and begged for more volunteers. Canada was born in the womb of such danger. A wave of intense feeling ran from one end of British North America to the other. Enough volunteers to fill every vacancy, and a hundred more battalions flooded in. War loans were oversubscribed twenty times. A soldier could not buy a drink. Even the French had come forward, realizing that the Crown's mild rule was infinitely preferable to that of Yankee conquerors.[5]

Wolseley commented on the last point, "We know how long that will last."

Grant drew his bow across his violoncello to test the instrument. He was worried how the cold might affect its tone, but clear, sweet notes scented the air, and he smiled. "Ah, you see, Joe, how well she plays. The army will play just as well in the spring. The battalions that are arriving will not be the last."

"But, sir–"

Grant waved his bow. "I am not worried. There is opportunity here. The key lies in your analysis of Hooker. I devoured your reports on the voyage over, Joe. First rate and the best preparation I've ever had before a campaign. The Crimea would have gone a damn sight better with such preparation."

"The key, sir?"

"Yes, Hooker is vainglorious and ambitious beyond a fault. From the American papers, he is riding as high as a balloon now, and I have no doubt it will go right to his head faster than sweet champagne on an empty stomach. I want him to come over the border on the first good day. A truly dangerous enemy would wait until he was ready.

"Now we shall make good use of the winter, mind you. The enthusiasm of the Canadians will be critical."

Wolseley said, "All fine and good, sir. The Canadians are in this to the knife. But Socrates put his finger on the problem. A collection of men is no more an army than a pile of building materials is a house. There's a limit to the training we can conduct in the winter, and Hooker will not give us a day of good weather before he's over the border and at our throats. The Americans will be pouring in from Detroit and Buffalo as well, and they will march up to relieve Portland again. Thank God fifty thousand Enfields arrived here earlier this year.

"Oh, I think the Canadians will be up to it. Now, gentlemen," he turned to the other three officers sitting with him, "Are we ready?" They bent to their instruments, and soon the delights of *Eine kleine Nachtmusik* wafted through the great stone hall.

PORT HUDSON, 8:45 AM, NOVEMBER 9, 1863

Franklin would have changed places without hesitation with Chamberlain, who was now shut up again in Fortress Portland. From the battery parapet, he could see the endless dark blue and red columns of French troops marching in from the east on Ponchatoula Road to join Taylor's Confederates already manning the old Union siege works. He was outnumbered at least four to one. His only trump was the Navy's Mississippi Squadron. In the weeks since he had brought his battered XIX Corps through the bayous and swamps from the Vermillionville disaster, he had done everything possible to put Port Hudson in a state to stand siege. The news filtered down from the north had been bad everywhere. No reinforcements. His orders were to hold with what he had. Crowding along the parapet was what gave him his greatest worry—one-third of his garrison, the black men of the Corps d'Afrique.

God knew he did not know what to make of them. He had to admit they maintained a sharp military bearing, and he found nothing to complain of in their guard duty or drill. What did take him aback was the intensity of their religious experience when their own preachers called them to God's work. It was a Sunday, and the power of their hymns thundered over the parapets and down across the fields.[6]

Bazaine was also thinking about black troops, his Sudanese battalion, as he rode with his escort surveying the defenses. The shame of their slaughter of prisoners at Vermillionville had stained the perfection of his victory. They must atone.

He raised his arm to halt the group and leaned over in the saddle to listen to the exotic rhythms pulsating from the fort. He asked what it was and was told by his Confederate escort that it was the black Union troops at church.

It occurred to him that there was a tidy solution to that little problem. It would be a very Gallic solution. Then he would take this place as he had stormed the Malakoff Heights in the Crimea. The emperor would deny him nothing.[7]

LOOKOUT CREEK, TENNESSEE, 7:45 PM, NOVEMBER 8, 1863

Longstreet sat his big sorrel on the banks of the creek as his veterans of Hood's and McClaw's divisions filed past in the early evening gloom. Bragg's "dramatic" removal from command left Jefferson Davis no choice. He recalled Longstreet from his expedition against Lexington and placed him in command of the Army of Tennessee. His arrival in camp was greeted with cheers that were heard down in besieged Chattanooga.

He knew his own army was as besieged as the Army of the Cumberland, nailed to the surrounding heights, now worse supplied than the Union troops below, with miserable shelter against this hard, early winter. Already the sick lists were enormous. It was not in James Longstreet's nature to see his army waste away from sickness. He would lose more men this way than in a battle. A battle was preferable, especially one that could end the siege with the enemy's capitulation.

That's why he was down by Lookout Creek. The great cloud-shrouded heights of Lookout Mountain towered above them as the men of his old corps massed for the blow that would shut up the enemy again, this time for good. A division of Sherman's corps faced them. Beyond their lines was Brown's Ferry, barely two miles away, across which life's blood flowed to the Army of the Cumberland. He was going to cut it and watch the enemy just bleed out.

His instrument, the most lethal offensive formation in North America, his mighty 1st Corps of the Army of Northern Virginia, would be his instrument of slaughter. Their ranks had been dreadfully thinned by Gettysburg and Chickamauga, but he had every faith in the hard, lean men filing past him now.

THE HOUSE OF COMMONS, LONDON, 2:30 PM, NOVEMBER 9, 1863

Disraeli sat on a green leather bench, the soul of calm, as the division of the House was announced. Parliament's method of voting had members counted as they came through one door signifying yea or another for nay, thus dividing.

The Liberal whips were as nervous as Disraeli was unmoved. Palmerston and Russell sitting opposite him appeared resigned to defeat. The clamor for their removal had shaken the pillars of the British establishment fast on the heels of the disaster at Claverack. Disraeli had done his subtle best to weaken those pillars in the public eye. Scandal had helped. Palmerston had had a randy reputation even into his old age. In the last few months, it has seemed he would be dragged into court over improper relations with a Mrs. Cane. "This prompted wags in the clubs of St. James to say of the septuagenarian Irish peer that, while she was certainly Cane, was he Able?"[8]

Now the entire Liberal political structure—Palmerston, Russell, Gladstone, and the rest—were pulled down by the weight of disaster, as if it were the temple whose house pillars had been snapped by a modern Samson. The analogy occurred to Disraeli, who relished its Old Testament ring.

The division was announced. Cheers thundered from the Tory and Radical benches. By a wide margin, the Liberals had lost a vote of confidence. Palmerston's ministry was dead. Now all that remained was for the queen to ask Disraeli to form a new government. He rose to speak. John Bright tried to catch his eye in this moment of their victory, but Disraeli looked away.

Men would later say it was his greatest speech. His once shrunken, used-up frame, his sharpened, wraith-like features, all seemed to melt away. Life flowed strong in him now, his black eyes glinted, and his movements were graceful, even elegant. His oiled hair shone, especially the curl so carefully draped over his forehead. He bowed slightly to the Speaker.

Bright's eyes glowed, then dimmed as he realized Disraeli was not giving the speech of peace. You could hear the drums roll in Disraeli's cadences as he called the nation to war for the Empire:

> I speak on this subject with confidence to the people of these isles because I know that they are men who are not ashamed of the empire which their ancestors created; because I know that they are not ashamed of the noblest of human sentiments, now decried by philosophers—the sentiment of patriotism; because I know they will not be beguiled into believing that that in maintaining their empire they may forfeit their liberties. One of the greatest of Romans, when asked what were his politics, replied, *Imperium et Libertas*. They would not make a bad program for a British Ministry. It is one from which Her Majesty's advisors will not shrink.[9]

> It is said that the working class of this country does not support this war and would be glad to end it under any conditions. I say that the working classes of England are proud of belonging to a great country, and wish to maintain its greatness—that they are proud of belonging to an imperial country and are resolved to maintain the Empire of England. I say with confidence that the great body of the working class of England utterly repudiate such sentiments. They have no sympathy with them. They are English to

the core. They repudiate such principles. They adhere to national principles. They are for maintaining the greatness of the Kingdom and the Empire, and they are proud of being subjects of our sovereign and members of such an empire. No Roman could have been prouder when he stated, "*Civis Romanus sum!*"[10]

Bright's self-control asserted itself. He coldly acknowledged Disraeli's mastery of the floor. He had severed the connection between freedom in America and the franchise at home and turned the issue into one of the bedrock patriotism of the working class and imperial glory. Disraeli's comparisons between the empire of Rome and that of Britain were brilliant in attaching the rest of British society to war. Such comparisons invariably resonated deeply with a country steeped in classical education. He could see the effect in the faces of the members hanging on Disraeli's every word:

> It has been said that the people of this country are deeply interested in the humanitarian considerations involved in the issue of slavery. All must appreciate such feelings. But I am mistaken if there be not a yet deeper sentiment on the part of the people of this country, one with which I cannot doubt the House will ever sympathize, and that is — the determination to maintain the Empire of England.[11]
>
> That sentiment forbids the surrender of any part of that empire, particularly one in which Her Majesty's subjects are so thickly settled. British North America is as much a jewel in the crown of empire as is India. We would not abandon the latter during the Great Mutiny. We will not abandon the former in this Great War.
>
> I will say to the nation that our aim is that embodied in the very name of our gracious sovereign — victory. We shall summon the might of this island race as our ancestors have in the past against the Armada and at Agincourt, Blenheim, Trafalgar, and Waterloo. We shall not fail history or posterity. Britannia shall be victorious.[12]

Once again Bright remembered a phrase of Disraeli's — "We are here for fame."

THE HOME OF CORNELIUS VANDERBILT, NEW YORK CITY, 9:22 PM, NOVEMBER 8, 1863

Ensign Nikolai Andreyevich Rimsky-Korsakov made love to the piano as his fingers danced across the keyboard. He was playing the "Intermezzo in Modo Classico" by his friend Modest Mussorgsky. The sensuous effect was not lost on the adoring young women in silk and crinoline who filled Vanderbilt's gilded music room.[13]

The performance of this good-looking young man with the short-cropped dark hair was a gift of the commander of the Russian squadron in New York Harbor, Rear Adm. Stefan Lisovsky, to his host, and most welcome it was. It would be the social event of the week. His audience also included the movers and shakers of New York society. Even Vanderbilt himself and his guest of honor had taken a break from their closeted meeting with the governor and both state senators to listen to him summon magic from the grand piano.

Half a world away, another piano's music had been silenced forever in an act of defenestration. In September, Polish revolutionaries in Warsaw had made an unsuccessful attempt on the life of the Russian military governor of Poland. Russian soldiers then sacked and burned the Zamoyski Palace for no other reason than their rage needed an object. As they rampaged through the grand old structure, they came across the piano of Frederick Chopin, who had once lived there. In a shower of broken glass, they had hurled it through a window to crash into the street below.

Now the street outside was the site of a gallows from which a dozen bodies swung in the cold wind that blew in from across the Russian steppes. On the gallows platform stood the Russian general commanding the suppression of the Polish Revolt, Mikhail Nikolayevich Muravyov. He personally fixed the noose on every Polish prisoner. Then Muravyov "the Hangman" stood back and grinned each time the trapdoor dropped.[14]

THE WHITE HOUSE, WASHINGTON, D.C., 10:30 AM, NOVEMBER 9, 1863

A month had passed since the dual victories at Washington and Claverack, with the belated news of Dahlgren's victory at Charleston making it a triple triumph of American arms. Vermillionville and Kennebunk were forgotten as a wave of elation surged through the North.

But Lincoln knew that Britannia's fist had only been warded off. Great Britain was still very much in the ring after this first round and doing much better than the victory celebrations warranted. That was the subject of Sharpe's formal report to the cabinet that morning. The report was something he called "National Strategic Estimate Number One." Much of what he said was known to his audience, but he tied it together into a coherent, seamless picture with a crisp objectivity that kept the studied attention of everyone at the table.[15]

Washington was half in ruins, many of its wounds concealed by the same blanket of snow that had shut down active operations along the Canadian border. The capital's role as the military logistics hub of the war had been broken. The premier arsenal of the Union was a ruin; the Navy Yard was hardly in better shape with its dry dock in ashes. The state of New York had been charred from Schenectady to Cold Spring. Its Upstate foundries and factories, as well as the arsenal at Watervliet, were heaps of rubble and ashes. Imports had ceased as the Royal Navy hovered off the coast.

For all the Navy's victory at Charleston, its blockade of the South had been shattered. The surviving ships of the North and South Atlantic Blockading Squadrons had poured into the safety of Norfolk, fighting their way past the Royal Navy's own blockaders with the monitors in the lead. It was only owing to the monitors that the Chesapeake Bay was not a British lake. But the Royal Navy had slammed the door to the sea shut on the U.S. Navy and the entire Eastern seaboard of the North as the heavy hand of its blockade settled in. Here the monitors were useless, for they dared not venture out into the heavy seas where the British watched. The Royal Navy was playing its trump. Where the balled fist had failed, the long, slow squeeze was far more dangerous. In past wars, it had strangled its opponents' commerce and confined their fleets to slow rust and rot in their ports through the inexorable pressure of blockade. And more than the U.S. Navy was shut up in its ports; the nation's merchant marine, the rival of Great Britain's, now swung idle at home, fled to neutral ports, or was hunted by the British and French navies off the oceans.

The South, now freed of its suffocating blockade, found its harbors from Wilmington to Savannah filled with British, French, and neutral ships gobbling up the three years of cotton harvest that was bursting from its warehouses. They brought in exchange a river of armaments and supplies that would banish tattered uniforms, bare feet, and empty haversacks from the Confederate armies. They also brought the iron rails and locomotives that would allow the South to begin rebuilding its worn-out rail system in order to bring its agricultural surplus to its armies. Britain's industrial base was ten times that of the North and could meet its own needs as well as the Confederacy's.

In the warm waters of the Gulf, there had been no victories to offset the bad news. The lightly armed West Gulf Blockading Squadron had been destroyed by the French off Galveston. The East Gulf squadron had fled into the safety of the Pensacola naval base. The French Navy now lurked off the mouth of the Mississippi. A pall had fallen over the cabinet room as Stanton announced the details of the French victory at Vermillionville. It was poor comfort that Bazaine's victory, coupled with that of the French Navy at Galveston, would create as much mortification in London as delight in Paris. What the first Napoleon had so fecklessly sold off, the third Napoleon seemed poised to snatch back. From Washington, the English and French seemed in firm alliance. It was an understandable conclusion at that point but one that failed to detect that the British had refused a formal alliance and were infinitely suspicious of French intentions. There was even less strategic coordination than with the Confederacy.

The effects of their reverses at Charleston, Washington, and Claverack, though, had caused London to be less fastidious about the French. The British cabinet had led the country to war on a wave of outrage over the Battle of Moelfre Bay, an outrage that had suppressed the natural sympathies for the Union held by significant parts of the British public and given full rein to the Confederate sympathies of the ruling and business classes. The unheard of reverses of British arms had stunned a nation that had come to assume that victory in battle was a national birthright. There were few voices that questioned the war. Yet they could be found and even at this early stage sought out—John Bright chief among them.

These doubts were only the faintest whispers drowned out by a nation and its empire that set themselves to the task ahead. Parliament voted vast sums for the war; factory, forge, shipyard, and recruiting station throbbed with energy and will of a great people at war. The British

Empire, like the Roman, was an implacable and relentless enemy. The Royal Navy's ships converged from every far-flung station of empire. Garrisons were stripped of their troops. Only India, where the embers of the Great Rebellion still glowed hot in British memory, was not asked for a single man. The garrisons of Ireland and Great Britain had been denuded for the twenty-thousand-man reinforcement under Maj. Gen. Hope Grant that by now had arrived in Canada. The militia and volunteers were being called up to fill their empty garrisons. So heavy was the volunteering that hardly a vacancy could be found in the militia, yeomanry, and volunteers.

There were even fewer doubts in the American North. It was worth a man's life now to voice Copperhead sentiments. He would be lucky to live long enough to be arrested by the authorities. The movement's blatant treason had damned it beyond redemption. Sherman had completed his march through the Midwest, stamping out the last few holdouts and was on his way to reinforce Grant at Chattanooga. He left the region under martial law, a measure Lincoln approved and showed no rush to lift. Too many dead men had littered the streets from Dayton to Chicago to trust the civil courts and state governments to resume the function they had so clearly failed to execute.

As soon as Lee had retreated from Washington, Lincoln had called Congress back into session, but it had taken weeks for that body to effectively reconvene. In that time, Lincoln ruled by presidential order and none too shyly. One problem that had simply evaporated was conscription. The draft was effectively suspended by the flood of volunteers who oversubscribed state conscription quotas three and four times. Prominent men who had stayed aloof from the war, such as New York aristocrat Theodore Roosevelt, Sr., now raised new regiments out of their own pockets and gladly accepted the commissions to command them. Another social barrier had also been breached by the war: enlistment of black regiments on the same pay scale as white units was implemented without opposition. With one stroke, Lincoln made available at least another two hundred thousand men for military service.

The disruption of the country's financial markets was only just being felt as the blockade hampered access to international loans and made U.S. Treasury bonds sink to their lowest rating ever. Cornelius Vanderbilt led a group of the wealthiest men in the country to offer the government a gift of fifty million dollars and a loan of a hundred million more at no interest, an act of patriotism that buoyed the shaken Treasury and banking system. With that example, the wealthy men of the North rushed to more than double Vanderbilt's gift; others underwrote the complete cost of warships. More than a few of these astute men of business recognized the opportunity to boost domestic war industries and expected a healthy return on their patriotism. Lincoln also set in motion statehood for the territory of Nevada, whose gushers of gold and silver were keeping the United States afloat. That the territory did not meet the minimal constitutional requirement of population was dismissed as a bagatelle.[16]

The war imports that had done so much to arm the new armies of the Union in the first year of the war had been severed at one blow. But the danger point had already passed in the summer. By then the Northern arsenals and factories were producing a steady flood of first-class weapons, from small arms to artillery. Four thousand tons of niter had been stockpiled from British and Chilean imports, guaranteeing the ability to fight for at least a year.[17]

Lincoln's problem now was to restrain the fury of the public and press demanding an immediate invasion of Canada. Headlines screamed, "On to Canada!" "Avenge Albany!" and "Remember Maine!" A blizzard had fallen from Wisconsin to Nova Scotia with such force that the first act of the war was over. That primal force of nature had had no noticeable effect on the press.

The siege of Portland had become the focus of the war for both the Americans and the British. For the Americans, it was the piece of Northern territory still under enemy occupation. For the British, it was the only place where British arms had not been driven from the field and the site of their only clear-cut victory. New York demanded the relief of Portland as much as London demanded its fall. For the British in North America, its capture was of the utmost strategic importance as well. Should they fail, they would lose the connecting railroad link between the Maritimes and the Canadas. It was through the ports of Maine that Hope Grant's reinforcements had poured. The status of the garrison and inhabitants of Portland were much on the mind of the cabinet.

Long faces lined the cabinet room table—with the exception of Lincoln who seemed remarkably unperturbed, a fact Stanton commented upon. "Now, gentlemen, it is I who should have the long face," Lincoln replied. "Mrs. Lincoln has insisted we go to the theater now that, as she put it, 'It would show confidence in our victories.' There you have it. A little confidence in our victories would do the country a good turn. And don't think I won't have to struggle to put on that good face tonight. Mrs. Lincoln is all atwitter over this young actor, Booth. All the ladies are, I gather. I would prefer to see his brother Edwin play in *Macbeth* or *Hamlet*. I guess I will have to settle for *The Marble Heart* tonight. I understand Edwin Booth's little brother plays the villain."[18]

But Stanton was determined to wear mourning and reminded Lincoln of the perilous state of Portland. "Why, you see," responded the president, "it reminds me of Mrs. Sallie Ward, a neighbor of mine who had a very large family. Occasionally one of her numerous progeny would be heard crying in some out-of-the-way place, upon which Mrs. Ward would exclaim, 'There's one of my children that isn't dead yet.'[19]

"Well, Portland is not dead yet, and I reckon that as long as Chamberlain commands, it will keep on wheezing along. I suggest you put your heads together to find a way to make sure Portland doesn't expire while you are wringing your hands. Why, Professor Lowe said to me yesterday that he could fly a thousand pounds of gunpowder into Portland a day, and it's gunpowder and not biscuit they need up there right now."

He winked slyly at Sharpe who had brought the idea to him from Lowe who was limping around the Navy Yard, trying to get his balloons repaired and new ones made. Lincoln had personally put the new shoulder straps with their stars on Lowe's uniform at the Yard the day before to the thunderous cheers of Yard workers, sailors, and Marines. The first man to sink warships from the air deserved no less. And even more important to Lowe than the star of a brigadier was the order signed by Lincoln for a hundred balloons and the sharp expansion of his corps.

Welles let Sharpe's conclusions sink home. His precious Navy had been dealt a strategic blow that could prove mortal if a way was not found to undo the logic of the British blockade. As if on cue, Welles proposed to Lincoln the establishment of a naval balloon corps. Lincoln surmised that Fox was behind it; most of the Navy's strategic and operational innovations found him an eager supporter. You did not have to hit the pugnacious Fox over the head for him to imagine the possibilities of aerial attack on the Royal Navy's blockaders. Then there was the gall that it had been the Army's Balloon Corps that had been so decisive in defeat of the enemy's naval descent on Washington. Thank God, he thought, a naval officer had gone up with Lowe. Welles had made sure that young Cushing had shared in Lowe's glory by jumping him up to the rank of captain and having Lincoln bestow the promotion at the same time as Lowe's.[20]

Matching the Army in promotions was simply not enough for Welles and Fox. It was brutally clear to them that despite the victory at Charleston, the Navy had been driven from the open sea and bottled up in its ports. The largest body of water it controlled, other than the Great Lakes, was the Chesapeake Bay and that none too securely. If the Navy didn't get back into the war in some dramatic fashion and soon, the war would be a replay of 1812 in which the Royal Navy ravaged the American coasts at will. Balloons had proved they could sink ships, and that was the Navy's job.[21]

Then Lincoln grew pensive. He stood up and waved his long arm across the wall map of the eastern United States and British North America. "Yes, new ideas. We need all the new ideas we can get. Try something. If it doesn't work, try something else. We must have an edge in this war, and it must come from the inventiveness and industry of our people. I've had young Carnegie putting his mind to how we can do better with these matters.

"But new ideas take time, and that is in short supply. In the spring, John Bull with little Napoleon will be on us in great force. We must get more time, and I can't think of a better way than setting fire to the Lion's tail in his own den."

He sat down again and leaned back in his chair. "You know, when a man's cookhouse and barn are on fire, he's got a lot less interest in bothering you. General Sharpe is looking into just how to do it for us. He thinks our Russian friends might be able to offer us a hand. We'll just let him work on it for a while before we talk it up anymore."

Seward laughed. "General, there's a heap of tinder in the Old World that is just begging for a match. Do your worst. And I guarantee that all those neutrals will pay attention. Our Russian friends would like us to keep our alliance close to the vest until the very last moment. They have their own plans for Europe that will set a lot of cookhouses and barns on fire."

Seward paused as if he were enjoying the taste of something. Then he added, "Let's also not forget we have as the president's guest His Royal Highness Prince Alfred. My sources tell me that Victoria is beside herself with anxiety but will not let on. Poor example that would be. I don't think the British have ever lost a royal prince, at least not since the Middle Ages. That issue alone has the courts of Europe all abuzz. It has been very positively received, even by the British press, that Prince Alfred is being nursed back to health in the White House by Mrs. Lincoln herself."

Lincoln smiled, "Well, his wound was just what Mrs. Lincoln needed. It was also what I needed. My poor wife had not recovered from the shock of a bomb being the main course at her breakfast followed by my 'altercation' with my late bodyguard. She just latched on to the idea of nursing Victoria's little boy like a life preserver. Snapped her right out of her funk it did. You will all be gratified to know that His Royal Highness is recovering from his wounds remarkably well."[22]

He added. "The royals appear to be a hardy bunch. Though from his abominable temper, lack of tact, sullen and brusque manner, Mrs. Lincoln is praying even harder than Victoria for his speedy recovery and even speedier departure. Most country people are better mannered, I must say. Why, I think that just to please Mrs. Lincoln, I will return him to his mother as soon as he's on his feet. It is a profitable day, gentlemen, when I can gratify my wife and annoy the enemy with one stroke. We will give back Prince Alfred and keep all the other British prisoners we have taken. Let Palmerston answer to the House how a royal prince escapes the cruel captivity his mother's subjects must endure."[23]

Stanton had remained uncharacteristically silent through most of the meeting. Sharpe had had the good sense to brief him thoroughly on his report beforehand so nothing would be a surprise. He was pleased that the War Department's interests had not been impinged, but then, they had not been exactly enhanced either. It was time to remember how the Army had saved the nation.

"Mr. President, I would like to add to Palmerston's problems. The Army has a little present for you that will surely cause the Prime Minister more difficult moments in the House." He signaled to one of the president's aides, who nodded and left the room. In a moment, the door opened wide to admit two color bearers carrying the torn and bloodied colors of the Grenadier Guards. They marched to the end of the room and dipped the colors. If Stanton hoped to please Lincoln, he failed. A look of pain crossed the president's face.

"Thank General Hooker for me; it is a most a handsome gift," he said almost perfunctorily. Then to the soldiers, he said, "Boys, just lean them in the corner by the window."

That was the signal for the meeting to come to an end. As the great men of the land moved to the door, young Tad rushed in past them, caught one look at the crimson and gold silk in the corner, and dashed over to it. He picked up the royal colors and ran shouting through the room. Stanton patted him on the head, glad to have pleased at least one Lincoln.

"General Sharpe," Lincoln said, "please stay a bit." He turned to Tad, who was making his third lap around the cabinet table. His hand snapped out and snatched the colors from the boy. He sat down and enfolded Tad with his other great arm. "Now, Tad, this is not a toy," he said gently. "Valiant and faithful men loved this flag and died for it. See the dark stains. That is their blood. It has made this a holy thing." He hugged the boy. "Now go lean it back up where you found it." Tad was used to being shamelessly indulged by his father, but even a spoiled child can sense when playtime is over. He propped it up against the frame of the nearest window and ran out to find some new mischief.

Lincoln just sat there, his large frame seeming to sink in on itself as he stared at the colors. There was a blanket of snow outside, but it was the sort of bright, clear day when the sky is so blue it hurts the eyes to look up. The light pulsed through the window and seemed to set the crimson flag on fire. The silk shone like a molten mist, and the light shining through it puddled a red glow on the carpet.

"General Sharpe, you see this thing, this object of military glory?"

"Yes, sir."

"Do you know what military glory is? It is 'that attractive rainbow, that rises in showers of blood—that serpent's eye, that charms to destroy.'[24] There I go, General, quoting myself again. I wrote that as a younger man when I was a congressman during the Mexican War. What I would have given to not have been so prescient." He stared a bit longer at the blood glow, his eyes gone blank. Sharpe had never seen him so withdrawn into himself, as if his body and mind had gone silent while a titanic struggle waged within for his soul.

Minutes passed as Sharpe waited silently with increasing unease. Then Lincoln was suddenly on his feet, his rangy frame radiating power and purpose. He seized the royal colors and pulled it out of the light. The serpent's eye suddenly faded away. It was now just ragged, stained crimson silk and gold thread. "We and the British will have our fill of this war long before it has had its fill of us. This war will girdle the world, Sharpe, with ropes of fire. This will be a war like no other, all kindled in the idea that one man can own another.

"Now we are at war with an empire that has fecklessly shackled itself to this evil idea, the very empire that first abolished the evil of slavery. Ask the average Briton if they should go to war for slavery, and he would recoil in disgust, but that is what they have done out of spite at our government of the people, by the people, and for the people. We are all gone mad. And we, who live and breathe freedom, have allied ourselves with the great autocrat, the 'czar of all the Russias,' who never saw a freedom he could not live without. Shame on us.

"Even the British mock the contradiction. Listen to this doggerel from *Punch*:

> Imperial son of Nicholas the Great
> We air in the same fix, I calculate,
> You with your Poles, with Southern rebels I,
> Who spurn my rule and my revenge defy."[25]

He turned to Sharpe. "Yes, this war will test us as nothing else before. I must tap this country's strength to the very bottom, Sharpe, as no free people have ever been tested since the Athenians gambled everything on their wooden walls against the great king's hordes.[26] In doing so, I will have to trample on the edges of freedom to save its substance. If we fail, the Constitution will not survive our fall. God help us."

He looked out the window bathed in the same sunlight that had fired the serpent's eye. He stood for a moment as the light washed around him like a great nimbus. Then Sharpe saw him bend his head and say, "Lord, abide with me."[27]

APPENDIX A

Order of Battle
at the Battle of Vermillionville
October 21st, 1863

Armée de Louisiane[1] (Franco-Confederate)
1st Division (6,500)
    1st Brigade
        1st *Régiment de Ligne*
        62nd *Régiment de Ligne*
        2nd Battalion *Infanterie Légère d'Afrique*
    2nd Brigade
        3rd *Régiment Zouave*
        7th *Battalion Chasseurs à Pied*
    Artillery (2 batteries)

2nd Division (6,800)
    1st Brigade
        7th *Régiment de Ligne*
        51st *Régiment de Ligne*
    2nd Brigade
        1st *Régiment Zouave*
        20th *Chasseurs à Pied*
        Tirailleurs Algériens (6 companies)
    Artillery (2 batteries)

3rd Division (5,900)
    1st Brigade
        95th *Régiment de Ligne*
        2nd *Régiment Zouave*

2nd Brigade
    18th Battalion *Chasseurs à Pied*
    1st *Régiment Étrangère*
    Sudanese Battalion
  Artillery (2 batteries)

Walker's Division (6,000)[2]
  Young's Brigade
    12th Texas Vol. Infantry
    13th Texas Vol. Infantry
    18th Texas Vol. Infantry
    22d Texas Vol. Infantry
    Halerman's Battery
  Randal's Brigade
    28th Texas Dismounted Cavalry
    11th Texas Vol. Infantry
    14th Texas Vol. Infantry
    Gould's Texas Infantry Battalion
  Flournoy's Brigade
    16th Texas Vol. Infantry
    16th Texas Dismounted Cavalry
    17th Texas Vol. Infantry
    19th Texas Vol. Infantry
    Edgar's Battery
  Polignac's Brigade (attached)
    Alexander's (Texas) Regiment
    Stevens's (Texas) Regiment
  Artillery (3 batteries)

Cavalry Division (1,900)
  1st Brigade
    5th Hussars (2 squadrons)
    Chasseurs d'Afrique (7 squadrons from 3 regiments)
  2nd Brigade
    6th Lancers (5 squadrons)
    12th Chasseurs à Cheval (4 squadrons)
  Harrison's Cavalry Brigade (attached) (900)

Green's Cavalry Division (2,500) (detached mission)
    Reserve Brigade (3,000)
        Zouaves of the Imperial Guard
        1st *Chasseurs à Pied*
        Guard artillery battery
    Artillery Reserve (3 batteries) (750)

Trains (4,000)

Total troops: 37,300
Total guns: 84

Department of the Gulf[3] (United States)
XIII Corps (16,200)
    1st Division (4,900)
        1st Brigade
            33rd Illinois
            99th Illinois
            8th Indiana
            18th Indiana
        2nd Brigade
            21st Iowa
            22nd Iowa
            23rd Iowa
            11th Wisconsin
        3rd Brigade
            49th Indiana
            69th Indiana
            7th Kentucky
            22nd Kentucky
            16th Ohio
            42nd Ohio
            120th Ohio
        Artillery (4 batteries)

    2nd Division (3,600)
        1st Brigade
            37th Illinois

     97th Illinois
     26th Indiana
     34th Iowa
     38th Iowa
   2nd Brigade
     94th Illinois
     19th Iowa
     20th Iowa
     13th Maine
     20th Wisconsin
  (3 batteries)

3rd Division (3,700)
   1st Brigade
     11th Indiana
     24th Indiana
     34th Indiana
     49th Indiana
     99th Wisconsin
   2nd Brigade
     47th Indiana
     24th Iowa
     28th Iowa
     56th Ohio
   Artillery (4 batteries)

4th Division (3,600)
   1st Brigade
     60th Indiana
     67th Indiana
     83rd Ohio
     96th Ohio
     23rd Wisconsin
   2nd Brigade
     77th Illinois
     97th Illinois
     130th Illinois

19th Kentucky
48th Ohio
Artillery (2 batteries)
Reserve Artillery (2 batteries) (400)

XIX Corps (9,000)

1st Division (5,800)
1st Brigade
30th Massachusetts
116th New York
161st New York
174th New York
2nd Brigade
12th Connecticut
75th New York
114th New York
160th New York
8th Vermont
Artillery (2 batteries)

3rd Division (3,000)
1st Brigade
110th New York
162nd New York
165th New York
173rd New York
2nd Brigade
14th Maine
26th Massachusetts
8th New Hampshire
133rd New York
Artillery (2 batteries)

Artillery Reserve (1 battery) (200)

Cavalry Division (3,300)
1st Brigade

> 118th Illinois
> 1st Louisiana (9 companies)
> 6th Missouri (7 companies)
> 14th New York (6 companies)

2nd Brigade

> 2nd Illinois (7 companies)
> 3rd Illinois (5 companies)
> 15th Illinois (1 company)
> 36th Illinois (1 company)
> 1st Indiana (1 company)
> 4th Indiana (1 company)

Not brigaded:

> 87th Illinois (infantry mounted)
> 16th Indiana (infantry mounted)
> 2nd Louisiana (infantry mounted)
> Artillery battery

Artillery Reserve (2 batteries) (400)

Trains (4,200)

Total Troops: 33,100
Total Guns: 102

APPENDIX B

Order of Battle
at the Battle of Kennebunk
October 25th, 1863

Portland Field Force (British)

Commander: Maj. Gen. Sir James Hope Grant
    Headquarters and Staff (75)

1st Division (7,900)
    1st Halifax Brigade[1]
        1/39th Foot
        Royal Canadian Regiment (detachment)
        Royal Newfoundland Company (detachment)
        52nd Bedford Battalion
        A Battery, 8th Brigade (Field)
    2nd Sherbrooke Brigade
        1/17th Foot
        53rd Sherbrooke Battalion
        54th Richmond Battalion
        55th Megantic Battalion
        1st Battery, 10th Brigade
    3rd Niagara Brigade
        1/63rd Foot
        56th Prescott Battalion
        57th Peterborough Battalion
        58th Compton Battalion
        6th Battery, 10th Brigade

Reserve: 1/62 Foot (450)

Military Train (1,065)
    3rd Battalion, Military Train (315)
    Canadian Military Train (500)
    Canadian Train Guards (250)
          5 Companies Canadian Militia Infantry

Total: 9,490
Guns: 18

Sixth Corps (US)

Commander: Maj. Gen. John Sedgwick
    Headquarters staff: 20
    1st Vermont Cavalry detachment (escort)

    1st Division (Wright) (6,200)
        1st Brigade (Torbert)
            1st New Jersey
            2nd New Jersey
            3rd New Jersey
            4th New Jersey
            15th New Jersey
        2nd Brigade (Bartlett)
            121st New York
            95th Pennsylvania
            96th Pennsylvania
        3rd Brigade (Russell)
            49th Pennsylvania
            119th Pennsylvania
            5th Wisconsin

    2nd Division (Howe) (4,500)
        2nd Brigade
            2nd Vermont
            3rd Vermont

           4th Vermont
           5th Vermont
           6th Vermont
     3rd Brigade
           43rd New York
           49th New York
           77th New York
           61st Pennsylvania

   3rd Division (Terry) (5,000)
     1st Brigade
           65th New York
           67th New York
           122nd New York
           23rd Pennsylvania
           82nd Pennsylvania
     2nd Brigade
           7th Massachusetts
           10th Massachusetts
           2nd Rhode Island
     3rd Brigade
           62nd New York
           93rd Pennsylvania
           98th Pennsylvania
           102nd Pennsylvania
           139th Pennsylvania

1st Cavalry Brigade (attached from 1st Division, Cavalry Corps) (1,200)
           8th Illinois
           12th Illinois
           3rd Indiana
           8th New York

Artillery (1,400)
           Massachusetts Light, 1st Battery (A)
           New York Light, 1st Battery
           New York Light, 3rd Battery

       1st Rhode Island Light, Battery C
       1st Rhode Island Light, Battery G
       5th United States, Battery F
       5th United States, Battery M

Trains (1,200)

Total: 19,520
Guns: 56

APPENDIX C

Order of Battle at the Battle of Claverack
October 28th, 1863

Hudson Field Force (British)

Commander: Maj. Gen. Frederick Lord Paulet
Headquarters and Staff (100)
The Royal Guides or the Governor General's Bodyguard (55)

1st Division (8,000)
    1st Montreal Brigade
        1/Rifle Brigade
        1st Battalion Prince of Wales Regt.
        2nd Battalion Queen's Own Rifles
        3rd Battalion Victoria Volunteers Rifles of Montreal
        G Battery, 4th Brigade (Field)
    2nd Montreal Brigade
        1/16th Foot
        4th Battalion *Chasseurs Canadiens*
        5th Battalion Royal Lieutenant Infantry Of Montreal
        6th Battalion Hochlega Lieutenant Infantry
        E Battery, 4th Brigade (Field)
    3rd Niagara Brigade
        1/25th Foot (King's Own Scottish Borderers)
        10th Battalion Volunteers Infantry
        18th Battalion Volunteers Infantry
        19th Battalion Volunteers Infantry
        H Battery, 4th Brigade (Field)

2nd Division (8,000)
  1st Kingston Brigade
    1/15 Foot
    14th Battalion Volunteers Infantry
    15th Battalion Volunteers Infantry
    16th Battalion Volunteers Infantry
    F Battery, 4th Brigade (Field)
  2nd St. John's Brigade
    1/30th Foot
    17th Levis Battalion Volunteers Infantry
    20th Battalion of Volunteers Infantry
    21st Battalion Richlieu Lieutenant Infantry
    D Battery, 4th Brigade (Field)
  3rd Hamilton Brigade
    1/47th Foot
    11th Battalion Volunteers Infantry
    12th Battalion Volunteers Infantry
    13th Battalion Volunteers Infantry
    8th Battery, 10th Brigade (Garrison)

Guards Brigade (2,125)
  1/Grenadier Guards
  2/Scots Fusilier Guards
  2nd Battery, 10th Brigade

Canadian Cavalry Brigade (600)
  1st Squadron (Upper Canada)
    1st Volunteer Militia Troop of the County of Wentworth
    2nd Volunteer Militia Troop of the County of Wentworth
    The Essex Volunteer Militia Troop of Cavalry
    1st Volunteer Militia Troop of Cavalry of Williamsburg
    1st Troop of Volunteer Militia Cavalry of the County of Leeds
    1st Volunteer Militia Troop of Cavalry of Guelph
    2nd Troop of Volunteer Militia Cavalry of the County of
    Northumberland
  2nd Squadron (Lower Canada)
    3rd Troop of Volunteer Militia Cavalry of Quebec

2nd Troop of Volunteer Cavalry of the County of Argeneuil
1st Troop of Volunteer Cavalry of the County of Laval
1st Troop of Volunteer Militia Cavalry of Laval
The St. Johns Volunteer Militia Troop of Cavalry

Artillery Brigade (1,125)
  1st Battalion
    3rd, 4th, Batteries, 7th Brigade (Heavy)
    3rd Battery, 10th Brigade
    1st, 2nd, Batteries, Battalion of Montreal Artillery
  2nd Battalion
    5th, 6th Batteries, 7th Brigade (Heavy)
    3rd, 4th Batteries, Battalion of Montreal Artillery

Engineer Battalion (500)
  4th Company, Royal Engineers
  15th Company, Royal Engineers
  Company of Canadian Volunteer Militia Engineers
  Company of Canadian Volunteer Militia Engineers

Trains (1,315)
  1st Battalion, Military Train (315)
  Canadian Military Train (500)
  Canadian Train Guards (500)
  10 Companies Canadian Militia Infantry

Total: 21,821
  British: 47%
  Canadian: 53%

Guns: 90

Army of the Hudson (American)

Commander: Maj. Gen. Joseph Hooker
Staff: (7)

XI Corps (Maj. Gen. Thomas F. Meagher)[1]
Staff: (53)
Independent Co., 8th New York (50)

    2nd Division (Maj. Gen. Adolph von Steinwehr) (2,764)
        1st Brigade (Col. Adolphus Buschbeck)
            33rd New Jersey
            134th New York
            154th New York
            27th Pennsylvania
            73rd Pennsylvania
        2nd Brigade (Col. Orlando Smith)
            33rd Massachusetts
            136th New York
            55th Ohio
            73rd Ohio
    3rd Division (Maj. Gen. Carl Schurz) (3,326)
        1st Brigade (Brig. Gen. Hector Tyndale)
            101st Illinois
            45th New York
            143rd New York
            61st Ohio
            82nd Ohio
        2nd Brigade (Col. Wladimir Krzysanowski)
            58th New York
            119th New York
            141st New York
            26th Wisconsin
        3rd Brigade (Col. Frederick Hecker)
            80th Illinois
            82nd Illinois
            68th New York
            75th Pennsylvania

    Corps Artillery (Maj. Thomas W. Osborn) (546)
        1st New York Light, Battery I
        New York Light, 13th Battery

1st Ohio Light, Battery I
1st Ohio Light, Battery K
4th United States, Battery G

XI Corps Total: 6,739

XII Corps (Maj. Gen. Henry Slocum)[2]
Staff: 159

    1st Division (Brig. Gen. Alpheus S. Williams) (4,565)
      1st Brigade (Brig. Gen. Joseph F. Knipe)
          5th Connecticut
          20th Connecticut
          3rd Maryland
          123rd New York
          145th New York
          46th Pennsylvania
      2nd Brigade (Brig. Gen. Thomas H. Ruger)
          27th Indiana
          2nd Massachusetts
          13th New Jersey
          107th New York
          150th New York
          3rd Wisconsin

    2nd Division (Brig. Gen. John W. Geary) (4,113)
      1st Brigade (Col. Charles Candy)
          5th Ohio
          7th Ohio
          29th Ohio
          66th Ohio
          28th Pennsylvania
          147th Pennsylvania
      2nd Brigade (Col. George A. Cobham, Jr.)
          29th Pennsylvania
          109th Pennsylvania
          111th Pennsylvania

3rd Brigade (Col. David Ireland)
      60th New York
      78th New York
      102nd New York
      137th New York
      149th New York

Corps Artilllery (Maj. John A. Reynolds) (354)
      1st New York Light, Battery M
      Pennsylvania Light, Battery E
      4th United States, Battery F
      5th United States, Battery K

XII Corps Total: 9,191

Reserves (600)
      120th New York (350)
      U.S. Military Academy Corps of Cadets (250)

3rd Cavalry Division (Brig. Gen. Judson Kilpatrick) (3,000)[3]
      1st Cavalry Brigade (Brig. Gen. Henry E. Davies, Jr.)
            2nd New York
            5th New York
            18th Pennsylvania
            1st West Virginia
            2nd United States Battery M
      2nd Cavalry Brigade "The Wolverines" (Brig. Gen. George A. Custer)
            1st Michigan
            5th Michigan
            6th Michigan
            7th Michigan
            1st Vermont
            New York Light, 6th Battery

Artillery Reserve (1st Volunteer Brigade) (Lt. Col. Freeman McGilvery) (430)[4]

Massachusetts Light, 9th Battery
New York Light, 4th Battery
Pennsylvania Light, Batteries C and F

Army of the Hudson Total: 19,967
Guns: 84

NOTES

INTRODUCTION

1. "History of Fort McNair," http://www.fmmc.army.mil/sites/about/history-mcnair.asp. Fort McNair now occupies the site of the Washington Arsenal, built 1803.

CHAPTER ONE: HANGING BILLY

1. *William Tecumseh Sherman, "The Liberation of Chicago," *Combat and Commanders of the Civil War*, vol. 3 (New York: The Century Company, 1885), 32–35.
2. Edwin C. Fishel, *The Secret War for the Union: The Untold Story of Military Intelligence in the Civil War* (Boston: Houghton Mifflin Company, 1996), 84. These were men of the 3rd Indiana Cavalry, Cline's own regiment, known for their skill in intelligence special operations mission. In 1862 they had earned the nickname of Hooker's Horse Marines for capturing a Confederate sloop.
3. *James W. Collier, *The White Terror* (Indianapolis: Hoosier Press, 1922), 202–10. Careful research by Collier showed that at least 8,200 men were summarily executed in the Loyalist reaction to Copperhead atrocities during the rising. Of these, over 2,500 were killed in Chicago and were not part of the military executions ordered by Sherman. The true number can never be known. Collier cites James Beard's study in *The Atlantic Monthly*, estimating the Copperheads had executed over 4,000 men in the few weeks of the uprising.
4. *Ulysses S. Grant, "Saving the Army of the Cumberland," *Combat and Commanders of the Civil War*, vol. 3 (New York: The Century Company, 1885), 293–95.
5. *Arthur Evans, *With Grant at Chattanooga: An Aide-de-Camp's Memoir* (New York: Charles L. Webster, 1880), 111.
6. Julia Keller, *Mr. Gatling's Terrible Marvel: The Gun That Changed Everything and the Misunderstood Genius Who Invented It* (New York: Viking, 2008), 95.
7. *Gatling's Guns and the Copperhead Mob," *New York Tribune*, October 25, 1863.

8. *John A. Dahlgren, "Official Report of the Battle of Charleston," February 13, 1864, National Archives. British losses included *Black Prince, St. George, Donegal, Shannon, Phaeton, Racoon,* and *Desperate,* which were sunk. *Sans Pareil, Melponeme, Ariadne,* and *Cadmus* were struck. The surviving ships, most of which were badly damaged, escaped. Of the ships that escaped, *Challenger* could not be saved and sank halfway to Bermuda. The Royal Navy lost twelve of the nineteen ships Sir Michael Seymour had led into action. The senior officer of the surviving ships was so anxious to seek the safety of Bermuda's naval base that he failed to dispatch one of his ships to take word of the defeat directly to Milne. That oversight allowed the American ships to slip into Norfolk without significant opposition.

9. *Dahlgren, "Official Report." U.S. Navy casualties were 250 dead, 32 missing, and 310 wounded. All but three of the 110 men on *Atlanta* were lost.

10. *Aaron C. Davis, *Sinking the* Black Prince: *First Victory of the Submersible Service* (New York: Webster, 2004), 211.

11. *Stephen Clegg Rowan, *With Dahlgren at Charleston: The Memoirs of the Captain of the USS* New Ironsides (New York: Webster, 1870), 276–77.

12. *Dahlgren, "Official Report." The British ships lost at the Battle of the Bar were crewed by over slightly over 5,000 men. Of these men, 3,870 were found alive with 1,397 wounded. HMS *Shannon* went down with almost her entire compliment of 560 men. The following are losses for each ship:

	Dead	Missing	Wounded POWs	Unwounded POWs
Black Prince	142	11	187	365
St. George	129	18	277	406
Donegal	101	12	238	679
San Pareil	122	9	256	239
Shannon	533	7	—	—
Phaeton	87	211	227	—
Ariadne	72	20	136	297
Racoon	47	5	36	152
Desperate	20	—	49	101
Totals	**1,253**	**293**	**1,406**	**2,239**

13. *Roger C. Atwith, *The Fighting Dahlgrens: Father and Son in the Civil War and Great War* (New York: Sheldon Publishers, 1899), 122–23.

14. Laird Brothers Shipbuilders were completing two double-turreted, armored ironclads, CSS *North Carolina* and CSS *Mississipp,i* for the Confederate agent in Britain, James Bulloch. They were the first turreted ironclads built in Britain, but their most notable feature was a steel ram, an odd mix of the ancient and modern.

15. George Macaulay Tevelyan, *The Life of John Bright* (Boston: Houghton Mifflin, 1913), 309.

16. Steve Sherman, "Karl Marx, Journalist: An Interview with Jim Ledbetter," *MSZine*, November, 1, 2008. *The People's Paper* was a supporter of

the Charterist Movement in Britain. However, Marx's chief source of income, aside from gifts from his friend Friedrich Engels, was the hundreds of articles he wrote as a foreign correspondent for the *New York Herald*. The editor of the *Herald*, Charles Dana, had met Marx in Germany and recruited him, and he had become one its most prolific contributors. Dana by this time had resigned from the paper and had become U.S. assistant secretary of war.

17. *National Intelligencer*, September 9, 1861; Albert A. Woldman, *Lincoln and the Russians* (Cleveland: The World Publishing Company, 1952), 129.

18. *Baron Edouard de Stoeckl, *Memoirs of Baron Stoeckl* (Boston: McNeal Publishers, 1893), 88–90.

19. *Woodrow Wilson, *The Russo-American Alliance in the Great War* (New York: D. Appleton, 1905) 115–118. Wilson relied heavily on notes of the meeting taken by John Hay, one of Lincoln's two secretaries. There were no substantial disagreements with the accounts of this meeting by Stoeckl and Hay.

20. Edwin C. Fishel, *The Secret War for the Union: The Untold Story of Military Intelligence in the Civil War* (Boston: Houghton Mifflin Company, 1996), 257–59, 303–302, 375–77.

21. *Alexander C. Rutledge, *Spymaster of the Republic: The Life of George H. Sharpe* (New York: Excelsior Press, 1934), 288.

22. *Thaddaeus Lowe, *Army Aeronautics in the Great War* (New York: The Century Company, 1878), 38. *Charles Dana, *Present at the Creation: A Memoir of George H. Sharpe* (Philadelphia: J.B. Lippincott, 1892), 125.

23. Anthony Gross, ed., *The Wit and Wisdom of Abraham Lincoln: The Best Stories by and about America's Most Beloved President* (New York: Barnes & Noble, 1994), 220.

24. "The Manifest Destiny of America and Russia," *New York Herald*, August 31, 1863.

25. *Sharpe, *Conversations with Abraham Lincoln, 1863–1868* (Philadelphia: L. B. Lippincott, 1886), 203–206.

26. The three joined fingers are to remind the believer of the Holy Trinity and the two folded fingers of the human and divine natures of Christ. Orthodox Christians cross themselves from right to left, while Catholics cross themselves from left to right.

27. *Ivan Dolgoruky, *The Great Tsar: Alexander II and the Great War* (New York: Beale Publishing, 1882), 102. Present on this occasion were Alexander's three older sons, Nicholas (19), Alexander (18), and Vladimir (16). All three would see active service in World War I and each would later state that this scene was the defining moment of their lives.

CHAPTER TWO: *LE BAL*

1. René Chartrand and Richard Hook, *The Mexican Adventure 1861–67* (London: Osprey Publishing, 1994), 18–19.

2. Stephen Shann and Louis Delperier, *French Army 1870–71 Franco-Prussian War (1)* (London: Osprey Publishing, 1991), 13, 44–47. The Zouaves had

been formed in 1830 from the Zougha tribe but by 1842 had been thoroughly Europeanized.

3. Bruce Bassett-Powell, *Maurice Toussaints Imperial Guard of Napoleon III* 3 (Waterford, TX: Uniformology, 2006) 3.

4. Shann and Delperier, *French Army*, 38.

5. Steve Wilson, *"We May Die, but Never Will Surrender" – The Battle of Cameron*, htpp://www.military.com/NewContent/0,13190,Wilson_022805-P1.html.

6. Chartrand, *The Mexican Adventure*, 19. Shann, *French Army*, 13.

7. Richard L. Hill and Peter C. Hogg, *A Black Corps d'Élite: An Egyptian Sudanese Conscript Battalion with the French Army in Mexico, 1863–1867, and Its Survivors in Subsequent African History* (East Lansing: Michigan State University Press, 1995).

8. *Emile DuPont, *The Prince de Polignac: Hero of Vermillionville* (New Orleans: Crescent City Press, 1890), 32–33.

9. *Richard Taylor, *Destruction and Reconstruction: Personal Experiences in the Civil War* (New York: Da Capo, 1995), 154.

10. The battle of Galveston on October 4, 1862, was as uneven a naval engagement as history has shown. The French squadron consisted of several of the French broadside ironclads of the Gloire class as well as ships-of-the line and frigates. The ships of the Union West Gulf Blockading Squadron were all lightly armed converted merchantmen. Nevertheless, the victory allowed Paris the immense satisfaction of comparing their overwhelming naval victory over the American "Anglo-Saxons" to the crushing British defeat at Charleston. The British did not know what stung worse—losing to the Americans or listening to the French cock crow over it. It put a great strain on the Anglo-French alliance of convenience. *Walter Davenport, *The Anglo-French Alliance in the Great War* (Boston: Brown & Brown Publishers, 1895), 43–47.

11. Bazaine had initially crossed into Texas at the beginning of the month at Brownsville as an immediate demonstration of French support to the Confederacy. The French naval victory in the Battle of Galveston had allowed his force to be quickly embarked and transported to Galveston, which was a short march of a little over a hundred miles to his rendezvous with Taylor. He had been advised that if you march through Texas, you simply never arrive, the distances were so great. Richard Taylor, *Destruction and Reconstruction: Personal Experiences of the Civil War* (New York: D. Appleton, 1879), 14–144.

12. *Official Records of the War of the Rebellion*, vol. 26, part 1 (Washington: Government Printing Office, 1880), 783.

13. Peter G. Tsouras, *Britannia's Fist: From Civil War to World War* (Washington: Potomac Books, 2008), 43.

14. Ian Sumner, *British Colours & Standards 1847–1881 (2)* (London: Osprey Publishing Ltd, 2001), 3, 10–11. The royal colors were not called the queen's (or later the king's) colors until 1892.

15. Philip Katcher, *American Civil War Armies 2: Union Troops* (London: Osprey Publishing, 1986) plates C & D, 45–46. Russ A. Pritchard, Jr. *The Irish Brigade: A Pictorial History of the Famed Civil War Fighters* (Philadelphia: Courage Books, 2004), 36–39.

16. "National Character of the Scottish Regiments," originally published in 1862, cited in http://www.btinternet.com/~james.mckay/account7htm

17. "The Gun: Rifled Ordnance—Armstrong," Royal New Zealand Artillery Old Comrades' Association, http://riv.co.nz/rnza/hist/gun/rifled3.htm.

18. Directorate of History, Canadian Forces Headquarters, *Report No. 6*, 30 June 1966, 147–48.

19. Desmond Morton, *A Military History of Canada: From Champlain to Kosovo* (Toronto: McClelland & Stewart Publishers, 1999), 88.

20. Register and Numeric Index of the Regiments and Corps of Canada and British North America since 1783, http://www.regiments.org.

21. *Official Records of the War of the Rebellion*, vol. 26, part 1 (Washington: Government Printing Office, 1888), 334.

22. Mark A. Snell, *From First to Last: The Life of Major General William B. Franklin* (New York: Fordham University Press, 2002), 109.

23. Mac Wyckoff, ed., *In Defense of Gen. William B. Franklin at the Battle of Fredericksburg, Virginia* (Fredericksburg, VA: Sergeant Kirkland's Museum and Historical Society, 1995), 47–48.

24. Michael Barthorp, *Queen Victoria's Commanders* (London: Osprey Publishing, 2000), 23.

25. George MacDonald Fraser, *Flashman and the Dragon* (New York: Plume, 1987).

CHAPTER THREE: NITER AND A ONE-EYED LAKE

1. Helen Nicolay, *Personal Traits of Abraham Lincoln: From the Notes of John Nicolay, Lincoln's Private Secretary* (Mechanicsburg, PA: Stackpole Books, 2006), 248–49.

 2. Harold Holzer, ed., *Lincoln as I Knew Him: Gossip, Tributes and Revelations from His Best Friends and Worst Enemies* (Chapel Hill, NC: Algonquin Books, 1999), 98.

 3. Abraham Lincoln, "Second Lecture on Discoveries and Inventions," February 11, 1859, in *Collected Works of Abraham Lincoln*, vol. 3 (Rutgers University Press, 1953, 1990), 357.

 4. Robert V. Bruce, *Lincoln and the Tools of War* (Indianapolis: Bobbs-Merrill Company, 1956), 270. The U.S. was now buying most of its niter from Chile instead of Great Britain's Indian sources.

 5. "Report of the Royal Commission upon the Volunteer Force," ([3053] HC (1862) xxvii), 89.

 6. Richard Aldous, *The Lion and the Unicorn: Gladstone and Disraeli* (New York: W. W. Norton & Co., 2007), 132.

 7. Wilfrid Meynell, *Benjamin Disraeli: An Unconventional Biography* (New York: D. Appleton, 1903), 146.

8. George Macaulay Trevelyan, *The Life of John Bright* (Boston: Houghton Mifflin Company, 1913), 245.

9. Aldous, *The Lion and the Unicorn*, 127.

10. Hesketh Pearson, *Dizzy: A Life of Benjamin Disraeli* (New York: Penguin Books, 2001), 161.

11. Trevelyan, *The Life of John Bright*, 207.

12. Aldous, *The Lion and the Unicorn*, 138.

13. G. W. E. Russell, *Collections and Recollections* (New York: Harper and Brothers Publishers, 1898) 224.

14. J. J. Colledge, *Ships of the Royal Navy* (London: Greenhill Books, 2003), 257. HMS *Prince Albert*, 3,687 tons, 240' x 48', four 9' MLR, 11.26 knots.

15. Meynell, *Benjamin Disraeli*, 405.

16. Richard Cobden (1804–1865), member for Rochdale in Parliament and one of the great economists of the era.

17. *Lord Rowton, *Disraeli: Recollections of a Private Secretary* (London: Blackpool & Sons, 1888), 402–404. *Edward Bulwer-Lytton, *A Friendship in Letters: The Correspondence of John Bright and Richard Cobden* (London: Wynslow Publishers, 1890), 216–17. Although written from two very different perspectives, these two accounts agree in the essentials of this historic conversation at Hughenden.

18. Clair Hoy, *Canadians in the Civil War* (Toronto: MacArthur & Company, 2004), 190–91.

19. *Arthur W. Williams, *The Life of Sir Charles Hastings Doyle* (Montreal: Mount Royal Press, 1922), 199.

20. *Ellis Spear, *With Chamberlain in the Portland Campaign* (New York: D. Appleton, 1885), 172–74.

21. *Nigel Wilkerson, *The Siege of Portland* (London: Blackbriar & Sons, 1879), 188–190.

22. William H. Roberts, *Civil War Ironclads: The U.S. Navy and Industrial Mobilization* (Baltimore: John Hopkins University Press, 2002), 159.

23. William Marvel, ed., *The* Monitor *Chronicles: One Sailor's Account & Today's Campaign to Recover the Civil War Wreck* (New York: Simon & Schuster, 2004), 22.

24. Ibid., 26–28. Roberts, 29.

25. Agnus Kostam, *Duel of the Ironclads: USS* Monitor *and CSS* Virginia *at Hampton Roads 1862* (London: Osprey Publishing, 2003) 94–95. The *Dictator* and *Puritan* were designed to be the largest, most powerful armed and armored ships in the Navy and in the world. The *Dictator* was designed at 4,438 tons, to do nine knots, and be armed with two fifteen-inch Dahlgren guns in a single turret with twelve-inch armor. The *Puritan* was even more ambitious with two twenty-inch Dahlgren guns.

26. Roberts, *Civil War Ironclads*, 105.

27. *David D. Porter, *The French Navy in the Great War* (Annapolis, MD: Naval Academy Press, 1877), 142–45.

28. *Richard Taylor, *The Louisiana Campaign* (Baton Rouge, LA: Dubois & Sons, 1886), 176–78.

29. *Edmund Allen, *Texas at the Gallop: The Brashear Raid*, (Lexington, VA: Washington and Lee University Press, 1905), 92.

CHAPTER FOUR: "WELL, THEY MIGHT HAVE STAYED TO SEE THE SHOOTING"

1. "Red Leg" is an old U.S. Army nickname for an artilleryman.
2. Eleanor Ruggles, *The Prince of Players: Edwin Booth* (New York: W. W. Norton & Company, 1953), 93, 156.
3. Raymond Lamont Brown, *Carnegie: The Richest Man in the World* (London: Sutton Publishing, 2005) 35, 44.
4. Anthony Smith, *Machine Gun: The Story of the Men and the Weapon That Changed the Face of War* (Waterville, ME: Thorndyke Press, 2002), 119.
5. Ibid., 118.
6. Robert V. Bruce, *Lincoln and the Tools of War* (Indianapolis: Bobbs-Merrill Company, 1956), 114.
7. Michael Burlingame, ed., *Inside the White House in War Times: Memoirs and Reports of Lincoln's Secretary* (Lincoln, NE: Bison Books, 2000), 21–23.
8. David Nasaw, *Andrew Carnegie* (New York: Penguin Press, 2006), 46–47.

CHAPTER FIVE: HONEY, VINEGAR, AND GUNCOTTON

1. Thomas Curson Hansard, *Hansard's Parliamentary Debates by Great Britain. Parliament*, http://hansard.millbanksystems.com/commons/1863/feb/23/the-navy-estimates.
2. HMS *Prince Albert*, launched May 1864, 3,880 tons, 144' x 48' 1" x 20' 5", four 9" rifled muzzle-loaders (RML). HMS *Royal Sovereign*, launched April 1957, a wooden ship-of-the-line, converted into ironclad August 1864, 5,080 tons, 240' 6: x 62' x 25', five 10.5" MLR. HMS *Wivern*, launched August 1863 as CSS *Mississippi*, seized by British government after war is declared and commissioned in the Royal Navy, 2,750 tons, 244' 6" x 421 6" x 17", four 9 RML. The launched date was simply the date the ship was dropped into the water; months and often years were required to ready the ship for active service in peacetime.
3. The American Method was the combination of mass production, specialized labor, and interchangeable parts.
4. David Pam. *The Royal Small Arms Factory, Enfield and Its Workers* (self-published, 1998), 50–58. Between 1859 and 1864, the factory produced 365,779 rifled muskets of the 1853 pattern. Private British arms manufacturers quickly followed the mass production model at Enfield.
5. Ibid., 58–59.
6. Thomas Boaz, *Guns for Cotton: England Arms the Confederacy* (Shippensburg, PA: Burd Street Press, 1996).
7. Robert V. Bruce, *Lincoln and the Tools of War* (Indianapolis: The Bobbs-Merrill Company, 1956), 196.

CHAPTER SIX: "BECAUSE I CAN'T FLY!"

1. *John H. Robson, "The Great Sortie," *Military Journal*, vol. 20, no. 7, June 23, 1912, 32–33.

2. *Joshua Lawrence Chamberlain, *The Defense of Portland* (New York: D. Appleton, 1880), 111–15.
3. *Edward Coddington-James, *Capt. Cowper Coles and the Royal Navy* (London: St. James Publishers, 1934), 83.
4. *"The Queen Asks Hard Questions of the Navy," *London Times*, October 25, 1863, 1.
5. *François Achille Bazaine, *Le Victoire de Vermillionville* (Paris: LeCroix et Fils, 1870), 299.
6. Peter F. Stevens, *The Voyage of the* Catalpa: *A Perilous Journey and Six Irish Rebels' Escape to Freedom* (New York: Carroll & Graf Publishers, 2002), 5.
7. Maj. Gen. George G. Meade, "Organization of the Army of the Potomac," vol. 29, part I, 226, October 10, 1863. Peter G. Tsouras, *Britannia's Fist: Civil War to World War* (Washington: Potomac Books, 2008). Sixth Corps was minus its original three Maine regiments (5th, 6th, 7th), which had been sent home on an ostensible recruiting mission.
8. *"Sedgwick Killed at Kennebunk," *New York Herald*, October 26, 1863, 1.
9. William H. Collins, *The Life of General Horatio Wright* (Philadelphia: L. B. Lippincott, 1897), 183.
10. *William Norquist, *Wisconsin in the Civil War and the Great War* (Madison: Wisconsin Historical Society, 1922), 119. Ulysses S. Grant once remarked that he would rather have one Wisconsin regiment than three from any other state.
11. J. J. Colledge, *Ships of the Royal Navy: The Complete Record of All Fighting Ships of the Royal Navy from the Fifteenth Century to the Present* (London: Greenhill Books, 2003), 48. HMS *Bacchante* was launched in 1859 and measured 235 by 50.5 feet. She carried thirty 8-inch rifles, one 68-pounder, and twenty 32-pounders.
12. *James Hope Grant, *The Maine Campaign in the Great War* (London: Blackstone, 1872), 188. The rescue of Hope Grant's army at Kennebunk by the daring of HMS *Bacchante* did much to restore the morale of the Royal Navy, badly shaken earlier that month by its disastrous defeat at the Third Battle of Charleston.

CHAPTER SEVEN: "LEE IS COMING!"

1. *Michael R. Hathaway, *From San Francisco Bay to Mount Vernon: My War Years with General Washington* (San Francisco: Knob Hill Publishing Company, 1905), 92.
2. Charles M. Evans, *War of the Aeronauts: A History of Ballooning in the Civil War* (Mechanicsburg, PA: Stackpole Books, 2002), 299–303.
3. Field Marshal Viscount Wolseley, *The American Civil War: An English View* (Mechanicsburg, PA: Stackpole Books, 2002), 35.
4. F. Stansbury Haydon, *Military Ballooning during the Early Civil War* (Baltimore: Johns Hopkins University Press, 2000), 238.
5. http://www.colonialwargames.org.uk/Miscenllany/Warships/Ironclads/EIroncladsRN.htm. The draft of the Warrior-class ships (*Warrior*

and *Black Prince*) was 26 feet and that of the Defence-class (*Defence* and *Resistance*) 25 feet.

6. "Chapter V: The Fortification System," *Civil War Defenses of Washington: Historic Resource Study*, National Park Service, http://www.cr.nps.gov/ history/online_books/civilwar/hrs1-5.htm.

7. Richard M. Lee, *Mr. Lincoln's City: An Illustrated Guide to the Civil War Sites of Washington* (McLean, VA: EPM Publications, Inc., 1981), 14. The Navy Yard still occupies the northern half of its original site; the southern half was turned over to the General Services Administration (GSA) and designated the Southeast Government Center.

8. The Eastern Branch was renamed the Anacostia River.

9. Lee, *Mr. Lincoln's City*, 14–16. Stephen M. Forman, *A Guide to Civil War Washington* (Washington: Elliott & Clark Publishing, 1995), 77–80. Foggy Bottom is now occupied by the Kennedy Center for the Performing Arts, The Watergate, George Washington University, and the State Department's Truman Building.

10. Robert V. Bruce, *Lincoln and the Tools of War* (Indianapolis: The Bobbs-Merrill Company, Inc., 1956), 89–92.

11. Margaret Leech, *Reveille in Washington* (New York: Harper Brothers, 1941), 11.

12. Ibid., 10.

13. Peter R. Penzcer, *Washington, DC: Past & Present* (Arlington, VA: Oneonta Press, 1998), 24–28.

14. The National Park Service, *The Civil War Defenses of Washington: Historic Resource Study*, part I, chapter V: The Fortification System, http://www. cr.nps.gov — The Civil War Defenses of Washington.

15. *Frederick R. Priestly, *To Assassinate the President* (New York: St. John's Press, 1948), 82.

16. *Edwin McGregor, *The Trial of John Wilkes Booth* (Philadelphia: D. Appleton, 173), 277.

17. Thomas J. Carrier, *Washington, D.C., A Historical Walking Tour* (New York: Arcadia Publishing, 1999), 72. "In 1853, this became the first equestrian statute cast in the United States. The sculptor, Clark Mills, melted the British cannons captured by Jackson at the Battle of New Orleans during the War of 1812 for the statue."

18. Julia Taft Bayne, *Tad Lincoln's Father* (Lincoln: University of Nebraska Press, 2001), 30.

19. *Michael D. Wilmoth, *Memories of Lincoln* (Indianapolis: Hoosier Press, 1888), 130.

20. *Henry J. Hunt, *The Artillery Revolution in the Great Wqr* (D. Appleton, 1876), 312. Hunt's enthusiasm for balloon-observed indirect fire ensured the full cooperation of the artillery establishment in the U.S. Army.

21. Abraham Lincoln, "Speech at the Republican Banquet," Chicago, IL, December 10, 1860, in *Collected Works of Abraham Lincoln*, vol. 3 (Rutgers University Press, 1953, 1990), 550.

22. *Sharpe, *Conversations with Abraham Lincoln,* 216–18.

23. Walter H. Taylor, *I Served With Lee* (Lexington, VA: Washington and Lee University Press, 1880), 324.

24. *"Hooker and Meagher Cheered in Wild Display," *Kingston Gazette,* October 12, 1863, 1. Two bronze statues face each other in the town square. One is of Hooker to commemorate his visit and role in the subsequent campaign. The other is of George H. Sharpe, famous son of Kingston.

25. *"Wild Parade of the Irish," *New York Herald,* October 12, 1863, 1. *"Victory at Cold Spring: Redcoats down Wall Street," *New York Tribune,* October 12, 1863, 1.

26. *Field Marshal Viscount Wolseley, *The Great War in North America* (London: Longmans, Green, 1890), 97. Wolseley was at pains to describe his strategic appraisal of the situation in this opening stage of the war as it would have a critical effect on subsequent operations.

27. With normal dredging operations interrupted by the war, the depth over the bar was reduced to 16 feet. The French ironclads had a draft of 26 feet.

CHAPTER EIGHT: FATEFUL NIGHT

1. James I. Robertson, Jr., *Stonewall Jackson: The Man, the Soldier, the Legend* (New York: Macmillan Publishing Company, 1997), 573.

2. *The War of the Rebellion: Official Records of the Union and Confederate Armies,* vol. 29, part 1 (Washington: Government Printing Office, 1899), 401.

3. Regis Courtemanche, *No Need for Glory: The British Navy in American Waters 1860–1864* (Annapolis, MD: Naval Institute Press, 1977), 203–204. *Greyhound* had been recently remodeled as a heavier armed corvette. The rest of the sloops had four to 11 guns. *Arthur Ramseur, "Preparations for the Raid on Washington," *International Naval Journal,* October 24, 1997, 142.

4. *"The Meeting of Milne and Lee," *Blackwood's Magazine,* December 1863, 92. It was obvious by this meeting that the British government's policy of no cooperation with the Confederacy had gone by the wayside. Milne was acting on his own authority to support his military operations. The Government acquiesced as the no-cooperation policy was made obviously unrealistic by the exigencies of the expanding war.

5. "Civil War Defenses of Washington: Fort Foote," National Park Service, http://www.nps.gov/archive/fowa/foote.htm.

6. *Milne to the Lord Commissioners of the Admiralty, October 10, 1863. Milne's private conversation with Lee is the only detailed record of the historic meeting as Lee never wrote his memoirs. His report to President Davis of the meeting was brief and essentially a summary, whereas Milne's letter included a deft character analysis of Lee as well a verbatim account of their conversation taken by his stenographer.

7. Fred Albert Shannon, *The Organization and Administration of the Union*

Army 1861–1865, vol. 1 (Cleveland: Arthur H. Clark Company, 1928), 265–67.

8. *Paulet to John C. Wilkinson, October 8, 1863, *The Papers of Lord Frederick Paulet* (London: Bartleby, 1882), 236. Paulet's letters and the recollections of his subordinates are the only source of his thinking that led to the battle of Hudson. Among his subordinates, the recollections of his aide, Captain Seymour, also a Coldstream Guardsman, were particularly revealing.

9. *Mark Serrano, "Intelligence and Reconnaissance during the Hudson Valley Campaign," *Army Review*, vol. 87 (June 12, 1888): 47.

10. *Judson Knight, "Scouting for Hooker," *National Tribune*, July 12, 1890, 12. Knight's series of articles under the column "Fighting Them Over," are a major primary source for the more adventuresome details of the campaign.

11. F. Stansbury Haydon, *Military Ballooning during the Early Civil War* (Baltimore: Johns Hopkins University Press, 2000), 249–50.

12. Spencer Tucker, *Arming the Fleet: U.S. Navy Ordnance in the Muzzle-Loading Era* (Annapolis, MD: Naval Institute Press, 1989), 244.

13. Robert J. Schneller, Jr., *Cushing: Civil War SEAL* (Washington: Potomac Books, 2004), 101.

14. Thomas S. Dickey and Peter C. George, *Field Artillery Projectiles of the American Civil War* (Atlanta: Arsenal Press, 1980), 440.

15. *Lowe, *The Battle of Washington from the Air*, 42–43.

16. *John R. Tappen, *The History of the 120th New York State Volunteer Regiment* (New York: The Neale Publishing Company, 1876), 236–38. Tappen and Sharpe were good friends, having served together as captains in the 20th New York State Militia Regiment when their unit was rushed to defend Washington in 1861 after the firing on Fort Sumter. They remained friends for life and to that association is due one of the finest prose portraits of Sharpe, much referred to by historians.

17. *Dwight D. Eisenhower, *The Coffee Mill Gun and the Revolution It Caused* (Washington: The Infantry Press, 1940), 121–23.

18. *George M. Miller, *History of the 20th New York State Militia Regiment* (Kingston, NY: Regimental Union, 1890), 187–88.

CHAPTER NINE: PERILOUS MORNING

1. *Knight, "Scouting for Hooker," 12.

2. *Mark Serrano, "Intelligence and Reconnaissance during the Hudson Valley Campaign," *Army Review*, vol. 87 (June 1888): 60.

3. *Martin Steinbach, *The Washington Campaign* (New York: Webster, 1979), 56–57. *Jackson O'Hara, "Running the Guns at Fort Washington, *Battles of the Civil War Magazine*, January 30, 1988, 23.

4. John Buchanan (1791–1868), the last president of the United States to be born in the eighteenth century, Buchanan was blamed for taking no serious action to arrest the South's secession.

5. Steuart acquired his nickname to distinguish him from the other Stuart—the dashing J. E. B. Stuart who commanded the cavalry of the Army of Northern Virginia. Steuart was a native Marylander and captain in the U.S. Army when the South seceded. Although Maryland did not follow that example, Steuart's loyalties were to the South. He resigned his commission, joined the Confederate service and was given command of the 1st Maryland Regiment, composed of other Marylanders expatriates.

6. John Manchip White, *Marshal of France: The Life and Times of Maurice, Comte de Saxe, 1696–1750* (New York: Rand McNally, 1962), 159. Attributed to a British sergeant of the Foot Guards (later Grenadier Guards) awaiting a volley from the French royal guard regiment *Maison du Roi* at the battle of Fontenoy on May 11, 1745.

7. *The War of the Rebellion: Official Records of the Union and Confederate Armies*, series 1, vol. 29, part 1 (Washington: Government Printing Office, 1890), 817–23. This entry gives the order of battle of the Army of Northern Virginia as of October 31, 1863. Steuart's brigade consisted of the 1st Maryland, 1st North Carolina, 33rd, 10th, and 37th Virginia Regiments.

8. *Lowe, *The Battle of Washington from the Air*, 45–47. This was the beginning of a lifelong friendship between Lowe and Zeppelin who collaborated on many improvements in the construction and use of lighter-than-air ships. This led to the development and joint production of the American-German Von–Steuben class bomber airships. It was an air fleet of over 200 German Steubens that raided London in 1890 so successfully in the great air raids of World War II.

9. *Heinrich Steiner, *Der deutsche Tat für Amerika*: *Der Mauer und die Deutscher in den grossen Krieg* (St. Louis, MO: Ostmann Publishing Company, 1889), 101.

10. The title of "Damned Dutch" persisted with XI Corps despite the fact that after Gettysburg, as an examination of its order of battle will show, many of its German regiments were replaced with other regiments. Although a significant German element remained, it was not as strong as before.

11. *Russell Alger, "Train-Busting in the Battle of Claverack," *Combat and Commanders of the Civil War* (New York: The Century Company, 1890), 297.

12. Longstreet had to go into battle with only the divisions of Hood and McLaws on the second day at Gettysburg. Pickett's division would not arrive until the evening of that day, long after the fighting stopped.

13. *Arthur Freemantle, *Paulet in the Hudson Valley Campaign: A Study in Command* (Edinburgh, UK: Blackwood and Sons, 1885), 146. Freemantle, who had been an observer at Gettysburg, continued to show a great interest in the fighting in North America after the war had widened. He maintained a heavy correspondence with Wolseley, who provided him much of the information and insights that appeared in Freemantle's book.

14. *George Armstrong Custer, *The Cavalry at Clavarack* (New York; Webster, 1880), 97.

15. Edward G. Longacre, *The Cavalry at Gettysburg: A Tactical Study of Mounted Operations during the Civil War's Pivotal Campaign, 9 June–14 July 1863* (Lincoln: University of Nebraska Press, 1993), 242. Davies had inherited Farnsworth's brigade; it was to the commander of the 5th New York that Farnsworth had said of Kilpatrick's criminal order, "My God, Hammond, Kil is going to have a cavalry charge. It is too awful to think of."

16. *"The Destruction of the Washington Arsenal," Committee on the Conduct of the War, U.S. House of Representatives, July 1, 1868, 322–28. *Sir Hugh Dunlop, *The Descent Upon Washington in the Great War* (London: Collins & Sons, 1876), 265–67; John Rogers Cooke, *Gallant Men: Cooke's Brigade in the War* (Richmond, VA: Longstreet Press, 1882), 311.

17. *Lowe, *The Battle of Washington from the Air*, 60. Lowe's panoramic description of the explosion and its effect on Washington is the most unique of the narratives of that horrific event.

18. *John Rogers Cooke, *Campaigning with Lee: The History of Cooke's Brigade* (Richmond, VA: Tidewater Press, 1888), 266.

19. *Joseph L. Cartwright, *Sailor and Aeronaut: The Life of William Cushing* (Annapolis, MD: Naval Academy Press, 1972), 132–33. William B. Cushing (1842–1874) had been expelled from the Naval Academy for his pranks and poor scholarship. With the attack on Fort Sumter, he pled successfully to Secretary Welles for reinstatement. He went on to win "a distinguished record, frequently volunteering for the most hazardous missions. His heroism, good luck, and coolness under fire were legendary."

20. *Emory Upton, *The Nation in Arms: Hooker and the Military Revolution* (New York: D. Appleton, 1887), 92–94.

21. *Oliver P. Campbell, *Old Slow Come: The Enigmatic Life of General John Slocum* (New York: Xenophon Books, 1996), 258.

22. *Upton, *The Nation in Arms*, 95.

23. *Custer, *The Cavalry at Clavarack*, 110.

24. * Upton, *The Nation in Arms*, 97.

25. *Wolseley, *The Great War in North America*, 230–32.

CHAPTER TEN: "PRETTIEST PARADE I'VE EVER SEEN"

1. *George H. Sharpe, *The Central Information Bureau in the Great War* (New York: Collier's Publishing Company, 1884), 89.

2. *Elizabeth Keckley, *My Life with the Lincolns* (New York: The Neale Publishing Company, 1875), 211–12. Keckley's is the only eyewitness account of the actual shooting, since the president downplayed it in his memoirs, and Mrs. Lincoln and Tad refused to ever comment on the incident.

3. *Michael D. Wilmoth, *Reminiscences of Lincoln* (New York: Dodd, Meade, 1886), 178–79. Wilmoth's account of events after he entered the room is largely in agreement with Keckley's.

4. *Keckley, *My Life with the Lincolns*, 212. *Jospeh R. Sanders, *The Lincoln Plot* (New York: Browning Books, 1955), 211–14. Sanders' book is the first reference to a letter Lincoln wrote to his friend, Admiral Dahlgren, in which he discusses details of his fight with Smoke. The letter was only found in the National Archives in 1953 by the author while searching naval administrative records.

5. *Ralph W. Kimball, "Defending the Navy Yard: Sailors, Marines, and Balloons," *Journal of Naval History*, vol. 23 (August 9, 1912): 23–24.

6. William B. Cushing, *Naval Aero-Power in the Great War: The Creation and Combat History of the Naval Aeronautics Service (NAS)* (New York: Appleton & Co., 1975), 24.

7. *Jason Martin, *From the Brink of Oblivion: General Henry Warner Slocum* (New York: Ultimate Books, 1977), 235. Slocum was reassigned to Sherman's command where he was given command of a corps, which he led with great credit against the French in the Second Battle of New Orleans.

8. *Official Records of the Great War*, series 1, vol. III, part 2 (Washington: Government Printing Office, 1878), 423. Alger had attacked the lead train carrying the 3rd Hamilton Brigade; in addition to the 932 prisoners taken, the wreck and subsequent attack had inflicted another 211 killed and wounded. Most of the casualties were in the 1/47 Foot and Canadian 11th Battalion Volunteer Militia. The remnant of the brigade was unable to take part in the fighting in Stottville.

9. *The War of the Rebellion: Official Records of the Union and Confederate Armies*, series 1. vol. 31, part 1 (Washington: Government Printing Office, 1890), 801. The corps present for duty was 8,702. The day before the battle, a brigade of New York regiments from the defenses of Washington arrived, to include the 20th New York State Militia Regiment.

10. *Wolseley, *The Great War in North America*, vol. 1, 225–26. Aldershot in Hampshire was the main maneuver area of the British Army in England established in 1854. Today it is known as the Home of the British Army.

11. *Edward Swinton, *The Battle for Washington: Lee's Great Gamble* (Philadelphia: National Publishing, 1878), 217–29.

12. *Francis X. Sweeny, *Hard Pounding: The XII Corps at Claverack* (New York; Francis D. Tandy Company, 1984), 200–202.

13. *John W. McGiver, *The Battle of "Out, Out!"* (New York: Scott & Sons, Publishers, 1886), 132–33. The nickname for the battle formerly known as the Battle of Claverack was the Battle of "Out, Out." McGiver wrote twenty years after the war and carefully interviewed hundreds of veterans to discover the origin of the shout. The best answer he could find was that a lieutenant of the brigade had tried to exhort his men with valor of the Saxons at Hastings who had shouted down at the Norman knights, "Out, Out!" The troops had overlooked the fact that the Saxons had lost, but had taken to the words. The reference to the magic arrow was the lucky shot that struck the Saxon king, Harold, in the right eye.

14. *John W. Winston, *The Royal Navy in the Battle for Washington* (London: Biddle & Marston, 1923), 173. The captain of *Spiteful* was awarded the Victoria Cross for his intrepidity in this action.

15. *Thaddeus Lowe, *The Triumph of Aeronautics* (Philadelphia: Henry T. Coates, 1880), 239. This book is a paean to the capabilities of the military balloon. However, Lowe does not stint his praise of Cushing. The two became fast friends and later collaborators in the development of military and naval balloons.

16. *Jacob van Dyke, *With Sharpe and the 120th at the Long Bridge: A Corporal's Story* (Albany: J. Munsell Publishers, 1875), 129. Surprisingly well-written, this soldier's-eye view of the action at the Long Bridge is a priceless part of the historical record for its close observation of Sharpe's skilled conduct of the fight as well as his portrait of Lincoln at the time.

17. *Joseph Hooker, *The Battle for New York in the Great War* (New York: D. Appleton, 1872), 382.

18. Peter G. Tsouras, ed., *The Book of Military Quotations* (London: Greenhill Books, 2005), 336.

CHAPTER ELEVEN: CLICK, BANG!

1. *Cushing, *Naval Aero-Power in the Great War*, 57.

2. "Sinking Ships from the Air," *Harper's Weekly*, October 12, 1863, 13. This article contained a lengthy interview with Cushing in the hospital and proved to be one of the most sought-after issues of the magazine during the war. Cushing was deluged with flowers, candy, fruit, and all sorts of knitted and embroidered items, not to mention hundreds of love letters from girls and young women across the North. The hospital commander finally had to put his ward off limits to female visitors.

3. *Friedrich Graf von Heinzen, *The Rise of German Air Power*, trans. Oscar Ritter (Boston: Roberts Brothers Publishers, 1936), 125–130. This issue, which also contained the coffee mill gun article, caused a sensation in Europe and was widely reprinted. In Prussia the king ordered copies of the articles for every officer at the suggestion of his army chief of staff, Gen. Helmuth von Moltke. The arrival of the *Harper's* issue coincided with the arrival of a detailed report and analysis of balloon operations by von Zeppelin. Von Moltke also wrote a lengthy analysis that was published in the prestigious *Berliner Beobacther*, a clear signal of government approval. Von Zeppelin was immediately recalled and put in charge of the development of the newly created Aeronautics Bureau of the Prussian general staff, with orders to develop a program along American lines.

4. *George H. Sharpe, "The Defense of the Long Bridge," *Journal of the Ulster Historical Society*, vol. xii (July 4, 1890): 36.

5. Gerald S. Henig and Eric Niderost, *Civil War Firsts: The Legacies of America's Bloodiest Conflict* (Mechanicsburg, PA: Stackpole Books, 2001), 77.

6. John R. Ivers, *The Coffee Mill Gunners: The Modern Fighting Man* (New York; Dodd, Meade & Company, 1870), 126–27.

7. *"The Coffee Gun Miracle," *Leslie's Weekly*, October 12, 1863, 25. *"Lincoln's Coffee Mill Guns: Baptism of Fire," *Harper's Weekly*, October 12, 1863, 7. Both magazines rushed engraved illustrations of the weapon into print, *Leslie's* being the more accurate in the depiction of the scene at the Long Bridge. Mathew Brady, however, immortalized the scene by rushing down to the bridge as the fighting had just ended to take pictures of the actual guns as well as the detritus of battle. *Mathew Brady, *Photographs of the Defense of Washington* (New York: Charles B. Richardson, 1864), 22–27.

8. *John R. Tappen, *The History of the 120th New York State Volunteer Regiment* (New York: Neale Publishing Company, 1876), 236–38.

9. *George Denison, *Charge to Glory: The Canadian Cavalry at Claverack* (Montreal: St. George's Press, 1868), 210.

10. *John L. Lambert, "Fighting in a Cloud: Close Combat at Claverack," *Journal of American Military History*, vol. 23 (July 7, 1966): 54–55.

11. The battle of Lundy's Lane took place on July 25, 1814, near Niagara Falls, Ontario. It could be considered a "narrow American tactical victory and a questionable British strategic victory." Losses were almost identical at 878 British and 860 Americans.

12. Joseph Lehmann, *The Model Major-General: A Biography of Field Marshal Lord Wolseley* (Boston: Houghton-Mifflin, 1964), 12.

13. *Wolseley, *The Great War in North America*, vol. 1, 259.

14. *Captain Nigel Atherton, *A History of the Scots Borderers* (Edinburgh, UK: Douglas & Wallace, 1912), 239.

15. *Joseph M. Kelly, *The Battle of Claverack* (New York: D. Appleton, 1876), 198–99. Kelly's work was one of the most popular of the D. Appleton series, Battles of the Great War. His assertion that the charge of the 2nd New York Cavalry was decisive in the outcome of the action at Stottville has never been challenged, especially since Meagher was of the same opinion.

16. Franklin Murphy (1846–1920) survived the battle to become a Republican politician and the thirty-first governor of New Jersey.

17. Capt. Geoffrey Wilson Brown (1842–1930) of the Scots Greys was a younger scion of the well-known Brown military family. There were rumors that he was actually the son of the famous Brig. Harry Paget Flashman (1822–1915), one of the most remarkable of all Victorian soldiers, whose life was immortalized in a brilliant novel series by George McDonald Fraser. Those in the know insisted the Geoffrey Brown was perfect double for Harry Flashman both in appearance and character, though Flashman never acknowledged him.

18. *Denison, *Charge to Glory*, 262

19. *Ibid., 237.

20. The modern Greek word for horse is *alogos*, which means "the creature without logic or reason."

21. *James P. McKenzie, *The Life of George Denison* (Toronto: Northern Lights Publishers, 1927), 190. Denison went on to become a Canadian hero but

immigrated to England rather than live in the newly acquired territories of the United States.

22. *Edmund St. Bury, ed., *British Military Poetry Through the Centuries* (London: Carlisle & Sons, 1883), 211.

23. *Thomas R. Foley, *The Cavalry at Claverack* (Carlisle Barracks, PA: Center for Military History Press, 1973), 187–192.

24. *William S. Johnson, Jr. *Immortal Charge: The Cadets at Claverack* (West Point: Press of the U.S. Military Academy, 1970), 261–63.

25. *Garrett L. Lydecker, *A Soldier's Tale: The Memoirs of Brig. Gen. Garrett L. Lydecker* (Boston: Lee and Shepard Publishers, 1900), 75. Lydecker recovered from his wounds and was immediately commissioned and served with the Army of the Hudson for the rest of the war being brevetted to captain.

26. The battle of Saratoga took place over September and October 1776 in Upstate New York, north of Albany, and resulted in the surrender on October 17th of the British army commanded by Maj. Gen. John Burgoyne.

27. It was this cry, after Wellington had repulsed the attack of Napoleon's Old Guard at Waterloo, that had dissolved the French army in panic.

28. To disengage from an enemy in combat is to retreat. To depart the field when not in contact with the enemy is to withdraw.

29. *Hooker, *The Battle for New York in the Great War*, 420.

30. *Wolseley, *The Great War in North America*, 270. John Renwick Davies immortalized Wosleley's bayonet charge at Claverack in a painting that is still a favorite of the visitors to the National Portrait Gallery in London.

CHAPTER TWELVE: THE SERPENT'S EYE

1. *Daniel Sickles, *The Life of Fighting Joe Hooker* (New York: Tammany Publishers, 1888), 238.

2. *Joseph Hooker, *Triumph on the Hudson: The Battle for New York in the Great War* (New York: D. Appleton, 1872), 433.

3. *John Geary, *The Battle of Claverack* (Boston: Liberty Publishers, 1873), 483–87. Hooker's estimate that night was not too far off. Losses for both sides, even by Civil War standards, had been enormous. The Army of the Hudson had suffered 6,487 casualties: 978 dead, 4,873, wounded, and 636 missing, mostly prisoners, totaling almost 32 percent. Enemy losses were 8,506: 1,311 dead, 4,830 wounded, and 2,365 unwounded prisoners. Wounded prisoners numbered 4,002. The British had had to leave almost all their wounded on the field to the clemency of the Americans. Total British losses were almost 42 percent.

4. *John W. Whitman, *Wolseley and the British Retreat from Claverack* (Washington: Infantry Journal Press, 1944), 199–200.

5. At Malplaquet, on September 11, 1709, the French volunteers under Marshal Claude de Villars had gutted Marlborough's invincible British and Dutch infantry. Writing to Louis XIV, Villars said that he hoped

God would grant the enemy more such victories. Marlborough's pyrrhic victory was his undoing. He fell from power, and his opponents quickly made peace.

6. *Adam Lefleur, *Franklin and the Corps d'Afrique* (Baton Rouge: Louisiana University Press, 1986), 92.

7. *Georges Delacroix, *The Life of Bazaine: A Marshal of Napoleon III* (New York: Chambers Publishers, 1933), 248.

8. Richard Aldous, *The Lion and the Unicorn*, 153–54.

9. William Flavelle Monypenny and George Earle Buckle, *The Life of Benjamin Disraeli, Earl of Beaconsfield: Volume II. 1860–1881* (London: John Murray, 1929), 1366–7.

10. *Archibald Makepeace, *The War Speeches of Benjamin Disraeli* (London: Blackwell Publishing Ltd, 1879), 38.

11. Monypenny, *The Life of Benjamin Disraeli*, 994.

12. *Makepeace, *The War Speeches*, 39.

13. *Nikolai A. Rimsky-Korsakov, *My Adventures in the Great War* (New York: Tudor Press, 1936), 82.

14. *Andrei M. Walendowski, *Muravyov the Hangman: The Man Who Made Poland Weep* (New York: Dobson Publishers, 1949), 211.

15. * Sharpe, *The Central Information Bureau in the Great War*, 198–205.

16. *Wilson M. Cartwright, *Keeping the Union Afloat: The Treasury, Vanderbilt, and Solvency in the Great War* (Washington: Government Printing Office, 1978) 89–90.

17. Robert V. Bruce, *Lincoln and the Tools of Victory* (Indianapolis: Bobbs-Merrill Company, 1956), 270.

18. Michael W. Kauffman, *American Brutus: John Wilkes Booth and the Lincoln Conspiracies* (New York: Random House, 2004), 125.

19. J.B. McClure, ed., *Anecdotes and Stories of Abraham Lincoln* (Chicago: Rhodes & McClure Publishing Company, 1888), 129.

20. *Edward L. Landsberg, *The Life of Will Cushing, American Hero* (Annapolis, MD: Naval Academy Press, 1939) 122.

21. *Alfred Thayer Mahan, *Gustavus Fox, William Cushing, and the Founding of the Naval Aeronautical Service* (Boston: Graham & Sons, 1912), 102.

22. *William H. Seward, *Lincoln as I Knew Him* (New York: D. Appleton Publishers, 1872), 322.

23. *"A Prince in the White House," *Harper's Weekly*, November 5, 1863, 5; *"Prince Arthur Nursed by Mrs. Lincoln," *Leslie's Illustrated*, November 6, 1863, 2; *Reginald P. Crawford, *HRH Arthur: Warrior Prince* (London: Carrington & Sons, 1902), 82–85. The Prince was none too discreet upon his return to Great Britain in December 1863 by referring to Mrs. Lincoln as "that insufferable woman" and worse. He returned to the Royal Navy to command a corvette to extract a highly publicized revenge only to be captured again in the Battle of Havana in 1864. Having heard of his remarks, Mrs. Lincoln sent her personal regards to the Prince in his new captivity, commenting on how nice it was to have him as a guest of the

United States again and asking him to call at the White House as soon as he was able.

24. Gabor S. Boritt, "War Opponent and War President," in *Lincoln: The War President: The Gettysburg Lectures* (New York: Oxford University Press, 1992), 190–92.

25. *Punch*, October 24, 1863.

26. Carl J. Richard, *Greeks and Romans Bearing Gifts: How the Ancients Inspired the Founding Fathers* (Lanham, MD: Rowman & Littlefield, Inc., 2008) 47.

27. *George H. Sharpe, *I Remember Lincoln* (Philadelphia: J.B. Lippincott, 1889), 353.

APPENDIX A

1. Chartrand, *The Mexican Adventure*,18–19; Shann and Delperier, *French Army 1870–71, Franco-Prussian War (1)*, 38–39.

2. *OR*, vol. 26, part 2 (Washington: Government Printing Office, 1880), 402, 465; History of the 12th Texas, http://wwwgeocities.com/rebel12th/history.html

3. *OR*, vol. 26, part 1, (Washington: Government Printing Office, 1880), 334–36, 398, 783.

APPENDIX B

1. Peter G. Tsouras, *Britannia's Fist: Civil War to World War* (Washington: Potomac Books, 2008). The Quebec Brigade was cut up badly in the First Battle of Portland. Its Imperial battalion, 1/62 Foot, took 50 percent casualties, and two of its three Canadian militia battalions were destroyed. The surviving 52nd Bedford Battalion was incorporated into the new Halifax Brigade composed of British and Canadian militia units in Newfoundland.

APPENDIX C

1. Peter Cozzens, *The Shipwreck of Their Hopes: The Battles for Chattanooga* (Urbana: University of Chicago Press, 1994) 401–402

2. Ibid., 402–404.

3. *The War of the Rebellion: Official Records of the Union and Confederate Armies*, vol. 29, part 1 (Washington: Government Printing Office, 1890) 224. Kilpatrick's Reserve Brigade had been at the cavalry remount depot in Washington since August.

4. *Maine Light, 6th Battery, was normally assigned to this brigade but was detached to accompany the rest of the Maine troops to Portland.

ABOUT THE AUTHOR

A former U.S. Army officer, Peter G. Tsouras is an intelligence analyst, a military historian, and the author or editor of two dozen works of military history and alternate history, including *Gettysburg: An Alternate History; Dixie Victorious: An Alternate History of the Civil War; Disaster at D-Day: The Germans Defeat the Allies, June 1944;* and *Military Quotations from the Civil War: In the Words of the Commanders*. Many of his books have been primary selections of the History Book Club and the Military Book Club and have been translated into numerous languages. A regular guest on the History Channel and similar venues in Britain and Canada, Mr. Tsouras is an analyst for the Defense Intelligence Agency and lives in Alexandria, Virginia.